Linda Howard is the award-winning author of many *New York Times* bestsellers. She lives in Alabama with her husband and two golden retrievers.

She is the author of *Dying To Please* and *Cry No More,* also published by Piatkus.

Also by Linda Howard

Dying to Please
Cry No More

Kiss Me While I Sleep

Linda Howard

PIATKUS

 *Visit the Piatkus website!*

Piatkus publishes a wide range of best-selling fiction and non-fiction, including books on health, mind, body & spirit, sex, self-help, cookery, biography and the paranormal.

If you want to:
- read descriptions of our popular titles
- buy our books over the Internet
- take advantage of our special offers
- enter our monthly competition
- learn more about your favourite Piatkus authors

VISIT OUR WEBSITE AT: www.piatkus.co.uk

Copyright © 2004 by Linda Howington

First published in Great Britain in 2004 by
Piatkus Books Ltd of
5 Windmill Street, London W1T 2JA
email: info@piatkus.co.uk

First published in the United States in 2004 by Ballantine Books, an imprint of
The Random House Publishing Group, a division of Random House Inc., New York

The moral right of the author has been asserted

A catalogue record for this book is available from the British Library

ISBN 0 7499 0713 4 (Hardback edition)
ISBN 0 7499 3544 8 (Trade paperback edition)

Printed and bound in Great Britain by
Butler and Tanner Ltd, Frome, Somerset

Kiss Me
While
I Sleep

1

Paris

LILY TILTED HER HEAD AND SMILED AT HER COMPANION, SALVAtore Nervi, as the maître d' silently and with grace seated her at the best table in the restaurant; her smile, at least, was genuine, though almost nothing else about her was. The pale arctic blue of her eyes was warmed to a hazel brown by colored contact lenses; her blond hair had been darkened to a rich mink brown, then subtly streaked with lighter shades. She touched up the roots every few days, so no telltale blond showed. To Salvatore Nervi she was Denise Morel, which was a common enough surname for there to be plenty of Morels in France, but not so common that the name set off subconscious alarms. Salvatore Nervi was suspicious by nature, a fact that had saved his life so many times he probably didn't remember all of the occasions. But if everything worked right tonight, at last he was caught–by his dick, as it were. How ironic.

Her manufactured background was only a few layers deep; she hadn't had time to prepare more. She had gambled that he wouldn't have his people dig any deeper than that, that he would run out of the patience required to wait for the answers before he made a move on her. Normally if a background was required, Langley prepared it for her, but she was on her own this time. She'd done the best she could in the time she had. Probably Rodrigo, Salvatore's oldest son and number two in the Nervi organization, was still digging; her time was limited before he found out that this particular Denise Morel had appeared out of thin air only a few months before.

"Ah!" Salvatore settled in his chair with a contented sigh, returning her smile. He was a handsome man in his early fifties; his looks were classic Italian, with glossy dark hair and liquid dark eyes, and a sensuous mouth. He made a point of keeping himself in shape, and his hair hadn't yet started to gray—either that or he was as skilled as she at touch-ups. "You look especially lovely tonight; have I told you that yet?"

He also had the classic Italian charm. Too bad he was a cold-blooded killer. Well, so was she. In that they were well-matched, though she hoped they weren't an exact match. She needed an edge, however small.

"You have," she said, but her gaze was warm. Her accent was Parisian; she had trained long and hard to acquire it. "Thank you again."

The restaurant manager, M. Durand, approached the table and gave a deferential bow. "It is so nice to see you again, monsieur. I have good news: we have procured a bottle of Château Maximilien eighty-two. It arrived just yesterday, and when I saw your name, I put it aside for you."

"Excellent!" Salvatore said, beaming. The '82 Bordeaux was an exceptional vintage, and very few bottles remained. Those that did commanded premium prices. Salvatore was a wine connoisseur and was willing to pay any price to acquire a rare wine. More than that, he loved wine. He didn't acquire bottles just to have them; he drank the wine, enjoyed it, waxed poetic about the different flavors and aromas. He turned that beaming smile on Lily. "This wine is ambrosia; you will see."

"That is doubtful," she calmly replied. "I have never liked any wine." She'd made that plain from the start, that she was an unnatural Frenchwoman who disliked the taste of wine. Her taste buds were deplorably plebeian. Lily, in fact, enjoyed a glass of wine, but when she was with Salvatore, she wasn't Lily; she was Denise Morel, and Denise drank only coffee or bottled water.

Salvatore chuckled and said, "We shall see." He did, however, order coffee for her.

This was her third date with Salvatore; from the beginning she had played it cooler than he wanted, refusing him the first two times he'd asked her out. That had been a calculated risk, one designed to allay his caution. Salvatore was accustomed to people seeking his attention, his favor; he wasn't accustomed at all to being turned down. Her seeming lack of interest in him had piqued his own interest, because that was the thing about powerful people: they expected others to pay attention to them. She also refused to cater to his tastes, as in the wine. On their two previous dates he had tried to cajole her into tasting his wine, and she had adamantly refused. He had never before been with a woman who didn't automatically try to please him, and he was intrigued by her aloofness.

She hated being with him, hated having to smile at him, chat with him, endure even his most casual touch. For the most part she'd managed to control her grief, forcing herself to concentrate on her course of action, but sometimes she was so sick with anger and pain that it was all she could do not to attack him with her bare hands.

She'd have shot him if she could, but his protection was excellent. She was routinely searched before being allowed anywhere near him; even their first two meetings had been at social occasions where all the guests were searched beforehand. Salvatore never got into a car in the open; his driver always pulled under a protected portico for him to enter, and he never went anywhere that required him to make an unprotected exit from the vehicle. If such an exit wasn't possible, then he didn't go. Lily thought he must have a secure, secret exit from his house here in Paris, so that he could move about without anyone knowing, but if he did, she hadn't spotted it yet.

This restaurant was his favorite, because it had a private, covered entrance that most of the patrons used. The establishment was also exclusive; the waiting list was long, and mostly ignored. The diners here paid well for a place that was familiar and safe, and the manager went to some lengths to ensure that safety. There were no tables by the front windows; instead there were banks of flowers. Brick columns throughout the dining floor broke up the space, interfering with any direct line of sight through the windows. The effect was both cozy and expensive. An army of black-suited waiters wove in and out among the tables, topping off wineglasses, emptying ashtrays, scraping away crumbs, and generally fulfilling every wish before most of them were even voiced. Outside, the street was lined with cars that had reinforced steel doors, bulletproof glass, and armored bottoms. Inside the cars were armed bodyguards who zealously watched the street and the windows of the neighboring buildings for any threat, real or otherwise.

The easiest way to take out this restaurant, and all its infamous patrons, would be with a guided missile. Anything short of that would depend on luck, and at best be unpredictable. Unfortunately, she didn't have a guided missile.

The poison was in the Bordeaux that would shortly be served, and it was so potent that even half a glass of the wine would be deadly. The manager had gone to extraordinary lengths to procure this wine for Salvatore, but Lily had gone to extraordinary lengths to get her hands on it first, and arrange for it to come to M. Durand's notice. Once she had known she and Salvatore were coming here for dinner, she had let the bottle be delivered.

Salvatore would try to cajole her into sharing the wine with him, but he wouldn't really expect her to do so.

He probably *would* expect her to share his bed tonight, but he was destined to be disappointed once again. Her hatred was so strong she had barely been able to force herself to let him kiss her and accept his touch with some warmth. There was no way in hell she could let him do more than that. Besides, she didn't want to be with him when the poison began to act, which should be between four to eight hours after ingestion if Dr. Speer was right in his estimation; during that time she would be busy getting out of the country.

By the time Salvatore knew anything was wrong, it would be too late; the poison would already have done most of its damage, shutting down his kidneys, his liver, affecting his heart. He would go into massive, multisystem failure. He might live a few hours after that, perhaps even a full day, until his body finally shut down. Rodrigo would tear France apart looking for Denise Morel, but she would have disappeared into thin air–for a while, at least. She had no intention of staying gone.

Poison wasn't the weapon she would normally have chosen; it was the one she had been reduced to by Salvatore's own obsession with security. Her preferred method was a pistol, and she would have used that even knowing she herself would be shot down on the spot, but she hadn't been able to devise any method of getting a weapon anywhere near him. If she hadn't been working alone, perhaps . . . but perhaps not. Salvatore had survived several assassination attempts, and had learned from each of them. Not even a sniper could get a clear shot at him. Killing Salvatore Nervi meant using either poison, or a massive weapon that would also kill any others nearby. Lily wouldn't have minded killing Rodrigo or anyone else in Salvatore's organization, but Salvatore was smart enough to always ensure there were innocents nearby. She couldn't kill so casually and indiscriminately; in that, she was different from Salvatore. Perhaps that was the only difference, but for her own sanity, it was one she had to preserve.

She was thirty-seven years old. She'd been doing this since she was eighteen, so for over half her life she'd been an assassin, and a damn good one at that, hence her longevity in the business. At first her age had been an asset: she had been so obviously young and fresh-faced that almost no one had seen her as a threat. She no longer had that asset, but experience had given her other advantages. That same experience, though, had also worn on her until she sometimes felt as fragile as a cracked eggshell: one more good thump would shatter her.

Or maybe she was already shattered, and just hadn't realized it yet. She knew that she felt as if she had nothing left, that her life was a desolate wasteland. She could see only the goal in front of her: Salvatore Nervi was going down, and so was the rest of his organization. But he was the first, the most important, because he was the one who had given the order to murder the people she'd loved most. Beyond this one aim, she could see nothing, no hope, no laughter, no sunshine. It meant almost nothing to her that she probably wouldn't survive the task she'd set for herself.

This in no way meant she would give up. She wasn't suicidal; it was a matter of professional pride that she not only do the job, but get away clean. And there still lurked in her heart the very human hope that if she could just endure, one day this bleak pain would lessen and she would again find joy. The hope was a small flame, but a bright one. She supposed that hope was what kept most people plugging along even in the face of crushing despair, why so relatively few actually gave up.

That said, she had no illusions about the difficulty of what she wanted to do, or her chances both during and after. After she'd finished the job, she would have to completely disappear, assuming she was still alive. The suits in Washington wouldn't be happy with her for taking out Nervi. Not only would Rodrigo be searching for her, but so would her own people, and she didn't figure the outcome would be much different if either caught her. She'd gone off the reservation, so to speak, which meant she was not only expendable–she'd always been that– but her demise would be desirable. All in all, this wasn't a good situation.

She couldn't go home, not that she really had a home anymore. She couldn't endanger her mother and sister, not to mention her sister's family. She hadn't spoken to either of them in a couple of years anyway . . . no, it was more like four years since she'd last called her mother. Or five. She knew they were okay, because she kept tabs on them, but the hard fact was she no longer belonged in their world, nor could they comprehend hers. She hadn't actually seen her family in almost a decade. They were part of Before, and she was irrevocably in After. Her friends in the business had become her family—and they had been slaughtered.

From the time that the word on the street had said that Salvatore Nervi was behind her friends' deaths, she had focused on only one thing: getting close enough to Salvatore to kill him. He hadn't even tried to hide the fact that he'd had them killed; he had used the deed to drive home the lesson that crossing him wasn't a good idea. He wasn't afraid of the police; with his connections, he was untouchable on that front. Salvatore owned so many people in high positions, not just in France but all across Europe, that he could and did act exactly as he pleased.

She became aware that Salvatore was speaking to her, and looking annoyed because she so obviously wasn't paying attention. "I'm sorry," she apologized. "I'm worried about my mother. She called today, and told me she had fallen down the steps at her home. She said she wasn't injured, but I think I should go there tomorrow to see for myself. She *is* in her seventies, and old people break their bones so easily, don't they?"

It was an agile lie, and not just because she'd been thinking about her real mother. Salvatore was Italian to the bone; he had worshipped his own mother, and understood family devotion. His expression immediately became concerned. "Yes, of course you must. Where does she live?"

"Toulouse," she replied, naming a city just about as far from Paris as you could get and still remain in France. If he mentioned Toulouse to Rodrigo, that might buy her a few hours while Rodrigo searched in the south. Of course, Rodrigo might just as easily assume she had mentioned Toulouse as a diversion; whether or not the ploy worked was a crapshoot. She couldn't worry about second-guessing the second-guessers. She would follow her plan, and hope it worked.

"When will you return?"

"Day after tomorrow, if all is well. If not—" She shrugged.

"Then we must make the most of tonight." The heat in his dark eyes told her exactly what he was thinking about.

She didn't dissemble. Instead she drew back slightly, and raised her eyebrows. "Perhaps," she said coolly. "Perhaps not." Her tone told him she wasn't quivering with eagerness to sleep with him.

If anything, her withdrawal sharpened his interest, deepened the heat in his eyes. She thought perhaps her reluctance reminded him of his salad days, when he had courted his late wife, the mother of his children. Young Italian girls of his generation had very closely guarded their virtue, perhaps still did, for all she knew. She hadn't had much contact with young girls from any country.

Two waiters approached, one bearing the bottle of wine as if a priceless treasure, the other bringing her coffee. She smiled her thanks as the coffee was placed in front of her, then occupied herself with adding rich cream to the brew and ostensibly paying no attention to Salvatore as the waiter made a production of uncorking the bottle and presenting the cork to be sniffed. In fact, her attention was sharply trained on that bottle and the ritual that was being played out. Wine connoisseurs were so earnest about these rituals; she didn't understand it herself. For her, the only ritual pertaining to wine was pouring it into the glass and drinking it. She didn't want to smell a cork.

After Salvatore nodded his pleased acceptance, the waiter, solemnly and with great awareness of his audience, poured the red wine into Salvatore's glass. Lily held her breath while Salvatore swirled the wine, sniffed its bouquet, then took an appreciative taste. "Ah!" he said, closing his eyes in pleasure. "Wonderful."

The waiter bowed, as if he were personally responsible for the wine's wonderfulness, then left the bottle on the table and took himself off.

"You must taste this," Salvatore told Lily.

"It would be a waste," she said, sipping her coffee. "For me, this is a pleasant taste." She indicated the coffee. "Wine . . . bah!"

"This wine will change your mind, I promise."

"So others have promised me before. They have been wrong."

"Just a sip, the merest taste," he cajoled, and for the first time she saw the flare of temper in his eyes. He was Salvatore Nervi, and he wasn't accustomed to anyone naysaying him, especially not a woman he had honored with his attention.

"I dislike wine—"

"You haven't tried *this* wine," he said, seizing the bottle and pouring a measure in another glass, then extending the glass to her. "If you don't think this is heaven, I will never again ask you to taste another wine. I give you my word."

That was true enough, since he would be dead. And so would she, if she drank that wine.

When she shook her head, his temper flared, and he set the

glass on the table with a sharp click. "You will do nothing I ask of you," he said, glaring at her. "I wonder why you are even here. Perhaps I should relieve you of my company and call an end to this evening, eh?"

She would have liked nothing better—if only he had drunk more of the wine. She didn't think one sip would deliver enough of the poison to do the job. The poison was supposed to be supertoxic, and she had injected enough of it through the cork into the bottle to fell several men his size. If he left in a temper, what would happen to that uncorked bottle of wine? Would he take it with him, or would he storm out and leave it sitting on the table? As expensive as this wine was, she knew it wouldn't be poured out. No, either another customer would drink it, or the staff would share it.

"Very well," she said, seizing the glass. Without hesitation she carried it to her mouth and tilted it, letting the wine wash against her closed lips, but she didn't swallow any. Could the poison be absorbed through the skin? She was almost certain it could; Dr. Speer had told her to wear latex gloves when she was handling it. She was afraid her night might now be very interesting, in a way she hadn't planned, but there was nothing else she could do. She couldn't even knock the bottle to the floor, because the wait staff would inevitably come in contact with the wine while they were cleaning up.

She didn't bother to repress the shudder that rolled through her at the thought, and hastily set the glass down before patting her lips with her napkin, then carefully folded the napkin so she wouldn't touch the damp spot.

"Well?" Salvatore asked impatiently, even though he'd seen the shudder.

"Rotten grapes," she said, and shuddered again.

He looked thunderstruck. "Rotten–?" He couldn't believe she didn't like his wonderful wine.

"Yes. I taste its antecedents, which unfortunately are rotten grapes. Are you satisfied?" She let a hint of temper show in her own eyes. "I dislike being bullied."

"I didn't–"

"You did. With the threat of not seeing me again."

He took another sip of wine, buying time before answering. "I apologize," he said carefully. "I am not accustomed to–"

"Being told 'no'?" she asked, mimicking him by sipping her coffee. Would the caffeine speed the poison? Would the cream in the coffee slow it down?

She would have been willing to sacrifice herself in order to take just one well-placed shot at his head; how was this any different? She had minimized the risk as much as she could, but it was still a risk, and poison was a nasty way to die.

He shrugged his burly shoulders and gave her a rueful look. "Exactly," he said, showing her some of his legendary charm. He could be a very charming man, when he chose. If she hadn't known what he was, she might have been taken in; if she hadn't stood beside three graves that contained two close friends and their adopted daughter, she might have philosophically decided that, in this business, death was a fairly normal outcome. Averill and Tina had known the risks when they got into the game, just as she had; thirteen-year-old Zia, however, had been an innocent. Lily couldn't forget Zia, or forgive. She couldn't be philosophic.

Three hours later, the leisurely meal consumed, the entire bottle of wine now sloshing in Salvatore's stomach, they rose to leave. It was just after midnight, and the November night sky was spitting out swirls of snowflakes that melted immediately on contact with the wet streets. Lily felt nauseated, but that could well have been from the unrelenting tension rather than the poison, which was supposed to take longer than just three hours before the effects began to be felt.

"I think something I ate isn't agreeing with me," she said when they were in the car.

Salvatore heaved a sigh. "You do not have to pretend illness in order to not go home with me."

"I'm not pretending," she said sharply. He turned his head and stared at the Parisian lights sliding by. It was a good thing he'd drunk all the wine, because she was fairly certain that he would have written her off as a lost cause in any case.

She leaned her head back against the cushion and closed her eyes. No, this wasn't tension. The nausea was increasing by the moment. She felt the pressure increase in the back of her throat and she said, "Stop the car, I'm going to be sick!"

The driver slammed on the brakes–odd how that particular threat made him instinctively go against his training–and she threw the car door open before the tires had rolled to a stop, then leaned out and vomited into the gutter. She felt Salvatore's hand on her back and another on her arm, holding her, though he was careful not to lean so far that he exposed himself to the line of fire.

After the spasms had emptied her stomach, she slumped back into the car and wiped her mouth with the handkerchief Salvatore silently passed to her. "I do beg your pardon," she said, hearing with shock how weak and trembly her voice sounded.

"It is I who must beg yours," he said. "I didn't think you

were truly ill. Should I take you to a doctor? I could call my own doctor–"

"No, I feel somewhat better now," she lied. "Please just take me home."

He did, with many solicitous questions and a promise to call her first thing in the morning. When the driver finally pulled to a stop in front of the building where she rented a flat, she patted Salvatore's hand and said, "Yes, please call me to-morrow, but don't kiss me; I might have caught a virus." With that handy excuse, she pulled her coat around her and dashed through the thickening snowfall to her door, not looking back as the car pulled away.

She made it to her flat, where she collapsed into the nearest chair. There was no way she could grab her necessities and make it to the airport, as she had originally planned. Perhaps this was best, after all. Endangering herself was the best cover of all. If she was also ill from poisoning, Rodrigo wouldn't suspect her, wouldn't care what happened to her when she re-covered.

Assuming she survived, that is.

She felt very calm as she waited for whatever would hap-pen, to happen.

2

Her door was kicked open with a splintering crash shortly after nine o'clock the next morning. Three men entered, all with weapons drawn. Lily tried to lift her head, but with a low moan let it drop back to the rug that covered the polished dark wood of the floor.

The faces of the three men swam in front of her as one knelt beside her and roughly turned her face toward him. She blinked and tried to focus. Rodrigo. She swallowed and reached for him with one hand, a silent plea for help.

She wasn't faking. The night had been long and difficult. She had vomited several times, and had been seized by alternating waves of hot and cold. Sharp pains had stabbed through her stomach, leaving her curled in a fetal ball, whimpering with distress. For a while she thought her dose must have been lethal after all, but now it seemed the pains were abating. She was still too weak and sick to climb from the floor onto the couch, or even to phone for help. Once last night she'd tried to get to the phone, but her effort had come too late, and she hadn't been able to reach it.

Rodrigo swore softly in Italian, then holstered his weapon and rapped out an order to one of his men.

Lily gathered her strength and managed to whisper, "Do not . . . get so close. I may be . . . contagious."

"No," he said in his very excellent French. "You aren't contagious." Moments later a soft blanket settled over her, and Rodrigo briskly wrapped it around her before gathering her into his arms and, with easy strength, rising to his feet.

He strode out of the flat and down the back stairs, where his car waited with the motor idling. The driver jumped out when he saw Rodrigo, and opened the rear door.

Lily was roughly bundled into the car, with Rodrigo on one side of her and one of the other men on the other. Her head lolled against the back of the car seat and she closed her eyes, whimpering in her throat as sharp pain once more daggered through her stomach. She didn't have the strength to stay upright and felt herself slowly begin to topple. Rodrigo made an exasperated sound, but shifted around so she could recline against him.

Most of her consciousness was taken up by her sheer physical misery, but one clear, cold portion of her brain remained separate and alert. She wasn't out of the woods yet, with either the poison or Rodrigo. For now, he was withholding judgment, but that was all. At least he was taking her somewhere for medical treatment–she hoped. He probably wasn't taking her anywhere to kill her and dump her body, because killing her in the apartment and walking away would have been far easier. She didn't know if anyone had seen him carrying her out, but the odds that someone had were good, even though he'd taken her out the back way. Not that he cared if anyone saw him, at least not much. She assumed Salvatore was either dead or dying, and Rodrigo was now the head of the Nervi organization; as such, he'd inherited a lot of power, both financial and political. Salvatore'd had a lot of people in his pocket.

She fought to keep her eyes open, to pay attention to the route the driver was taking, but her lids kept drifting shut. Finally she thought to hell with it and gave up the effort. No matter where Rodrigo was taking her, there was literally nothing she could do about it.

The men in the car were silent, not making even idle comments. The atmosphere seemed heavy and strained, with grief or worry or even rage. She couldn't tell which, and since they weren't talking, she couldn't eavesdrop. Even the outside noise of the traffic seemed to fade away, until at last there was nothing.

The gate to the compound slid open as the car approached, and the driver, Tadeo, slotted the white Mercedes through the gap with only inches to spare on each side. Rodrigo waited until they were stopped under the portico and Tadeo had jumped out to open the passenger door before he shifted Denise Morel around. Her head lolled back and he realized she was unconscious. Her face was a pasty yellowish-white, her eyes sunk back in her head, and an odor clung to her–the same odor he'd noticed on his father.

Rodrigo's stomach clenched as he fought to contain his grief. He still couldn't quite believe it–Salvatore was dead. Just that fast, he was gone. The news hadn't got out yet, but it was only a matter of time. Rodrigo wouldn't be allowed the luxury of grieving; he had to move fast, consolidate his position and take up the reins, before their rivals moved in like a pack of jackals.

When the family doctor had said Salvatore's ailment looked like mushroom poisoning, Rodrigo had moved quickly. He dispatched three men to take M. Durand from the restaurant and bring him to the house, while he himself, with Tadeo driving, took Lamberto and Cesare to find Denise Morel. She was the last person his father had been with before falling ill, and poison was a woman's weapon, indirect and indefinite, depending on guesswork and happenstance. In this case, though, the weapon had been effective.

But if his father had died at her hand, she had then poisoned herself, too, instead of fleeing the country. He hadn't truly expected her to be at her flat, since Salvatore had said she was going to Toulouse to visit her ailing mother; Rodrigo had taken that as a handy excuse. It seemed he'd been wrong—or at least the possibility of error was strong enough that he hadn't shot the woman on sight.

He slid out of the car and hooked his hands under her arms, then dragged her out behind him. Tadeo helped support her until Rodrigo could slide his arm under her knees and lift her against his chest. She was of normal height, about five and a half feet, but on the lanky side; even though she was dead weight, he handled her easily as he carried her inside.

"Is Dr. Giordano still here?" he asked, and received an affirmative reply. "Tell him I need him, please." He took her upstairs to one of the guest bedrooms. She would be better off in a hospital, but Rodrigo wasn't in the mood to answer questions. Officials could be so annoyingly *official*. And if she died, then she died; he had made all the effort he was willing to make. It wasn't as if Vincenzo Giordano wasn't a real medical doctor, even if he no longer had a practice and instead spent all his time in the lab on the outskirts of Paris that Salvatore had funded–though, perhaps if Salvatore had called for help earlier and asked to be taken to a hospital, he would still be alive. Still, Rodrigo hadn't questioned his father's decision to have Dr. Giordano brought in, had even understood it. Discretion was everything, when vulnerability was involved.

He laid Denise on the bed and stood looking down at her, wondering why his father had been so besotted with her. Not that Salvatore hadn't always had an eye for the ladies, but this one was nothing out of the ordinary. Today she looked awful, her hair lank and uncombed, her color as terrible as if she were already dead, but even at her best she wasn't beautiful. Her face was a bit too thin, too austere, and she had a slight overbite. The overbite, however, made her upper lip look fuller than the lower one, and that alone gave her features a piquancy she would otherwise have lacked.

Paris was full of women who were better looking and had a better sense of style than Denise Morel, but Salvatore had wanted this one, to the point that he'd been too impatient to completely investigate her background before approaching her. To his astonishment, she'd refused his first two invitations, and Salvatore's impatience had turned into obsession. Had his preoccupation with her caused him to relax his guard? Was this woman indirectly responsible for his death?

So great was Rodrigo's pain and rage that he might have

strangled her just because of the possibility, but beneath those feelings was the cool voice that said she might be able to tell him something that would lead him to the poisoner.

He would have to find out who had done this, and eliminate him—or her. The Nervi organization could not let this go without retaliation, or his reputation would suffer. Since he was just now stepping into Salvatore's shoes, he couldn't afford the least doubt about his ability, or his resolve. He had to find his enemy. Unfortunately, the possibilities were endless. When one dealt in death and money, all the world was involved. Because Denise had also been poisoned, he even had to consider whether the perpetrator could be a jealous ex-lover of his father's—or one of Denise's old lovers.

Dr. Vincenzo Giordano tapped politely on the frame of the open door, then stepped inside. Rodrigo glanced at him; the man looked haggard, his usually neat salt-and-pepper curls disordered, as if he'd been pulling at them. The good doctor had been his father's friend since boyhood, and he'd wept unashamedly when Salvatore had died not two hours ago.

"Why isn't she dead, too?" Rodrigo asked, indicating the woman on the bed.

Vincenzo took Denise's pulse, and listened to her heart. "She might still die," he said, rubbing a hand over his weary face. "Her heartbeat is too fast, too weak. But perhaps she didn't ingest as much of the poison as your father did."

"Do you still think it's mushrooms?"

"I said it *looked* like mushroom poisoning—for the most part. But there are differences. The speed with which it acted, for one thing. Salvatore was a big, robust man; he wasn't feeling ill when he returned home last night at almost one o'clock. He died just six hours later. Mushrooms are slower acting; even the deadliest will take almost two days to kill. The symptoms were very similar; the speed was not."

"It wasn't cyanide or strychnine?"

"Not strychnine. The symptoms weren't the same. And cyanide kills within minutes, and causes convulsions. Salvatore wasn't convulsive. The symptoms of arsenic poisoning are somewhat similar, but different enough to rule that out also."

"Is there any way to tell for certain what was used?"

Vincenzo sighed. "I'm not certain it is a poison at all. It could be a virulence, in which case we have all been exposed."

"Then why hasn't my father's driver become ill? If this is a virus that works within hours, then he, too, should be ill by now."

"I said it *could* be, not that it *is*. I can do tests, with your permission examine Salvatore's liver and kidneys. I can compare his blood analysis with that of . . . What is her name?"

"Denise Morel."

"Ah, yes, I remember. He talked about her." Vincenzo's dark eyes were sad. "I think he was in love."

"Bah. He would have lost interest in her eventually. He always did." Rodrigo shook his head, as if clearing his mind. "Enough of that. Can you save her?"

"No. She will either survive, or she will not. There is nothing I can do."

Rodrigo left Vincenzo to his tests and went to the basement room where his men were holding M. Durand. The Frenchman was already the worse for wear, with thin rivulets of blood trickling from his nose, but for the most part Rodrigo's men had concentrated on punches to the body, which hurt more and weren't as readily visible.

"Monsieur Nervi!" the restaurant manager croaked when

he saw Rodrigo, and began weeping with relief. "Please, whatever has happened, I know nothing about it. I swear to you!"

Rodrigo pulled up a chair and sat down in front of M. Dur-
and, leaning back and crossing his long legs. "My father ate
something in your restaurant last night that disagreed with
him," he said with massive understatement.

An expression of total bewilderment and astonishment
crossed the Frenchman's face. Rodrigo could read his thoughts:
He was being beaten to a pulp because Salvatore Nervi had *in-
digestion*? "But–but," M. Durand sputtered. "I will refund his
money, of course, he had only to ask." Then he dared to say,
"This wasn't necessary."

"Did he eat mushrooms?" Rodrigo asked.

Another look of bewilderment. "He knows he did not. He
ordered chicken in wine sauce, with asparagus, and Mademoiselle Morel had the halibut. No, there were no mushrooms."

One of the men in the room was Salvatore's regular driver,
Fronte; he bent down and whispered in Rodrigo's ear. Rodrigo
nodded.

"Fronte says that Mademoiselle Morel became ill just after
leaving your restaurant." So she'd been stricken first, Rodrigo
thought. Had she been the first to take whatever poison they'd
ingested? Or had it worked faster on her, because of her lower
body weight?

"It was not my food, monsieur." Durand was highly insulted.
"None of the other patrons became ill, or had any complaint.
The halibut had not gone bad, and even if it had, Monsieur
Nervi didn't have it."

"What food did they share?"

"Nothing," M. Durand replied promptly. "Except perhaps

the bread, though I didn't see Mademoiselle Morel eat any. Monsieur drank wine, an exceptional Bordeaux, Château Maximilien's eighty-two vintage, and Mademoiselle drank coffee as usual. Monsieur did prevail upon her to taste the wine, but it wasn't to her liking."

"So they shared the wine."

"A small sip only. As I said, she didn't care for it. Mademoiselle does not drink wine." Durand's very Gallic shrug said he didn't understand such peculiarity, but there it was.

But last night she had drunk wine, even if it was only a small sip. Was the poison so potent that one sip would threaten her life?

"Was there any wine left?"

"No. Monsieur Nervi drank it all."

That wasn't unusual. Salvatore's head had been remarkably hard, with the result that he drank more than most Italians.

"The bottle. Do you still have the bottle?"

"It will be in the refuse box, I'm certain. Behind the restaurant."

Rodrigo ordered two men to go search through the trash and find the empty Bordeaux bottle, then turned back to M. Durand. "Very well. You will remain my guest"—he gave a humorless smile—"until this bottle and the dregs have been analyzed."

"But that can—"

"Take days, yes. I'm sure you understand." Perhaps Vincenzo could get his answers faster than that, in his own lab, but that remained to be seen.

M. Durand hesitated. "Your father . . . he is very ill?"

"No," said Rodrigo, rising to his feet. "He is dead." And once more the words arrowed straight through his heart.

* * *

By the next day, Lily knew she would live; it took Dr. Giordano another two days to make the same pronouncement. She needed the entire three days before she felt well enough to get out of bed and take a much-needed bath. Her legs were so shaky she had to hold on to furniture to make her way to the bathroom, her head swam and her vision was still a little blurry, but she knew the worst was past.

She had fought desperately for consciousness, refusing the drugs Dr. Giordano tried to give her to ease her pain, give her sleep. Even though she had passed out during the drive over to what was obviously the Nervi compound, she hadn't been drugged. Despite the excellence of her French, it wasn't her first language; if she were sedated, her native American English might slip out. She had pretended to be afraid she would die in her sleep, that she felt she could fight the poison so long as she remained alert, and though Dr. Giordano knew that was medically ridiculous, he had nevertheless bowed to her wishes. Sometimes, he'd said, the patient's mental condition meant more to recovery than the physical condition.

When she slowly, laboriously made her way out of the lavishly appointed marble bathroom, Rodrigo was sitting in the chair by the bed, waiting for her. He was dressed all in black, turtleneck and trousers, a dark omen in the white-and-cream bedroom.

Immediately all her instincts went to a higher stage of alertness. She couldn't play Rodrigo the way she had Salvatore. For one thing, as wily as Salvatore had been, his son was smarter, tougher, more cunning—and that was saying something. For another, Salvatore had been attracted to her, and Rodrigo wasn't.

For the father she had been a younger woman, a conquest, but she was three years older than Rodrigo and he had plenty of conquests of his own.

She was wearing a set of her own pajamas, brought from her flat yesterday, but she was glad of the extra covering of the thick Turkish robe she'd found hanging on a hook in the bathroom. Rodrigo was one of those overtly sexual men who made women very aware of him, and she wasn't immune to that facet of his personality, even though she knew enough about him to make her cold with disgust. He wasn't innocent of the majority of Salvatore's sins, though he *was* innocent of the murders that had moved her to vengeance; by chance, Rodrigo had been in South America at the time.

She struggled to the bed and sat on it, clinging to one of the posts at the foot for support. She swallowed and said, "You saved my life." Her voice was thin and weak. *She* was thin and weak, in no shape to protect herself.

He shrugged. "As it happens, no. Vincenzo–Dr. Giordano– says there was nothing he could do to help. You recovered on your own, though not without some damage. A heart valve, I believe he said."

She already knew that, because Dr. Giordano had told her the same thing that very morning. She had known the possibilities when she took the risk.

"Your liver, though, will recover. Already your color is much better."

"No one has told me what was wrong. How did you know I was sick? Did Salvatore become ill, too?"

"Yes," he said. "He didn't recover."

Some reaction other than, "Oh, good," was expected of her,

so Lily deliberately thought of Averill and Tina, of Zia with her adolescent gangliness, her bright, cheerful face and nonstop chatter. Oh, God, she missed Zia so much; it was an ache in the center of her chest. Tears filled her eyes, and she let them drip down her cheeks.

"It was poison," Rodrigo said, both his expression and tone as calm as if he'd commented on the weather. She wasn't deceived; he had to be in a rage. "In the bottle of wine he drank. It appears to be a synthetic, designer poison, very potent; by the time the symptoms occur, it's already too late. Monsieur Durand from the restaurant said you tasted the wine."

"Yes, one sip." She wiped the tears from her face. "I dislike wine, but Salvatore was insistent, and he was becoming angry because I didn't want to taste it, so I did . . . just one very small sip, to please him. It was nasty."

"You are lucky. According to Vincenzo, the poison is so potent that had you drunk any more than that, if the sip hadn't been very small, you would be dead."

She shuddered, remembering the pain and vomiting; she had been that sick without actually swallowing any of the wine, just letting it touch her lips. "Who did this? Anyone could have drunk that wine; was it some terrorist who didn't care who he killed?"

"I think my father was the target; his love of wine was well-known. The eighty-two Château Maximilien is very rare, yet a bottle mysteriously became available to Monsieur Durand the day before my father's reservation at his restaurant."

"But he might have offered the wine to anyone."

"And taken the risk that my father would hear about it and take umbrage that this rare wine wasn't offered to him? I think not. This tells me the poisoner is very familiar with Monsieur Durand and his restaurant, and the clientele."

"How was it done? The bottle was uncorked in front of us. How was the wine poisoned?"

"I imagine a very thin hypodermic needle was used to inject the poison through the cork. It wouldn't have been noticeable. Or the bottle could have been uncorked, then resealed if the proper equipment was available. To Monsieur Durand's extreme relief, I don't believe either he or the waiter who served you are culpable."

Lily had been out of bed so long that she was trembling with weakness. Rodrigo noticed the tremors that shook her entire body. "You may stay here until you are fully recovered," he said politely, rising to his feet. "If you need anything, you have only to ask."

"Thank you," she said, then uttered the biggest lie of her life: "Rodrigo, I'm so sorry about Salvatore. He was . . . he was–" He was a murdering asshole son of a bitch, but now he was a dead murdering asshole son of a bitch. She managed to produce one more tear, thinking of Zia's little face.

"Thank you for your condolences," he said without expression, and left the room.

She didn't do a victory dance; she was too weak, and for all she knew there were hidden cameras in the room. Instead she climbed back into bed and tried to seek refuge in strength-restoring sleep, but she was feeling too triumphant to do more than doze.

Part of her mission was accomplished. Now all she had to do was disappear before Rodrigo discovered Denise Morel didn't exist.

3

TWO DAYS LATER, RODRIGO AND HIS YOUNGER BROTHER, DAMONE, stood beside their parents' graves at their boyhood home in Italy. Their mother and father were once more side by side in death as they had been in life. Salvatore's grave was covered in flowers, but both Rodrigo and Damone had taken some of the flowers and put them on their mother's grave, too.

The weather was cool but sunny, and a light breeze was blowing. Damone put his hands in his pockets and stared up at the blue sky, his handsome face drawn with grief. "What will you do now?" he asked.

"Find who did this and kill him," Rodrigo said without hesitation. Together they turned and began walking away from the gravesite. "I'll also put out a press release about Papa's death; it can't be kept quiet much longer. The news will make some people nervous, wondering about the status of various agreements now that I am in charge, and I will have to deal with that. We may lose some revenue, but nothing that we can't absorb. And the losses will be short-term. The revenues from the vaccine will make up the difference, and more. Much more."

Damone said, "Vincenzo has made up the lost time?" He was more of a businessman than Rodrigo, and it was he who handled the majority of their finances from his own head-quarters in Switzerland.

"Not as much as we had hoped, but work is progressing. He assures me he will be finished by next summer."

"Then he is doing better than I'd expected, considering how much was lost." An incident at Vincenzo's lab had destroyed much of his current project.

"He and his people are working very long hours." And would be working even longer ones if Rodrigo saw they were falling behind schedule. The vaccine was too important to let Vincenzo miss the deadline.

"Keep me abreast of the situation," said Damone. By agree-ment, because of security issues, they wouldn't be together again until after the poisoner was identified and apprehended. He turned and looked back at the new grave, his dark eyes filled with the same pain and rage Rodrigo felt. "It's still so hard to believe," he said, almost inaudibly.

"I know." The two brothers hugged, unashamed of their emotion, then got into separate cars for the trip back to their private airfield, where they would each take a corporate jet home. Rodrigo had taken comfort in his younger brother's presence, in having what was left of his immediate family next to him. Despite the sadness of their purpose for being together, there had also been an ease of companionship. Now each returned to their linked but separate empires, Damone to watch over the money, Rodrigo to find their father's killer and exact revenge. Whatever steps he took, he knew, Damone would support him.

But the fact was, he hadn't been able to make any progress in finding who had killed Salvatore. Vincenzo was still analyzing the poison, which might give them an idea of its origin, and Rodrigo had been closely watching his rivals for any hint of knowledge that Salvatore had died, any aberration in their usual pattern of doing business. One might think their less legitimate associates would be seen as the most likely suspects, but Rodrigo didn't eliminate anyone from suspicion. It could even be someone within their own organization, or someone in the government. Salvatore had had his fingers in many pies, and evidently someone had got greedy enough to want the whole pie to himself. Rodrigo just had to discover which one.

"Drive Mademoiselle Morel home," Rodrigo told Tadeo after she had been there a week. She was steady on her feet now, and though she seldom left her bedroom, he wasn't comfortable having a stranger under his roof. He was still busy consolidating his position—unfortunately, a couple of people had felt he wasn't the man his father had been and were impelled to challenge his authority, which had in turn impelled him to have them killed—and there were some things a stranger shouldn't accidentally see or hear. He would feel more comfortable when the house was once more a total haven.

It took only a matter of minutes for the car to be brought around and the woman and her few belongings loaded inside. After Tadeo had left with the Frenchwoman, Rodrigo went into

Salvatore's study—his study now—and sat behind the huge carved desk that Salvatore had loved. Vincenzo's report on the poison, analyzed from the dregs in the wine bottle recovered from the restaurant's refuse, lay in front of him. He had looked over the report when he first received it, but now he picked it up again and thoroughly studied it, going over every detail.

According to Vincenzo, the poison was chemically engineered. It contained some of the properties of orellanine, the poison in the deadly galerina mushroom, which was why he had first suspected mushrooms. Orellanine attacked several internal organs, most notably the liver, kidneys, heart, and the nervous system, but orellanine was also notoriously slow. Symptoms wouldn't appear for ten hours or more, then the victim would appear to recover, only to die several months later. There was no known treatment or antidote for orellanine. The poison had also shown some relation to minoxidil, with the effects of bradycardia, heart failure, hypotension, and depressed respiration—which would help to render the victim unable to recover from the orellanine lookalike. Minoxidil worked fast, orellanine worked slowly; somehow the two properties had been combined in such a way that there was a delay, but of only a few hours.

Also according to Vincenzo, there were only a few chemists in the world capable of doing this work, and none of them worked in reputable drug corporations. Because of the nature of their work, they were both expensive to hire and difficult to contact. This particular poison, at such a potency that less than an ounce would kill a hundred-and-fifty-pound man—or woman—would cost a small fortune to produce.

Rodrigo steepled his fingers and thoughtfully tapped them

against his lips. Logic told him the killer he sought would almost certainly be a business rival or someone seeking to avenge
a past grievance, but instinct kept him looking at Denise Morel.
There was something about her that nagged at him. He couldn't
identify the source of his faint discomfort; so far his investigations had told him she was exactly what she purported to
be. Moreover, she, too, had been poisoned and very nearly died,
which any logical man would say proved she wasn't the villain.
And she had wept when he told her of Salvatore's death.

Nothing pointed to her. The waiter who had served the
wine was a far more likely suspect, but exhaustive questioning
of both M. Durand and the waiter had produced nothing but the
information that M. Durand himself had put the bottle in
the waiter's hands and watched him take it, without detour, to
the Nervi table. No, the person he sought was the one who had
brought the availability of the bottle of wine to M. Durand's attention, and so far there was no record of that person. The bottle had been bought from a company that didn't exist.

Therefore, the killer was fairly sophisticated in the trade,
with the means of procuring both the poison and the wine. He–
for convenience' sake Rodrigo thought of the killer as a "he"–
had researched both his victim and his victim's habits; he had
known Salvatore frequented that particular restaurant, known
when he had a reservation, and known with some certainty
that M. Durand would of course hold this particular bottle
for his very important customer. The killer also had the skill
to present a believable facsimile of a legitimate company. All
of this pointed to a level of professionalism that practically
screamed "competitor."

And yet, he still couldn't quite disregard Denise.

It wasn't likely, but this could still be a crime of passion. No one was beyond suspicion until he knew for certain who had killed his father. Whatever his father had seen in Denise, perhaps some other man had seen the same thing, and been just as obsessed.

As for Salvatore's past lovers . . . Rodrigo mentally reviewed them, and all but categorically dismissed them from contention. For one thing, Salvatore had been like a honey bee, never staying long enough with one lover for any real connection to be formed. Since his wife's death, some twenty years before, he had been amazingly active in the romance department, but no woman had come close to joining his wife in his regard.

Moreover, Rodrigo had investigated every woman who spent time with his father. Not one of them had shown any signs of obsessive behavior, nor would they have had the knowledge of such an exotic poison, or the means of acquiring it, much less the hideously expensive wine. He would investigate them again, just to be certain, but he thought they would all check out clean. However, what about the people in *Denise's* past?

He had questioned her about that, but she hadn't provided any names, merely saying, "No, there's no one."

Did that mean she'd lived virtuous and nunlike all her life? He didn't think so, though he did know for a fact that she'd refused Salvatore's propositions. Or did it mean there had been lovers but no one she considered capable of such a thing? He didn't care what she thought; he wanted to draw his own conclusions.

Ah, there it was. Why wouldn't she tell him about anyone in her past? Why was she so secretive? *That* was what bothered him about her; there was no reason for her not to give him the name of everyone she had been with since adolescence. Was she protecting someone? Did she have an idea of who could have put the poison in that bottle, knowing her dislike of wine and never dreaming she might drink some of it?

He hadn't investigated her as thoroughly as he would have liked; first Salvatore had been too impatient to wait, and then their dates had been so noneventful—until the last one—that Rodrigo had basically put the matter aside. Now, however, he would find out everything there was to know about Denise Morel; if she had ever even thought about sleeping with any-one, he would know it. If anyone was in love with her, he would find the man.

He picked up the telephone and dialed a number. "I want Mademoiselle Morel watched at all times. If she moves an inch outside her door, I want to know about it. If anyone calls her, or she places any calls, I want the call traced. Is that understood? Good."

In the privacy of the guest bedroom's bathroom, Lily had worked hard to regain her strength. A thorough search of the room had revealed neither camera nor microphone, so she knew she was safe from observation there. At first she'd been able to do only stretching exercises, but she'd pushed herself hard, jogging in place even when she had to hold on to the mar-ble vanity to keep her balance, doing push-ups and sit-ups and ab crunches. She forced herself to eat as much as she could, fu-eling her recovery. She knew pushing herself could be danger-ous, with her damaged heart valve, but it was a calculated risk, as was almost everything else in her life.

The first thing she did once she was back in her flat was

subject it to the same exhaustive search that the bathroom had received. To her relief, she didn't find anything. Rodrigo must not suspect her, or he would have had the place bugged seven ways from Sunday while she'd been incapacitated. No, he would have killed her on just suspicion alone.

That didn't mean she was safe. When he asked about her past lovers, she'd known she had only a few days to get away, because he would be digging deeper into Denise's past and finding out there *was* no past.

If her flat had been searched—and she had to assume it had been—the searchers had been very neat. But they hadn't found her stash of getaway items, or she wouldn't be standing here now.

The old building had once been heated by fireplaces, which at some time after World War II had been replaced by radiators. The fireplace in her flat had been bricked over, and a chest shoved in front of it. She had put a cheap rug under the chest, not to prevent the floor from being scarred, but so she could silently move the chest about by pulling the rug. She pulled the rug away from the wall now, and got down on her belly to inspect the bricks. Her repair job wasn't noticeable; she'd dirtied the mortar so it looked as aged as the mortar around it. There wasn't any mortar dust on the floor, either, to indicate that anyone had tapped on the bricks.

She got a hammer and chisel, lay down on her belly again, and began gently tapping the mortar from around one of the bricks. When it was loosened, she worked it free, then another, then another. Reaching her hand into the cavity of the old fireplace, she pulled out an array of boxes and bags, each item safely wrapped in plastic to keep it clean.

One small box held her alternate identities: passports, credit cards, driver's licenses, ID cards, depending on which nationality she chose. A bag held three wigs. There were distinctive changes of clothes, kept hidden because they were so memorable. Shoes were a different matter; she'd simply put the shoes she'd need in her closet, dumped in a pile with all her other shoes. How many men would pay any attention at all to a tangle of shoes? She also had a supply of cash, in euros, pounds sterling, and American dollars.

In the last box was a secure cell phone. She turned it on and checked the battery: LOW. Taking out the charger, she plugged it into a wall outlet and set the phone in the cradle.

She was exhausted, sweat beading her forehead. She wouldn't go tomorrow, she thought; she was still too weak. But day after tomorrow, she would have to move, and move fast.

So far she'd been lucky. Rodrigo had kept the news of Salvatore's death quiet for several days, which had bought her some time, but with every minute that passed, the danger grew that someone in Langley would see a photograph of Denise Morel, scan it into a computer, and the computer would spit out the report that, hair and eye color aside, Denise Morel's features matched those of one Liliane Mansfield, contract agent for the U.S. Central Intelligence Agency. Then the CIA would be hot on her trail, and the Agency had resources Rodrigo Nervi could only dream about. For practical reasons, Salvatore had been left in place with the Agency's blessings; no one there would look kindly on her for taking him out.

It was a toss-up who would come after her first, Rodrigo or someone sent by the CIA. She would have a better chance against Rodrigo, because he would probably underestimate her. The Agency wouldn't make that mistake.

Because it would look odd if she didn't, and also because she wanted to see if she was under surveillance, she bundled up against the chill and walked to the neighborhood market. She'd spotted one guard as soon as she came out of her building; he was sitting in a nondescript gray car parked halfway down the block, and as soon as she walked out, he lifted a newspaper to cover his face. Amateur. But if there was one in front, she could assume there was also one in back. The good news was there wasn't a guard inside her building, which would have made matters a bit more iffy. She didn't want to have to go out a third-story window, as weak as she was.

She carried a cloth shopping bag into which she put some produce and fruit. An Italian-looking man–who didn't really stand out unless you were specifically looking for him– meandered around in her wake, always keeping her in view. Okay, that made three. Three were enough to do a competent job, but weren't so many that she couldn't handle them.

After paying for her selections, she walked back to her flat, careful to keep her gait rather slow and laborious. She walked with her head down, the picture of dejection, and not the way anyone who was the least alert would walk. Her watchers would think she was completely unaware of them and, moreover, that her health was still so precarious she could scarcely get around. Since they weren't extraordinarily skilled in surveillance, that meant they would somewhat relax their guard without realizing it, because she was such a poor challenge.

When her cell phone was fully charged, she took it into the bathroom and turned on the tap water to mask sound, in case a parabolic microphone was aimed at her flat. The chance of that was admittedly small, but in her business paranoia saved lives. She booked a first-class one-way ticket to London, disconnected, then called back and, under another identity, booked a flight out of London that left within half an hour of her arrival, headed back to Paris, where absolutely no one would expect her to go. After that, she would see, but that little maneuver should buy her some more time.

Langley, Virginia

Early the next morning, a junior analyst named Susie Pollard blinked at what the computer facial-recognition program had just told her. She printed out the report, then wove her way through a maze of cubicles to stick her head inside another cubicle. "This looks interesting," she said, handing the report to a senior analyst, Wilona Jackson.

Wilona slid her glasses into place and swiftly looked over the document. "You're right," she said. "Good catch, Susie. I'll kick this upstairs." She stood, a six-foot-tall black woman with austere features and a no-bullshit attitude honed to perfection on her husband and five rowdy sons. Without another woman in the household for backup, she said, she had to stay on top of things. That carried over to her work, where she tolerated no nonsense. Anything she kicked upstairs was given proper consideration, or else.

By noon, Franklin Vinay, director of operations, was reading the report. Salvatore Nervi, the head of the Nervi organization— he couldn't call it a corporation, though corporations were involved—was dead of an undisclosed ailment. The exact date of his death was unknown, but Nervi's sons had buried him at their home in Italy before releasing the news. His last sighting was at a Parisian restaurant, with a lapse of four days between then and the announcement of his death. He had apparently been in perfect health, so the unknown ailment had occurred rather abruptly. It happened, of course; heart attacks or strokes struck down seemingly healthy people every day.

What set the alarm bells to clanging was the facial-recognition program, which said that, without doubt, Nervi's newest lady friend had been none other than one of the CIA's best contract agents in disguise. Liliane Mansfield had darkened her wheat-blond hair and put in dark contacts to hide her distinctive pale blue eyes, but it was undoubtedly her.

Even more alarming was the fact that, a few months ago, two of her closest friends and their adopted daughter had died at Nervi's hands. All of the indications were that Lily had gone off the reservation and taken matters into her own hands.

She'd known the CIA wouldn't sanction the kill. Salvatore Nervi was a disgusting example of humanity who deserved killing, but he'd been smart enough to play both ends against the middle and make himself useful, as insurance against just this sort of thing. He had passed along extremely useful information, and done so for years. That information pipeline was now lost, perhaps irrevocably; it would take them years, if they could at all, to develop the same relationship with the heir apparent. Rodrigo Nervi was notoriously suspicious, and not apt to jump at any partnership. Frank's only hope in that direction was that Rodrigo would prove to be as pragmatic as his father.

Frank hated working with the Nervis. They had some legitimate business concerns, yes, but they were like Janus: everything they did had two faces, a good side and a bad side. If their researchers were working on a cancer vaccine, another group in the same building was working to develop a biological weapon. They gave huge amounts of money to charitable organizations that did a lot of good work, but they also funded terrorists groups that killed indiscriminately.

Playing in the pool of world politics was like playing in a sewer. You had to get dirty in order to play. Privately, Frank thought the end of Salvatore Nervi was good riddance. In the realm of his work, though, if Liliane Mansfield was responsible, he had to do something about it.

He pulled up her security-coded file and read it. Her psychological profile said that she'd been operating under some strain for a couple of years now. In his experience there were two types of contract agents: those who did their work with no more emotion than they would expend on swatting a fly, and those who were convinced of the good they did but whose souls, nevertheless, wore thin under the constant assault. Lily was in the latter group. She was very good, one of the best, but each hit had left its mark on her.

She had stopped contacting her family years ago, and that wasn't good. She would feel isolated, cut off from the very world she'd worked to protect. Under those circumstances, her friends in the business had become more than just friends; they'd become her surrogate family. When they were hit, her tattered soul had perhaps taken one blow too many.

Frank knew some of his colleagues would laugh at him, thinking in terms of souls, but he'd been in this business a long time and he not only knew what he saw, he *understood* it.

Poor Lily. Perhaps he should have pulled her out of the field when she first started showing signs of psychological strain, but it was too late now. He had to deal with the situation that existed.

He picked up the phone and had his assistant locate Lucas

Swain, who, wonder of wonders, was actually in the building. The fickle Fates must have decided to smile on Frank.

Some forty-five minutes later, his assistant buzzed him. "Mr. Swain is here."

"Send him in."

The door opened and Swain sauntered in. Actually, he sauntered everywhere. He walked like a cowboy who had nowhere to go and wasn't in any hurry to get there. Ladies seemed to like that about him.

Swain was one of those good-looking people who seemed to be perpetually good-natured, too. There was a goofy smile on his face as he said hello and took the chair Frank indicated. For some reason, the smile worked in the same way as the walk: people liked him. He was a devastatingly effective field officer because he went in under people's radar. He might be a happy man, he might have a walk that looked like the definition of laziness, but he got the job done. He'd been getting the job done in South America for the better part of a decade, which explained the deep tan and rock-hard leanness.

He was beginning to show his age, Frank thought, but then, weren't they all? There was gray at the temples and along the hairline of Swain's brown hair, which was kept cropped short because of an unruly cowlick in front. There were lines bracketing his eyes and on his forehead, creases in his cheeks, but with his luck, the ladies probably thought that was as cute as his walk. *Cute.* It was a sad day in hell, Frank reflected, when he was mentally describing one of his best male field officers as *cute.*

"What's up?" Swain asked, stretching his long legs out as he relaxed, his spine curving so he sank down in his chair. Formality wasn't Swain's way.

"A delicate situation in Europe. One of our contract agents has gone off the reservation, killed a valuable asset. We need her stopped."

"Her?"

Frank handed the report over the desk. Swain took it and swiftly read through it, then passed it back. "The deed's done. What's there to stop?"

"Salvatore Nervi wasn't alone in the situation that ended with the death of Lily's friends. If she's on a rampage to get all of them, she could wreck our entire network. She's already done considerable damage by eliminating Nervi."

Swain screwed up his face and briskly rubbed both hands over it. "Don't you have some irrascible rogue agent, forcibly retired under a cloud, with some special skill that makes him the only choice possible for locating Ms. Mansfield and stopping her killing ways?"

Frank bit the inside of his cheek to control a smile. "Does this look like a movie production to you?"

"A man can hope."

"Consider your hopes dashed."

"Okay, then, how about John Medina?" Swain's blue eyes were full of laughter as he got into the spirit of deviling Frank.

"John's busy in the Middle East," Frank said calmly.

His reply brought Swain upright in his seat, all hint of laziness gone. "Wait a minute. Are you saying there really is a Medina?"

"There really is a Medina."

"There's no file on him—" Swain began, then caught himself, grinned, and said, "Oops."

"Meaning you've checked."

"Hell, everyone in the business has checked."

"That's why there's no file in the computer system. For his protection. Now, as I was saying, John's deep cover in the Middle East, and in any case, I wouldn't use him for a retrieval."

"Meaning he's way more important than I am." Swain had that goofy grin again, meaning he took no offense.

"Or that he has different talents. You're the man I want, and you'll be on a plane to Paris tonight. Here's what I want you to do."

4

After spending an entire day eating, resting, and doing light workouts to increase her stamina, Lily got up the morning of her departure feeling much better. She carefully packed her carry-on bag and shopping tote, making sure she was leaving nothing crucial behind. Most of her clothes were left hanging in the closet; the odd photographs of complete strangers that she had put in cheap frames and set around the flat, to give herself the appearance of a background, were left in place.

She didn't strip the bed linens or wash the single bowl and spoon she'd used for breakfast, though she did take the precaution of thoroughly wiping the place down with oil-dissolving disinfectant, to destroy her fingerprints. That was something she'd been doing for nineteen years, and the habit was strongly ingrained. She had even wiped down her surroundings before leaving the Nervi compound, though she hadn't been able to

use a disinfectant. She had also always wiped her eating uten-
sils and drinking glasses with a napkin before they were collected, and cleaned her hairbrush every morning, flushing the
stray hairs that collected in the bristles.

She was uncomfortably aware she couldn't do anything
about the blood Dr. Giordano had drawn for analyzing, but
DNA wasn't used for identification the same way that fingerprints were; there was no extensive database. Her fingerprints
were on file in Langley, but nowhere else; except for the occasional assassination, she'd been a model citizen. Even fingerprints were no good unless there was a file somewhere to match
them to, and get a name. One slipup meant nothing. Two provided a means of identification. To the best of her ability, she
tried never to provide even a starting point.

Probably Dr. Giordano would find it odd in the extreme if
she called him and asked for the return of any leftover blood. If
she were in California, now, she could claim she was a mem-
ber of a weird religious cult and needed the blood, or even that
she was a vampire, and probably get any remnants returned.

The ghoulish thought made her mouth curve into a wan
smile, and she wished she could share that thought with Zia,
who'd had a rich sense of the absurd. With Averill and Tina,
and especially with Zia, she'd been able to relax and act silly
occasionally, like a normal person. For someone in her line of
work, relaxation was a luxury, and done only with others of
her kind.

The faint smile faded. Their absence left such a huge void
in her life that she didn't think she'd ever be able to fill it. Over
the years her affection had been given to an ever-shrinking circle, until finally there had been just five people in it: her

mother and sister—and she no longer dared visit them for fear of bringing the danger of her job to their doorsteps—and three friends.

Averill had once been her lover; for a very brief time they had staved off the loneliness together. Then they had drifted apart, and she met Tina during a job that required two agents. She had never bonded instantly with anyone before the way she had with Tina, as if they had been twins meeting for the first time. They had only to look at each other to know they were thinking the same things at the same times. They had the same sense of humor, the same silly dreams that someday, when they weren't in this line of work any longer, they'd get married and own their own businesses—not necessarily in that order—and maybe even have a kid or two.

Someday had come for Tina when, like helium balloons floating around in a closed room, Averill eventually floated across her path. Lily and Tina might have had tons in common, but chemistry was one thing that was different; Averill took one look at slim, brunette Tina and fell in love, and the feeling was mutual. For a while, between jobs, they had bummed around together and generally had a blast. They were young and healthy and good at their jobs; admittedly, being assassins made them feel tough and invincible. They were professional enough not to swagger, but young enough to feel the rush.

Then Tina was shot, and reality crashed down on them. The job was deadly. The rush was no longer there. Their own mortality stared them in the face.

Averill and Tina reacted to it by getting married, as soon as Tina was well enough to walk down the aisle. They set up housekeeping together, first in a flat here in Paris, then they bought a small house on the outskirts. They began taking fewer and fewer jobs.

Lily usually came back to visit whenever she could, and one day she brought Zia with her. She'd found the baby, abandoned and starving to death, in Croatia, just after Croatia had declared its independence from Yugoslavia, when the Serb army was already decimating pockets of the new country in the beginning of the bitter war. No one Lily had asked seemed to have any knowledge of the baby's mother, or none they'd admit to, and they had even less interest. It was either take the baby with her or know she was leaving it to die a miserable death.

Within two days she loved the infant as fiercely as if she'd given birth to it herself. Getting out of Croatia hadn't been exactly easy, especially since she was lugging a baby. She'd had to find milk, and diapers, and blankets. She hadn't worried about clothes at that point, just some means, any means, of keeping the baby fed and dry and warm. She named her Zia, just because she liked the name.

Then there was the problem of getting paperwork for Zia, finding a forger good enough, and getting her into Italy. Once out of Croatia, caring for her was less difficult, the supplies Lily needed more readily available. The task of caring for her was never easy, though. The baby jerked and went rigid whenever Lily touched her, and often spat up almost as much milk as she swallowed. Rather than subject the infant to even more travel, when she'd had so few constants in her very short life, Lily decided to stay in Italy for a while.

She thought Zia had been only a few weeks old when she'd found her, though it was possible lack of food and care had made her smaller than average. After staying in Italy for three months, though, Zia had gained enough weight to have dimples on her plump little hands and legs, she was drooling incessantly as she began to cut teeth, and she looked at Lily with the openmouthed, wide-eyed expression of sheer joy that only the very young could achieve and not look like total idiots.

Finally she took Zia to France to meet Uncle Averill and Aunt Tina.

The changeover in custody happened very gradually. Whenever Lily had a job, she would leave Zia with them; they loved the baby and she was content with them, though it still broke Lily's heart every time she had to leave her, and she lived for the moment when she returned and Zia saw her for the first time. That little face would light up and she'd squeal in delight, and Lily thought she'd never heard a sound so beautiful.

But then the inevitable happened: Zia was growing up. She needed to attend school. Lily was sometimes gone for weeks at a time. It was only logical that Zia spend more and more time with Averill and Tina, until finally they all realized they had to get some more papers forged, showing the couple as Zia's parents. By the time Zia was four, Averill and Tina were Daddy and Mom to her, and Lily was Aunt Lil.

For thirteen years Zia had been the emotional center of Lily's life, and now she was gone.

What on earth had caused Averill and Tina to get back into a game they were well out of? Had they needed money? Surely they had known all they had to do was ask Lily, and she'd have given them every euro and dollar she had—and after nineteen years of the very lucrative work she did, she'd had a hefty balance in a Swiss bank. But something had lured them out of retirement, and they'd paid with their lives. And so had Zia.

Now Lily had used up most of her savings getting that poison and setting up the situation. Good papers cost money, and the better they were the more they cost. She'd had to rent the flat, get an actual job–because not having one would have been suspicious–then put herself in Salvatore Nervi's path and hope he took the bait. That hadn't been a sure bet, by any means. She could make herself look very attractive, but she knew she wasn't a beauty. If that hadn't worked, she would have thought of something else; she always did. But it *had* worked, beautifully, right up until the moment Salvatore insisted she taste his wine.

Now she had one-tenth the money she'd had before, she had a damaged heart valve that, as Dr. Giordano had explained, would eventually have to be replaced, her stamina was laughable, and her time was running out.

From a logical standpoint, she knew her odds weren't good. This time not only did she not have Langley's resources behind her, the Agency would actually be working against her. She wouldn't be able to use any of her known safe havens, she couldn't call for either backup or extraction, and she would have to be on guard against . . . everyone. She had no idea whom Langley would send after her; they might simply locate her and have a sharpshooter take her out, in which case she had nothing to worry about, because there was no way she could protect herself from something she couldn't see. She wasn't Salvatore Nervi, with a fleet of steel-reinforced cars and protected entrances. Her only hope was not to let them locate her.

On the plus side . . . Well, there was no plus side.

That didn't mean she'd walk out into the open and make

herself an easy target. They might take her down, but she'd make it as difficult for them as possible. Her professional pride was at stake. With Zia and the others gone, pride was just about all she had left.

She waited as long as she dared before using her cell phone to call for a taxi to the airport. She had to cut it as close as possible, to limit the time Rodrigo would have to get people in place. At first the men tailing her wouldn't know where she was going, but as soon as they realized she was headed to the airport, they'd call Rodrigo for instructions. The chance of Rodrigo already having someone–or several someones–on the payroll at the airport was at least fifty-fifty, but de Gaulle was a large airport and, without knowing exactly which airline she was taking or her destination, heading her off would be difficult. All they could do was follow, but only so far before security would stop them.

If Rodrigo had the passenger list checked, the jig would be up, because she wasn't flying under the name of Denise Morel, or even her own name. She had no doubt he'd check; the only question was how soon he'd do it. At first, he might not even be suspicious enough to do more than have her followed.

By leaving so openly, and taking so little luggage, she hoped he'd be curious but not suspicious, at least not for the short amount of time it would take her to disappear.

If the gods were smiling on her, he wouldn't be unduly suspicious even when his men lost track of her in busy Heathrow. He might wonder why she flew instead of taking a ferry or tunnel, but a lot of people flew the short hop from Paris to London, and vice versa, if they were short of time.

In the best possible scenario, he wouldn't think anything of her trip for at least a couple of days, until she failed to return home. The worst possible scenario would be if he had his men grab her in de Gaulle airport, regardless of witnesses and possible repercussions. Rodrigo wouldn't worry about either of those. She was betting he wouldn't go to that extent; so far he hadn't discovered she wasn't who she said she was, because he hadn't had his men storm her flat. In the absence of that knowledge, there was no reason for him to cause a public disturbance.

Lily went downstairs to wait for the taxi, standing where she could see the street but her watchers couldn't see her. She had thought about walking the several blocks to a taxi rank and waiting in line, but that would have given Rodrigo time she didn't want him to have, and also tired her. Once—only a little over a week ago—she could have sprinted the distance and not even been winded.

Perhaps her heart had sustained little damage, just enough for Dr. Giordano to detect the murmur, and this insidious weakness would eventually go away. She'd been very sick for over three days, eating nothing, flat on her back. The human body lost strength much faster than it gained it. She'd give it a month; if she wasn't back to normal in that length of time, she'd have some tests run on her heart. She didn't know where, or how she'd pay for it, but she'd manage.

Of course, that was assuming she was still alive a month from now. Even after she escaped from Rodrigo, she'd still have to evade her former employer. She hadn't computed those odds yet; she didn't want to discourage herself.

A black taxi stopped outside. Picking up her carry-on bag, Lily murmured, "Show time," and calmly stepped outside. She didn't hurry, didn't in any way appear nervous. When she was seated, she took a mirrored compact out of her tote and angled it so she could watch her watchers.

As the taxi pulled away, so did a silver Mercedes. It slowed, a man darted over and practically leaped into the passenger seat, then the Mercedes accelerated until it was right behind the taxi. In the mirror, Lily could see the passenger talking on a cell phone.

The airport was about thirty kilometers out of the city; the Mercedes stayed behind the taxi all the way. Lily didn't know if she should be insulted or not; did Rodrigo think she was too stupid to notice, or that she would simply not care if she did? On the other hand, normal people didn't check to see if they were being followed, so the fact that her watchers were so blatant could mean Rodrigo still didn't really suspect her of anything, despite having her watched and followed. Judging from what she knew about him, she thought he would do that until he discovered who killed his father. Rodrigo wasn't one to let a loose end go untied.

When they reached the airport, she walked calmly to the British Airways desk to check in. Her passport said her name was Alexandra Wesley, British citizen, and the passport photo matched her current coloring. She was flying first class, she wasn't checking any luggage, and she had carefully built up this identity, over several years, with numerous stamps on her passport showing she visited France several times a year. She had several such identities, prudently kept private even from her contacts at Langley, for just such emergencies.

Boarding for the flight had already been called by the time she went through all the security checks and got to the designated gate. She didn't look around her, instead carefully studying her surroundings with her peripheral vision. Yes, that man there; he was watching her, and he held a cell phone in his hand.

He didn't make any move toward her, just made a call. Her luck was holding.

Then she was safely on the plane, effectively in the hands of the British government. Her designated seat was next to the window; the aisle seat was already occupied by a stylishly dressed woman who looked to be in her late twenties or early thirties. Lily murmured an apology as she slid past the woman to the window seat.

Within half an hour they were in the air for the hour's flight to London. She and her seatmate exchanged pleasantries, Lily using a public-school accent that seemed to put the woman at ease. The British accent was easier to maintain than the Parisian one, and she almost sighed with relief as her brain seemed to relax. She dozed briefly, tired from all the airport walking.

When they were fifteen minutes out of London, she leaned over and pulled her carry-on bag from underneath the seat. "I'm sorry to disturb you," she said hesitantly to the woman beside her, "but I've a bit of a problem."

"Yes?" the woman said politely.

"My name is Alexandra Wesley, perhaps you've heard of Wesley Engineering? That's my husband, Gerald. The thing is–" Lily looked down, as if embarrassed. "Well, the thing is, I'm leaving him and he isn't taking it at all well. He's set men to following me, and I'm afraid he'll have them grab me. He's a bit abusive, set on having his way, and . . . and I really can't go back."

The woman looked both uncomfortable and intrigued, as if she didn't like hearing such intimate details from a stranger but was fascinated in spite of herself. "You poor dear. Of course you can't go back. But how can I help?"

"When we leave the plane, will you take this bag for me and go to the nearest public loo? I'll follow you and take it back. It has a disguise in it," she said quickly, when the woman's face showed alarm at being asked to take a stranger's bag in this age of terrorism. "See, look through it." She quickly unzipped the bag. "Clothes, shoes, wigs. Nothing else. The thing is, they might think of that–that I'd disguise myself, I mean–and pay attention to the bags I take into the loo with me. I read a book on how to evade a stalker and it mentioned this. He'll have men at Heathrow waiting for me, I know it; as soon as I step out for transportation they'll take me." She wrung her hands, hoping she looked suitably distressed. It helped that her face was still thin and drawn from illness, and that she was normally lanky anyway, making her look more frail than she was.

The woman took the bag from Lily and carefully went through every item. A smile broke over her face when she examined one of the wigs. "Hiding in plain sight, are you?"

Lily smiled back. "I hope it works."

"We'll see. If not, we'll share a taxi. Safety in numbers, and all that." The woman was getting into the spirit of things now.

If her seatmate hadn't been a woman, Lily would have improvised, taken her chances, but this gambit slightly increased her chances, and at this point she was willing to grab at the least advantage. Agency men could be waiting for her, as well as Rodrigo's goons, and they wouldn't be as easy to fool.

Depending on how they wanted to play it, they could have her arrested as soon as she stepped off the plane, in which case there was nothing she could do. They usually played it much

closer to the vest than that, though. If they could avoid involving the British government in what was essentially a housekeeping chore to them, then they would.

The plane landed and went to the gate with a minimum of
fuss. Lily took a deep breath, and her cohort patted her hand.
"Don't worry," she said cheerfully. "This will work, you'll see.
How will I know if they've spotted you?"

"I'll tell you where the men are standing. I'll look for them
when I go into the loo. Then I'll leave before you, and when you
come out, if they're still there, then you'll know it worked."

"Oh, this is exciting!"

Lily really hoped not.

The woman took the carry-on bag and exited the plane two
people ahead of Lily. She walked briskly, looking at the signs
but not staring at the people waiting at the gate. Good girl, Lily
thought, hiding a smile. She was a natural.

There were two of them waiting for her, and again they
made no particular effort to disguise their interest. Glee rose in
her. Rodrigo still didn't suspect anything truly unusual, didn't
think she would notice she was being followed. This might
really work.

The two men trailed in her wake, staying about twenty or
thirty feet back. Up ahead, her cohort went into the first public
restroom. Lily paused just outside at a water fountain, giving
her followers time to choose their positions, then entered.

The woman was waiting just inside and handed over the
bag. "Is anyone there?" she asked.

Lily nodded. "Two of them. One is about six feet tall, larg-
ish, and he's wearing a light gray suit. He's standing directly
across from the door, against the wall. The other is smaller,

short dark hair, double-breasted blue suit, and he's in position about fifteen feet ahead."

"Hurry and change. I can't wait to see you."

Lily went into a stall and swiftly began her identity change. The severe dark suit and low heels came off; in their place went a bright pink tank top, painted-on turquoise leggings, stiletto knee-high boots, a fringed turquoise jacket, and a short, spiky red wig. She dumped the clothes she'd removed into the carry-on, and stepped out of the stall.

A huge smile lit the woman's face, and she clapped her hands. "Wonderful!"

Lily couldn't help grinning. She swiftly added blusher to her pale cheeks, a thick coating of pink lipstick, and dangling feathered earrings. Slipping a pair of pink shades over her eyes, she said, "What do you think?"

"My dear, I wouldn't have recognized you, and I knew what you were about. I'm Rebecca, by the way. Rebecca Scott."

They shook hands, each delighted for different reasons. Lily took a deep breath. "Here I go," she murmured, and strode boldly out of the restroom.

Both of her followers involuntarily stared at her; everyone did. Looking directly beyond the dark-haired man who stood practically in front of her, Lily waved enthusiastically. "I'm here!" she squealed to no one in particular, though in this crowd that would have been difficult to determine. This time she used her own distinctly American accent, and dashed past her watchers as if joining someone.

As she went by the dark-haired man, she saw him jerk his gaze back to the restroom entrance, as if afraid that moment of inattention had allowed his quarry to escape.

Lily walked as rapidly as she could, losing herself in the crowd. The five-inch heels put her close to six feet tall, but there was no way she intended to wear them any longer than necessary. As she neared her departure gate, she ducked into yet another public restroom, and changed out of the eye-grabbing disguise. When she left that bathroom, she had long black hair and wore black jeans and a thick black turtleneck sweater, with the same low-heeled shoes she'd worn on the flight over. She had wiped off the pink lipstick, replaced it with red gloss, and exchanged the pink shades for gray ones. Her papers as Alexandra Wesley were stowed in her tote, and the ticket and passport in her hand stated she was Mariel St. Clair.

Soon she was on a plane headed back across the Channel to Paris, this time in coach. She leaned her head back against the seat and closed her eyes.

So far, so good.

5

RODRIGO WAS FURIOUS. HE SAID, CAREFULLY, "HOW, PRECISELY, did you manage to lose her?"

"She was followed from the moment she exited the plane," replied the British voice on the phone. "She entered the public facilities, and never came out."

"Did you send someone in to look for her?"

"After some length of time, yes."

"Exactly *what* length of time?"

"Perhaps twenty minutes passed before my men became alarmed, sir. Then I had to wait until a female could be brought to the location to enter the facilities and search."

Rodrigo closed his eyes as he tried to rein in his temper. Bumblers! The men following Denise must have become distracted and not noticed her leaving the facilities. There were no other exits, no windows or trash chutes or anything else. She could only have left the same way she entered, yet these idiots had somehow completely overlooked her.

The matter wasn't terribly important, but inefficiency annoyed him. Until he got the answers he wanted about Denise's background, he wanted to know exactly where she was and what she was doing. In fact, he'd expected to have those answers the day before, but the bureaucracy was being as inefficient as usual.

"One thing is puzzling, sir."

"And that is?"

"When my men lost her, I immediately checked with Customs, but we have no record of her."

Rodrigo sat upright, a sudden frown drawing his brows together. "What does that mean?"

"It means she disappeared. When I checked the passenger list of the inbound flight, there was no Denise Morel listed. She did get off the plane, but then she somehow disappeared. The only plausible explanation is that she got on another plane, but I have no record of her doing that."

Alarm bells rang in Rodrigo's head so loudly they were almost deafening. He went cold, frozen by the sudden horrible suspicion. "Check the records again, Mr. Murray. She must have done."

"I have already double-checked, sir. There is no record of her entering or leaving London. I was very thorough with my search."

"Thank you," Rodrigo said, and hung up the phone. He was so enraged he was dizzy from the force of his emotions. The bitch had played him for a fool!

Just to make certain, he called his contact in the Ministry. "I need that information immediately," he barked, not identifying either himself or the information in question. He didn't need to.

"Yes, of course, but there is a problem."

"You can't find where this particular Denise Morel exists?" Rodrigo asked sarcastically.

"How did you know? I'm certain I can—"

"Don't trouble yourself. You won't find her." His suspicions confirmed, Rodrigo hung up again and sat behind the desk trying to contain the sulfuric rage that blasted through him. He had to think clearly, and at the moment that was beyond him.

She was the poisoner. How clever of her, to also poison herself, but with such a small dose that she would be sick for a time but would survive. Or perhaps she hadn't intended to sip the wine at all, but his father had insisted and she accidentally took a larger swallow than she'd intended. That part didn't matter; what mattered was that, ultimately, she had succeeded in killing his father.

He couldn't believe how she had fooled him, fooled them all. Her paperwork had been perfect, as far as it went. Now that it was too late, he saw with perfect clarity how it had worked. Salvatore had been lulled into carelessness by her apparent indifference to his advances, and Rodrigo, too, had allowed himself to relax after Salvatore's first few meetings with her were so ordinary. If she had appeared eager for his father's company, he would have been much more vigorous in demanding answers, but she had played them all perfectly.

She was obviously a professional, no doubt paid by one of his rivals. As a professional, she had other identities to use when she disappeared afterward, or perhaps she simply used her own real name, since *Denise Morel* was an alias. She had definitely been on that plane to London—his men had seen her there—therefore, one of the passengers listed was her. He simply had to discover which one, and follow the path from there. The task before him now—or rather, before his people who would be doing the actual work—was daunting, but he had a starting point. He would have them investigate every person on that plane, and he would find her.

No matter how long it took, he *would* find her. And then he would make her suffer far more than his poor father had suffered. Before he finished with her, she would not only tell him everything she knew about who had hired her, she would also die cursing her own mother for giving birth to her. This he swore on the memory of his father.

Lucas Swain moved silently about the flat that Liliane Mansfield, aka Denise Morel, had abandoned.

Oh, her clothes were still here, or most of them, anyway. Food still in the cupboard, a bowl and spoon in the sink. It looked as if she'd gone to work, or was just out shopping, but he knew better. He knew a professional job when he saw one. There wasn't a fingerprint in the place, not even on the spoon left in the sink. The wipe-down was perfect.

Judging from the file he'd read on her, the clothes she'd left behind weren't her type, anyway. The clothes belonged to Denise Morel, and now that Denise had served her purpose, Lily had shed her like a snake shedding its skin. Salvatore Nervi was dead; there was no reason for Denise to exist any longer.

What puzzled him was why she'd hung around for so long. Nervi had evidently been dead for a week or longer, but the landlord reported Mlle. Morel had taken a taxi this very morning. No, he did not know to where, but she was carrying a small bag. A weekend trip, perhaps.

Hours. He'd missed her by mere hours.

The landlord hadn't let him into the flat, of course; Swain'd had to sneak in, then quietly spring the lock on Lily's flat. The landlord had obligingly told him which flat it was, saving Swain from having to break in during the night and look at the records, which would have wasted time.

As it was, this was wasted time anyway. She wasn't here, and she wasn't coming back.

There was a bowl of fruit on the table. He selected an apple, polished it on his shirt, and bit into it. Damn, he was hungry, and if she'd wanted the apple, she'd have taken it with her. Curious, he opened the icebox to see what else she had in the way of food, and closed the door again in disappointment. Chick food: fruit, some fresh produce, and what was either cottage cheese or yogurt that was way too old. Why didn't women who lived alone ever have real food around? He'd kill for a pizza, loaded with pepperoni. Or a grilled steak, with a huge baked potato dripping with butter and sour cream. Now, that was *food.*

While he pondered what his next step should be in locating his quarry, he ate another apple.

According to her file, Lily was very comfortable in France and spoke the language like a native. She supposedly had a talent for accents, too. She had spent some time in Italy and traveled all over the civilized world, but when she settled down for a rest, it was in either France or Great Britain, where she felt most at home. Logic would say she had got the hell out of Dodge, meaning she was no longer in France. That left Great Britain as the most likely place to start looking.

Of course, since she was very good at her job, she might have considered the same logic and gone someplace else entirely, such as Japan. He grimaced. He hated it when he outthought himself. Well, he might as well play it by the numbers and start with the most likely place first; even a blind hog sometimes found an acorn.

There were three common ways to cross the Channel: ferry, train, and airplane. He picked air, because it was the fastest, and she'd be wanting to put some space between her and the Nervi organization. London wasn't the only G.B. destination she could have chosen, of course, but it was the closest, and she'd want to give any pursuers the shortest length of time possible in which to organize an interception. Information could be relayed instantly, but moving human beings around still took time. That made London the logical destination, which left him with two major airports to cover, Heathrow and Gatwick. He opted for Heathrow first, because it was the busiest and most crowded.

He took a seat in the cozy little parlor–no recliners, damn it–and pulled out his trusty secure cell phone. After punching in a long series of numbers, he pressed the *send* button and waited to connect. A brisk British voice said, "Murray here."

"Swain. I need some info. A woman named Denise Morel may or may not have–"

"This is certainly a coincidence."

Adrenaline surged through Swain, the kick felt by a hunter who has suddenly found the trail he'd been seeking. "Someone else has asked about her?"

"Rodrigo Nervi himself. We were told to follow her when she deplaned. I put two men on it; they tailed her as far as the first public facility. She went in, and never came out. She didn't go through Customs, and I show no record of her taking another flight out. She's a very resourceful woman."

"More than you know," Swain said. "You told Nervi all of this?"

"Yes. It's my standing order to cooperate with him—up to a point. He didn't ask to have her killed, just followed."

But the fact that she had disappeared so thoroughly would have tipped Nervi off to her capabilities, which in turn would put her in an entirely new light. By now Nervi would have discovered there was no Denise Morel of this particular description, and worked out for himself that she was almost certainly the person who had killed his father. The heat on Lily had just been turned up a couple of thousand degrees.

How had she slipped away in Heathrow? A secure-access door? First she would have had to slip out of the restroom undetected, and that meant a disguise. A clever woman like Lily would have figured out how to do that, been prepared for it. And she would have had an alternate identification to use, too.

"A disguise," he said.

"I thought the same, though I didn't say so to Mr. Nervi. He's a smart man, so he'll eventually think of it, even though airport security isn't his milieu. Then he'll want me to look at all the film."

"Have you?" If the answer wasn't yes, then Murray wasn't as sharp as he used to be.

"Immediately after my men failed to spot her when she left the facility. I can't fault them, however, because I've been over the film twice and I haven't spotted her yet, either."

"I'll be there on the next available flight."

Because of travel time to the airport, the availability of seats, et cetera, that was some six hours later. Swain passed the time by catching a nap, but he was aware that every passing minute was to Lily's advantage. She knew how they worked, what their resources were; she'd be building herself a tidy little hidey-hole, adding more and more layers to her camouflage. The delay was also giving her time to procure funds from some unknown bank account that he assumed she had. If he'd been in her line of work, he sure as hell would have had several numbered accounts. As it happened, he himself had a little liquid security deposited offshore. You just never knew when something like that might come in handy. And if it never needed to be used, well, it would make retirement a trifle more comfortable. He was all for a comfortable retirement.

As promised, Charles Murray was waiting at the gate when Swain finally arrived at Heathrow. Murray was of medium height, trim, with short iron-gray hair and hazel eyes. His bearing said he was ex-military; his demeanor was always calm and capable. He'd been unofficially on Nervi's payroll for seven years, and on the government's for a lot longer than that. Over the years Swain had occasionally dealt with Murray, enough so that they were fairly informal with each other. That is, Swain was informal; Murray was a Brit.

"This way," said Murray after a brief handshake.

"How are the wife and kids?" Swain asked, talking to Murray's back as he ambled along in the British wake.

"Victoria is beautiful, as always. The children are teenagers."

"Enough said."

"Quite. And you?"

"Chrissy is a junior in college now; Sam's a freshman.

They're both great. Technically Sam's still a teenager, but he's out of the worst of it." Actually, both of them had turned out pretty damned good, considering their parents had been divorced for a dozen years and their father was out of the country a lot. To a large degree that was because their mother, bless her heart, had steadfastly refused to make him the bad guy in their breakup. He and Amy had sat the kids down, told them the divorce was for a lot of reasons, including getting married way too young, blah blah blah. Which was all perfectly true. The bottom line, though, was that Amy was tired of having a husband who was mostly somewhere else, and she wanted to be free to look for someone else. Ironically, she hadn't remarried, though she dated some. The kids' lives hadn't changed all that much from when he and Amy were still married: they lived in the same house, went to the same school, and saw their father just about as often as they had before.

If he and Amy had been older and wiser when they married, they never would have had kids together, knowing how his work would affect their marriage, but unfortunately age and wisdom seem to increase at about the same rate and by the time they were old enough to know better, it was too late. Still, he couldn't regret having his kids. He loved them with every cell in his body, even if he got to see them only a few times a year, and he accepted that he wasn't nearly as important in their lives as their mother was.

"One can only do one's best, and pray the demon seed eventually morph back into human beings," Murray observed as he turned down a short corridor. "Here we are." He blocked the view of a keypad and punched in a code, then opened a plain steel door. Inside was a vast array of monitors and sharp-eyed personnel watching the ebb and flow of people inside the huge airport.

From there they went into a smaller room, which also had several monitors, as well as equipment for reviewing what the numerous array of cameras caught on film. Murray seated himself in a blue chair on wheels and invited Swain to pull up another one just like it. He typed in a keyboard command and the monitor directly in front of them glowed to life. Frozen on it was a frame of Lily Mansfield getting off the plane from Paris that morning.

Swain studied every detail, noting that she didn't wear any jewelry at all, not even a wristwatch. Smart girl. Sometimes people would change everything except their wristwatch, and that one detail would trip them up. She was dressed in a plain dark suit and wore low-heeled black pumps. He thought she looked thin and pale, as if she'd been sick or something.

She didn't look left or right, just walked with the rest of the crowd getting off the plane, and went into the first restroom she came to. A steady parade of women came out of the restroom, but none of them looked like Lily.

"I'll be damned," he said. "Run it again. In slow motion."

Murray obligingly set the video back to the beginning. Swain watched her come off the plane carrying a medium-sized black tote, the kind that didn't stand out because millions of women carried them every day. He focused on the tote, looking for any means of identifying it: a buckle, the way the straps fit, anything. After Lily vanished into the restroom, he looked for that tote coming out. He saw a lot of black bags of all sizes and shapes, but only one looked as if it might be that particular one. It was carried by a six-foot-tall woman whose clothes,

hair, makeup all shouted, "Look at me!" But she wasn't carrying just that tote, she was also hauling around a carry-on bag,
and Lily hadn't had one of those.

Huh.

"Run it again," he said. "From the beginning. I want to see
everyone who got off that plane."

Murray obliged. Swain studied every face, and particularly
noted what bags they carried.

Then he saw it. "There!" he said, leaning closer to the
screen.

Murray froze the image. "What? She hasn't come into view
yet."

"No, but look at this woman." Swain jabbed his finger at the
screen. "Look at her carry-on bag. Okay, let's pay attention to
what she does, too."

The stylishly dressed woman was several passengers ahead
of Lily. She walked straight to the restroom, which wasn't
unusual. A fair number of women from that flight did the
same thing. Swain watched the video until the woman left the
restroom—without the carry-on bag.

"Bingo," he said. "She took the bag in; the clothes for the
disguise were in it. Back it up some. There. That's our girl. She
has the bag now."

Murray blinked at the fantastic creature on the monitor.
"My word," he said. "Are you certain?"

"Did you see this particular woman go into the restroom?"

"No, but I wasn't looking for her." Murray paused. "I could
scarcely have missed her, could I?"

"Not in that get-up." The feathered earrings alone would

pull a second look. From the short red spiky hair to the stiletto boots, that woman was an attention-getter. If Murray hadn't seen her enter the restroom, it was because she hadn't. But no wonder Murray's men hadn't seen beneath the disguise; how many people, trying to hide their true self, would invite scrutiny like that?

"Look at the nose and mouth. That's her." Lily's nose wasn't exactly hooked, but it was the closest it could get and still be feminine. It was thin but strong, and oddly appealing when paired with that mouth, with the full upper lip.

"So it is," Murray said, and shook his head. "I'm off my game, not to have seen it before."

"It's a good disguise. Smart. Okay, let's see where our Technicolor cowgirl goes."

Murray worked the keyboard, pulling up the necessary video to follow Lily's progress through the airport. She walked for a while, then went into another restroom. And didn't come back out.

Swain rubbed his eyes. "Here we go again. Just concentrate on finding those particular bags."

Because of the swarm of foot traffic occasionally blocking the camera's view, they had to watch the tape several times to narrow their list of possibilities down to three women, and track them until they could get a better view. At last they had her, though. She had long black hair now, and was wearing black pants and a black turtleneck. She was shorter, the stiletto boots gone. The sunglasses were different, too, and the feathered earrings had been replaced with gold hoops. She still had those two particular bags, though.

The cameras tracked her to another gate, where she boarded

another plane. Murray swiftly checked which flight had left the gate at that particular time. "Paris," he said.

"Son of a bitch," Swain uttered in astonishment. She'd gone back. "Can you get that passenger list for me?" It was a rhetorical question; of course Murray could. It was in his hands a few minutes later. He skimmed down the names, noting that neither Denise Morel nor Lily Mansfield was listed, meaning she had yet another identity going.

Now would come the fun part, going back to Paris and going through this same process with the authorities at de Gaulle airport. The prickly French might not be as accommodating as Murray, but Swain wasn't without a few resources.

"Do me a favor," he said to Murray. "Don't pass this information along to Rodrigo Nervi." He didn't want that bunch getting in his way, plus he had a natural dislike of doing anything to help people like that. Circumstances might force the United States government to occasionally look the other way about the dirtier parts of the Nervi organization, but he didn't have to help them out one bit.

"I don't know what you're talking about," said Murray blandly. "What information?"

It would be, of course, just as much hassle getting back across the Channel as it had been getting to London. He couldn't get off one plane and get right back on another the way she had done; oh, no, it was never that simple. She had planned ahead; he was scrambling around behind her, trying to find an available seat. She'd known exactly what would confuse and delay anyone tracking her, of course.

Still, it was discouraging to find out he had another long wait before the next flight with an empty seat.

Murray clapped him on the shoulder. "I know someone who can get you there much faster than that."

"Thank God," said Swain. "Bring him on."

"You don't mind flying backseat, do you? He's a NATO pilot."

"Holy shit," Swain blurted. "You're putting me in a *fighter*?"

"I did say 'much faster,' didn't I?"

6

LILY LET HERSELF INTO THE SUBLET APARTMENT IN MONTMARTRE that she had rented several months ago, before she had assumed the Denise Morel identity. The apartment was tiny, really more a studio than a true apartment, but had its own minuscule bathroom. She had her own clothes here, plus privacy and relative safety. Because the sublet predated Denise's appearance, no computer search was likely to go back far enough to put her on any sort of list, plus she had concocted yet another identity: Claudia Weber, a German national.

Because Claudia was a blonde, Lily had stopped at a hairdresser and had the artificial coloring removed from her hair. She would have bought the products and done it herself, but removing color was much more complicated than adding it and she was afraid she might do all sorts of damage to her hair. An inch had had to be trimmed as it was, to get rid of the dry ends after the bleaching process.

But when she looked in the mirror, she saw herself again, at last. The colored contact lenses were gone and her own pale blue eyes looked back at her. Her straight hair was once more wheat blond, reaching just to her shoulders. She could walk right past Rodrigo Nervi and he probably wouldn't recognize her–she hoped, because she might be doing exactly that.

Wearily she set her bags on the neatly made fold-out bed, then tumbled down beside them. She knew she should check to make certain the apartment hadn't been bugged, but she had been pushing herself relentlessly all day and she was shaking with fatigue. If she could sleep for just an hour, that would make a world of difference.

All in all, though, she was pleased with how her stamina had held out today. She was tired, yes, but not gasping for breath, as Dr. Giordano had warned she would be if that heart valve was severely damaged. Of course, she hadn't been unduly exerting herself, either; she hadn't been sprinting. So the jury was still out on the heart thing.

She closed her eyes and in the quiet concentrated on her heartbeat; it seemed normal to her. *Thump-thump, thump-thump.* With his stethoscope Dr. Giordano could hear a murmur, but she didn't have a stethoscope and as far as she could tell the rhythm was completely normal. So maybe the damage was minimal, just enough to produce a faint murmur. She had other things to worry about.

She drifted into a half-doze in which her body relaxed while her mind began to circle around the situation, probing and rearranging facts as she knew them, trying to find answers to the unknown factors.

She didn't know what Averill and Tina had stumbled across, or what they'd been told, but it was something they felt strongly

enough about to bring them back into a business they'd abandoned. She didn't even know who had hired them. Not the CIA,
she was almost certain. Probably not MI-6 either. While they
didn't live in each other's pockets, the two governments and
agencies maintained a strong degree of cooperation between
them, and in any case, there were plenty of active agents available to them, so there wouldn't have been any need to bring in
two inactive ones.

In fact, she didn't think any government had hired them; instead, it looked like a private hire. Somewhere along the way—
hell, *all* along the way—Salvatore Nervi had stepped on toes,
bullied, brutalized, and killed. Finding his enemies wouldn't be
difficult; sorting them out could take a year or longer. But who
had gone to the trouble of hiring two professionals, albeit retired ones, to hit back? Moreover, who had known about her
friends' backgrounds? Averill and Tina had lived ordinary lives,
had gone out of their way to provide that kind of life for Zia;
they hadn't exactly advertised their pasts.

But someone had known about them, known their capabilities. That suggested someone who had been in the business,
too, she thought, or at least been in a position to know names.
Whoever it was had also known not to approach an active contract agent, not to bring attention to himself or herself in that
manner. Instead the unknown someone had picked Averill and
Tina because . . . why? Why them? And with Zia to consider,
why had they accepted?

Her friends had been young enough to still be in good
physical shape—that was one possible reason for their selection
that came to mind. They had also been skilled at what they did,
coolheaded, experienced. She could see why they had been

tapped, but what had swayed them to get involved? Money? They had been doing okay, not rich but not hurting for cash, either. A truly astronomical amount could have swayed them, but over the years they'd developed the same casual attitude about money that she had. From the time she'd begun her career, money had always been there. She didn't worry about it, and neither had Averill and Tina. She knew for a fact that between them the two agents had salted away enough cash to live in relative comfort for the rest of their lives, plus Averill had been doing okay for himself with a computer-repair shop.

She wished one of them had picked up the telephone and called her, told her what they were considering. Their motivation had to have been strong and she wanted to know what it was, because then she'd know how to attack. Her revenge wasn't complete just because Salvatore was dead; he was just the first act. She wouldn't be satisfied until she found out what was bad enough that her friends had become involved, something that would make the entire world turn against the Nervi organization, and even the people in power who had been in Salvatore's pocket would rush to distance themselves. She wanted to bring down the entire rotten deck of cards.

She had the fleeting thought that if Tina had told her about the job they were taking, if it had been something important enough to bring them out of retirement, she might well have joined them. She might have made the difference between success and failure—or she herself might be dead alongside them.

But they hadn't mentioned a thing, even though she'd had dinner with them not a week before their murders. She had been going out of town on a job that would take a few days or a little longer, yes, but she'd told them when she expected to be back. Had they already known then, or had this job offer come out of the blue and needed doing immediately? Averill and Tina didn't operate that way. Neither did she. Anything involving the Nervi organization required study and preparation, because the layers of security were so dense.

None of this was anything she hadn't mentally gone over and over during many sleepless nights since they had been killed. Sometimes, when Zia's cheerful little face formed in her mind's eye, she wept with a violence that frightened her. In her grief she'd needed to strike back immediately, to cut off the head of the snake. She'd done that, focusing on nothing else for three months, and now she would concentrate on the rest of it.

First, she needed to find out who had hired Averill and Tina. A private hire meant someone with money . . . or maybe not. Maybe the need had been the motivating factor. Maybe this person had come to them with proof of something particularly nasty in which Salvatore was involved. With Salvatore, that could be anything; she couldn't imagine anything so low and dirty that he would balk at it. His only requirement had been that he make money.

But Averill and Tina had both retained an idealistic core, and she could see them being so alarmed at something that they were moved to action, even though in their former occupations they'd seen so much that it was difficult to shock them. What could that have been?

Zia. *Something that threatened Zia.* To protect her, they would have fought tigers bare-handed. Anything involving her would explain both their urgency and their motivation.

Lily sat up, blinking. Of course. Why hadn't she seen it before? If it wasn't money that drew them back in, then what else had been important to them? Their marriage, their love for each other, Lily herself . . . but most of all, Zia.

She had no proof. She didn't need it. She had known her friends, known how much they loved their daughter, known what was important in their lives. This conclusion was an intuitive leap, but it felt right. Nothing else had.

This gave her a direction. Among the Nervi holdings were several labs, engaged in all sorts of medical, chemical, and biological research. Since Averill and Tina had evidently felt this was something that had to be taken care of immediately, whatever it was had been imminent. But even though they'd failed, nothing unusual that had happened since then came to mind; no catastrophes locally. She couldn't think of anything other than the usual terrorist bombings, which seemed to need no reason.

But maybe they hadn't failed. Maybe they had succeeded in their mission, but Salvatore had discovered who they were and had them killed, to teach others not to interfere with the Nervis.

The target might not have been one of the laboratories, though they seemed the most likely targets. Salvatore had many properties, scattered all over Europe. She needed to search the back issues of some newspapers, to see if any incidents involving a Nervi property had been reported during the week between when she'd last seen her friends alive and their deaths. Salvatore had been powerful enough to keep media attention to a minimum, even black it out completely if he saw the need, but there might still be a small mention of . . . something.

Her friends hadn't taken any trips immediately prior to their deaths. She had talked to their neighbors; Averill and Tina had been at home, Zia had been in school. So whatever was involved was local, or at least close by.

She would go to an Internet café tomorrow and do a search. She could do it now, but common sense told her to rest after such a long day. She was relatively safe here, even from the Agency. No one knew about Claudia Weber, and she wasn't doing anything to attract attention. She'd had the foresight to grab something to eat at the airport, knowing she was in for a long session with the hairdresser, and she'd also bought a few snacks for tonight, plus enough coffee for tomorrow. She was set for right now. Tomorrow she'd need to shop for food, something best done early in the morning before all the best choices were taken. After that, she'd hit an Internet café and get started.

The Internet was a wonderful thing, Rodrigo thought. If one knew the right people—and he did—almost nothing on it was safe from scrutiny.

First his people had created a list of the rogue chemists available for hire who had the skill to create such a lethal poison. That last requirement had shrunk the list from several hundred down to nine, which was a much more manageable number.

From there it had simply been a matter of investigating finances. Someone would have received a large amount of money recently. Perhaps the person in question would be intelligent enough to put the money in a numbered account, but perhaps not. Even so, there would be evidence of an influx of cash.

He found that evidence with Dr. Walter Speer, a German national who lived in Amsterdam. Dr. Speer had been fired from a reputable company in Berlin, then from another in Hamburg. He had then relocated to Amsterdam, where he had been getting by but not making a fortune. Dr. Speer, however, had recently purchased a silver Porsche, and paid for it in full. It was child's play to discover where Dr. Speer banked, and not much more difficult than that for the experts on Rodrigo's staff to get into the bank's computer system. A little more than a month ago, Dr. Speer had deposited a million American dollars. The conversion rate had made him a very happy man.

American. Rodrigo was stunned. The *Americans* had paid to have his father killed? That didn't make sense. Their agreement was too valuable to the Americans for them to interfere; Salvatore had seen to that. Rodrigo hadn't necessarily agreed with his father on their dealings with the Americans, but it had worked for a number of years and nothing had happened to upset the status quo.

Denise—or whoever she was—had effectively disappeared today, but now he had another link to her, to finding out who she really was and whom she was working for.

Rodrigo wasn't a man who wasted time; that very night he flew in his private jet to Amsterdam. Locating Dr. Speer's apartment was child's play, as was forcing the lock on the door. He was waiting in the dark when Dr. Walter Speer finally came home.

From the moment the door opened, Rodrigo smelled the strong odor of alcohol, and Dr. Speer stumbled a bit as he turned to switch on a lamp.

Rodrigo hit him from behind a split second later, slamming him into the wall to stun him, then throwing him to the floor and straddling him, his fists delivering powerful one-two punches to the doctor's face. Explosive violence stuns the in-experienced, throws them into such a state of confusion and shock that they are helpless. Dr. Speer was not only inexperienced but inebriated. He couldn't manage anything in the way of self-defense, not that it would have done any good. Rodrigo was bigger, younger, faster, and skilled at what he did.

Rodrigo hauled him to a sitting position and thrust him against the wall, making sure that his head once more banged hard. Then he gripped the doctor's coat and pulled him closer for a good look. He liked what he saw.

Huge red lumps were already swelling on the doctor's face, and blood trickled from both his nose and mouth. His glasses had been broken and hung askew from one ear. The expression in his eyes was one of total incomprehension.

Other than that, Dr. Speer looked to be in his early forties. He had a shock of thick brown hair and was stocky in build, making him slightly bearlike. Before Rodrigo's art work on them, his features had probably been ordinary.

"Let me introduce myself," Rodrigo said in accented German. He didn't speak it well, but could make himself understood. "I am Rodrigo Nervi." He wanted to let the doctor know exactly with whom he was dealing. He saw the doctor's eyes widen in alarm; he wasn't so drunk that he was beyond all good sense.

"A month ago, you received a payment of a million American dollars. Who paid you, and why?"

"I–I . . . What?" Dr. Speer stammered.

"The money. Who gave it to you?"

"A woman. I don't know her name."

Rodrigo shook him so hard his head wobbled on his neck, and his broken glasses went flying. "Are you certain of that?"

"She–she never told me," Speer gasped.

"What did she look like?"

"Ah–" Speer blinked as he tried to focus his thoughts. "Brown hair. Brown eyes, I think. I did not care how she looked, you understand?"

"Old? Young?"

Again Speer blinked, several times. "Thirties?" he said, making it a question, as if he wasn't certain of his memory.

So. It had definitely been Denise who had given him the million dollars. Speer didn't know who had given her the money–that was another trail to follow–but this confirmed everything. Rodrigo had known instinctively from the moment she disappeared that she was the killer, but it was good to know he wasn't wasting time chasing down false leads.

"You made a poison for her."

Speer swallowed convulsively, but a spark of professional pride lit his blurry gaze. He didn't even deny it. "A masterpiece, if I do say so. I took the properties of several deadly toxins and combined them. One hundred percent lethal, if even a half ounce is taken. By the time the delayed symptoms are presented, the damage is so severe there is no effective treatment. I suppose one could try a multiorgan transplant, assuming there just happened to be that many organs available at one time and they were all a match, but if there was any toxin left in the system it would attack those organs, too. No, I don't think that would work."

"Thank you, Doctor." Rodrigo smiled, a cold smile that, if the doctor had been more sober, would have frightened him senseless. Instead he smiled back.

"You're welcome," he said. The words were still hanging in the air when Rodrigo broke his neck and let him drop like a rag doll.

7

SWAIN LAY IN HIS HOTEL BED THE NEXT MORNING STARING AT THE
ceiling and trying to logically connect the dots. Outside a cold
November rain was pelting the windows; he hadn't yet adjusted from the much warmer climate of South America, so he
was definitely feeling a chill, even though he was snug in bed.
Between the rain and jet lag, he figured he deserved a rest. Besides, it wasn't as if he was totally slacking off; he was thinking.

He didn't know Lily, so he was hampered in his effort to figure out what she would do. So far she'd proven herself to be in-
ventive, bold, and coolheaded; he'd have to be on top of his
game to outthink her. But he did love a challenge, so instead of
running around Paris flashing a photograph of her and asking
strangers on the street if they'd seen this woman—yeah, like that
would work—he tried instead to anticipate what she would do
next, so he could get just that one half-step ahead of her that he
needed.

Mentally he listed what he knew so far, which wasn't much.

Point A: Salvatore Nervi had killed her friends.
Point B: She had then killed Salvatore Nervi.

Logically, that should be the end of it. Mission accomplished, except for the little detail of getting away from Rodrigo Nervi alive. But she'd managed that; she had made her escape to London, pulled that slick disguise switcheroo and then doubled back. She could possibly have gone to ground here in Paris, using yet another of her seemingly endless supply of alternate identities. It was also possible she'd left the airport, changed her appearance yet again, then returned and taken yet another flight out. She had to know that everything any passenger did in an airport, outside of the restrooms, was caught on some camera somewhere, so she would expect that eventually anyone looking for her would nail down the switches she'd made, and from there be able to run the passenger list and deduce the identities she'd used. She had been forced to do her quick changes to throw off Rodrigo Nervi and buy some time, even though that meant she'd burned three aliases and wouldn't be able to use them again without raising all sorts of red flags that would get her caught.

With that time, however, she could have left the airport and assumed yet another name and appearance, one that hadn't been caught on the airport cameras. Her paperwork was good; she knew some talented people. She'd be able to sail through security checkpoints and Customs with no problem. She could be anywhere by now. She could be back in London, snoozing on a red-eye flight back to the States, or even sleeping in the room next to his.

She'd come back to Paris. There had to be some signifi-
cance in that. Logistically, it made sense; the flight was short,
giving her time to land and get away before security could
painstakingly go over and over the video to tell how she'd done
it, then by process of elimination narrow the list of passenger
names down to the one she'd used. By coming back to Paris,
she'd also involved yet another government and bureaucracy,
slowing the process even more. She could, however, have done
the same thing by flying to any other European country. Though
the London-to-Paris flight was just an hour, Brussels was even
closer. So were Amsterdam and The Hague.

Swain locked his hands behind his head and scowled at the
ceiling. There was a great big gaping hole in that reasoning.
She could have gone through Customs in London and walked
out of the airport long before there was any chance of someone
watching the security tapes and figuring out which disguise
she'd used. If she didn't want to stay in London, she could then
have simply changed her disguise and gone back a few hours
later to catch another flight, and absolutely no one would have
made the connection. She'd have been home free. In fact, that
would have been a much smarter move than staying in the airport with all those surveillance cameras. So why hadn't she
done that? Either she didn't think anyone would be able to pick
up her identity switch, or she'd had a compelling reason for
coming back to Paris at that particular time.

Granted, she wasn't a field officer, trained in espionage;
contract agents were hired for each individual job, sent in to
perform a specific duty. Her file mentioned nothing about her
being schooled in disguise or evasion techniques. She had to
know the Agency would be after her for screwing up the Nervi

deal, but it was possible she didn't know the extent of surveillance in major airports.

He wouldn't bet the farm on it.

She was too smart, too on top of things. She'd known cameras were watching her every move, though she'd thrown enough curve balls at them to keep them occupied for a while. And she might have decided that giving them more time, by leaving Heathrow and returning later, would give them a chance to . . . do something. He didn't know what. Scan her face into the facial-recognition data bank, maybe? She *was* in the Agency's data bank, but not anywhere else. If, however, someone had scanned her facial structure into Interpol's database, the cameras at the airport entrances would then have been able to come up with a match before she could get to her gate. Yeah, that could be it. She could have been afraid Rodrigo Nervi would try to have her entered into Interpol's data.

How could she avoid that danger? By having cosmetic surgery, for one thing. Again, that would be the smart thing for a woman on the run to do. She hadn't opted for that, though; instead she'd come back to Paris. Maybe going into hiding and not coming out until after she'd had cosmetic alterations would have taken too long. Maybe there was some kind of time limit for something she wanted to get accomplished.

Such as? See Disneyland Paris? Tour the Louvre?

Maybe killing Salvatore Nervi was just the opening act, instead of an end unto itself. Maybe she knew the Agency's best of the best—namely himself, not that she knew him from Adam's house cat—was on the job, and it was only a matter of time before she was grabbed. That kind of faith in his abilities made him feel all warm inside. At any rate, say his thinking was on the right track: she had something she wanted to do, something so urgent that hours counted, and she was afraid she wouldn't have time to do it.

Swain groaned and sat up, rubbing his hands over his face. There was a flaw in that logic, too. She'd have had a better chance of accomplishing whatever it was if she'd gone to ground and had the cosmetic surgery. He kept coming back to that. The only thing that made sense of her actions was if there was a metaphoric time bomb somewhere, something that wouldn't wait a few months and had to be accomplished *right now,* or at least in a short period of time. But if there really was something along those lines, something that posed a world danger, all she had to do was pick up a phone and call it in, let a group of experts handle whatever it was rather than her trying to pull a Lone Ranger.

Scratch "world danger" as a motivation.

Something personal, then. Something she wanted to do herself, and felt a compelling urge to get done as soon as possible.

He thought about the contents of her file. Her motivation for killing Salvatore Nervi was the deaths of a couple of her friends and their adopted daughter a few months ago. She'd done the smart thing and laid her groundwork for that, taken her time, got close enough to Nervi to do the job. So why wasn't she doing the smart thing now? Why was an intelligent, professional agent doing something so dumb it would ultimately get her caught?

Forget motivation, he suddenly thought. He was a man; he'd go crazy trying to figure out what was going through a woman's mind. If he had to pick the most likely scenario, he'd say she wasn't finished with the Nervi family. She'd struck them hard, but now she'd circled back for a killing blow. They had pissed her off big-time, and she was going to make them pay.

He heaved a sigh of satisfaction. There. That felt right. And damn if it didn't provide motivation, too. She'd lost people she loved, and she was striking back no matter what the cost to herself. He could understand that. The reasoning was simple and clean, without all the why-do-this and not-do-that second-guessing.

He'd run it by Frank Vinay in a few hours when sunrise hit D.C., but his gut told him he was on the right track and he'd start nosing around before he talked to Vinay. He just needed to decide on a starting point.

It all went back to her friends. Whatever they'd been doing that got on Nervi's bad side, that same thing would be her target as a sort of poetic justice.

He thought back to the file he'd read in Vinay's office. He hadn't brought any paperwork with him, because it could compromise security; unsanctioned eyes couldn't read what wasn't there. He relied instead on his excellent memory, which produced the names *Averill* and *Christina Joubran,* retired contract agents. Averill had been Canadian, Christina from the States, but they'd lived in France full-time and been completely retired for over twelve years. What could have spurred Salvatore Nervi to kill them?

Okay, first he had to find out where they'd lived, how they'd died, who their friends were other than Lily Mansfield, and if they'd talked to anyone about something unusual going on. Maybe Nervi was manufacturing biological weapons and selling them to the North Koreans, though again, if Lily's friends had stumbled across something like that, why the hell wouldn't they have simply called their old bosses and reported it? Idiots might try to handle things themselves, but successful contract agents weren't idiots, because if they were, they'd be dead.

That wasn't a good thought, because the Joubrans *were* dead. Uh-oh.

Before he thought himself in circles again, Swain got out of bed and showered, then called room service for breakfast. He'd elected to stay at the Bristol in the Champs-Élysées district because it had hotel parking space and twenty-four-hour room service. It was also expensive, but he needed the parking for the car he'd rented last night, and the room service because he might be keeping some very odd hours. Besides, the marble bathrooms were cool.

It was while he was eating his croissant and jam that something obvious occurred to him: the Joubrans hadn't stumbled across anything. They'd been *hired* to do a job and either it had gone bad on them or they'd succeeded at it and been killed afterward when Nervi struck back.

Lily might already know what that something was, in which case he was still playing catch-up. But if she didn't–and he thought that was likely, since she'd been away on a job when the kills went down–then she'd be trying to find out who had hired her friends, and why. Essentially, she'd be asking the same questions of the same people that Swain intended to interview. What were the odds that their paths would cross at some point?

He hadn't liked those odds before, but they were looking better and better by the minute. A good starting point would be finding out what, if anything, had happened to any Nervi-owned facility in the week preceding the Joubrans' deaths. Lily would be checking newspaper reports, which might or might not have any mention of a problem pertaining to the Nervis; he was in a position to go straight to the French police, but he'd just as soon they not know who he was or where he was staying. Frank Vinay wanted this kept as quiet as possible; it wouldn't be good for diplomatic relations for the French to know that a CIA contract agent had apparently assassinated someone as politically connected as Salvatore Nervi, who hadn't been a French citizen, but had nevertheless lived in Paris and had many friends in the government.

He checked in the phone directory for the Joubrans' address, but there was nothing listed. No surprise there.

Swain's good luck was that he worked for an agency that collected the most minute bits of news from all over the world, then cataloged and analyzed everything. Another bit of good luck was that the information highway in that agency was open twenty-four hours a day.

He used his secure cell phone to call Langley, going through the usual process of identification and verification, but within a minute he was talking to a person in the know, by the name of Patrick Washington. Swain told him who he was and what he needed, Patrick said, "Hold on," and Swain waited. And waited.

Ten minutes later Patrick came back on the line. "Sorry it took so long, I had to double-check something." Meaning he'd checked on Swain. "Yeah, there was an incident at a lab on August twenty-fifth, a contained explosion and fire. According to the reports, the damage was minimal."

The Joubrans had been killed on August 28. The lab incident had to be the trigger.

"Do you have an address on the lab?"

"Coming up."

Swain heard computer keys clicking; then Patrick said, "Number Seven Rue des Capucines, just outside Paris."

That covered a lot of ground. "North, east, south, or west?"

"Uh–let me pull up a street-finder–" More clicking keys. "East."

"What's the name of the lab?"

"Nothing fancy. Nervi Laboratories."

Yeah, right. Mentally Swain translated the name into French.

"Need anything else?"

"Yeah. The street address of Averill and Christina Joubran. They were retired contract agents. We used them occasionally."

"How long ago?"

"Early nineties."

"Just a minute." More clicking keys. Patrick said, "Here it is," and recited the address. "Anything else?"

"No, that's it. You're a good man, Mr. Washington."

"Thank you, sir."

The "sir" verified that Patrick had indeed double-checked Swain's identity and clearance. He put Patrick's name down in his mental file of go-to people, because he liked that the man was cautious enough that he didn't take anything for granted.

Swain looked out the window: still raining. He hated that. He'd spent too many hours in the steaming tropical heat after a sudden downpour had drenched him to the skin, and the experience had given him an intense dislike of getting his clothes wet. It had been a long time since he'd been cold and wet, but as he remembered, it was even more miserable than being hot and wet. He hadn't brought a raincoat with him, either. He wasn't even certain he owned one, and he didn't have time to go shopping.

He checked his watch. Ten after eight; shops weren't open yet, anyway. He solved that problem by calling down to the front desk and arranging to have a raincoat in his size delivered to his room and charged to his account. That wouldn't prevent him from getting wet this morning, since he couldn't wait for it to arrive. At least he would be in the rain only going to and from his rental car, not slogging through miles of jungle.

He'd rented a Jaguar because he'd always wanted to drive one, and also because only the more expensive cars had been available by the time he got to the rental office last night, even though he'd crossed the Channel "much faster" than usual, thanks to Murray's NATO friend. He figured he'd write off the usual amount of a rental on expenses and eat the rest of it himself. He'd never seen a rule he didn't like to finesse, but he was scrupulously honest on his expenses. He figured his ass was more likely to be raked over the coals because of money than for any other reason. Being fond of his ass, he tried to spare it unnecessary stress.

He left the Bristol behind the wheel of the Jaguar, deeply inhaling the rich leather scent of the upholstery. If women really wanted to smell good to men, he thought, they'd wear perfume that smelled like a new car.

With that happy idea lingering in his mind, he plunged headlong into Parisian traffic. He hadn't been in Paris in years, but he remembered that the bravest and most foolhardy won the right-of-way. The rule was you yield to traffic on the right, but screw the rule. He deftly cut off a taxi whose driver slammed

on the brakes and screamed Gallic curses, but Swain accelerated and shot through a gap. Damn, this was fun! The wet
streets raised the unpredictability factor, adding to his adrenaline level.

He battled his way south of the Montparnasse district to
where the Joubrans had lived, occasionally consulting a city
map. Later in the day he would check out the Nervi lab, eyeball
the layout and more obvious security measures, but right now
he wanted to go where he figured Lily Mansfield was most
likely to be.

It was time to get this show on the road. After the merry
chase she'd led him the day before, he couldn't wait to match
wits with her again. He had no doubt he'd win—eventually—but
all the fun was in the run.

8

RODRIGO SLAMMED DOWN THE PHONE, THEN PROPPED HIS ELBOWS on the desk and buried his face in his hands. The urge to strangle someone was strong. Murray and his band of merry idiots had evidently gone both blind and stupid, to let one woman so thoroughly make fools of them all. Murray swore he'd had experts look at the airport video, and none could tell where Denise Morel had gone. She had effectively vanished into thin air, though Murray was gracious enough to admit that she must have used a disguise, but one so clever and professional that there were no visible similarities for them to track.

She could *not* be allowed to get away with killing his father. Not only would his reputation suffer, but everything in him demanded vengeance. Grief and wounded pride roiled together, giving him no peace. He and his father had always been so careful, so thorough, but this one woman had somehow slipped under their defenses and dealt Salvatore a nasty, painful death. She hadn't even given him the dignity of a bullet, but had chosen poison, a coward's weapon.

Murray might have lost her, but he, Rodrigo, hadn't given up. He refused to give up.

Think! he commanded himself. To find her he first had to identify her. Who was she, where did she live, where did her *family* live?

What were the usual means of identification? Fingerprints, obviously. Dental records. The last wasn't an option, because he would need to know not only who she was but who her dentist was, and at any rate, that method was used mainly for identifying someone already dead. To find someone alive . . . how to do that?

Fingerprints. The room where she'd slept while she was here had been thoroughly cleaned by his staff the day she went back to her flat, destroying any prints, nor had he thought to lift a print from any of the drinking glasses or silverware she'd used. Her flat was a possibility, though. Feeling faintly heartened, he contacted a friend in the Parisian police department who didn't ask questions, just said that he would take care of it immediately himself.

The friend called within the hour. He hadn't gone over every inch of the flat, but he'd checked the most obvious places and there were no prints at all, not even smudged ones. The flat had been thoroughly wiped down.

Rodrigo swallowed his rage at being so completely thwarted by this woman. "What other means are there of finding someone's identity?"

"None that are guaranteed, my friend. Fingerprints are of

use only if the subject has previously been arrested and his prints are in the database. It is the same with every method. DNA, as accurate as it is, is good only if there is another DNA sample to which it can be compared so you can say, yes, these two samples did or did not come from the same person. The facial recognition programs will identify only those people who are already in the database, and is targeted mostly toward terrorists. It is the same with voice recognition, retina patterns, everything. There must be a database from which matches can be made."

"I understand." Rodrigo rubbed his forehead, thoughts racing. Security video! He had Denise's face on security video, plus much clearer pictures on her identity paperwork and the investigations he'd done. "Who has these facial-recognition programs?"

"Interpol, of course. All the major organizations such as Scotland Yard, the American FBI and CIA."

"Are their data banks shared?"

"To some extent, yes. In a perfect world, speaking from an investigational standpoint, everything would be shared, but everyone likes to keep some secrets, no? If this woman is a criminal, then Interpol might very well have her in their data banks. And one other thing—"

"Yes?"

"The landlord said that a man, an American, was here yesterday asking about the woman. The landlord didn't get a name, and his description is so vague as to be useless."

"Thank you," said Rodrigo, trying to think what this meant. The woman had been paid in American dollars. An American man was looking for her. But it followed that if this man had been the one to hire her, he would already know where she was—and why search for her anyway, when she had completed her mission? No, this had to be something totally unconnected, an acquaintance perhaps.

He disconnected the call, a grim smile twisting his lips, and punched in a number he'd called many times before. The Nervi organization had contacts all over Europe, Africa, and the Middle East, and were expanding into the Orient. As an intelligent man, it behooved him to make certain one of those contacts was very conveniently placed within Interpol itself.

"Georges Blanc," said a quiet, steady voice, which was indicative of the man himself. Rodrigo had seldom met anyone more competent than Blanc, whom he'd never met face-to-face.

"If I scan a photograph and send it to your computer, can you run it through your facial identification program?" He had no need to identify himself. Blanc knew his voice.

There was a short pause; then Blanc said, "Yes." There were no qualifications, no explanation of the security measures he might have to sidestep, just that brief affirmative.

"I will have it to you within five minutes," Rodrigo said, and hung up. From the file on his desk he took the photo of Denise Morel—or whoever she was—and scanned it into his computer, which was properly safeguarded with every security measure known. He typed a few lines, and the photograph was on the way to Lyon, where Interpol was headquartered.

The phone rang. Rodrigo picked up the receiver. "Yes."

"I have it," said Blanc's quiet voice. "I will call you as soon as I have an answer, but as to how long it will take . . ." His voice trailed off, and Rodrigo imagined him shrugging.

"As soon as possible," said Rodrigo. "One other thing."

"Yes?"

"Your contact with the Americans—"

"Yes?"

"There's a possibility the person I'm seeking is an American." Or had been hired by an American, thus the payment in United States dollars. While he didn't think the United States government had anything to do with his father's murder, until he knew for certain who had hired the bitch, he intended to keep his cards close to his chest where they were concerned. He could have gone directly to his American liaison and asked the same favor he was asking of Blanc, but it was better, perhaps, that he approach this from a more oblique angle.

"I will have my contact check their data banks," Blanc said.

"Discreetly."

"Of course."

9

DESPITE THE COLD RAIN BLOWING IN UNDER THE PROTECTION OF her umbrella, Lily kept her head high so she could see what was going on around her. She strode briskly, pushing herself to see how her stamina held up. She was gloved, booted, and wrapped against the chill, but she left her head uncovered so her blond hair was visible. If by chance Rodrigo's men were looking for her here in Paris, they'd be looking for a brunette. She doubted Rodrigo had followed her path back here, though, at least not yet.

The Agency, however, was a different matter entirely. She was almost surprised she hadn't been detained in London as soon as she got off the plane. But she hadn't been, and she hadn't spotted a tail, either when she'd left de Gaulle airport or this morning.

She began to think that she might have been incredibly lucky. Rodrigo had kept Salvatore's death secret for several days, then released the news only after Salvatore's funeral. There hadn't been any mention of poison, just that he had died after a brief illness. Was it possible the dots hadn't been connected?

She didn't dare let herself hope, couldn't afford to let down her guard. Until she'd finished the job, she would stay alert for trouble from every corner. After the job–well, she really had no idea. At this point, all she hoped for was survival.

She hadn't chosen an Internet café close to her sublet studio, because for all she knew there might be a trap on any on-line requests for information pertaining to anything about the Nervi organization. Instead she had taken the Metro to the Latin Quarter, and opted to walk the rest of the way. She had never used this particular Internet café before, which was one of the reasons she'd chosen it. One of the basic rules for evasion was to not follow a set routine, not be predictable. People got caught because they went where they were most comfortable, where things were familiar.

Lily had spent quite a lot of time in Paris, so that meant there were a lot of places and people that she would now have to avoid. She'd never actually had a residence here, instead staying with friends–usually Averill and Tina–or at a B and B. Once, for about a year, she'd rented a flat in London but gave it up because she'd spent twice as much time traveling as she had at the flat and it was just an added expense.

Her theater of work had been primarily in Europe, so going home to the States hadn't happened very often, either. As much as she liked Europe and was familiar with it, truly settling down there had never occurred to her. If she ever bought a home–a very big "if"–it would be in the States.

Sometimes she thought longingly of retiring as Averill and

Tina had, of living a normal life with a nine-to-five job, of staying in a community and becoming part of its fabric, knowing her neighbors, visiting with relatives, chatting on the phone. She didn't know how she had come to this, to being able to snuff out a human life as easily as most people would step on an insect, to being afraid to even call her mother, for God's sake. She had started so young, and that first time hadn't been easy at all—she'd been shaking like a leaf—but she'd gotten the job done, and the next time had been easier, and the time after that easier still. After a while the targets had become less than human to her, an emotional remoteness that was necessary for her to be able to do the job. Perhaps it was naive of her, but she trusted her government not to send her after any of the good guys; it was a necessary belief, the only way she could work. And still she had become someone she feared, this woman who probably couldn't be trusted to enter normal society.

It was still there, that dream of retiring and settling down, but Lily recognized it as just that, a dream, and unlikely ever to happen. Even if she got through this situation alive, settling down was something normal people did, and Lily was afraid she herself had become less than human. Killing had become too easy, too instinctive. What would happen to her if she had to deal with the same frustrations every day, a nasty boss or a vicious neighbor? What if someone tried to mug her? Could she control her instincts, or would people die?

Even worse, what if she inadvertently brought danger to someone she loved? She knew she literally wouldn't be able to bear it if anyone in her family was harmed because of her, because of what she was.

A car horn beeped, and Lily started, jerking her attention

back to her surroundings. She was appalled that she'd let her thoughts wander, instead of keeping herself alert and focused. If she couldn't hold her concentration, there was no way she'd be able to successfully pull this off.

She might have squeaked under the Agency's radar so far–she hoped–but that couldn't last. Eventually someone would come for her, and she thought sooner rather than later.

Looked at realistically, there were four possible outcomes for this situation. In the best-case scenario, she would discover what it was that had lured Averill and Tina out of retirement, and whatever it was, would be so horrible that the civilized world would distance itself from the Nervis and they would be put out of business. The Agency would never use her again, of course; no matter how justified, a contract agent who went around killing assets was too unstable for the job. So she'd win, but be unemployed, which threw her back to her earlier concern about whether she could actually live a normal life.

In the next-best-case scenario, she wouldn't find anything suitably incriminating–selling weapons to terrorists wouldn't be bad enough, because everyone knew about it anyway–and would be forced to live out her life under an alias, in which case she'd be unemployed, and back to the question of whether she could hold down a regular job and be Jane Citizen.

The last two possibilities were bleak. She might accomplish her aim, but get killed. Finally, worst of all, she might get killed before she got anything accomplished.

She would have liked to say the odds were fifty-fifty that she'd have one of the first two outcomes, but the four possibilities weren't equal in *probability*. She thought there was something like an eighty percent chance she wasn't going to survive this, and that might be an optimistic guess. She was going to try like hell for the twenty percent, though. She couldn't let Zia down by giving up.

The Latin Quarter was a maze of narrow cobbled streets, usually teeming with students from the nearby Sorbonne and shoppers who came for the odd boutiques and ethnic stores, but today the cold rain had thinned the crowds. The Internet café, however, was already busy. Lily surveyed the café as she closed her umbrella and removed her raincoat, scarf, and gloves, looking for an unoccupied computer where she was least likely to be observed. Beneath the lined raincoat she wore a thick turtleneck sweater in a rich blue that darkened the shade of her eyes and drapey knit slacks over low boots. An ankle holster carrying a .22 caliber revolver was strapped around her right ankle, easily accessible in the low boot, and the drapey fit of the trousers hid any telltale line. She had felt horribly defenseless during the weeks when she hadn't been able to carry a weapon because of those damn searches every time she got close to Salvatore; this was better.

She located a machine situated at such an angle that she could watch the door while she was there, plus it was as private as she was likely to get in this particular café. It was, however, being used by a teenage American girl who was evidently checking her e-mail. It was usually easy to spot Americans, Lily thought; it wasn't just their clothing or style, it was some-thing about them, an innate confidence that often edged into arrogance, and had to be irritating as hell to a European. She herself might still have the attitude–she was almost certain of it–but over the years her style of dress and outward manners had changed. Most people mistook her for Scandinavian, given her coloring, or perhaps German. No one, looking at her now, would automatically think of apple pie and baseball.

She waited until the teenager had finished with her e-mail and left, then slid into the vacated seat. The rate per hour here was very reasonable, doubtless because of the hordes of college students. She paid for an hour, expecting to take at least that long or longer.

She began with *Le Monde*, the biggest newspaper, searching the archives between August 21, when she had dinner with the Joubrans for the last time, and the 28th, when they were murdered. The only mention of "Nervi" was of Salvatore in connection with a story on international finances. She read the article twice, searching for any detail that might indicate an underlying story, but either she was in the dark concerning financial matters or there was nothing.

There were fifteen newspapers in the Parisian area, some small, some not. She had to research all of them, covering the archives for those seven days in question. The task was time-consuming and sometimes the computer would take forever to download a page. Sometimes the connection was broken and she would have to log on again. She had been there three hours when she logged on to *Investir*, a financial newspaper, and hit the jackpot.

The item was just a sidebar, only two paragraphs long. On August 25, a Nervi research laboratory had suffered an explosion and subsequent fire that was described as "small" and "contained," with "minimal damage" that would in no way affect the lab's ongoing research in vaccines.

Averill had specialized in explosives, to the point of being a true artist. He'd seen no point in wanton destruction when, with care and planning, it was possible to design a charge that would take out only what was needed. Why blow up an entire building when one room would do? Or a city block when one building would do? "Contained" was a word often used to describe his work. And Tina had been skilled at bypassing security systems, in addition to being talented with a pistol.

Lily couldn't know for certain it was their work, but it felt right. At least this was a lead she could follow, and hope it went down the correct path.

While she was online, she pulled up what information there was on the research laboratory, and found precious little more than the address and the name of the director, her pal Dr. Vincenzo Giordano. Well, well. She typed his name into the search engine and came up dry, but then she hadn't really expected he would have his home phone number published. That would have been the easiest way to locate him, but it certainly wasn't the only way.

Logging off line, she flexed her shoulders and rolled her head back and forth to loosen the tight muscles in her neck. She hadn't moved from the computer terminal in over three hours and every muscle felt stiff, plus she really needed to use the facilities. She was tired, but not as tired as she'd been the day before, and she was satisfied with the way her stamina had held up during the brisk walk from the Metro.

The rain was still falling when she left the café, but had slowed to little more than a drizzle. She opened her umbrella, thought for a moment, then struck out in the opposite direction from which she'd come earlier. She was hungry, and though she hadn't had one in years, she knew exactly what she wanted for lunch: a Big Mac.

*　　*　　*

Swain second-guessed himself again. He was getting damn tired of doing that, but couldn't seem to help himself.

He'd located the Joubrans' old address, and found that the space had evidently been cleaned up, cleaned out, and either rented or sold to another family. He'd had a vague notion that he might break in and see what he could find, but that would have been useful only if no one else had moved there in the meantime. He had watched a young mother welcome a babysitter—her mother, from the resemblance—and two pre-school children erupt out of the door into the rain before she could stop them. The two adults had, with much clucking and shooing, rounded up the two giggling curtain-climbers and got them indoors; then the young woman had dashed out again, clutching an umbrella and bag. Whether she was going to work or going shopping didn't matter to him. What mattered was the residence was no longer empty.

That's where he second-guessed himself. He'd also planned to question the neighbors and the proprietors of the local mar-kets about the Joubrans, who their friends were, that kind of thing. But it occurred to him that if he beat Lily to the punch with those questions, when she did come around, someone was bound to tell her an American man had asked those same questions just the day before, or even a few hours before. She wasn't stupid; she'd know exactly what that meant, and go to ground somewhere.

He'd been chasing around after her the day before, trying to catch up, but now he had to adjust his thinking. He was no longer necessarily behind her, which was good only if he knew what her next move would be. Until then, he couldn't afford to alarm her or she would disappear on him again.

Through channels—with Murray dealing with the French—

he knew that Lily had flown back to Paris using the identity of Mariel St. Clair, but the address listed on her passport had turned out to be a fish market. Just a little humor on her part, he thought. She wouldn't be using the St. Clair identity again; she had probably slid effortlessly into yet another persona, one he had no way of finding. Paris was a big city, with over two million inhabitants, and she was far more familiar with it than he was. He had only this one chance where their paths might intersect, and he didn't want to ruin it by jumping in too fast.

Disgruntled, he drove around the neighborhood getting the lay of the land, so to speak, and more than casually studying pedestrians as they hurried up and down the streets. Unfortunately, most of them carried umbrellas that partially hid their features, and even if they hadn't, he had no idea what disguise Lily might be using now. She'd been just about everything except an elderly nun, so maybe he should start looking for those.

In the meantime, maybe he should take a look at that Nervi lab, eyeball the outward security measures. Who knew when he might need to get inside?

After an unhealthy and extremely satisfying lunch, Lily took the SNCF train to the suburb where Averill and Tina had lived. By the time she arrived there, the rain had stopped and a weak sun was making fitful efforts to peek through the dull gray clouds. The day wasn't any warmer, but at least the rain wasn't making everyone miserable. She remembered the brief snow flurry the night Salvatore had died, and wondered if Paris would see more snow this winter. Snow events didn't happen in Paris all that often. How Zia had loved playing in the snow! They'd taken her skiing in the Alps almost every winter, the three adults who'd loved her more than life itself. Lily herself never skied, because an accident could put her out of commission for months, but after they'd retired, both her friends had taken to the sport like fiends.

Memories flashed in her mind like postcards: Zia as an adorable, chubby three-year-old in a bright red snowsuit, patting a small and extremely lopsided snowman. That was her first trip to the Alps. Zia on the bunny trails, shrieking, "Watch me! Watch me!" Tina taking a header into a snowbank and emerging laughing, looking more like the Abominable Snowman than a woman. The three of them enjoying drinks around a roaring fireplace while Zia slept upstairs. Zia losing her first tooth, starting school, her first dance recital, showing the first signs of changing from child to adolescent, getting her period last year, fussing with her hair, wanting to wear mascara.

Lily briefly closed her eyes, shaking with pain and rage. Desolation filled her, the way it often had since she'd learned they were all dead. Since then she could see the sunshine but hadn't been able to feel it, as if its warmth never touched her. Killing Salvatore had been satisfying, but it wasn't enough to bring back the sun.

She stopped outside the place where her friends had lived. There was someone else living in the house now, and she wondered if they knew three people had died there just a few months before. She felt violated, as if everything should have been left the way it had been, their things untouched.

That very first day she'd returned to Paris and discovered they'd been murdered, she herself had taken some of the photographs, some of Zia's games and books, a few of her childhood toys, the baby album she had started and Tina had lovingly continued. The house had been cordoned off, of course, and locked up, but that hadn't stopped her. For one thing, she had her own key. For another, if necessary she would have torn the roof off with her bare hands to gain entrance. But what had happened to the rest of their belongings? Where were their clothes, their personal treasures, their ski equipment? After that first day she had been busy for a couple of weeks finding out who had killed them, and beginning her plan for vengeance; when she'd returned, the house had been cleaned out.

Averill and Tina had each had some family, cousins and such, though no one close. Perhaps the authorities had notified those family members, and they had come to pack up everything. She hoped so. It was okay if family had their possessions, but she hated the idea of some impersonal cleaning service coming and boxing things up to be disposed of.

Lily began knocking on doors, talking to neighbors, asking if they'd seen anyone visiting that week before her friends were murdered. She had questioned them before, but hadn't known the right question to ask. She was known to them, of course; she'd been visiting for years, had nodded hello, stopped for brief chats. Tina had been a friendly person, Averill more aloof, but to Zia there'd been no such thing as a stranger. She'd been on very friendly terms with all the neighbors.

Only one had seen anything that she remembered, though; it was Mme. Bonnet, who lived two doors down. She was in her mid-eighties, grumpy with age, but she liked to sit by the front window while she knitted—and she was constantly knitting—so she saw almost everything that happened on the street.

"But I have already told all of this to the police," she said impatiently when she answered the door and Lily posed her question. "No, I saw no one the night they were killed. I am old; I don't see so well, I don't hear so well. And I close my curtains at night. How could I have seen anything?"

"What about before that night? Any time that week?"

"That, too, I told the police." She glared at Lily.

"The police have done nothing."

"Of course they have done nothing! Worthless, the lot of them." With a disgusted wave of her hand she dismissed a small army of public servants who every day did the best they could.

"Did you see anyone you didn't know?" Lily repeated patiently.

"Just that one young man. He was very handsome, like a movie star. He visited one day, for several hours. I hadn't seen him before."

Lily's pulse leaped. "Can you describe him? Please, Madame Bonnet."

The old lady glared some more, muttered a few uncomplimentary phrases like "incompetent idiots" and "bumbling fools," then barked, "I told you, he was handsome. Tall, slim, black-haired. Very well dressed. He arrived by taxi, and another came for him when he left. That is all."

"Could you guess his age?"

"Young! To me, anyone under fifty is young! Don't bother me with these silly questions." And with that, she stepped back and closed the door with a bang.

Lily took a deep breath. A young, handsome, dark-haired man. And well-dressed. There were thousands who met that description in Paris, which abounded with handsome young men. It was a start, a piece of the puzzle, but as a stand-alone clue it meant absolutely nothing. She had no list of usual suspects, nor a selection of photographs she could show Mme. Bonnet and hope the old lady could pick out one and say, "This one. This is the man."

And what did this tell her, really? This handsome young man could have hired them to blow up something at the Nervi lab, or he could have been no more than a friendly acquaintance who happened to visit. Averill and Tina could have gone somewhere else to meet the person who hired them, rather than letting him come to their home. In fact, that would have been more likely.

She rubbed her forehead. She hadn't thought this out, but she didn't know if it could *be* thought out. She didn't know if it mattered why they'd taken the job, or what the job was. She couldn't even be certain there *was* a job, but it was the only scenario that made sense and she had to go with her instinct on that. If she started doubting herself now, she might as well pack it in.

Deep in thought, she walked back to the train platform.

10

GEORGES BLANC BELIEVED STRONGLY IN LAW AND ORDER, BUT HE was also a pragmatic man who accepted that sometimes there were difficult choices and one just did the best one could.

He didn't like providing information to Rodrigo Nervi. He did, however, have a family to protect and an older son who was in his first year at Johns Hopkins University, in the United States. The tuition at Johns Hopkins was almost thirty thousand American dollars every year; that alone would have beggared him. But he would have managed, somehow, if Salvatore Nervi hadn't approached him over ten years ago and genially suggested that Georges would greatly benefit from a second, very generous income, for which he would have to do nothing but share information now and then, and perhaps do some small favors. When Georges had politely refused, Salvatore had kept smiling, and had begun reciting a bone-chilling list of mis-

fortunes that could befall his family, such as his house burning
down, his children being kidnapped or perhaps even physically
harmed. He told how a gang of thugs had broken into an old
woman's house and blinded her by throwing acid in her face,
how savings could disappear like smoke, how automobiles had
accidents.

Georges had understood. Salvatore had just outlined the
things that *would* happen to him and his family if he refused to
do what Salvatore demanded. So he had nodded, and tried over
the years to limit the damage he did with the information he
passed on and the favors he did. With those threats as motivation, Salvatore could have had the information for free, but he
had established an account for Georges in Switzerland, and the
equivalent of twice his yearly salary was paid into it every year.

Georges was careful to outwardly live on his Interpol salary,
but pragmatic enough to dip into the Switzerland account to
pay for his son's education. There was a healthy amount in the
account now, having accumulated for ten years and drawn interest as well. The money was there; he wouldn't use it to buy
luxuries for himself, but he would use it for his family. Eventually, he knew, he would have to do something with the money,
but he didn't know what.

Over the years he had dealt mostly with Rodrigo Nervi, Salvatore's heir apparent, and now heir in fact. He would almost
rather have dealt with Salvatore. Rodrigo was colder than Salvatore, smarter, and, Georges thought, probably more ruthless.
The only advantage Salvatore had had over his son was experience, and more years in which to accumulate a devil's list of
sins.

Georges checked the time: one PM. With the six hours'

time difference between Paris and Washington, that made it seven AM there, just the right time for reaching someone on a cell phone.

He used his own cellular phone, not wanting a record of the call on Interpol's records. Marvelous inventions, cell phones; they made pay phones almost obsolete. They weren't as anonymous, of course, but his was secure against eavesdropping and far more convenient.

"Hello," a man said after the second ring. In the background Georges could hear a television, the modulated tones of newscasters.

"I'll be sending you a photograph," Georges said. "Would you please run it through your facial-recognition program as soon as possible?" He never used a name, and neither did the other man. Whenever one of them needed information, he would call on a personal phone, rather than going through channels, which kept their official contact at a minimum.

"Sure thing."

"Please send all pertinent information to me by the usual channel."

They each rang off; conversations were always kept to a minimum as well. Georges knew nothing about his contact, not even his name. For all he knew, his counterpart in Washington cooperated for the same reason he himself did, out of fear. There was never any hint of friendliness between them. This was business, which they understood all too well.

"I need a definite answer. Will you have the vaccine ready by the next influenza season?" Rodrigo asked Dr. Giordano. There was a huge report on Rodrigo's desk, but he was concerned with the bottom line, and that was whether the vaccine could be produced in the volume needed, before it was needed.

Dr. Giordano had a hefty grant from several world health organizations to develop a reliable vaccination against avian influenza. Theirs wasn't the only laboratory working on this problem, but it was the only one that had Dr. Giordano. Vincenzo had become fascinated with viruses and had left his private practice behind for a chance to study them, becoming an acknowledged expert and seen as someone who was either a remarkable genius or remarkably lucky in working with the microscopic nasties.

A vaccine for any strain of avian flu was difficult to develop, because avian flu was fatal to birds and vaccines were made by growing the influenza virus in eggs. Avian flu, however, killed the eggs; therefore, no vaccine. The developer of a process for producing an effective, reliable vaccine against avian flu would have a huge cash cow.

This was, potentially, the biggest moneymaker in the entire Nervi corporate structure, more lucrative even than opiates. So far avian flu itself was following dead-end paths: The virus would pass from an infected bird to a human, but it lacked the means of human-to-human infection. The human host would either die or get well, but without infecting anyone else. Avian flu, as it was now, was still incapable of causing an epidemic, but the American CDC and the World Health Organization were greatly alarmed by certain changes in the virus. The experts were betting that the next influenza pandemic, the influenza virus against which humans had no immunity because they'd never come in contact with it before, would be an avian influenza virus—and they were holding their breaths with each successive flu season. So far, the world had been lucky.

If the virus made the necessary genetic changes that would enable it to jump from human to human, the company that could make a vaccine for that influenza would be able to name its price.

Dr. Giordano sighed. "If there are no more setbacks, the vaccine can be ready by the end of next summer. I cannot, however, guarantee there will be no more setbacks."

The explosion in the lab last August had destroyed several years of work. Vincenzo had isolated a recombinant avian virus and painstakingly developed a means of producing a reliable vaccine. The explosion had not only destroyed the product, it had also taken out a huge amount of information. Computers, files, hard copy notes—gone. Vincenzo had started again from scratch.

The process was going faster this time, because Vincenzo knew more about what worked and what didn't, but Rodrigo was concerned. This season's influenza was of the ordinary variety, but what about next season? Producing a batch of vaccine took about six months, and a large quantity of it had to be ready by the end of next summer. If they missed that deadline and next season the avian virus made the genetic mutation it needed to jump from human to human, they would have missed the opportunity to make an incredible fortune. The infection would flash around the world, millions would die, but in that one season the immune systems of those who survived would adjust and that particular virus would reach the end of its brief success. The company that was ready with a vaccine when the virus mutated was the company that would reap the benefits.

They might be lucky once again, and the avian virus wouldn't mutate in time for the next influenza season, but Rodrigo refused to rely on luck. The mutation could happen at any time. He was in a race with the virus, and he was determined to win.

"It's your job to make certain there aren't any more set-backs," he told Vincenzo. "An opportunity such as this comes once in a lifetime. We will *not* miss it." Left unsaid was that if Vincenzo couldn't get the work done, Rodrigo would bring in someone who could. Vincenzo was an old friend, yes–of his father's. Rodrigo wasn't burdened by the same sentimentality. Vincenzo had done the most important work, but it was at a point where others could take over.

"Perhaps it isn't once in a lifetime," said Vincenzo. "What I have done with this virus, I can do again."

"But in these particular circumstances? This is perfect. If all goes well, no one will ever know and, in fact, we'll be praised as saviors. We're perfectly positioned to take advantage *this one time.* With the WHO funding your research, no one will be amazed that we have the vaccine. But if we go to the well too many times, my friend, the water will become muddied and questions will be asked that we don't want answered. There cannot be a pandemic every year, or even every five years, without someone becoming suspicious."

"Things change," Vincenzo argued. "The world's population is living in closer contact with animals than ever before."

"And no disease has ever been studied as thoroughly as influenza. Any variation is examined by thousands of microscopes. You're a doctor, you know this." Influenza was the great killer; more people had died in the 1918 pandemic than during the four-year Great Plague that had devastated Europe during the Middle Ages. The 1918 influenza had killed, it was estimated, between forty and fifty million people. Even in normal years influenza killed thousands, hundreds of thousands. Every

year two hundred and fifty million doses of vaccine were produced, and that was only a fraction of what would be needed
during a pandemic.

Labs in the United States, Australia, and the U.K. worked
under strict regulations to produce the vaccine that targeted
the virus researchers said would most likely be dominant in
each influenza season. The thing about a pandemic, however,
was that it was always caused by a virus that hadn't been pre-
dicted, hadn't been seen before, and thus the available vaccine
wouldn't be effective against it. The whole process was a giant
guessing game, with millions of lives at stake. Most of the time,
the researchers guessed right. But about once every thirty years
or so, a virus would mutate and catch them flat-footed. It had
been thirty-five years since the Hong Kong influenza pandemic
of 1968–69; the next pandemic was overdue, and the clock was
ticking.

Salvatore had used all his influence and contacts to win the
WHO grant to develop a reliable method of vaccine production
for avian influenza. The selected labs that normally produced
vaccine would be focusing on the usual strains of viruses, not
the avian virus, so their vaccines would be useless. Because of
the grant and Vincenzo's research, only the Nervi labs would
have the know-how to produce the avian vaccine and–here
was the important part–have doses ready to ship. With millions
of people worldwide dropping like flies from the new strain,
any effective vaccine against it would be priceless. The sky was
literally the limit to how much profit could be made in a few
short months.

There was no way to produce enough to protect everyone,
of course, but the world's population would benefit by some ju-
dicious thinning, Rodrigo thought.

The explosion in August had threatened all of that, and Salvatore had moved swiftly to control the damage. The ones who had set the explosion had been eliminated, and a new security system installed, since obviously the old one had huge flaws. But despite all his efforts, Rodrigo had never been able to discover who hired the husband-and-wife team to destroy the lab. A rival for the vaccine? There was no rival, no other laboratory working on this particular project. A general business rival? There had been bigger targets that could have been selected, but were ignored.

First the explosion, then three months later Salvatore was murdered. Could the two be linked? Over the years there had been many attempts on Salvatore's life, so perhaps there was no connection between the two events. Perhaps this was simply a very bad year. And yet . . . the Joubrans had been professionals, the husband a demolitions expert and the wife an assassin; Denise Morel was probably also a professional assassin. Was it beyond the realm of possibility that they'd been hired by the same person?

But the two events were very different in nature. In the first, Vincenzo's work had been deliberately targeted and destroyed. Since it was no secret he was working on a different method of producing influenza vaccine, who would benefit from that destruction? Only someone who was also working on the same project, knew Vincenzo was close, and wanted to steal a march on him. Undoubtedly there were private laboratories that were trying to develop an avian flu vaccine, but who among the many researchers would not only know how close Vincenzo was but have the financial wherewithal to hire two professionals to stop him?

One of the regular sanctioned laboratories that produced influenza vaccines, perhaps?

Killing Salvatore, on the other hand, in no way affected Vincenzo's work. Rodrigo had simply stepped into Salvatore's place. No, his father's murder served no purpose in that arena, so he couldn't see a connection.

The phone rang. Vincenzo got up to leave, but Rodrigo stayed him with a lifted hand; he had more questions about the vaccine. He picked up the receiver. "Yes."

"I have an answer to your question." Again, no names were used, but he recognized Blanc's quiet voice. "There was nothing in our data banks. Our friends, however, came up with a match. Her name is Liliane Mansfield, she is American, and she is a contract agent, a professional assassin."

Rodrigo's blood ran cold. "*They* hired her?" If the Americans had turned on him, matters had just become enormously complicated.

"No. My contact says our friends are greatly disturbed and are themselves trying to find her."

Reading between the lines, Rodrigo interpreted that to mean that the CIA was trying to find her to eliminate her. Ah! That explained the American man who had been to her flat searching for her. It was a relief to have that mystery explained, as well; Rodrigo liked to know who all the players were on his chessboard. With the vast American resources and extensive knowledge they must have about her, they were far more likely to succeed before he did . . . but he wanted to personally oversee the solution to her breathing problem. She breathed, therefore she was a problem.

"Is there any way your contact can share their knowledge

with you, as they receive it?" If he knew what the CIA knew, he could let them do the legwork for him.

"Perhaps. There is one other thing that I thought would be of great interest to you. This woman was a very close friend of the Joubrans."

Rodrigo closed his eyes. There it was, the one detail that made sense of everything, that tied it all together. "Thank you," he said. "Please let me know if you can work out this other matter with our friends."

"Yes, of course."

"I'd like a copy of all the information you have on her."

"I will fax it to you as soon as I am able," Blanc replied, meaning when he returned home that night. He would never send information to Rodrigo from the Interpol building itself.

Rodrigo hung up and leaned his head back against his chair. The two events were connected, after all, but not in any way he'd imagined. Vengeance. So simple, and something he understood with every cell in his body. Salvatore had killed her friends, so she had killed Salvatore. Whoever had hired the Joubrans to destroy Vincenzo's work had set in motion a chain of events that had ended with his father's murder.

"Her name is Liliane Mansfield," he told Vincenzo. "Denise Morel's real name, that is. She is a professional assassin, and she was friends with the Joubrans."

Vincenzo's eyes widened. "And she took the poison herself? Knowing what it was? Brilliant! Foolhardy, but brilliant!"

Rodrigo didn't share in Vincenzo's admiration for this Liliane Mansfield's actions. His father had died a very painful, difficult death, robbed of dignity and control, and he would never forget that.

So. She had accomplished her mission and fled the country. She was perhaps out of his reach now, but she wasn't out of the reach of her own countrymen. With Blanc on the job, he would be able to stay abreast of their search for her, and when they were closing in on her, he would step in and do the honors himself. With great pleasure.

11

When Rodrigo received the faxed papers, he stared for a long time at the picture of the woman who had killed his father. His machine was a color printer, so he received the full impact of the skillfulness of her disguise. Her hair was wheat blond and very straight, her eyes a piercing pale blue. She was very Nordic in looks, with a strong, lean face and high cheekbones. He was amazed at how changing her coloring to dark hair and brown eyes had softened her face; her facial structure had remained unchanged, but one's perception of her was definitely altered. He thought she could have walked into the room and sat next to him, and it would have taken him a moment to recognize her.

He had wondered what his father had seen in her. As a brunette, she had left Rodrigo cold; his reaction to her as a blonde was very different. It wasn't just the normal Italian reaction to blond hair, either. It was as if he was truly seeing her for the first time, seeing the intellect and strong will so evident in those pale eyes. Perhaps Salvatore had been more perceptive than he himself was, because his father had respected strength as he'd respected nothing else. This woman was strong. Once she had crossed his path, it was almost inevitable that Salvatore would have been attracted to her.

Rodrigo leafed through the other pages Blanc had sent him. He was interested in the Mansfield woman's employment history with the American CIA; she was a hired killer, period. He wasn't shocked that governments used such people; he would have been shocked if they *didn't*. This was information he could use at a later date if he needed a particular favor from the American government, but nothing that would help him right now.

He was more interested in the information about her family: a mother and a sister. The mother, Elizabeth Mansfield, lived in Chicago; the younger sister, Diandra, lived with her husband and two children in Toledo, Ohio. If he couldn't locate Liliane, he thought, he could use her family to flush her out of hiding. Then he read that she hadn't been in contact with her family in years, and had to allow for the possibility that she might not care about their welfare.

The last page indicated what Blanc had told him, that his father's murder had not been ordered by the Americans. She had acted alone, seeking vengeance for the deaths of her friends the Joubrans. The CIA had dispatched an operative to terminate the problem.

Terminate. That was a very good word, but he wanted to do the terminating himself. If possible, he would have that satisfaction. If not, he would accept with good grace that the Americans had handled the situation.

The very last paragraph made him sit up straight. The subject had fled to London using an alias, then evidently switched identities once again and returned to Paris. Search efforts were focusing there. The operative on location believed she was preparing for yet another strike against the Nervi organization.

Rodrigo felt as if he'd been electrified; every fine hair on his body lifted, and chills ran down his spine.

She had come back to Paris. She was *here,* within his reach. It was a bold move, and if not for M. Blanc, he would have been caught unawares. His personal security was as tight as he could humanly make it, but what about the Nervi holdings scattered around Europe? More particularly, what about the ones here in the Paris area? The security systems in place were good, yes, but where this woman was concerned, extra precautions were called for.

What was her most likely target? The answer came immediately to mind: Vincenzo's laboratory. He *knew* it; the flash of intuition too strong to ignore. That was where her friends had struck, and gotten shot for their efforts. She would see it as poetic justice if she completed the job, perhaps setting a series of explosive charges and completely demolishing the laboratory complex.

Losing the projected profits from the influenza vaccine wouldn't bankrupt him, but he was looking forward to that huge influx of cash. Money was the real power in the world, behind the kings and oil princes, the presidents and prime ministers, with each group trying to get more than the other. But even greater than the lost profits would be the insult, the loss of face. Another incident at the lab and the WHO would begin questioning the security, at best simply withdrawing the funding, at worst insisting on on-site inspections. He didn't want anyone from the outside looking through the laboratory. Vincenzo could probably hide or disguise what he was doing, but any further delay would wreck their plans.

He couldn't let her win. Aside from everything else, word would reach the streets that Rodrigo Nervi had been bested– and by a woman. He could perhaps keep it quiet for a time, but eventually someone would talk. Someone always talked.

This could not have happened at a worse time. He had just buried his father no more than a week before. As well as he knew what needed to be done, nevertheless he was aware that on some fronts there was still a lingering doubt that he could step into Salvatore's shoes. And he himself had taken over a lot of the everyday work of Salvatore's; he had no one in position to do the same for him.

He was in the middle of arranging a shipment of weapons-grade plutonium to Syria. There were opiates to funnel into various countries, arms deals to be made, in addition to all the legitimate work of running a multifaceted corporation. He had to attend board meetings.

But to apprehend Liliane Mansfield, he would make the time, if he had to clear his slate of everything else. By tomorrow morning, every employee of his in France would have a photograph of her. If she walked down the street, eventually someone would recognize her.

The security at the laboratory was common, at least on the outside. Fenced and gated–with one entrance in front and one in back, both manned by two guards—the lab itself was a series of connected buildings that were mostly windowless. The architecture was graceless, the buildings themselves constructed of ordinary red brick. The parking lot on the left contained about fifty vehicles.

Swain noted all of this on one drive-by. The Jaguar was kind of noticeable, so he couldn't do an immediate repeat without the guards noticing. Instead he waited until the next day to do another drive-by, and in the meantime, he used all his contacts to locate the building specs so he could figure out how Lily was most likely to try to gain entrance. For the exterior grounds, security was pretty much what he could see: the fence, the gated entrances, the guards. At night, the grounds were patrolled by a guard with a leashed German shepherd, and the grounds were well-lit.

For obvious reasons, he thought she would try for a night entrance, despite the dog. The night lighting was good, but created shadows that provided concealment. There weren't as many people around at night, plus people naturally got tired in the wee hours. She was an expert with a pistol, and could take out both the guard and the dog with well-placed sedation darts. Not instantaneously, true, and the guard might be able to yell or otherwise attract attention. Of course, she could also kill them; if she used a silencer, the guards at the gate wouldn't hear a thing.

Swain didn't like that thought. He wouldn't bat an eyelash if she killed the guard, but it made him queasy to think about harming the dog. He was a sucker for dogs, even trained attack dogs. People were a different story; some of them just cried out for killing. He excluded most kids from that theory, lumping them in with dogs, though he'd met some kids he'd thought the world would be better off without. He was just glad his own kids hadn't turned out to be jerks, because it would've been embarrassing.

He just hoped Lily didn't shoot dogs. A lot of his natural sympathy for her would go down the drain if she did.

There was a nice little park across the street from the laboratory. On warm summer days, a lot of the employees from the nearby shops would find their way there to relax during their lunch breaks. There were a few hardy souls there even on a brisk November day, walking their dogs, reading; enough of them, in fact that one more man wouldn't be noticeable.

The streets here were wider than in the older parts of Paris, but parking was still at a premium. Finally Swain found a parking space nearby, and walked to the park. He bought a cup of coffee and found himself a nice bench in the sun where he could watch the comings and goings at the lab, familiarize himself with the routine, maybe notice some security weakness he hadn't already spotted. If he was lucky, Lily might choose today to do the same thing. There was no telling what garb she'd be wearing, or what color wig, so he might wander around and study the park-goers' noses and mouths. He thought he'd recognize the shape of Lily's mouth anywhere.

The laboratory complex looked ordinary enough; the external security was what one would expect at any manufacturing facility: a perimeter of fencing, limited access, uniformed guards at the gates. Anything more, such as twelve-foot concrete walls with barbed wire on the top, would only attract attention.

The sophisticated security, Lily thought, would be inside.

Fingerprint scans or retinal scans for entry into the most re-
stricted areas. Motion sensors. Laser beams. Sensors for broken glass, weight sensors, you name it. She needed to know
exactly what was inside, and she might have to hire someone
who could bypass those systems. She knew several people in
the business, but she wanted to stay away from acquaintances.
If the word had gone out that she was now persona non grata at
the Agency, none of them would be inclined to help her. They
might even actively work against her, dropping a word in interested ears about her location and intentions.

The neighborhood was an interesting mix of ethnic shops,
trendy little boutiques–like there was ever any other kind–
cafés, coffee shops, and cheap apartment housing. A small park
gave the eye a break from the urban sprawl, though most of the
trees had been denuded by approaching winter and the brisk
wind made the limbs rattle like bones against each other.

She felt much better today, almost normal. Her legs had
held up well on the brisk walk from the train, and she wasn't
breathless. Tomorrow, she thought, she would try a slow jog,
but today she was content to walk.

She stopped in a coffee shop and bought a cup of strong
black coffee, as well as a pastry with a buttery, flaky crust that
almost melted in her mouth as soon as she took a bite. The park
was just fifty meters distant, so she walked there and selected a
bench in the sun, where she devoted herself to the sinful pastry
and her coffee. When she was finished, she licked her fingers,
then took a thin notebook from her tote, opened it in her lap,
and bent her head over it. She pretended to be engrossed in
what she was reading, but in reality her eyes were busy, her
gaze moving from point to point, noting the people in the park
and the placement of certain things.

There was a score of people in the little park; a young mother with an energetic toddler, an elderly man walking an elderly dog. Another man sat alone, sipping a cup of coffee and looking at his wrist watch several times, as if he was waiting, none too patiently, for someone to join him. Others walked among the trees: a young couple holding hands, two young men kicking a soccer ball back and forth as they went, people enjoying the sunny day.

Lily took a pen from her tote and drew a rough diagram of the park, marking the locations of benches, trees, shrubbery, the concrete trash receptacles, the small fountain in the middle. Then she flipped a page and did the same with the laboratory complex, marking where the doors were in relation to the gate, the windows. She would need to do the same for all four sides of the complex. This afternoon she would rent a motorbike and wait for Dr. Giordano to leave the complex, assuming he was even there, of course–she had no idea what hours he kept. She didn't even know what model and make of car he drove. She was betting, however, that he would keep fairly regular hours, close to the national average. When he left, she would follow him home. Simple. His phone number might not be published, but old-fashioned methods still worked.

Again, she knew nothing about the man's family life, or if he even had family here in Paris. He was her ace in the hole. He knew about the complex's security and, as director, would have access to every part of it; what wasn't certain was how easily he would divulge that information. She preferred not to use him, however, because once she grabbed him, she would have to move quickly, before anyone noticed he was missing. She would try to find out about the internal security methods by other means, try to get in without using Dr. Giordano. But she wanted to know where he lived sooner rather than later, just in case.

Lily was sharply aware of her shortcomings in this area. She'd never dealt with anything more than the most basic security systems. She wasn't an expert in anything, except reading her target and getting close enough to execute the mission. The more she thought about this undertaking, the more she realized how uneven the odds were, but that didn't lessen her determination. There was no perfect security system in the world; there was always someone who knew how to bypass it. She would find that someone, or she would learn how to do it herself.

The two young men were no longer kicking the soccer ball. Instead they were talking on a mobile phone as they looked at a sheet of paper, then at her.

Alarm skittered through her. She slid the notebook and pen back into her tote, then pretended to accidentally knock the tote to the ground beside her right leg. She bent down and, using the tote to hide her movements, slid her hand inside the top of her boot and pulled out her weapon.

She used the tote to keep the weapon concealed as she got to her feet, moving at an angle away from the two men. Her heart was thumping in her chest. She was accustomed to being the hunter, but this time she was the prey.

12

LILY SPRINTED, HER SUDDEN BURST OF SPEED CATCHING THEM BY surprise. She heard a shout, and instinctively dived to the ground a split second before the sharp, deep crack of a large-caliber pistol shattered the drone of everyday business. She rolled behind one of the concrete trash receptacles and came up on one knee.

She wasn't fool enough to stick her head up, though most people weren't all that accurate with a pistol. Instead she took a quick peek around the side and squeezed off a shot of her own. At that distance, some thirty or thirty-five meters, she wasn't all that accurate herself; her bullet went into the ground just in front of the two men, kicking up a spray of dirt and sending both of them diving for cover.

She heard tires squealing, people screaming as they realized the sharp sounds were those of gunfire. Out of the corner of her eye she saw the young mother swoop down on her toddler and snatch him up as if he were a football, holding him under her arm as she scrambled for safety. The little boy squealed with joy, thinking it was a game. The old man stumbled and fell, losing his hold on the leash. The old dog, however, was long past making a dash for freedom, and it sat down on the grass.

Quickly she looked around for any threat coming at her from the rear, but all she saw was people running away, not toward her. Safe from that quarter, at least for right now, she looked around the other side of the receptacle and saw two uniformed guards running from the complex gate, weapons in their hands.

She squeezed off a shot at the guards and made them dive for the pavement, though again they were too far away for accuracy. She used a modified Beretta model 87, shooting .22-caliber long rifle bullets, with a ten-round clip. She had just used two rounds, and she hadn't brought any extra ammo with her, because she hadn't been expecting to use it. *Fool!* she berated herself. She didn't know if these two guys were Agency or some of Rodrigo's men, but she was betting on Agency, for them to have found her so fast. She should have been better prepared, instead of underestimating them and perhaps overestimating herself.

She snapped her attention back to the two soccer players. They both had weapons, and when she peeked around again, both fired off shots; one shot missed completely, and she heard glass shatter behind her, followed by more screams and the sudden shocked cries of someone who had been wounded. The other bullet struck the trash receptacle, sending a chunk of concrete into the air and peppering her face with stinging shards. She fired a shot herself–*three*–and checked the guards. They had both found cover, one behind a tree and the other behind a trash receptacle like the one she crouched behind.

They weren't changing their position, so she turned back to the soccer players. The one to her left had moved even further to her left, hampering her aim at him, since she was right-handed and the concrete that protected her was to some extent also protecting him.

This was *not* good. There were four weapons to her one, therefore theoretically at least four times as much ammunition as she had. They could keep her pinned here until she ran out of ammo, or until the French police arrived–which should be any minute now, because even with the ringing in her ears from the gunfire, she could hear the sirens–and took care of her themselves.

Behind her, traffic had snarled as drivers stopped their cars and jumped out to hide behind them. Her only chance was to run for the cover of the cars and use them to hide her movements; she'd have to shortcut through a shop, probably, or hope someone came by on a bicycle, so she could relieve them of it. She didn't think she could trust her ability to run for any distance.

The old man who had fallen was trying to get up and at the same time gather his trembling pet to him. "Stay down!" Lily yelled at him. He looked at her with terrified incomprehension on his face, his white hair wildly disordered. "Stay down!" she yelled again, making a downward motion with her hand.

Thank God, he finally understood, and flattened himself on the ground. His little dog crept to him and lay down by his head, getting as close to him as it could.

For a moment, time seemed frozen, the sharp smell of

cordite seeming to hang over the park despite the chill breeze. She heard the two soccer players say something to each other, but she couldn't make out the words.

From her right came the purr of a well-tuned, powerful engine. She glanced in that direction and saw a gray Jaguar jump the curb, heading straight toward her.

Her heartbeat thundered in her ears, almost deafening her. She had only a few seconds; she had to time her jump perfectly or the car would crush her. She gathered her legs under her, preparing to spring–

The driver spun the wheel and the Jaguar slid sideways between her and the soccer players, the tires slinging clots of dirt and grass as they tried to grab traction, the rear end of the car swinging around so that it ended up facing in the same direction from which it had come. The driver leaned over and thrust open the passenger door.

"Get in!" he yelled in English, and Lily dived into the front seat. Over her head came the deep boom of a large-caliber weapon, and the spent cartridge bounced off the seat into her face. She swatted the hot shell away.

He floored the accelerator and the Jaguar leaped forward. There were more shots, several of them, the cracks and booms of different caliber weapons overlapping. The driver's side rear window splintered, and the driver ducked as glass sprayed behind him. "Shit!" He grinned, then swerved to miss a tree.

Lily had a dizzying image of a tangle of cars as they shot forward into the street. The driver spun the wheel again and the Jaguar once more swapped ends, throwing Lily onto the floorboard. She tried to grab the seat, the door handle, anything with which to anchor herself. The driver was laughing like a maniac as the car once more leaped a curb, fishtailed, then shot through a gap and briefly went airborne before coming down on the street with a hard thump that rattled her teeth and made the chassis groan. Lily gulped for air.

He slammed on the brakes, made a hard left turn, and accelerated out of it. The G-force pressed Lily into the floorboard, preventing her from climbing into the seat. She closed her eyes as squealing brakes sounded directly beside her door, but there was no collision. Instead he made a right turn, bumping along a very uneven surface; with the buildings looming so close on each side that she thought they were going to lose the side-view mirrors, Lily knew they must be in an alley. Dear God, she'd gotten into a car with a maniac.

At the end of the alley he slowed, stopped, then smoothly pulled out into traffic and measured his speed to that of the other cars around him, driving as sedately as any grandmother on Sunday morning.

But he was grinning, and he threw back his head on a full-throated laugh. "Damn, that was fun!"

He had both hands on the wheel, the big automatic lying on the seat beside him. This was likely the best chance she'd have. Lily stayed in the close confines of the floorboard. She fished around for her pistol, which she'd dropped when he was slinging her around as if she were on a carnival ride. She found it under the passenger seat and, with a smooth, economical motion, brought the weapon up and aimed it between his eyes. "Pull over and let me out," she said.

He glanced at the pistol, then turned his attention back to the traffic. "Put that peashooter away before you piss me off. Hell, lady, I just saved your life!"

He had, which was why she hadn't already shot him. "Thank you," she said. "Now, pull over and let me out."

The soccer players hadn't been Agency; she'd heard them call to each other in Italian, so they were Rodrigo's men. Which meant this man was maybe, probably, Agency. He was definitely American. She didn't believe in coincidence, or at least not in massive coincidence, and for this man to show up just as she was pinned down, with driving skills like a professional and toting a Heckler and Koch nine millimeter that cost close to a thousand bucks . . . yeah, like he was anything else except Agency. Or more likely he was a contract agent, a hired killer just like herself.

She frowned. That didn't make sense. If he was a contract agent sent to terminate her, then all he'd had to do was stay out of it and she would likely have been dead very shortly, and he wouldn't have had to lift a finger. She would have tried to make a run for it, though how far she'd have gotten with four gunmen after her and her stamina more than a little questionable, she didn't know. Her heart was still hammering, and to her dismay she was still trying to drag in air.

There was also the possibility that he was a lunatic. Considering how he'd been laughing, that was more than a little likely. Either way, she wanted out of this car.

"Don't make me pull the trigger," she said softly.

"Wouldn't think of it." He glanced at her again, the corners of his eyes crinkling in another of those grins. "Just let me get farther away from the scene of the crime, okay? In case you didn't notice, I was involved in that little fracas, too, and a Jag with a shot-out window is kind of noticeable. Shit. It's a rental, too. American Express is gonna be pissed."

Lily watched him, trying to get a read. He seemed genuinely unperturbed by the fact that she had a weapon trained on him. In fact, he seemed to think the entire situation was a lark. "Have you ever spent any time in a mental hospital?"

"What?" He laughed and shot her another of those quick glances.

She repeated the question.

"You're serious. You think I'm a lunatic?"

"You were laughing like one, in a definitely non-funny situation."

"One of my many faults, laughing. I'd been about to die of boredom, and here I was, sitting in a little park minding my own business, when a shoot-out starts behind me. It's four against one, and the one is a blond woman. I'm bored, I'm horny, so I think maybe if I drive my Jag over there and get it shot up while I'm saving her life, I'll get a little excitement and the blonde might jump my bones out of gratitude. So, what about it?" He waggled his eyebrows at her.

Startled, Lily laughed. He looked remarkably silly, waggling his eyebrows like that.

He stopped waggling and winked at her. "You can get up in the seat now. You can hold the pistol on me from that position, too."

"The way you drive, I may be safer on the floorboard." But she hoisted herself into the seat, and didn't buckle her seat belt because she would have had to put down the pistol in order to do it. She noticed he didn't have his seat belt buckled, either.

"Nothing's wrong with my driving. We're alive, aren't we? Not leaking from any new holes—well, maybe just a little."

"You were hit?" she asked sharply, twisting toward him.

"No, just some glass cut the back of my neck. It's minor." He reached back and swiped his right hand across his neck. His fingers came away smeared with blood, but not a lot of it. "See?"

"Okay." Smooth as silk, she reached out her left hand to confiscate the weapon lying beside his leg.

Without looking down, he snapped his right hand around her wrist. "Uh-uh," he said, all playfulness gone from his voice. "That's mine."

He was fast, amazingly so. In a flash the good-natured goofiness had vanished, replaced by a cool, hard look that said he meant business.

Oddly, she was reassured by this glimpse, as if now she was seeing the real man and knew what she had to deal with. She moved farther away from him, as close to the door as she could get, not because she was afraid of him but to make it more difficult for him to grab her weapon with one of those lightning moves. And maybe she *was* a little afraid of him; he was an unknown, and in her business what she didn't know could get her killed. Fear was good; it kept her on her toes.

He rolled his eyes at her action. "Look, you don't have to act like I'm psycho or something. I'll let you out safe and sound, I promise—unless you shoot me, in which case we'll crash into something and I can't make any guarantees."

"Who are you?" she asked in a flat tone.

"Lucas Swain, at your service. Most people just call me Swain. For some reason, *Lucas* never really caught on."

"I didn't mean your name. Who do you work for?"

"Myself. I'm not real good at the nine-to-five routine. I'd been in South America for ten years or so and things got kind of tense there, so I thought taking in the sights in Europe for a while would be a good idea."

He *was* darkly tanned, she noticed. If she read between the lines, he was telling her he was either an adventurer, a mercenary, or a contract agent. She was still betting on the latter. But then why had he intervened? That was what made no sense. If his orders were to kill her, he could have done that when she first dived into the car if he hadn't wanted to let Rodrigo's goons do the deed for him.

"Whatever you're involved in," he said, "from the looks of it you're outnumbered and could use some help. I'm available, I'm good, and I'm bored. So what was going on back there?"

Lily wasn't an impulsive person, at least not in her work. She was careful, she did her homework, and she planned. But she'd already realized she'd need help in getting into the laboratory complex, and despite his unsettling good humor, Lucas Swain had proven himself to be skilled at a lot of things. She had been so alone these past few months that her solitude was a constant ache in her heart. There was something about this man that invited trust, something that eased the ache of loneliness.

She didn't answer his question. Instead she said, "Are you any good with security systems?"

13

HE PURSED HIS LIPS, CONSIDERING HER QUESTION. "I KNOW enough to get by, but I'm no expert. Depends on the actual system. I do, however, know some real experts who can tell me anything I need to know." He paused. "Are you talking about doing something illegal?"

"Yes."

"Oh, good. I'm feeling more cheerful by the minute."

If he got any more cheerful, she thought, she'd have to shoot him to protect her own sanity.

He made another turn, looked around, then said thoughtfully, "Do you know where the hell we are?"

Lily turned sideways and swung her legs up in the seat, blocking any move he might make to grab her pistol, then dared a quick glance around. "Yes. At the next traffic signal turn right, then about a mile farther turn left. I'll tell you when."

"Where will we be then?"

"At the train station. That's where you can let me out."

"Aw, come on. We've been getting along so great. Don't abandon me so soon. I had my hopes up we were going to be partners."

"Without checking you out?" she asked incredulously.

"I guess that would be stupid."

"No joke." Ten minutes with an American and she found herself easily falling back into the vernacular, like putting on comfortable slippers. "Where are you staying? I'll call you."

"At the Bristol." He took the right turn she'd indicated. "Room seven-twelve."

She lifted her brows. "You rented a Jag, you stay at one of the most expensive hotels in Paris. Your day job must pay well."

"All of my jobs have paid well, plus I had to have some-where to park the Jag. Damn. Now I have to rent another car, and I can't turn this one in yet or I'll be busted when the dam-age is reported."

She glanced back at the broken window, through which cold air was rushing. "Break it out the rest of the way and tell the rental company some punk broke it with a bat."

"That'll work, unless someone got the license number."

"The way you were fishtailing?"

"There is that, but why take the chance? In France you're assumed guilty unless you can prove otherwise. I'll just try to stay out of the clutches of the gendarmes, thank you."

"Your choice," she said indifferently. "You're the one who'll be paying for two rental cars."

"Don't sound so sympathetic; I'll start thinking you care."

That quip pulled an unwilling smile from her. He didn't

take himself seriously; she didn't know if that was an asset or a liability, but he was definitely amusing. He'd all but fallen into her lap just when she'd been trying to decide whom she should pull in to help her, so she'd have to be a fool to categorically turn him down. She would check him out, and if there was the slightest hint of Agency or untrustworthiness, then she would simply never contact him. He hadn't acted as if he'd been hired to kill her; she was beginning to feel easy about that. As for whether or not he was any good, or reliable, that remained to be seen. She couldn't call her normal source with the Agency and have him investigated, but she knew a couple of shady guys who could find out for her.

She used the short time left before they reached the train station to study him. He was a good-looking man, she noticed with faint surprise; when he'd been talking, that was what she'd paid attention to, not his face. He was tallish, around six-one or so, and lean. His hands were sinewy, long-fingered, ringless, with prominent veins and short, clean nails. His hair was short, brown with gray around his temples; his eyes were blue, much bluer than her own. Lips a bit thin, but well-shaped. Strong chin that stopped just short of being cleft. A noble nose, thin and high-bridged. Except for the gray in his hair, he looked younger than he probably was. She guessed his age to be close to her own, late thirties, possible early forties.

He was dressed the way millions of men on the Continent dressed, nothing that would make him stand out or shout "American," no Levi's or Nikes or a sweatshirt imprinted with his favorite professional football team. Instead he wore taupe slacks, a blue shirt, and a great black leather blazer. She envied him that blazer. And his Italian leather loafers were clean and shiny.

If he was newly arrived from South America, he'd adopted the style of the locals pretty fast.

"The next left," she said as they neared the turn.

He'd also picked up the Parisian style of driving pretty fast, too; he drove with nerve, verve, and reckless abandon. As someone tried to cut him off, she saw that he'd also been fast to pick up some of the local gestures. He was smiling as he cut in front of the other car; a glint in his eyes that said he enjoyed the challenge of Parisian traffic. He was definitely a lunatic.

"How long have you been in Paris?" she asked.

"Three days. Why?"

"Pull over there." She directed him to the curb in front of the train platform. "You already drive like a native."

"When you swim with the sharks, you gotta show your teeth so they know you mean business." He pulled to the curb. "It's been a pleasure, Ms. . . . ?"

Lily didn't leap into the opening. Instead she returned her pistol to its holster in her boot and continued the movement, opening the door and sliding out. She leaned in to look at him. "I'll call you," she said, then closed the door and strode away.

He wasn't in a parking slot, so he couldn't wait to see which train she got on; he had to pull away, and though he looked back, already her blond head was gone from view. He didn't think she'd pulled a wig out of her pocket and clapped it on, so he assumed she had deliberately lost herself behind some taller passengers.

He could have pushed it, left the car where it was and followed her, but his gut told him that persistence right now wasn't a smart idea. If he tried to follow her, she would bolt. Let her come to him.

She was going to check him out. Shit. He pulled out his cell phone and made an urgent call stateside so some computer geek could earn his salary and make sure no one could learn anything about Lucas Swain except for some highly edited, and mostly fabricated, details.

That taken care of, Swain put his mind to solving another less pressing problem: the Jag. That window needed to be replaced before he turned it in to the rental company, because he'd been serious about not wanting the French cops to know about him. It wasn't good politics, and he also had to figure an organization like the Nervis' would have informants everywhere it mattered, which certainly included the cops.

He loved the Jag, but it would have to go. It was just too damn noticeable. Maybe a Mercedes–no, still too noticeable. A French-made car, then, a Renault or something like that; though, come to think of it, he'd love to drive an Italian sports car. He had to think of the job first, damn it, and Lily might balk at running around with him if he was driving something flashy.

God, he'd almost choked on his coffee when he saw her walking casually into the park as if she weren't being hunted all over Europe. He'd always been a lucky son of a bitch, and that luck was holding. Forget any fancy computer work, deductive reasoning, shit like that–all he'd had to do was sit down on a bench in a dinky park and she walked up before he'd been there fifteen minutes. Okay, so deductive reasoning had helped him pick out the laboratory complex as the place where she was most likely to show; he was still lucky.

He hadn't been shot, either, which was damn lucky. Too bad about the Jag. Vinay would say he'd been hotdogging again, and the charge would be true. He liked a little excitement in his life. Vinay would also ask him what the hell he was thinking, playing games like this instead of doing the job he'd been sent to do, but he'd always been curious as well as lucky. He wanted to know what Lily was planning to do, what there was at that laboratory that was so interesting. Besides, she'd got the drop on him.

Strange, but he hadn't been worried. Lily Mansfield was a hired assassin, and just because she hired out to the good guys didn't make her any less dangerous. But she hadn't wanted that old guy in the park to get hurt, and she hadn't recklessly fired where innocent bystanders could have been hurt–unlike the soccer guys, who had done exactly that. Just because of that, he'd have been inclined to help her even if she hadn't been his quarry.

He guessed he wouldn't tell Vinay anything just yet, because Vinay might not understand his letting Lily go without getting any idea of how to get in touch with her again.

In betting that she'd call him in a day or so, he was trusting in human nature. He'd helped her, he'd made her laugh, and he hadn't done anything threatening. He'd offered to help her further. He'd given her information about himself. The reason she hadn't put down that damn pistol of hers was that she'd been expecting him to use his weapon on her, and by not even trying to, he'd muddied the waters of suspicion.

She was just good enough, just dangerous enough, that if he made a move too soon, he might end up with some extra ventilation holes, which would spoil his reputation for being lucky. And if he was wrong about her calling him, then he'd have to go back to the boring way of finding people: computers and deductive reasoning.

He spent the rest of the day locating someone who would replace the Jaguar's side window, then renting another car. He started to get one of the ordinary little Renaults, but at the last moment decided on the Mégane Renault Sport, a hot little turbo-charged number with a six-speed transmission. It wasn't ex-actly a nondescript car, but he figured there might be another occasion when he needed speed and handling and he didn't want to get caught a few horses short. The rental office had had a red one that really caught his eye, but he went with the silver. There was no sense in waving a red flag and shouting, "Here I am, look at me!"

He ended up back at the Bristol just as daylight faded completely. He was hungry, but he wasn't in the mood for com-pany, so he went up to his room and called room service. While he waited for his food to be delivered, he took off his shoes and jacket and flopped on the bed, where he lay staring at the ceiling–he'd done some good thinking while looking at that ceiling–and thinking about Lily Mansfield.

He'd recognized her immediately from the color photo in her file. No photograph, however, could have conveyed the en-ergy and intensity that permeated every move she made. He liked her face, almost thin but strongly structured, with very high cheekbones, that proud nose, and Lord God Almighty, that mouth. Just looking at that mouth gave him a woody. Her eyes were like pieces of blue ice, but her mouth was tender and vul-nerable and sexy and a lot of other things he could feel but couldn't put into words.

He hadn't been kidding when he told her he hoped she'd jump his bones. If she'd said the word, he'd have had her back here at the Bristol in record time.

He could remember exactly how she'd looked, what she was wearing: dark gray pants with black boots, a blue oxford-cloth shirt, and a dark blue pea jacket. He should probably also commit to memory that when she was wearing those boots, she was armed. Her hair was simply cut, just to her shoulders, and framed her face with long wisps. Even though the pea jacket had hidden most of her figure, from the length and build of her legs, he figured she was on the lean side. She had also looked a little frail, with bluish circles under her eyes, as if she'd been sick or wasn't getting enough rest.

Having the hots for her wouldn't make his job any easier; in fact, he felt a little sick at what he had to do. He'd finesse the rules, but he wouldn't break them. Well, not much. He'd accomplish the job on his own timetable, and if there were a couple of detours along the way, so be it. It wouldn't hurt to find out what was behind the Joubrans' murders, who had hired them and why. The Nervis were scum, and if he could get some really nasty goods on them, so much the better.

That would buy him time with Lily. Too bad in the end he'd have to betray her.

14

"There was trouble yesterday," Damone said softly from the library doorway. "Tell me what is happening."

"You shouldn't be here," Rodrigo said instead, rising to greet his brother. He'd been astonished when the guards had called to announce Damone's arrival. The agreement was that they wouldn't be together again until after their father's murderer had been caught. Learning that Liliane Mansfield, alias Denise Morel, had killed Salvatore in revenge for the deaths of her friends, in no way abrogated that agreement. In fact, other than telling Damone the woman's identity, Rodrigo hadn't passed along any other information other than to say they were searching for her.

Damone wasn't a weak man, but Rodrigo had always felt protective of his younger brother, first because he *was* younger, and second because Damone had never been in the trenches with their father the way Rodrigo had. Rodrigo knew the ways of urban and corporate warfare, while Damone knew the ways of stock markets and mutual funds.

"You have no one to help you the way you helped Papa," Damone replied, sitting down in the chair Rodrigo had always used when Salvatore was alive. "It isn't right that I should spend my time studying money markets and moving funds around when you're shouldering the entire responsibility for operations." He spread his hands. "I also receive news from both the Internet and print sources. The item I read early this morning wasn't very informative, just a small mention of an incident at a park yesterday, of several people exchanging gunfire. None of the culprits were identified, other than two guards from a nearby laboratory who heard the shots and ran to help." His intelligent dark eyes narrowed. "The name of the park was given."

Rodrigo said, "But why are you here? The incident was handled."

"Because this is the second incident at Vincenzo's lab. Am I supposed to think that is coincidence? We are depending on the influx of profits from the influenza vaccine. There are several opportunities pending that I'll have to let go by if the funds aren't there. I want to know what's going on."

"A phone call wouldn't have sufficed?"

"I can't see your face over the phone," Damone replied, and smiled. "You're a talented liar, but I know you too well. I've watched you from the time we were small, looking up at Papa and denying we had done whatever thing had happened, though of course we were always guilty. If you lie to me in person, I'll know it. So I am capable of adding more than two dig-

its together. There is an ongoing problem at Vincenzo's laboratory, and in the middle of this, our father is murdered. Are the
two connected?"

That was the problem with Damone, Rodrigo thought; he
was too damned intelligent, and intuitive into the bargain. It annoyed Rodrigo that he'd never been able to successfully lie to his
younger brother; everyone else in the world, yes, but not to Damone. And perhaps being protective of his younger brother had
been good when they were seven and four, but they were both
grown men now. That was a habit he should perhaps break.

"Yes," he finally said. "They are."

"How so?"

"The woman who killed Papa, Liliane Mansfield, was a
close friend of the Joubrans, the couple who broke into the
laboratory in August and destroyed a great portion of Vincenzo's work."

Damone rubbed his eyes as if he was tired, then pinched
the bridge of his nose before lowering his hand. "So it was
vengeance."

"That part of it, yes."

"And the other part?"

Rodrigo sighed. "I still don't know who hired the Joubrans
in the beginning. Whoever it is could well hire someone else to
attack the laboratory again. We cannot afford another such
delay. This woman who killed Papa wasn't working for anyone
at the time, I don't think, but she could well be by now. My men
spotted her at the park yesterday; she was surveilling the
grounds of the complex. Whether she was hired or is doing this
on her own, the result is the same. She will try to sabotage the
vaccine."

"Can she possibly know what the vaccine is?"

Rodrigo spread his hands. "There is always the possibility of betrayal from within, someone who works at the laboratory, in which case she would know. Supposedly mercenaries such as the Joubrans don't work cheaply, so I'm investigating the financial circumstances of all the laboratory employees, to see if any of them had the means of hiring them."

"What do you know about this woman?"

"She is an American, and she was a hired killer, a contract agent, for their CIA."

Damone paled. "The Americans hired her?"

"Not to kill Papa, no. She did that on her own and, as you can imagine, they are very upset with her. They have, in fact, dispatched someone to 'terminate the problem,' I believe is the phrase that was used."

"And in the meantime she is trying to devise a way to get inside the laboratory. How did she get away yesterday?"

"She has an accomplice, a man driving a Jaguar. He drove the car between her and my men, shielding her while he returned fire."

"License plate?"

"No; the angle was wrong for my men to see it. There were witnesses, of course, but they were too busy cowering to take down a license number."

"The most important question: *Has she tried to harm you personally?*"

"No." Rodrigo blinked in surprise.

"Then it follows that I am in less danger than you. Therefore I will stay here, and you may delegate some of your duties to me. I will oversee the search for this woman, or any of your other problems if you would rather see to that yourself. Or we can work together on everything. I wish to be of help. He was my father, too."

Rodrigo sighed, realizing he had been wrong to keep Damone away from everything; his brother was, after all, a Nervi. He must long for vengeance as deeply as did Rodrigo himself.

"There is another reason I want this matter taken care of," Damone continued. "I am thinking of getting married."

Astonished, Rodrigo stared at him in silence for a moment, then burst into laughter. "Married! When? You haven't said anything about a special woman!"

Damone laughed, too, and color darkened his cheeks. "I don't know when, because I haven't asked her yet. But I think she will say yes. We have been seeing each other for over a year—"

"And you didn't tell us?" *Us* included Salvatore, who would have been delighted that one of his sons intended to settle down and provide him with grandchildren.

"—but exclusively only in the past few months. I wanted to be certain before I said anything. She is Swiss, of a very good family; her father is a banker. Her name is Giselle." His voice deepened when he said her name. "I have known from the very first that she is the one."

"But she took longer, eh?" Rodrigo laughed again. "She didn't take one look at your handsome face and decide you would make beautiful babies with her?"

"She knew that immediately, yes," Damone said with cool confidence. "It was my ability to be a good husband that she doubted."

"All Nervis make good husbands," Rodrigo said, and it was

true, if the wife didn't mind the occasional mistress. Damone, though, would probably be faithful; he was just that type.

This happy news did explain why Damone was anxious to put this problem of Liliane Mansfield to rest. While it was true that wanting retribution was also part of it, he might well have been patient enough to let Rodrigo handle things had events in his personal life not spurred him to action.

Damone looked at Rodrigo's desk and saw the photograph lying on it. Walking over, he turned the file around and studied the woman's face. "She's attractive," he said. "Not pretty, but . . . attractive."

He flipped through the rest of the file, reading rapidly. He looked up in astonishment. "This is the CIA's file on her. How did you get it?"

"We have someone there on our payroll, of course. Also in Interpol, and Scotland Yard. It has, on occasion, been convenient to know certain things in advance."

"The CIA calls here? You call them?"

"No, of course not; every call going in or out of there is logged and perhaps recorded. I have a private number for our Interpol contact, Georges Blanc, and he contacts the CIA or FBI through normal channels."

"Have you thought of asking Blanc to get the mobile phone number of the person the CIA has sent to track Mansfield? The CIA doesn't do this itself; it hires others to do the work, am I correct? I'm certain he or she would have a mobile, everyone does. Perhaps this person would be interested in making a considerable sum of money in addition to what the CIA pays, if certain information comes our way first."

Intrigued by the idea, chagrined that he hadn't thought of it himself, Rodrigo stared at his brother in admiration. "Fresh eyes," he murmured to himself. And Damone was a Nervi; some things were inborn. "You have a devious mind," he said, and laughed. "Between the two of us, this woman has no chance."

15

FRANK VINAY ALWAYS ROSE EARLY, BEFORE DAWN. SINCE THE death of his wife, Dodie, fifteen years before, it had been increasingly difficult for him to find reasons *not* to work. He still missed her, dreadfully at times; at other times it felt more like a distant ache, as if something in his life wasn't quite right. He'd never considered remarrying, because he thought it would be grossly unfair to a woman to marry her when he still loved his dead wife with all his heart and soul.

He wasn't alone, anyway; he had Kaiser for company. The big German shepherd's chosen sleeping place was in a corner of the kitchen–maybe the kitchen felt like home to him, since that was where he'd been kept as a puppy until he became accustomed to his new surroundings–and he rose from his bed, tail wagging, as soon as he heard Frank's footsteps coming down the stairs.

Frank entered the kitchen and rubbed Kaiser behind the ears, murmuring silly things that he felt safe in saying because Kaiser never betrayed a secret. He gave the dog a treat, checked the water in the bowl, then switched on the coffeepot that Bridget, his housekeeper, had prepared the evening before. Frank himself had no domestic skills at all; it was a complete mystery to him how he could take water, coffee, and filter and concoct an undrinkable brew, while Bridget could use the same components to make a pot of coffee that was so good it almost made him weep. He'd watched her do it, tried to do the same things, and ended up with sludge. Accepting that any further efforts of his to make coffee would fit the definition of insanity, Frank had acknowledged defeat and saved himself from further humiliation.

Dodie had made things easy for him, and he still followed her guidelines. All his socks were black, so he wouldn't have to worry about matching them. All his suits were neutral in color, his shirts either white or blue so they'd go with any suit, and his ties were likewise of the mix-and-match variety. He could pull out any item of clothing and be assured that it would go with anything else in his closet. He'd never win any awards for style, but at least he wouldn't embarrass himself.

He'd tried to vacuum the house . . . once. He still wasn't certain how he'd managed to explode the vacuum cleaner.

All in all, it was best to leave the domestic front to Bridget, while he concentrated on paperwork. That was what he did now, paperwork. He read, he digested facts, he gave his learned opinion—which was another phrase for "best guess"—to the director, who then gave it to the president, and he made decisions about operations based on what he'd read.

While the coffee was brewing, he turned off the outside security lights and let Kaiser out into the backyard to do a
perimeter patrol and also take care of nature's call. Kaiser was
getting old, Frank realized as he watched his pet, but then so
was he. Maybe both of them should think about retiring, so that
Frank could read something besides intelligence reports and
Kaiser could give up his guard duties and just be a companion.

Frank had been thinking about retiring for several years
now. The only thing that held him back was the fact that John
Medina wasn't ready to come in from the field, and Frank
couldn't think of anyone else he wanted to see fill his shoes. Not
that the position was his to bestow, but his choice would carry
a lot of weight when the decision was made.

Maybe soon, Frank thought. Niema, John's wife of the past
two years, had commented rather testily to Frank that she
wanted to get pregnant and she'd like for John to be there when
she did. They had done a lot of operations together, but John's
current assignment was one in which she couldn't participate,
and the long separation was grating on both of them. Add that
to the ticking of Niema's biological clock, and Frank rather
thought that John would finally be turning over his spurs to
someone else.

Someone like Lucas Swain, perhaps, though Swain had
spent a long time in the field, too, and his temperament was totally different from John's. John was patience itself; Swain was
the type who would prod a tiger with a stick, just to get some
action going. John had trained from the time he was eighteen–
in truth, even before that–to become as superlative at his job as
he was. They needed someone young to replace him, someone
who could stand up under the rigorous physical and mental

discipline. Swain was a genius at getting results–though he usually got those results in surprising ways–but he was thirty-nine, not nineteen.

Kaiser trotted up to the back door, his tail wagging. Frank let the dog in and gave him another treat, then poured himself a cup of coffee and carried it into his library, where he sat down and began catching up on the news of the day. By that time his morning papers had been delivered and he read them while he sat at the table eating a bowl of cereal–he could manage that without Bridget's aid–and drinking more coffee. Breakfast was followed by a shower and shave, and at seven-thirty on the dot he was heading out the door just as his driver pulled to the curb.

Frank had resisted being driven for a long time, preferring to take the wheel himself. But D.C. traffic was a nightmare, and driving tied up time he could devote to work, so he'd finally given in. His driver, Keenan, had been his regular driver for six years now, and they'd settled into a comfortable routine, like an old married couple. Frank rode up front–it made him nauseous to sit in back and read–but other than greeting each other, they never talked during the morning commute. The afternoon drive was different; that was when Frank had found out Keenan had six kids, that his wife, Trisha, was a concert pianist, and that his youngest child's cooking experiment had almost burned down the house. With Keenan, Frank could talk about Dodie, about the good times they'd had together, and what it was like growing up before the advent of television.

"Morning, Mr. Vinay," Keenan said, waiting until Frank was buckled in before pulling smoothly away from the curb.

"Good morning," Frank absently replied, already absorbed in the report he was reading.

He glanced up occasionally, a precaution against getting carsick, but for the most part he was oblivious of the thick traffic as people in the hundreds of thousands poured into the capital for the day's work.

They were in an intersection, in the right lane of two turn lanes making a left turn on a green arrow, hemmed in by vehicles directly ahead, behind, and to the left, when a screech of brakes to his right made him lift his head and search out the sound. Frank saw a white-paneled florist delivery truck barreling through the intersection, ignoring the double lanes of traffic turning left, with the flashing lights of a police car directly behind him. The grill of the truck loomed in his vision, heading directly toward him. He heard Keenan say, "Shit!" as he fought the wheel to angle the car to the left, into the line of traffic beside them. Then there was a bone-jarring crash, as if he'd been picked up and flung to the ground by a giant, his entire body assaulted all at once.

Keenan regained consciousness with the taste of blood in his mouth. Smoke seemed to fill the car, and what looked like an enormous condom spilled profanely from the steering wheel. There was a buzzing in his head, and every movement was such an effort that he couldn't lift his head off his chest. He stared at the huge condom, wondering what in hell it was doing there. An irritating blare was sounding in his left ear, making his head feel as if it might explode, and there was some other noise that sounded like shouting.

For what seemed like forever Keenan stared blankly at the steering-wheel condom, though it was only a few moments. Awareness seeped back into him, and he realized that the condom was an air bag and the "smoke" was powder from the bag.

With an almost audible pop, reality snapped back into place.

The car was in the middle of a tangle of metal. To his left were two other cars, steam rising from the broken radiator of one. A panel truck of some kind was squashed against the right side. He remembered trying to turn the car so they wouldn't be T-boned, then an impact harder than anything he'd ever imagined. The truck had been aimed right at Mr. Vinay's passenger door—

Oh, my God.

"Mr. Vinay," he croaked, the sound nothing like his own voice. He turned his head and stared at the director of operations. The entire right side of the car was smashed in, and Mr. Vinay lay in an impossible tangle of metal, seat, and man.

Someone finally silenced the maddening car horn, and in the sudden relative quiet he could hear a distant siren.

"Help!" he yelled, though again it was nothing more than a croak. He spat blood out of his mouth, drew a deep breath that hurt like hell, and tried again. "Help!"

"Just hold on, buddy," someone called. A uniformed officer climbed over the hood of one of the vehicles on the left, but the two were so crunched together that he couldn't get between them. Instead he got on his hands and knees on the hood and peered at Keenan's face. "Help's on the way, buddy. Are you hurt bad?"

"I need a phone," Keenan gasped, realizing the cop couldn't see their license plates. His cell phone was somewhere in the wreckage.

"Don't worry about making any calls—"

"I need a damn phone!" Keenan repeated, his tone fierce.

He fought for another breath. CIA people never identified themselves as working for the CIA, but this was an emergency. "The man beside me is the director of operations–"

He didn't need to say more. The cop had worked in the capitol area a long time, and he didn't ask, "What kind of operations?" Instead he whipped out his radio and barked a few terse words into it, then turned around and yelled, "Anyone have a cell phone?"

Silly question. Everyone did. In just a moment the cop was stretching out on the hood to hand Keenan a tiny flip-phone. Keenan reached out a shaky, bloodstained hand and took the phone. He punched in a few numbers, realized this wasn't a secure phone, then mentally said, "Shit," and punched the rest of them.

"Sir," he said, fighting back the black edges of unconsciousness. He still had a job to do. "This is Keenan. The director and I have been in an accident and the director is severely injured. We're at . . ." His voice trailed off. He had no idea where they were. He held the phone out to the cop. "Tell him where we are," he said, and closed his eyes.

16

Even though her regular contacts were out of the question, over the years Lily had met a number of people of questionable character with unquestionable skills who, for the right amount of money, would dig up dirt on their mothers. She still had some money left but not a huge amount, so she hoped that "right" translated to "reasonable."

If Swain checked out okay, that would help her financial situation, because he'd volunteered to work with her. If she had to hire someone, that would put a serious dent in her bank account. Of course, she had to remember that Swain had admitted he wasn't an expert at security systems, but he said that he knew people who were. The big question was, would those people want to be paid? If they did, then she'd be better off hiring someone from the beginning, rather than wasting money having Swain investigated.

Unfortunately, that was something she wouldn't know until it was too late to do anything about it. She wanted Swain to check out okay. She wanted to find out he hadn't escaped from a psychiatric ward somewhere or, even more important, he hadn't been hired by the CIA.

It was as she was going to an Internet café that she realized she'd made a tactical error in walking away from Swain the day before. If the CIA *had* hired him, Swain had now had the opportunity to call and have his file sanitized to fit whatever story he told. No matter what she or anyone else was able to find out about him, she couldn't be certain the information was correct.

She stopped dead in her tracks. A woman bumped into her from behind and gave her a nasty look for stopping so abruptly. *"Excusez-moi,"* Lily said, detouring to a small bench so she could sit while she thought this out.

Damn it, there was so much about spy craft that she didn't know; she was at a huge disadvantage here. There was now no point in investigating Swain; he either was or wasn't CIA. She simply had to make up her mind to contact him or not.

The safest thing to do was not call him. He didn't know where she lived, didn't know what name she was using. But if he was CIA, then he had somehow figured out that she'd be after the Nervi laboratory complex and he had staked it out, waiting for her to appear. Either she abandoned her plan completely, or he'd eventually find her there again.

As far as the laboratory went, the circumstances there had become enormously complicated. Rodrigo had obviously found out who she really was and somehow gotten a photo of her sans disguise, otherwise the soccer players wouldn't have recognized her so readily. The little fracas at the park would put him on double alert, and security at the complex had undoubtedly been doubled.

She needed help. There was no way now she could accomplish anything on her own. The way she saw it, she could either walk away and let Rodrigo Nervi continue to flourish, without making any more effort to find out what had been so important to Averill and Tina that it had cost them their lives, or she could cross her fingers for luck and accept Swain's aid.

She wanted him to be on the level, she realized with a jolt. He seemed to get so much *enjoyment* out of life, and joy had been in short supply in her life for several long months. He'd made her laugh. He might not realize how long it had been since that had happened, but she did. The tiny human spark in her that grief hadn't extinguished wanted to laugh again. She wanted to be happy again, and Swain radiated happiness like the sun. Okay, so he might be certifiable, but the hint of steel he'd shown when he stopped her from getting his weapon reassured her. If he could make her laugh, if she could find joy again, perhaps that alone was worth the risk of taking him as a partner.

There was also an element of physical attraction. That aspect took her a little by surprise, but she recognized the little flare of interest for what it was. She had to factor that into any decision she made concerning him, not let it cloud her mind. But did it make any difference if she wanted to accept his offer of help because he made her laugh or because she found him attractive? The fact was, the emotional need was greater than the physical. Besides, she doubted she would act on the physical attraction. She hadn't had many lovers in her life, going through long periods of abstinence and not minding at all. Her last lover, Dmitri, had tried to kill her. That had been six years ago, and since then, trust had been a real issue for her.

So the sixty-four-thousand-dollar question was, since she had no way of reliably determining if he was CIA and her only alternative now was to walk away and do nothing else about the Nervis, did she call him because he was cute and made her laugh?

"What the hell. Why not?" she muttered, and gave a rueful laugh that earned her a startled glance from a passerby.

He was staying at the Bristol, in the Champs-Élysées. On impulse she went into a café and ordered a cup of coffee, then asked to look up a number in their telephone directory. She scribbled down the Bristol's number, then finished her coffee and left.

She could have called and had him meet her somewhere, but instead she took the train, and was just up the street from the hotel when she stopped at a public phone and used her Télécarte phone card to call the hotel. If he was CIA and had all of his incoming calls traced, this would deny him not only her cell phone number but any hint of where she was staying.

She gave his room number to the clerk who answered, and Swain answered on the third ring–a sleepy "Yeah," followed by a yawn. She felt a glow of pleasure at his accent, the pure American informality of his greeting.

"Can you meet me at Palais de l'Élysée in fifteen minutes?" she asked without identifying herself.

"Wha–? Where? Wait a minute." She heard another jaw-cracking yawn; then he said unnecessarily, "I've been asleep. Is this who I think it is? Are you blond and blue-eyed?"

"And I tote a peashooter."

"I'll be there. Wait a minute. Where in hell is this place?" he asked.

"Just down the street. Ask the doorman." She hung up, and positioned herself so she could watch the front door of the hotel. The palace was close enough that only a fool would drive instead of walk, but just distant enough that he wouldn't be able to tarry and still make the fifteen-minute deadline. When he came out of the hotel, he would turn in the opposite direction from where she was positioned, and she could fall in behind him.

He was out the door in five minutes; if he'd made any calls, they had been on his cell phone as he walked down the hall, because otherwise he hadn't had time. He stopped to speak to the doorman, nodded, then set off down the street. Or rather, he ambled down the street, a loose-hipped gait that made her wish she could see his butt while he walked. Unfortunately he was wearing that great leather blazer again, and it covered his rear.

Lily walked swiftly, the sound of her soft-soled boots covered by the traffic. No one was with Swain, and he wasn't talking on the phone as he walked, so that was good. Maybe he really was on his own. She closed the distance between them, and with one long stride fell into step beside him. "Swain."

He glanced at her. "Hi, there. I spotted you when I came out of the hotel. Any reason why we're going to the Palais?"

Caught, she had to smile and shrug. "None at all. Let's walk and talk."

"I don't know if you've noticed, but the weather's cold and the sun has almost set. Remember I told you I've been in South America? That means I'm used to warmth." He shivered. "Let's find a café and you can tell me what's going on over a nice cup of hot coffee."

She hesitated. Though she knew she was being paranoid, that Rodrigo couldn't possibly have someone on his payroll in every shop and café in Paris, his influence was broad enough that she didn't want to take the chance. "I don't want to talk in public."

"Okay, let's go back to the hotel. My room is private, and it's warm. And there's room service. Or, if you're afraid you can't control yourself if you're in the same room with me and a bed, we can get the car and drive aimlessly around Paris, burning gas that costs forty bucks a gallon."

She rolled her eyes. "It does not. And it's liters, not gallons."

"I notice you didn't deny the part about controlling yourself." He wasn't smirking, but it was close.

"I'll manage," she said drily. "The hotel it is." If she was going to trust him, she might as well start now. Besides, seeing his hotel room without him having time to neaten it and put away things he didn't want to be seen might be enlightening—not that he would have asked her back to his room if there was anything incriminating lying about anyway.

They retraced their steps, and when they reached the hotel, the impassive doorman opened the door for them. Swain led the way to the elevators, stepping aside to let her enter first.

He unlocked his door, and she stepped into a bright, cheerful room with two floor-to-ceiling windows overlooking a courtyard. The walls were cream colored, the bed had a soft-blue-and-yellow spread, and to her relief there was a fairly spacious sitting area, with two chairs and a sofa arranged around a coffee table. The bed was made, but one of the pillows bore the imprint of his head and the spread was wrinkled where he'd been napping. His suitcase wasn't in sight, so she assumed it was tucked away in the closet. Other than a water glass on the bedside table and the rumpled condition of the spread, the room was as neat as if no one was staying there.

"May I see your passport?" she asked as soon as he'd closed the door behind him.

He gave her a quizzical glance, but reached inside his coat. Lily tensed; she barely moved, but he caught her sudden tension and froze in the act of pulling out his hand. Very deliberately he reached up with his left hand and pulled his coat open so she could see that his right hand was filled with nothing more than his blue passport.

"Why do you want to see my passport?" he asked as he handed it over. "I thought you were going to check me out."

She flipped open the cover, not bothering to check the photo, but instead looking at the entry stamps. He had indeed been in South America–all over it, in fact–and had returned to the States about a month ago. He'd been in France four days. "I didn't bother," she said briefly.

"Why the hell not?" He sounded indignant, as if she'd said he wasn't worth checking out.

"Because I made a mistake in letting you go yesterday."

"*You* let *me* go?" he asked, lifting his brows.

"Who had the gun on whom?" She mirrored his expression as she gave the passport back to him.

"You have a point." He tucked the folder in his inside coat pocket, then shrugged out of the coat and tossed it across the bed. "Have a seat. How was *letting me go* a mistake?"

Lily sat on the sofa, which put a wall at her back. "Because if you're CIA, or were hired by the CIA, that gave you time to have them sanitize whatever information on you is out there."

He put his hands on his hips and glared at her. "If you know that, then what in hell are you doing here in my hotel room? My God, woman, I could be anyone!"

For some reason, his scolding struck her as funny, and she began to smile. If he'd been hired to kill her, would he be fussing about her not being careful enough?

"It's not funny," he groused. "If the CIA's after you, you have to be on your toes. Are you a spy or something?"

She shook her head. "No. I killed someone they didn't want killed."

He didn't blink an eye at the fact that she'd killed someone. Instead he picked up the room menu and tossed it into her lap. "Let's order some food," he said. "My stomach hasn't adjusted to this time zone, either."

Though it was very early for supper, Lily briefly glanced through the menu and made her choice, then listened as Swain phoned in the order. His French was passable, but no one would ever mistake him for a native speaker. He hung up the phone, then came to sit down in one of the blue-patterned chairs. Pulling up his right leg to prop his ankle on top of his left knee, he asked, "Who did you kill?"

"An Italian businessman-slash-hoodlum named Salvatore Nervi."

"Did he need killing?"

"Oh, yes," she said softly.

"Then what's the problem?"

"It wasn't a sanctioned hit."

"Sanctioned by whom?"

"The CIA." Her tone was ironic.

He gave her a thoughtful glance. "*You're* CIA?"

"Not exactly. I'm—I *was* a contract agent."

"So you've put your killing ways behind you?"

"Let's just say I doubt any more jobs will be coming my way."

"You could hire out to someone else."

She shook her head.

"No? Why not?"

"Because the only way I could do the job was if I thought it was right," she said in a low tone. "Maybe it was naive, but I trusted my government in this. If it sent me out, then I had to believe the hit was righteous. I wouldn't have that same trust with anyone else."

"Not naive, but definitely idealistic." His blue eyes were kind. "Don't you trust them to overlook this Nervi thing?" he asked, and again she shook her head.

"I knew he was an asset. He passed information to them."

"So why'd you kill him?"

"Because he had some of my friends killed. There's a lot I don't know, but—they were retired from the business, raising their daughter, being normal. For some reason they broke into the laboratory complex where we were yesterday—or I think they did—and he had them killed." Her voice thickened. "Also their thirteen-year-old daughter, Zia. She was killed, too."

Swain blew out a breath. "You have no idea why they broke in?"

"Like I said, I'm not even certain they did. But they crossed Salvatore somehow, and that's the only thing I can find happening to any of the Nervi holdings that falls in that time frame. I think someone hired them to do it, but I don't know who or why."

"I don't mean to sound callous, but they were pros. They had to know the risks."

"Them, yes. If it was just them, I'd be angry, I'd miss them terribly, but I wouldn't—I don't know if I'd have gone after Salvatore. But Zia . . . no way could I let that go." She cleared her throat, and the words seem to pour out of her. She hadn't been able to talk about Zia to anyone since the murders, and now it was like water going over a spill gate. "I found Zia when she was just a few weeks old. She was starving, abandoned, almost dead. She was *mine,* she was *my* daughter even though I let Averill and Tina adopt her because there was no way I could take care of her or provide her with a stable home while I was off on a job. Salvatore killed my little girl." Despite her best effort to hold them back, tears welled in her eyes and spilled down her cheeks.

"Hey," he said in alarm. With the tears blurring her vision, she didn't see him move, but suddenly he was beside her on the sofa, putting his arm around her and pulling her close so her head nestled in the curve of his shoulder. "I don't blame you. I'd have killed the son of a bitch, too. He should have known you don't touch the innocents." He was rubbing her back, the motion comforting.

Lily let herself be held for a moment, closing her eyes as she savored his closeness, the heat of his body, the man-smell of his skin. She was starved for human contact, for the touch of someone who cared. He might not care, but he sympathized, and that was close enough.

Because she wanted to stay where she was just a little too much, she sat up out of his embrace and briskly rubbed her cheeks dry. "I'm sorry," she said. "I didn't mean to cry on your shoulder—literally."

"You can use my shoulder anytime. So, you killed Salvatore Nervi. I assume the guys trying to kill you yesterday are after you because of that. Why are you still here? You've done what you set out to do."

"Only part of it. I want to know why Averill and Tina did what they did, what was so important to them that they took the job when they'd been retired for so long. It had to be bad, and if it was bad enough for them to act, I want the whole world to know what that something is. I want the Nervi organization broken up, destroyed, made a pariah in the business world."

"So you're planning on breaking into that lab and seeing what you can find?"

She nodded. "I don't have a firm plan on how to do it; I've just started gathering information."

"You know the security had to be upgraded after your friends broke in."

"I know, but I also know there's no foolproof system. There's always a weakness, if I can just find what it is."

"You're right about that. I'd say the first step is finding out who did the security work, then getting your hands on the specs."

"Assuming they haven't been destroyed."

"Only an idiot would do that, when the system might need repair sometime. If Nervi was really smart, though, he would have the specs instead of letting the security company keep them."

"He was smart, and suspicious enough that he probably thought of that."

"Not *quite* suspicious enough, or he wouldn't be dead," Swain pointed out. "I've heard of Nervi, even though I've been in a different hemisphere for ten years. How did you get close enough to him to use that peashooter of yours?"

"I didn't use it," she replied. "I poisoned his wine, and almost killed myself in the bargain, because he insisted I taste it, too."

"Holy shit. You knew it was poison and you still drank it? Your balls must be bigger than mine, because I wouldn't have done it."

"It was either that or let him storm out without drinking enough for me to be sure it would kill him. I'm okay, except for some damage to a heart valve, but I don't think it's serious." Except, yesterday she'd been gasping for breath in his car, which wasn't good. She hadn't even been running, though she guessed being shot at would get the adrenaline flowing and speed up her heartbeat just as running would.

He was looking at her in astonishment, but before he said anything else, there was a knock on the door. "Good, the food's here," he said, getting up and going to the door. Lily slipped her hand into her boot, ready to act if the room service waiter made a wrong move, but he wheeled in the cart and set out the food with swift precision; Swain signed the ticket and the waiter let himself out.

"You can take your hand off the peashooter," Swain said as he pulled two chairs up to the cart. "Why don't you carry something with some stopping power?"

"My peashooter gets the job done."

"Assuming you put the shot right where it counts. If you miss, someone's gonna be pissed and still able to come after you."

"I don't miss," she said mildly.

He glanced at her, then grinned. "Ever?"

"Never when it counts."

* * *

News that the director of operations had been critically injured in a car accident didn't send ripples through the intelligence community, it sent tsunamis. The first possibility to
investigate was that the accident wasn't an accident at all.
There were more efficient ways to kill someone than an automobile accident, but still, the idea had to be considered. That
suspicion was laid to rest after swift but thorough interviews
with the cop who had been chasing the florist van for speeding
through a red traffic light. The driver of the van, who was killed
in the accident, had an outstanding warrant for unpaid speeding tickets.

The director was taken to Bethesda Naval Hospital, where
the security would be tighter, and rushed into surgery. Simultaneously, his house was secured, arrangements made for the
director's housekeeper, Bridget, to take care of Kaiser, and the
deputy director stepped up to take Mr. Vinay's place until, and
if, he returned. The accident site was carefully combed for any
sensitive papers, but Mr. Vinay was extremely careful about paperwork and nothing classified was found.

For long hours in surgery, his survival was very much in
question. If Keenan hadn't managed to angle the car slightly
away just before the van collided with them, the director would
have died on the spot. His right arm suffered two compound
fractures, his collarbone was broken, five ribs were broken,
and his right femur was broken. His heart and lungs were
severely bruised, his right kidney ruptured. A shard of glass
had pierced his throat like an arrow, and he had a concussion
that had to be watched closely for signs of developing pressure in his skull. That he was alive at all was because the side

air bag had deployed, shielding his head from part of the impact.

He survived the various surgeries needed to repair his broken body and was taken to SICU, where he was kept heavily
sedated and closely monitored. The surgeons had done the best
they could; the rest was up to Mr. Vinay.

17

M. BLANC WASN'T HAPPY TO HEAR FROM RODRIGO AGAIN SO SOON. "How may I be of service?" he asked somewhat stiffly. He disliked what he did anyway; to have to do it very often was salt in an open wound. He was at home, and receiving a call there made him feel as if he'd brought evil much too close to his loved ones.

"First, my brother, Damone, will be working with me," Rodrigo said. "There may be times when he will call instead of me. I trust there will be no problem?"

"No, monsieur."

"Excellent. This problem I asked your help with the other day. The report said that our friends in America had dispatched someone to handle it. I would like very much to contact this person."

"Contact him?" Blanc echoed, suddenly uneasy. If Rodrigo

met with the contract agent—at least Blanc assumed it was a contract agent, that was usually how a "problem" was handled—it was possible Rodrigo would say something that the contract agent would then carry back to his employers, and that wouldn't do at all.

"Yes. I'd like his mobile phone number, if you please. I'm certain there is some way of contacting him. Do you know this person's name?"

"Ah . . . no. I don't believe it was listed in the report I received."

"Of course it wasn't," Rodrigo snapped. "Or I wouldn't ask, would I?"

He actually thought, Blanc realized, that he had been sent everything Blanc received. That wasn't the case, however, and had never been. To minimize the damage he did, Blanc always removed important pieces of information. He knew that if he was found out, the Nervis would have him killed, but he'd become very skillful at balancing on that high wire. "If the information is available, I will get it," he assured Rodrigo.

"I'll be waiting for your call."

Blanc checked the time and calculated the time in Washington. It was the middle of the workday there, perhaps his contact was even having lunch. After disconnecting the call from Rodrigo, he walked outside so no one—mainly his wife, who was an insatiably curious woman—could overhear, then punched in the required sequence of numbers.

"Yes." The voice wasn't as friendly as it was when Blanc caught him still at home, so he was probably where someone could hear his side of the conversation.

"In the matter I spoke to you about before, is it possible to have the mobile phone number of the person who was dispatched here?"

"I'll see what I can do."

No questions, no hesitation. Perhaps there wouldn't be a number, Blanc thought, walking back inside. The temperature had dropped with the sun, and he was shivering slightly, not having put on a coat.

"Who was that?" his wife asked.

"It was work," he said, dropping a kiss on her forehead. Sometimes he could talk about what he did, sometimes not, so although she clearly wanted to ask more questions, she did not.

"You could at least have put on a coat before going outside," she scolded in a fond tone.

Less than two hours later Blanc's mobile phone rang. Quickly he grabbed a pen, but couldn't find a scrap of paper. "This wasn't easy, buddy," his contact said. "Something about different cell phone systems. I had to dig deep to find the number." He read off the number, and Blanc scribbled it on his left palm.

"Thank you," he said. After hanging up, he found some paper and wrote down the number, then washed his hands.

He should call Rodrigo Nervi immediately, he knew, but he didn't. Instead he folded the paper and put it in his pocket. Perhaps he would call him tomorrow.

When Lily left his hotel room, Swain started to follow her back to her lair but decided against it. It wasn't that he thought she would spot him; he knew she wouldn't. She was good, but he was damn good. He didn't follow her because it just didn't feel right. It was crazy, but he wanted her to trust him. She had come to him, and that was a start. She had also given him her cell phone number, and he'd given her his. Funny how that felt the same as giving a friendship ring to a girlfriend in high school.

He hadn't done what Vinay had told him to do. He kept putting it off, partly out of curiosity, partly because she was battling giants and needed all the help she could get, and partly because he was seriously interested in getting her into bed. She was playing a dangerous game with Rodrigo Nervi, and Swain was enough of a risk-taker to be intrigued and want to play, too. He was supposed to take her out of the equation, but instead he wanted to know what was going on in that lab. If he could find out, maybe Vinay wouldn't demote him to desk jockey for not doing his job the first time he got close to Lily.

But all in all, he was enjoying himself. He was staying in a great hotel, driving a spitfire of a car, and eating French food. After some of the shit holes he'd stayed in during the past ten years, he needed some fun.

Lily was quite a challenge. She was wary and clever, with a streak of recklessness in her, and he never forgot that she was one of the best assassins working in Europe. Never mind that she'd had some pie-in-the-sky ideal about only making sanctioned hits until she'd gone after Salvatore Nervi; he was aware that he couldn't afford a single misstep around her.

She was also sad, grieving for her friends and the young girl she'd thought of as her own. Swain thought of his own kids, and how he'd feel if one of them was murdered. No way would the murderer escape, or even make it to trial—no matter who it was. He was totally in sympathy with her on that score, not that it changed the final outcome.

He lay in bed that night and thought of her drinking the wine she knew was poisoned, just so Salvatore Nervi would continue drinking it. Damn, she'd skated close to the edge. From what she'd told him about the poison, how potent it was, he knew she'd had a very rough time and was probably still weak. There was no way she could get into that lab on her own, not in her shape, so that was probably why she'd called him. He didn't care what her reason was; he was just glad she'd done it.

She was beginning to trust him. She'd cried in his arms, and he got the feeling she didn't often let anyone get that close to her. She gave off a strong DO NOT TOUCH signal, but from what he could tell, that was more out of self-defense than coldness. She wasn't a cold person at all, just wary.

Maybe he was crazy for being so attracted to her, but, hell, some male spiders willingly let their mates chew their heads off while they are going at it, so he figured he was ahead of the game in that respect: Lily hadn't killed him yet.

He wanted to know what made her tick, what made her laugh. Yeah, he definitely wanted her to laugh. She looked as if she hadn't had much fun lately, and a person should always have something to enjoy. He wanted her to relax and drop her guard around him, laugh and tease, make jokes, make love. He'd seen flashes of a dry sense of humor, and he wanted more.

He was well on his way to being obsessed, no doubt about it. He might lose his head yet, and die happy.

A gentleman wouldn't plan the seduction of a woman he'd been sent to take down, but he'd never been a gentleman. He'd grown up a rowdy west Texas shit-kicker, refused to listen to adults who knew better and married Amy when they were both eighteen and fresh out of high school, was a father at nineteen, but he'd never quite got the hang of settling down. He'd never cheated on Amy, because she was a great girl, but he hadn't exactly been there for her, either. Now that he was older, he was more responsible and felt ashamed of how he'd basically left her to raise their two kids by herself. The best he could say for himself was that he'd supported his family, even after the divorce.

Over the years he'd traveled a lot, become more sophisticated, but good manners and knowing how to order off a menu in three different languages didn't make a gentleman. He was still rowdy, he still didn't like rules, and he did like Lily Mansfield. He hadn't often met women who could hold their own with him, but Lily could; her personality was as forceful as his. She decided what she was going to do and did it, come hell or high water. She had a steel backbone, but at the same time she had a real feminine warmth and tenderness. Finding out everything about her would take a man a lifetime. He didn't have a lifetime, but he'd take what he could get. He was beginning to think that a few days with Lily would pack more of a punch than ten years with any other woman.

The big question was: What would he do afterward?

Blanc tensed when his phone rang early the next morning. "Who could that be?" his wife asked, annoyed that their breakfast was interrupted.

"It will be the office," he said, and got up to take the phone outside. He punched the *talk* button and said, "This is Blanc."

"Monsieur Blanc." The voice was smooth and calm, one he had never heard before. "I am Damone Nervi. Do you have the number my brother requested?"

"No names," Blanc said.

"Of course. This one time it seemed necessary, as we haven't spoken before. Do you have the number?"

"Not yet. Evidently there is some difficulty—"

"Get it. Today."

"There is a six-hour time difference. It will be afternoon at the earliest."

"I'll be waiting."

Blanc hung up and for a moment stood with his fists clenched. Damn the Nervis! This one spoke better French than the other one, he sounded smoother, but underneath they were all the same: barbarians.

He would have to give them the number, but he would try to impress upon Rodrigo that it would be ill-advised to call the CIA's man, that it could easily result in both him and his contact being prosecuted. Perhaps not, perhaps the man the CIA had sent didn't care about who hired him, but that wasn't something Blanc felt confident about.

He went back inside and looked at his wife, her dark hair still tousled from bed, a robe cinched around her trim waist. She slept in flimsy, low-cut nighties because she knew he liked it, though in the winter she put an extra blanket on her side of the bed because she felt the cold. What if something happened to her? What if Rodrigo Nervi followed through on the threats that had been made years ago? He couldn't bear it.

He would have to give them the number. He would stall as long as he could, but in the end he had no choice.

18

Swain had a brilliant idea in the middle of the night: instead of finding who had installed the Nervi security system, breaking into the office, and somehow getting the schematics, why not just use the resources at his fingertips? The boys–and girls–and their toys could find and access just about anything. If it was on a computer somewhere, and that computer was online, they could get it. It stood to reason that any security company Nervi used would be up to snuff on all the latest bells and whistles, which meant they were probably computerized. Password protected, yeah, but how tough was that? The hackers on the payroll in Langley would consider that no more worrisome than a mosquito bite.

Besides, that meant they'd have to do the work, and he wouldn't. All in all, he thought it was a great idea. He was so pleased with it that he sat up and switched on the bedside lamp, plucked his cell phone from the charger, and called right then. Going through the security checks seemed to take longer than ever, but finally he was talking to someone who had some authority.

"I'll see what I can do," the woman said. She'd identified herself, but Swain had been preoccupied and hadn't caught her name. "Things are in an uproar around here, though, so I don't know when—wait a minute. This is listed as a holding of Salvatore Nervi, deceased, and now Rodrigo and Damone Nervi. They're listed as assets. Why do you need the breakdown on their security system?"

"They may not be assets much longer," Swain said. "The word is they've just received a shipment of weapons-grade plutonium." That sounded ominous enough to stir some action.

"Have you generated a report on this?"

"Earlier today, but then no one got back to me—"

"That's because of Mr. Vinay. I told you things were in an uproar."

"What about Mr. Vinay?" Jesus, had Frank been replaced?

"You haven't heard?"

Obviously not, or he wouldn't have asked. "Heard what?"

"He was in a car accident this morning. He's in critical condition at Bethesda. The DDO is taking over until and if he comes back. Word is the doctors aren't optimistic."

"Shit." The news hit him like a blow to the solar plexus. He'd worked for Frank Vinay for years, and respected him as he did no one else in the pickle factory. Frank might dance through the daisies when he was dealing with politicians, but with the field officers under him, he'd never been anything but straight, and willing to stand up for them. In Washington, that was not only unusual but almost suicidal, careerwise. That Frank had not only survived but advanced in his job, first as DDO and now as director, was a testament to his worth—and his skill as a dancer.

"Anyway," the woman said, "I'll see what I can do."

Swain had to be satisfied with that, because he could imagine the uncertainty and jockeying for position that was going on across the pond. He knew the deputy director, Garvin Reed; Garvin was a good man, but he wasn't Frank Vinay. Frank had forgotten more about spy craft than Reed had ever known, plus Frank was a genius at reading people and seeing layers, patterns, where no one else did.

Swain felt uneasy about his own status, as well. Frank's solution for handling the Lily problem might not be the same as Garvin's. Garvin's view of the Nervis might not be the same as Frank's. Swain felt as if his tether to the mother ship had been cut and he was drifting away; or, to use another metaphor, he had already been skating on thin ice by delaying the purpose of his mission, and now he could hear the ice cracking beneath him.

Fuck it. He'd keep to the same course until he was either jerked off the mission or told to alter it—not that he hadn't already altered it, or at least delayed it, but no one knew that except him. When in doubt, plow ahead. Of course, the captain of the *Titanic* had probably had the same philosophy.

He didn't sleep well the rest of the night, which made him crabby when he woke up the next morning. Until, and if, the computer geeks came through for him, he didn't have anything to do, other than driving by the lab and mooning the guards. Since the weather was chilly, his ass would get cold, so mooning was out unless he was really provoked.

On impulse he grabbed his cell phone and dialed Lily's cell number, just to see if she'd answer.

"Bonjour," she said, making him wonder if perhaps she didn't have Caller ID on her cell phone. He couldn't imagine her *not* having it, but maybe she answered in French out of habit, or precaution.

"Hi, there. Have you had breakfast yet?"

"I'm still in bed, so no, I haven't eaten."

He glanced at his watch: not quite six. He'd forgive her for being lazy. In fact, he was glad he'd caught her in bed because she sounded sleepy and soft, without the usual crispness to her voice. He wondered what she wore to bed, maybe a skinny little tank top and her panties, maybe nothing at all. She definitely wouldn't wear something slinky and see-through. He tried to imagine her in a long nightgown or a sleep shirt, and couldn't. He could, however, imagine her naked. He imagined it so well that his johnson perked up and began to swell, requiring a firm hand to keep it under control.

"What are you wearing?" His own voice came out slower and deeper than usual.

She laughed, a startled sound that seemed to burst out of her. "Is this an obscene phone call?"

"It could be. I think I feel some heavy breathing coming on. Tell me what you're wearing." He imagined her sitting up against the pillows, tucking the covers under her arms, pushing her tousled hair out of her face.

"A flannel granny gown."

"Liar. You aren't a granny-gown type of woman."

"Did you call for any reason other than to wake me up and find out what I'm wearing?"

"I did, but I got sidetracked. C'mon, tell me."

"I don't do phone sex." She sounded amused.

"Pretty please with sugar on top."

She laughed again. "Why do you want to know?"

"Because my imagination is killing me. You sounded so sleepy when you answered, and I pictured you all soft and warm under the covers. Everything grew out of that." He gave his erection a wry glance.

"You can stop imagining. I don't sleep raw, if that's what you're asking."

"Then what are you wearing? I really need to know, so I can be accurate in my fantasies."

"Pajamas."

Damn, he'd forgotten about pajamas. "Shorty pajamas?" he asked hopefully.

"I switch to long ones in October, and back to short ones in April."

She was bursting all of his bubbles. He pictured her in tailored pajamas, and the effect just wasn't the same. He sighed. "You could have said you were bare-assed naked," he groused. "What would it have hurt? I was having fun here."

"Maybe a little too much," she said drily.

"Not enough, though." His erection was subsiding, a wasted effort.

"Sorry I couldn't be more accommodating."

"That's okay. You can make it up to me in person."

"You *wish*."

"Honey, you don't know how much I wish. Now, about why I called–"

She chuckled, and he felt a kind of squirrely feeling in the pit of his stomach. His insides were actually jumping around just because he'd made her laugh. Again.

"I don't have anything to do today, and I'm bored. Why don't we go to Disneyland?"

"What?" she asked blankly, as if he'd been speaking a foreign language.

"Disneyland. You know, the one right outside the city. I've never been to either one in the States. Have you been to this one?"

"Twice," she said. "Tina and I took Zia twice. Averill wouldn't go, because he didn't like standing in lines."

"It takes a real man to stand in lines."

"And not bitch about it," she added.

"And not bitch about it." What else could he do but agree? "I have someone looking into the security system thing, but I'm not likely to find out anything today. I have time to kill, you have time to kill, so why should we stare at the walls when we can see Cinderella's castle?"

"Sleeping Beauty, not Cinderella."

"Whatever. Myself, I always thought Cinderella was prettier than Sleeping Beauty, because she was blond. I have a thing for blondes."

"I hadn't noticed." She sounded as if she might laugh again.

"Look at it this way: Will anyone be looking for you in Disneyland?"

There was a small silence as she considered the real truth behind his proposal. He couldn't tell her that he was restless and worried about Frank, and that he thought he'd go crazy if he had to sit around his hotel room all day. He wasn't big on amusement parks, but it was something to do and they wouldn't have to watch their backs. Nervi would never think to have people watching the entrances to Disneyland, because what idiot would stop in the middle of a deadly cat-and-mouse game to go ride Thunder Mountain?

"The weather is supposed to be sunny today. Let's go," he cajoled. "It'll be fun. We can ride the teacups and get dizzy and puke."

"It sounds marvelous, I can't wait." She was snickering and trying to control it, but he could hear the little gulping sounds she was making.

"Then you'll go?"

She sighed. "Why not? It's either a dumb idea or a brilliant one, and I'm not certain which."

"Great. Why don't you put on a hat and sunglasses and sneak over here, and we'll have breakfast before we start out? I've been itching to let the hammer down on this little car I got to replace the Jag. It has two hundred and twenty-five horses, and I want to let at least two hundred of them run."

"Ah-ha. Now I know why you called. You want to drive like a maniac with a woman along to watch you show off, and to make appropriate oohing and aahing noises."

"Indulge me. I've been a little short on those kinds of noises lately."

"I'll try my best. I'll be there around eight; if you get hungry before then, go ahead and order. I can eat later."

Her two-hour time limit didn't tell him squat about where she was. In two hours, she could get here from anywhere in the area. Hell, she could probably get here from Calais in that length of time. "I'll wait for you. Tell me what you want and I'll order it about twenty minutes before eight."

All she wanted was a pastry and coffee, and he made a mental note to add some protein to the order. Just as she started to hang up he said, "By the way–"

She paused and said, "What?"

"In case you're wondering, I *do* sleep naked."

Lily closed her flip-top phone, stared at it, then flopped back on the pillows and burst into laughter. She didn't know when she'd last been teased and flirted with so relentlessly, maybe never. It felt good; just as it felt good to laugh. She *was* alive, then, after all. She even felt a little guilty for laughing, because Zia would never laugh again.

She sobered on that thought, and the familiar pain squeezed her heart. The pain would never go away, she thought, but there would be times when perhaps she could forget for just a little while. Today, she would try to forget.

She got out of bed and stretched, then did the set of exercises she'd been doing every day in an effort to regain her strength. She was getting better, her stamina improved a bit every day. After thirty minutes of exercise she was damp with sweat but not breathless; the old ticker was holding up. She got into the shower without having to take off any clothes, because she slept nude. Lying to Swain had seemed like a good idea, plus it was fun.

Fun. There was that word again. It seemed to come up often in connection with him.

She hadn't wondered before about whether he slept raw, but now her imagination supplied an image of *him* just waking up, stretching, his jaw dark with stubble. His skin smelled warm and musky, and his morning erection jutted up, demanding attention–

For a moment she could almost smell that warm man-scent, the memory so fresh and so specific she was briefly puzzled that she knew how he smelled. Then she remembered crying on his shoulder, with his arms around her. She must have sub-consciously noticed his scent then, and her brain had filed the memory away for future reference.

She couldn't believe she'd agreed to spend the day with him—at Disneyland, of all places. She hadn't thought she would ever go back there. This past summer Zia hadn't wanted to go; she was too old for that baby stuff, she'd said with the wither-ing scorn only a thirteen-year-old could muster and completely ignoring the fact that most of the people who went to the amusement park were older than she.

There were always a lot of Americans there, too, which al-ways surprised Lily, because she'd have thought if any Ameri-can wanted to go to a Disney attraction, one of those back home would have been closer than Paris. She and Swain wouldn't be noticed; they would be just two more Americans.

She blow-dried her hair, then found herself picking through her makeup bag for just the right items. She was primping for him, she thought with equal parts amusement and amazement—and she was enjoying it. She had always made herself up for her dates with Salvatore, but that had been more like applying a theater mask. This felt like a date, and she felt as nervous with excitement as she had in high school.

She had good skin, having never been a sun worshipper. She didn't need a base, though she did need mascara if she didn't want her lashes to look nonexistent. She had nice long lashes, but without mascara they were a light brown that made them almost invisible. She lined her eyes with a light touch, dusted on shadow, rubbed just a hint of a rose-hued liquid tint

on her cheeks and more on her mouth. A dusting of transpar-
ent powder and a coat of ego-saving mascara finished the job.

Lily looked at herself in the mirror as she put on her earrings, tiny gold hoops that seemed appropriate for a day at the
amusement park. She would never be really pretty, but on her
good days she was more than passable. Today was a good day.

With luck, it would get better.

19

THE CLOSER THEY GOT TO DISNEYLAND, THE MORE TENSE LILY BE-
came as her excitement began to fade and memories shoved
their way back to the forefront. "Let's not go to Disneyland," she
blurted.

He quirked his brows. "Why not?"

"Too many memories of Zia."

"Are you going to avoid everything that reminds you of
her?"

His tone was practical, nonchallenging. Lily stared out the
window. "Not everything. Not forever. Just not . . . right now."

"Okay. Where do you want to go instead?"

"I'm not certain I want to go anywhere. There should be
something we can do other than wait for your friend to dig up
something on the lab's security system."

"Other than driving back and forth in front of the lab and

giving the guards a good look at this car, I can't think of any-thing."

Was the man incapable of picking out a car that wasn't no-ticeable? Yes, this Renault was gray, just as the Jag had been, but the Mégane Renault Sport wasn't exactly a run-of-the-mill car. At least he hadn't got a red one.

"How many ways are there to get into a building?" she asked reasonably. "Doors and windows, obviously. You could also go in through a hole in the roof–"

"No one would notice you on top of the building with a chain saw?"

"–but that isn't feasible," she finished, giving him a dirty look. "How about from underneath? The complex has to be connected to the sewer system."

He looked thoughtful. "That's a possibility. I don't like it, but it's a possibility. In the movies it always looks like they're splashing around in water, but when you think about what goes into sewers, I'll bet they're splashing around in something else."

"Historic Paris is riddled with underground tunnels, but the lab is on the outskirts, so there probably isn't a decent tunnel anywhere near there."

"Just out of curiosity, in case we do end up in the sewer, what kind of laboratory is this? What do they do?"

"Medical research."

"And how is their waste dumped? Is it treated first? All the nasty little critters killed?"

She sighed. Common sense said the waste would be treated before it was dumped into the sewer, in which case there wouldn't be a direct connection between the complex and the sewer system. Instead, the waste material would go into some sort of holding tank where it was treated, and from there to the sewer. Common sense also said they didn't want to come in contact with any of the raw sewage.

He said, "I vote we stay out of the sewer."

"Agreed. Doors and windows are best. Or . . . we could find some big boxes and have ourselves shipped to the lab." That idea came out of nowhere.

"Huh." He considered the idea. "We'd have to find out if all packages and boxes are x-rayed or something, if they're opened immediately, if they ever get large shipments–things like that. See, we wouldn't want to come out of our boxes until late at night, at least after midnight, when there are fewer people around. Or does the lab operate on an around-the-clock basis?"

"I don't know, but that's something for us to check out. We'll have to know anyway, even if we get the specs on the security system."

"I'll drive by tonight, check out how many cars are in the parking lot, try and get an idea of how many people work there at night. I'm sorry, I should have done that last night," he apologized. "In the meantime, we have today. Disneyland's out. Do we just turn around and go back to our respective rooms, where we spend the day being bored? What else is there to do? Now that you've been made, I wouldn't advise walking around Paris, shopping."

No, she didn't want to go back to her little studio apartment. It didn't even have the advantage of being old and interesting; it was just convenient and safe. "Let's just drive. We can stop to have lunch when we get hungry."

They kept driving east, and when they were well away from

Paris and the heavy traffic, he picked a straight stretch of road and let the horses run. It had been a long time since Lily had gone fast just for the enjoyment of it, and she settled back in her seat, securely buckled in, while a pleasant sense of faint alarm made her pulse quicken. She felt like a teenager again, when she and seven or eight of her friends would cram into one car and bullet down the highway. It was a miracle all of them made it through high school alive.

"How did you get in this business?" he asked.

Startled, she looked at him. "You're driving too fast to talk. Pay attention to the road."

He grinned and let up on the gas pedal, and the needle dropped down to a hundred kph. "I can walk and chew gum at the same time," he said in mild protest.

"Neither of which requires much in the way of a brain. Talking and driving are different."

He said thoughtfully, "For someone in this business who takes as many risks as you do, you aren't really much of a risk-taker, are you?"

She watched the scenery zipping by. "I'm not a risk-taker at all, I don't think. I plan carefully; I don't take chances."

"Who drank wine she knew was poisoned, taking the chance that the dose wasn't lethal? Who is being hunted all over Paris but stays there anyway because she's got a vendetta going?"

"These are unusual circumstances." She didn't mention the risk she had taken in deciding to trust him, but he was smart enough to figure out that one, too.

"Was it something unusual that got you started killing people?"

She was silent for a moment. "I don't think of myself as a murderer," she said quietly. "I've never harmed an innocent. I've made the sanctioned hits that I was hired by my country to make, and I don't believe the decision was ever lightly made. I never thought so when I was young, but now I know there are people who are so inherently evil they don't deserve to live. Hitler wasn't a one-time phenomenon, you know. Look at Stalin, Pol Pot, Idi Amin, Baby Doc, bin Laden. Can you say the world isn't or wouldn't be better off without them in it?"

"And hundreds of other tin-pot dictators, plus the drug lords, the perverts and pedophiles. I know. I agree. But had you already decided this when you made your first hit?"

"No. Eighteen-year-olds generally don't get into heavy philosophy."

"Eighteen. Man, that's young."

"I know. I think that's why I was chosen. I used to look like such a rube," she said, smiling a little. "All fresh-faced and innocent, not an ounce of sophistication to me, though at the time I thought I was cool and world-weary. I was even flattered that I was approached."

He shook his head at such naivete. When she didn't continue, he said, "Go on."

"I came to their notice because I joined a shooting club. The boy I had a huge crush on at the time was an avid hunter and I wanted to impress him by being able to talk about different makes of weapons, caliber, range, all that stuff. But I turned out to be darn good; a pistol felt natural in my hand. Before long I was outshooting almost everyone else in the club. I don't know where that came from," she said, looking at her hands as if they held the answer. "My dad wasn't a hunter, had never been in the military. My mother's father was a lawyer, not at all an out-doorsman, and my other grandfather worked in a Ford factory in Detroit. He went fishing sometimes, but he never hunted that I knew of."

"It's just a particular blend of DNA, I guess. Maybe your dad wasn't interested in hunting, but that doesn't mean he wouldn't have found he had a natural talent for shooting. Hell, you could have gotten it from your *mother.*"

Lily blinked, then chuckled. "I never even thought of that. Mom's a peacemaker, but personality doesn't have anything to do with physical skill, does it?"

"Not that I ever noticed. Back to the shooting club."

"There isn't much to tell. Someone noticed how I shot, mentioned it to someone else, and one day a nice middle-aged man came to talk to me. First he told me about this person, a man, everything he'd done and the people he'd killed, and backed it up with newspaper clippings and copies of police reports, things like that. When I was properly horrified, the nice man offered me a lot of money. I was horrified all over again, told him no, but I couldn't stop thinking about everything he'd told me. He must have known, because he called me two days later and I said yes, I'd do it. I was *eighteen.*"

She shrugged. "I went through a cram course on what to do, and like I said, I looked like such a wet-behind-the-ears baby that no one saw me as a threat. I got close to the guy with no trouble, did the job, walked away. I threw up for a week every time I thought about it. I had nightmares for longer than that."

"But when the nice man offered you another job, you took it."

"I took it. He told me what a service I'd done for my country with the first job, and the thing is, he wasn't lying or manipulating me. He was sincere."

"But was he right?"

"Yes," she said softly. "He was. What I've done is illegal, I know that, and I have to live with what I am. But he was right, and what it comes down to is I was willing to do the dirty work. Someone has to do it, so why not me? After the first time I was already muddy anyway."

Swain reached over and took her hand, raised it to his mouth, and pressed a gentle kiss on her fingers.

Lily blinked in astonishment, opened her mouth to say something, then shut it and stared wide-eyed out the window instead. Swain chuckled and laid her hand back in her lap, then for thirty exhilarating minutes devoted himself to driving as fast as he could.

They stopped for lunch at a small sidewalk café in the next town they came to. He asked for a table in the sun but out of the slight breeze, and they were quite comfortable sitting outside. She had a salad topped with grilled goat cheese, he had lamb chops, and they each had a glass of wine followed by strong coffee. As they lingered over the coffee she said, "What about you? What's your story?"

"Nothing unusual. Wild west Texas boy who couldn't settle down, which is a real shame because I got married and had two kids."

Startled, she said, "You're married?"

He shook his head. "Divorced. Amy–that's my ex-wife–finally decided I was never going to settle down, and she got tired of raising the kids by herself while I was off in some other country doing things she didn't want to know about. I don't blame her. Hell, I'd have divorced me, too. Now that I'm older I know what an ass I was, and I could kick myself for missing my kids growing up. I can't get those years back. Thank God, Amy did a good job with them . They turned out great, no thanks to me."

He pulled out his wallet and fished out two small photographs, put them on the table in front of her. They were both high school graduation pictures, of a boy and a girl, and both of them looked a lot like the man sitting across from her. "My daughter Chrissy and my son Sam."

"They're good-looking kids."

"Thank you," he said with a grin. He knew very well they strongly resembled him. He picked up the photographs and studied them before putting them back in his wallet. "Chrissy was born when I was nineteen. I was way too young and too stupid to get married, much less have a baby, but being young and stupid means you don't listen to people who know more than you. And if it comes to that, I'd do it over again, because I can't imagine not having my kids."

"Are you close to them now?"

"I doubt I'll ever be as close to them as their mother is, because she's way more important to them than I am. She was there when I wasn't. They like me, they even love me because I'm their dad, but they don't know me the way they know Amy. I was a lousy husband and father," he said frankly. "Not abusive or lazy or anything like that, but just never at home. The best that can be said is that I always supported them."

"That's more than some men do."

He muttered his opinion of those men, something that started with "stupid" and ended with "sons of bitches," with several even more uncomplimentary words in between.

Lily was touched by the way he didn't cut himself any slack. He'd made mistakes and with maturity he could both see them and regret them. As the years had passed he'd been able to appreciate all the things in his children's lives that he'd missed out on, and he was grateful to his ex-wife for minimizing the damage he'd done to them with his absence.

"Are you thinking about settling down now, going home and living near your children? Is that why you left South America?"

"Nah, I left because I was ass-deep in alligators and they were all hungry." He grinned. "I like a little excitement in my life, but sometimes a man needs to climb a tree and reassess the situation."

"So what exactly do you do? For a living, I mean."

"I'm kind of a jack-of-all-trades. People want something to happen, they hire me to make it happen."

There was a lot of room in that statement, she thought, but sensed he'd been as specific as he was willing to be. She was comfortable not knowing every detail of his life. She knew he loved his kids, that he walked on the shady side but had a conscience, liked fast cars, and made her laugh. And he was willing to help her. For now, that was enough.

After lunch they walked around for a while. He spotted a small chocolate shop and immediately developed a craving for chocolate, even though they'd just left the café. He bought a dozen pieces in different flavors, and as they walked around he alternately fed her and himself until the chocolate was gone. Somewhere along the way, he caught her hand and simply held it in his for the rest of their walk.

In a way the day felt strangely disconnected from reality, as if they were in a bubble. Instead of pitting her wits against Rodrigo's, she was walking around a small town with nothing more pressing to do than window-shop. She had no worries here, no stress; a handsome man was holding her hand and probably planning to make a move on her before the day was over. She hadn't yet decided if she was okay with that or not, but wasn't worried about it. If she said no, he wouldn't sulk. She didn't think Swain had ever sulked in his life. He would simply shrug and move on to the next entertainment.

She had been under unremitting stress for months, and it was only now, when she could relax, that she realized what a mental toll it had taken. She didn't want to think today, didn't want to dredge up hurtful memories. She just wanted to be.

By the time they walked back to the car, the sun was low and the brisk day was turning cold as the temperature dropped. She reached to open the car door, but he caught her hand and gently tugged, turning her around, and in one smooth move he released her hand and cupped her face in both of his big warm hands, tilting her chin up as he lowered his mouth.

She didn't say no. Instead Lily grasped his wrists and simply held him while he was holding her. His mouth was surprisingly gentle, the kiss tender rather than demanding. He tasted like chocolate.

She sensed that the kiss was an end unto itself, that he had no further agenda—not at this moment, anyway. She could kiss him in return and he wouldn't try to tear off her clothes or pin her against the car. Leaning into him a little, she felt the warmth of his body, enjoyed the closeness. It was she who lightly teased him with her tongue, asking for more. He gave it, not plunging deep but teasing in return as they learned each other's taste and feel, how their mouths fit together. Then he released her lips, smiled, and wiped his thumb across her mouth before opening the car door and letting her slide inside.

"Where to now?" he asked as he got in the car. "Back to Paris?"

"Yes," she said, with obvious regret. The day had been a welcome escape, but it was almost at an end. She had decided something important, however: Swain couldn't be CIA, in any capacity, because she was still alive. It was always a bonus if, at the end of a date, the guy didn't kill you.

20

Late that afternoon, Georges Blanc received another call from Damone Nervi. He knew who was calling and his stomach tightened with dread. He was in his car, so he wasn't in danger of being overheard, which was a small blessing and the only one he'd found so far in this situation. He pulled to the side of the road and answered the call.

Damone's tone was very even. "I am a more reasonable man than my brother. I am not, however, one who can be safely ignored. Do you have the information I requested?"

"Yes, but–" Blanc hesitated, and took the plunge. "My advice, my hope, is that you do not use this number."

"Why is that?"

To Blanc's relief, Damone sounded more curious than angry. He took a deep breath. Maybe there was hope. "There is only one way you could get this number, and that is if someone in the American CIA gave it out. This man you want to call works for them. Do you think he won't wonder how you came to have his mobile phone number? Do you think he is, perhaps, so stupid he cannot add two and two? The question you must ask yourself is if he is loyal to his employers, will he not report this to his superiors? And will they not investigate? If you use this number, monsieur, you may very well destroy both my contact and me."

"I see." The connection was silent for a moment as Damone considered all of the ramifications. After a moment he said, "Rodrigo is impatient; I think it's best if he doesn't know this. Sometimes his desire for action can outweigh prudence. I will tell him that this person was to rent a mobile phone here, and hasn't contacted anyone yet."

"Thank you, monsieur. Thank you." Blanc closed his eyes in relief.

"But," Damone said, "it now occurs to me that you owe me a favor."

Blanc was reminded that, reasonable or not, Damone was still a Nervi, and therefore dangerous. Tension knotted his stomach again. What else could he do except agree? "Yes," he said heavily.

"This is private. There's something I want you to do for me, something you can never tell anyone. The lives of your children depend on it."

Tears burned Blanc's eyes and he rubbed them away. His heart was pounding so hard he thought he might faint. He had never made the error of underestimating the brutality of which the Nervis were capable. "I understand. What is it I am to do?"

* * *

They were near the hotel when Swain said, "Let me take you home. You shouldn't have to take the Metro when you're so much safer in a car no one recognizes."

Lily hesitated, instinctively not wanting to disclose the location of her apartment. "I took the Metro this morning," she pointed out. "The trains are faster, anyway." She had put her hair up under a cloche and worn sunglasses, as he'd suggested, just in case Rodrigo had people watching the train stations. There were a lot of stations in Paris; covering them would require a lot of manpower, but of course Rodrigo wouldn't have to supply the men. With his influence, he could have others do the job.

"Yeah, but this morning the sun was shining, and now it's dark. The sunglasses will make you conspicuous." He grinned. "Plus I want to check out your bed and make sure it's big enough for me."

She rolled her eyes. One kiss and he expected her to fall into bed with him? She enjoyed kissing him, but she had merely been charmed, not rendered stupid. "It isn't," she said, "so there's no point in you seeing it."

"That depends. Is it narrow, or short? If it's just narrow that's no problem, because we'll be double-decker anyway. But if it's a short bed, I'll have to rethink my infatuation with you, because there's something wrong with a woman who doesn't buy a bed long enough for a man to stretch out his legs."

"It's both," she said, trying to control a giggle. She hadn't giggled since she was eighteen, but one was building in her throat. "Short *and* narrow. I bought it from a convent."

"Nuns sell their beds?"

"They had a huge garage sale as a fund-raiser."

He threw back his head and laughed, not at all put out by her refusal. All of his lines and proposals were so outrageous she thought he must be at least half-joking, though if she took him up on any of them, like most men he'd jump at the opportunity to have sex.

He'd distracted her from his original suggestion, but she hadn't forgotten it. She had to weigh her natural caution about divulging the location of her apartment against the risk of taking the Metro. Sometimes she wouldn't be able to avoid taking the train, but why push her luck if she didn't have to? What it came down to was, who did she think was more of a danger to her, Swain or Rodrigo? No contest there. So far, Swain had been solidly on her side, even though he didn't have a compelling reason for helping her other than boredom and wanting to sleep with her. "I live in Montmartre," she said. "It's out of your way."

He shrugged. "So what?"

If he didn't care, why should she? The safety factor was the only reason to let him drive her, because the trains were a much more convenient way of getting around Paris, but it was a big reason.

She gave him directions and settled back in her seat; let him worry about fighting the traffic. He did it with his usual verve, shouted insults, and assorted gestures. He got a little too much into the spirit of things, actually accelerating once when a group of tourists tried to cross a street in front of him. Because this was Paris, naturally the car beside him speeded up, too. They barreled down on a portly middle-aged woman, and Lily gasped in horror. The woman's eyes bugged out as the two cars bore down on her.

"Shit!" Swain yelled. "You son of a bitch!" He swerved sharply toward the car beside them, and its panicked driver jerked the steering wheel to the left as he slammed on his brakes. Swain downshifted into a lower gear and shot into the gap between the pedestrian and the fishtailing car, even as the woman scrambled to get back on the curb.

Brakes were screeching behind them, and Lily twisted in her seat to see what sort of carnage they were leaving behind. The car that had tried to block them from getting into the left lane was turned sideways in the broad street, with other vehicles at various angles around it. Horns were blaring, and angry drivers were already jumping out of their cars waving their arms and shaking their fists. She didn't see any bodies on the ground, so evidently all the pedestrians were safe.

"Let me out," she said furiously. "It'll be safer on the trains with Rodrigo's men than riding in a car that you're driving!"

"I had room to swerve around them until that asshole beside me speeded up," he said in sheepish defense.

"Of course he speeded up!" she yelled. "This is Paris! He'd have died before he just *let* you cut in front of him."

She sank back, breathing hard in her fury. A few minutes later she said, "I told you to let me out."

"I'm sorry," he said contritely. "I'll be more careful. I promise."

Since he showed no signs of slowing down to let her out, she supposed she'd have to stay in the car with the lunatic. Her only other option was to shoot him, and that was looking more attractive by the minute. That poor woman! If she'd had a bad heart, the fright might have killed her. She'd *looked* okay, though, because she had been one of the fist-shakers, stepping back into the street to glare at their taillights as they sped away from the mayhem Swain had caused.

After five minutes of careful driving and total silence in the car, Swain said, "Did you see her face?"

Lily burst out laughing. It was awful of her, she knew, but the image of the woman's red, choleric face going bug-eyed with panic would stay with her forever. She tried to control herself, because what he'd done wasn't funny at all and she didn't want him to think he'd got away with it.

"I can't believe you're laughing," he said in disapproval, though the corners of his mouth were twitching. "That's cold."

It was, even though he was teasing. She gulped, wiped her eyes, and with sheer willpower forced herself to stop laughing.

She made the mistake of looking at him. As though he'd been waiting for her to do just that, he bugged out his eyes at her in perfect imitation of the woman's expression, and Lily went off into whoops again. She rocked against the constraint of her seat belt, holding her stomach. To punish him she punched him in the arm, but she was laughing so hard there wasn't any force behind the blow.

He turned sharply, off the main boulevard, and by some miracle found a place to pull the car off the road. Lily stopped laughing. "What's happening?" she asked in alarm, looking around for a threat even as she reached down to her ankle holster.

Swain turned off the engine and grabbed her shoulders. "You don't need a weapon," he said in a rough tone as he dragged her as far over the console as her seat belt would allow. He kissed her hungrily, fiercely, cupping the back of her head in his left hand while with his right he kneaded and stroked her breasts. After an initial squeak of surprise, Lily let herself sink against him. The gearshift was digging into her hip, one knee was awkwardly bent, and she didn't care.

She hadn't felt passion in so long that it took her by surprise, both his and her own. She hadn't realized how starved she was, how much she'd wanted someone to hold her. Needing more, she opened her mouth for him and wrapped her arms around his neck.

He made love the same way he drove, fast and with great enthusiasm. He barely paused at second base, then drove for third, slipping his hand between her legs and gently massaging. In sheer reflex she grabbed his wrist, but she couldn't make herself push his hand away. He set the heel of his palm against the center seam of her pants and rocked it back and forth, and Lily went boneless.

Only the fact that they were in the car saved her. Her bent leg began cramping under her and with a gasp she pulled away from his mouth, clumsily trying to twist so she could straighten out her leg, hampered by the seat belt and his arms. She gave one hoarse cry of pain, then ground her teeth together.

"What's wrong?" he asked sharply as he tried to right her in the seat. They flailed around, elbows banging steering wheel, console, and dashboard, getting in each other's way and generally looking like idiots. Finally Lily managed to fight her way back into her seat and with a groan of relief stretched out her aching leg as far as she could. It wasn't far enough; she released the seat latch and pushed the seat back as far as it would go.

Panting, she tried to catch her breath as she massaged her thigh. "Cramp," she muttered in explanation. Her knotted muscles began to relax and the pain receded. "I'm too old to be making out in a sports car," she said, heaving a sigh. Leaning her head back against the seat, she gave a tired laugh. "I hope no one videotaped that little comedy."

He was still turned toward her, the streetlights illuminating his face. He was smiling, his expression strangely tender. "You think we could be blackmailed with it?"

"Oh, yeah. Think how our reputations would suffer. What brought that on, anyway?"

His smile turned wry. "Have I mentioned that I get turned on when you laugh?"

"No, I don't believe you have. I'm sure I'd have remembered." He was wrong; she had definitely needed her weapon. She should have shot him before letting him kiss her like that, because now she wasn't sure she could get through a day without having more of his kisses.

She returned her seat to its original position and smoothed her hair. "If you try, do you think you can manage the rest of the trip without scaring any more pedestrians half to death, almost killing us, or making another detour to attack me? I'd like to get home before midnight."

"You liked being attacked. Admit it." He reached for her left hand and took it, lacing her fingers with his. "If it hadn't been for that cramp in your leg, you'd have liked it a lot more."

"We'll never know now, will we?" she asked.

"Wanna bet?"

"No matter how much I liked it, I'm not sleeping with someone I met just a few days ago. Period. So don't get your hopes up, or anything else for that matter."

"Too late, on both accounts."

She swallowed a laugh, sucking hard on the insides of

her cheeks. He gently squeezed her hand, then released it and restarted the engine. A U-turn put them back on the main boulevard.

Montmartre used to be thick on the ground with artists of all descriptions, but a lot of the area had deteriorated since its salad days. There were narrow, twisting one-lane streets with a groove down the middle for water to run off, buildings crowded close on each side, and a lot of tourists in search of nightlife. Lily guided him through the maze and finally said, "There, the blue door. That's my apartment building."

He pulled up outside the door. There was no place to park the car without blocking the street, so there was no question of him coming upstairs with her. She leaned over and pressed a quick kiss to his cheek, then his mouth. "Thank you for today. It's been fun."

"It was my pleasure. Tomorrow?"

She hesitated, then said, "Call me. We'll see." Perhaps his friend would come through with the information they needed about the lab's security. Swain was just as likely to come up with yet another impractical invitation that would for some reason appeal to her, though she thought they'd be safer if she drove instead of him—and *her* driving skills were sadly rusty.

He watched until she was inside the building, then lightly tapped the horn before driving away. Lily climbed the stairs, taking them slower than she once would have, pleased that she was only a little out of breath when she reached her little apartment on the third floor. She let herself in and locked the door behind her, then heaved a big sigh.

Damn him. He was getting inside her defenses and they both knew it.

*   *   *

As soon as Swain picked his way out of the maze that was Montmartre and could pay attention to something other than where he was, he turned on his cell phone to check for messages. There weren't any, so he called Langley as he drove, and asked for Director Vinay's office; maybe his assistant was still at her desk, though the time there was pushing five o'clock. When he recognized her voice, he was relieved. "This is Lucas Swain. Can you tell me the director's condition?" Then he held his breath, praying that Frank was still alive.

"He's still in critical condition," she said. She sounded shaken. "He doesn't have any immediate family, just two nieces and a nephew who live in Oregon. I contacted them, but I don't know if any of them will be able to come."

"Do you know the prognosis?"

"The doctors are saying that if he makes it through twenty-four hours, his odds get better."

"Will you mind if I call you again for an update?"

"Of course not. I don't have to tell you that this is being kept very quiet, do I?"

"No, ma'am."

He thanked her and hung up, then breathed a combined thank-you and prayer. He had succeeded in distracting both himself and Lily today, but the knowledge that Frank could die had stayed in the back of his mind, gnawing at him. He didn't know what he might have done, if it hadn't been for Lily. Just being with her, devoting himself to making her laugh, had given him something to focus on other than his worries.

It broke his heart to think of her as an eighteen-year-old, just the age his son Sam was now, being recruited to kill someone in cold blood. God, whoever had done that should be taken out and shot. That man had robbed her of a normal life when she was still too young to realize how high the cost would be to herself. He could see how she would have been the perfect weapon, young and fresh and largely innocent, but that didn't make it right. If he ever got the man's name from her–assuming she'd been given his correct name and not an alias–he'd make it a point to hunt the bastard down.

His cell phone rang. He frowned, the bottom dropping out of his stomach. Surely to God, Frank's assistant wasn't calling him to say that Frank had just died–

He grabbed the phone and glanced at the number showing in the window. It was a French number, and he wondered who in hell could be calling, because it wasn't Lily–she'd have used her own cell phone–and no one else here had his number.

He flipped it open and cradled it between his jaw and shoulder as he pushed in the clutch and downshifted for a turn. "Yeah."

A man said in a quiet, even tone, "There is a mole in your CIA headquarters feeding information to Rodrigo Nervi. I thought you should know."

"Who is this?" Swain asked, stunned, but there was no answer. The call had been disconnected.

Swearing, he closed the phone and slipped it back into his pocket. A mole? Shit! He couldn't doubt it, though, because otherwise how had the Frenchman gotten this number? And the caller had definitely been a Frenchman; he'd spoken in English, but the accent was French. Not Parisian, though; Swain'd picked up on the Parisian accent within a day.

A chill ran down his spine. Had everything he'd requested been fed straight to Rodrigo Nervi? If so, any action he and Lily took could be taking them straight into a trap.

21

SWAIN PACED BACK AND FORTH IN HIS HOTEL ROOM, HIS USUAL good-humored expression replaced by one that was cold and hard. No matter how he looked at it, he was literally on his own. The mole at Langley could be anyone: Frank's assistant; Patrick Washington, whom Swain had liked so much that one time he'd talked to him; any of the analysts; the case officers— hell, even the DDO, Garvin Reed. The only person there Swain totally trusted was Frank Vinay, who was in critical condition and might not live. With this revelation from his mysterious caller, Swain had to consider that Frank's automobile accident might not have been accidental, after all.

But if he had thought of that, then probably several thousand others at Langley had thought the same thing. What if the mole was conveniently placed to divert suspicion from the accident?

The thing was, though, auto accidents were tricky, definitely not the most reliable method of eliminating someone;
people had been known to walk away from accidents that to-
taled their cars. On the other hand, if you killed someone and
didn't want anyone to know it was deliberate, you staged events
to make it *look* like an accident. How well it was staged depended on the reliability of the parties involved, and the amount
of money behind it.

But how could anyone stage an auto accident that would
take out the DO? Logically, predicting where someone would
be at any given moment in the D.C. traffic was impossible,
what with the fender benders, mechanical troubles, and flat
tires all over the city that delayed and diverted traffic to other
routes. Add in the human factor, such as oversleeping, stopping
for a latte–he didn't see how it could be done, how anyone
could time things so perfectly.

At any rate, surely to God, Frank's driver hadn't taken the
same route to work every day. That was basic. Frank wouldn't
have allowed it.

So–logically, the accident had to be just what it seemed: an
accident.

The result was the same. Whether or not Frank lived, he
was out of commission, unreachable. Swain had been a field
officer for a long time, but he'd been *in* the field, working with
various insurgents and military groups in South America; he
hadn't actually spent much time in CIA headquarters. He didn't
know very many people there, and they didn't know him. He'd
always considered it a bonus that he was seldom at headquarters, but now that put him in a bind, because he had no
one he knew well enough to trust.

So there would be no more help from Langley, no more requests for information. He tried to work the angles on what this meant to his particular situation. The way he saw it, he had two options: he could pull the plug on Lily right now and complete his stated mission, then hope to God that Frank lived so he could root out this damned mole—or he could stay here, work with Lily in cracking the Nervis' security, and try to find out from this end who the mole was. Of the two, he preferred staying here. For one thing, he was already here, and no matter how good the security was at the Nervi complex, it wouldn't be anything compared to the security at Langley.

Then there was Lily. She touched him and amused him and turned him on way more than he'd expected. Yeah, he'd found her attractive from the get-go, but the more time he spent with her, the better he knew her, the more intense the attraction became. He was getting in deeper with her than he'd ever planned, but it still wasn't deep enough. He wanted more.

So he'd stay here and do the best he could to work things from this end, totally on his own. He'd been playing along with Lily's scheme to break into the lab complex out of his own curiosity—that, and a strong desire to get into her pants—but now he needed to get serious about it. And he wasn't totally alone; he had Lily, who was no novice, and he also had his unknown caller. Whoever he was, the man was well-placed enough to know what was going on, and by warning Swain he'd placed himself on the side of the angels.

Thanks to the handy-dandy little cell-phone feature that listed incoming calls, Swain had the guy's number, both literally and figuratively. A person almost couldn't make a move today without leaving an electronic or paper footprint somewhere. Sometimes that was a blessing, sometimes a curse, depending on whether you were searching or hiding.

It was possible the guy even knew the name of the mole, but Swain doubted it. Otherwise, why give him a generic heads-up? If it had mattered enough for him to warn Swain, then he'd have given the name if he'd had it.

But you never knew how much information anyone had that they didn't know they had, bits and pieces they simply hadn't put together yet into a cohesive whole. The only way to find out was by asking.

He didn't want to call his unknown informant back using his cell phone, on the off chance that the guy didn't want to talk to him and wouldn't answer after seeing his phone number listed as incoming. Likewise, he didn't want this guy to know he was staying at the Bristol; just seemed safer that way. He'd bought a telephone card the day he'd arrived in France, figuring he'd never use it but wanting to have it just in case his cell phone batteries died unexpectedly or something. Leaving the hotel, he walked down Faubourg-Saint-Honoré, bypassing the first public phone for one farther down the street.

He was smiling as he dialed the number, but this smile was totally lacking in humor. It was more like the smile of a shark as it closed in on lunch. He glanced at his wristwatch as he listened to the phone ringing: 1:43 AM. Good. He was probably getting the guy out of bed, which is what he deserved for hanging up the way he had.

"Yes?"

The tone was wary, but Swain recognized the voice. "Hi there," he said cheerfully, in English. "I didn't disturb anyone, did I? Don't hang up, now. Play along and all you'll get is a phone call. Hang up on me and you'll get a visit."

There was a pause. "What do you want?" Unlike Swain, the

guy on the other end spoke in French; Swain was glad he knew
enough of the language to get by.

"Nothing much. I just want to know everything you know."

"One moment, please." Swain heard the man speaking quietly to someone, a woman. Though it was difficult to tell what
he was saying with the phone away from his mouth, Swain
thought he caught something about "taking the call downstairs."

Ah. So he was at home.

Then the man returned to the phone, saying briskly, "Yes,
what may I do for you?"

Smoke screen for the wife's sake, Swain thought. "You can
give me a name, for starters."

"The mole's?" He must be out of earshot of his wife, because the guy had switched to English.

"Definitely, but I was thinking of yours."

The man paused again. "It would be better if you do not
know."

"Better for you, yes, but I'm not worried about making
things better for you."

"But *I* am, monsieur." Firmness there now; the man wasn't
a milquetoast. "I am risking my life and the lives of my family.
Rodrigo Nervi is not one to take betrayal lightly."

"You work for him?"

"No. Not in that sense."

"I'm feeling a little dense, here. Either he pays you or he
doesn't. Which is it?"

"If I give him certain information, monsieur, he does not
kill my family. Yes, he pays me; the money further incriminates
me, yes?" Bitterness entered the quiet voice. "It is an insurance
that I will not talk."

"I see." Swain eased off on the smart-ass tough-guy act–or at least he racheted down his behavior–though, it came so naturally to him, it probably wasn't an act. "Something puzzles me. How did Nervi even know I was here, that he would be asking about me? I assume that's how my name came up, and how you got my phone number."

"He was searching for the identity of one of your contract agents. I believe it was a facial-recognition computer program that identified her. The mole accessed her file, and there was a notation that you had been dispatched to handle the problem she caused."

"How did he know she was a contract agent?"

"He did not. He was exploring several different means of identifying her."

So that was how Rodrigo had acquired a photo of Lily without the disguise she had used when she was with Salvatore. He knew what Lily looked like, and he knew her real name. Swain asked, "Does Nervi know my name?"

"I cannot say. I am the conduit between the CIA and Nervi, but I haven't given your name to him. He did ask for a way to contact you."

"In God's name, why?"

"To offer you a deal, I believe. A lot of money in exchange for any information you have about the whereabouts of the woman he is seeking."

"What made him think I would take the deal?"

"You are for hire, yes?"

"No," Swain said briefly.

"You are not a contract agent?"

"No." He didn't say more. If the CIA had sent him, and he wasn't a contract agent, then there was only one other category for him: field officer. He suspected this guy was bright enough to figure it out.

"Ah." There was the sound of a sharply drawn breath. "Then I have made the correct decision."

"Which is?"

"I did not give him your phone number."

"Even though your family is in danger?"

"I have a cover. There is another Nervi, a younger brother, Damone, who is . . . not quite in the family mold. He is intelligent, and reasonable. When I pointed out the inherent dangers in contacting someone who worked for the CIA, that this person would realize the only way Rodrigo could have his telephone number was if someone with the CIA had given it to him—moreover, this person could be very loyal to his country—Damone saw the wisdom of what I was saying. He said he would report to Rodrigo that the CIA person—that is yourself, of course—had rented a mobile here and had not yet contacted headquarters, so there was no current number available."

That made sense, even though the explanation was a tad convoluted. Rodrigo likely didn't know that field officers, when outside their own country, would use either secure international cell phones or satellite phones.

Another piece also fit neatly into this little piece. For information to be routed from the CIA through this man to Rodrigo Nervi, then the man Swain was talking to had to be in a position to request such sensitive information—and have quite a lot to lose if anyone found out. "What are you?" he asked. "Interpol?"

He heard a quick intake of breath and triumphantly thought, *Bingo!* Got it in one. Looked as if Salvatore Nervi had poked his fingers into a lot of pies that he shouldn't have.

"So what you're doing," he said, "is getting back at Nervi

without endangering your family. You can't overtly refuse to do anything he asks, can you?"

"I have children, monsieur. Perhaps you don't understand–"

"I have two of my own, so, yes, I understand perfectly."

"He would kill them without hesitation if I don't cooperate. In this matter with his brother, I did not refuse a request; his brother made a decision concerning it."

"But since you had my number anyway, you thought you'd put it to good use by making an anonymous call to warn me of the mole."

"*Oui*. An investigation prompted by an internal suspicion is far different from one instigated from outside, no?"

"Agreed." This guy wanted the mole caught; he wanted that contact closed off. He must be feeling guilty about the information he'd passed along over the years and was trying to somewhat atone. "How much damage have you done?"

"To national security, very little, monsieur. When asked I must provide at least a *soupçon* of reliable information, but always I have removed more sensitive items."

Swain accepted that. After all, the guy had a conscience or he wouldn't have called him with a warning. "Do you know the mole's name?"

"No, we have never used names. He does not know mine, either. By that I mean our real names. We have identifiers, of course."

"Then how does he get information to you? I assume he sends it through channels, so anything that is faxed or scanned would have to be sent to your attention."

"I set up a fictitious identity on my home computer for those things that must be sent electronically, which is most things.

Only rarely is anything faxed. Such a thing could be traced, of course–assuming one knew what to look for. I can access the account from my . . . the word escapes me. The small hand-computer in which one puts one's appointments–"

"PDA," Swain said.

"*Oui*. The PDA." Said with a French accent, it was *pei d'ay*.

"The number you use to contact him–"

"It is a mobile number, I believe, as I am always able to reach him on it."

"Have you had the number traced?"

"We do not investigate, monsieur; we coordinate."

Swain was well aware that Interpol's constitution directly prohibited the organization from conducting its own investigations. His guy had just confirmed that he was indeed Interpol, not that Swain had doubted it.

"I am certain the mobile phone would be registered under a false name," the Frenchman continued. "That would be easy for him to do, I think."

"A snap of the fingers," Swain agreed, pinching the bridge of his nose. A fake driver's license was easy to come by, especially for people in their line of work. Lily had used three sets of iden-tification running from Rodrigo. For someone who worked at Langley, how hard could it be?

He tried to think of the various means available for nabbing this guy. "How often are you in contact?"

"Sometimes not for months. Twice in the past few days."

"So a third contact so soon would be unusual?"

"Very unusual. But would he be suspicious? Perhaps, per-haps not. What are you thinking?"

"I'm thinking, monsieur, that you're between a rock and a hard place and would like to get out. Am I right?"

"A rock and a–? Ah, I understand. I would like that very much."

"What I need is a recording of your next conversation with him. Turn off the recorder while you're talking, if you want. The content of the conversation isn't important, just his voice."

"You will get a voiceprint."

"Yeah. I'll also need the recorder you use. Then all I have to do is find a match." Voiceprint analysis was fairly exact; that and facial-recognition programs had been used to differentiate Saddam Hussein from his doubles. A voice was a product of the structure of each individual's throat, nasal passages, and mouth, and hard to fake. Even impressionists couldn't exactly match a voice. Variables came in with the differences between microphones, recorders, audio feed, and so on. By having the same recorder, he took that variable out of the equation.

"I am willing to do this," the Frenchman said. "It is a danger to me and my loved ones, but I think the risk is manageable, with your cooperation."

"Thank you," Swain said sincerely. "Are you willing to go a step further, and perhaps remove the threat from existence?"

There was a very long pause; then he said, "How would you do this?"

"You have contacts you trust?"

"But of course."

"Someone who could maybe find out the specs of the security system at a certain complex?"

"Specs . . . ?"

"Blueprint. Technical details."

"I assume this complex belongs to the Nervi organization?"

"It does." Swain gave him the name of the laboratory, and the address.

"I will see what I can do."

22

LILY SMILED WHEN HER CELL PHONE RANG THE NEXT MORNING. Expecting another half-humorous half-serious obscene call from Swain, she didn't check the number of the incoming call before she answered. Just to jerk his chain, she changed her voice to a deep, almost masculine tone, and barked an impatient, "Hello!" into the phone.

"Mademoiselle Mansfield?" The voice she heard wasn't Swain's; it was one that had been electronically altered so the voice was distorted, and the words sounded as if they were coming out of a drum.

Lily went cold with shock and without thinking she started to disconnect the call, but calm reason reasserted itself. Just because someone had her cell phone number didn't mean he knew where to locate her. The phone was registered in her real name; the apartment and everything connected to it was in

Claudia Weber's name. It was, in fact, reassuring that the caller had referred to her as "Mansfield"; her *Claudia* persona was still secure.

Who had access to this phone number? It was her private cell phone, one she used only for personal business. Tina and Averill had had the number, of course, and Zia; Swain had it. Who else? Once she'd had a large circle of acquaintances, but that had practically been pre–cell phone; since the day she'd found Zia, the circle had grown smaller and smaller as she devoted herself to the baby, and smaller still after the debacle with Dmitri. She couldn't think of anyone now who had this number other than Swain.

"*Mademoiselle Mansfield?*" the distorted voice asked again.

"Yes?" Lily replied, forcing herself to sound calm. "How did you get this number?"

He didn't answer, instead saying in French, "*You do not know me, but I knew your friends, the Joubrans.*"

The words sounded strange, above and beyond the distortion that disguised the voice, as if the speaker had difficulty talking. She tensed even more at the mention of her friends. "Who are you?"

"*Forgive me, but that must remain private.*"

"Why?"

"*It is safer.*"

"Safer for whom?" she asked drily.

"*Both of us.*"

Okay, she could go with that. "Why did you call?"

"*It is I who hired your friends to destroy the laboratory. I never intended for what happened, to happen. No one was supposed to die.*"

Shocked once more, Lily groped behind her for a chair, sank down onto it. She had wanted answers, and without warning they were dropping into her lap. The phrase "never look a gift horse in the mouth" warred with "beware of Greeks bearing gifts." So which was the caller, figuratively, a horse or a Greek?

"Why did you hire them?" she finally asked. "More to the point, why are you calling me?"

"Your friends succeeded in their mission—temporarily. Unfortunately, research has resumed, and it must be stopped. You have reason to want to succeed: revenge. That is why you killed Salvatore Nervi. Therefore, I would like to hire you to complete the mission."

A cold sweat trickled down her spine. How did he know she'd killed Salvatore? She licked suddenly dry lips, but didn't explore that avenue. Instead she focused on the rest of his statement. This man wanted to hire her to do what she planned to do anyway. The irony of it almost made her laugh, except she felt more bitter than amused. "What exactly is this mission?"

"There is a virus, an avian influenza virus. Dr. Giordano has altered it so it may be passed from human to human, to create a pandemic and therefore a huge demand for the vaccine he has also developed. People do not have a resistance to this virus; mankind has not encountered it before. To create even greater panic, Dr. Giordano has somehow specifically engineered this virus to cause the greatest harm to children, who do not have immune systems as fully developed as adults. Millions will die, mademoiselle. It will be a pandemic greater than the one in 1918, which is believed to have killed between twenty and fifty million people."

. . . Cause the greatest harm to children. Zia. Lily felt sick that she had been right, that it was something concerning Zia that had spurred Averill and Tina to the act that had eventually resulted in their deaths. In trying to protect Zia, they had caused her death. She wanted to scream at the unfairness of it, at the ultimate irony. She clenched her fist, fighting for control, fighting to contain the fury and pain that rose into her throat like lava.

"The virus has been perfected. As soon as the vaccine is ready, packages will be delivered worldwide to the largest cities in the world, where human contact is greatest. The influenza will spread rapidly. By the time there is worldwide panic, thousands, perhaps millions, will have died. Then Dr. Giordano will announce that he has developed a vaccine for avian influenza, and the Nervi organization will be able to name its price for it. They will make an enormous fortune."

Yes, they would. It was classic. Control the supply, then create a demand for it. De Beers did it with diamonds; by carefully limiting the diamonds available on the market, they kept the price artificially high. Diamonds weren't rare at all, but the supply was controlled. It was roughly the same situation with crude oil and OPEC, except in the case of oil, the world had created its own demand.

"How do you know all this?" she asked angrily. "Why haven't you told the authorities?"

There was a pause; then the distorted voice said, *"Salvatore Nervi had many political connections, people in high positions who owed him many favors. This same laboratory is developing the vaccine against the virus, so the virus's existence there is explained. There is no proof that would outweigh his influence. That is why I was forced to hire professionals."*

Unfortunately, that was true; there were many influential

politicians who had set up housekeeping in Salvatore's pocket, making him all but untouchable.

It was also true that she had no idea whom she was talking to, if he was on the level, or if Rodrigo had found her cell phone number and was using this as a ruse to draw her out. She would have to be a fool to take everything this man said at face value.

"Will you do it?" he asked.

"How can I say yes when I don't know who you are? How can I possibly trust you?"

"I understand the difficulty, but I have no solution."

"I am not the only person you could hire."

"No, but your motivation is greater, perhaps, and also you are here now. I do not have to waste time looking for someone else."

"Tina Joubran was an expert with security systems. I am not."

"You do not need to be. It was I who provided the Joubrans with the details of the security system in place at the laboratory."

"It would have been changed after the incident in August."

"Yes, it was. I have acquired that information, also."

"If you know all of this, you must work at the laboratory. You could destroy the virus yourself."

"There are reasons why I could not."

Again she caught some strange difficulty in his speech, and abruptly she wondered if perhaps the speaker was handicapped in some fashion.

"I will pay you one million American dollars to do this."

Lily rubbed her forehead. That was wrong, the amount was way too much. Her inner alarm bells began ringing.

When she didn't say anything, the man continued, *"There is one other thing. Dr. Giordano must also be killed. If he lives, he will replicate his success with some other virus. Everything must be destroyed: the doctor, his research papers, computer files, the virus. Everything. That is a mistake I made the first time, not being thorough."*

Abruptly one million dollars didn't seem so far out of line. Everything he had said so far was reasonable and answered many of the questions she'd had, but innate caution held her back. There had to be some way she could safeguard herself in case this was a trap, but this entire conversation had taken her unawares and she hadn't been able to properly marshal her thoughts. She needed to think everything out before she made a decision.

"I can't give you an answer now," she said. "I have several things to consider."

"I understand. This could be a trap. You are wise to consider all possibilities, and yet time is a factor. I believe the job I have offered you is a goal you have in any case, one that you have a greater chance of attaining with my help. The longer you wait, the greater the odds that Rodrigo Nervi will locate you. He is intelligent and ruthless, and money is no object. He has people all over Paris, all over Europe, in shops and police departments. Given enough time, he will find you. With the money I will pay you, you will have the means to effectively disappear."

He was right. A million dollars would improve her situation beyond all measure. Yet she still couldn't jump at the offer, couldn't ignore the possibility that the bait might blind her to the trap.

"Consider these things. I will call you again tomorrow. I must have your answer then, or pursue other avenues."

The connection was broken. Automatically Lily checked

her incoming call log for the number, but she wasn't surprised to see that the information had been blocked; a man who had a million dollars available to hire a saboteur would also be able to afford layers of security.

But would someone that wealthy *work* at the laboratory? Not likely. So how did he have this information? How could he get the schematics of the security system?

Who he was, and how he got his information, was all-important. He could be a partner in Salvatore's scheme who got cold feet when he thought about all the innocents who would die–though in Lily's experience, people like the Nervis and their ilk simply didn't care who or how many died, so long as they achieved their aim.

Or had the caller been Rodrigo Nervi himself, telling her the truth about what was going on in order to draw her into a trap? He was intelligent enough, bold enough, to conceive and enact such a plot, to make it realistic down to the last detail, such as telling her he wanted her to kill Dr. Giordano.

Rodrigo Nervi also had the means to acquire her cell phone number, which for the sake of privacy she had not had listed in the *Pages Blanches.*

Her fingers were trembling as she punched in Swain's number.

On the third ring she heard his sleepy, "Good morning, sexy."

"Something has happened," she said in a tense voice, ignoring his greeting. "I need to see you."

"Do you want me to pick you up, or do you want to come here?" He sounded instantly alert.

"Pick me up," she said; her caller's warning about Rodrigo

having people everywhere had made her nervous. She had *known* that, had felt safe riding the trains by covering her hair and wearing sunglasses, yet having been tracked down so easily by someone who evidently knew everything made her nervous. Most Parisians used the train service, because traffic was such a nightmare. Having people watch the trains for someone of her description was a no-brainer.

"Depending on the traffic, I'll be there in . . . oh, anywhere between an hour and two days."

"Call when you get close and I'll meet you on the street," she said, and disconnected without responding to his joke.

She showered and dressed, in her usual pants and boots. A peek out the window showed a sunny sky, thank goodness, so she wouldn't look odd wearing sunglasses. She pinned up her hair so she could cover it with a hat, then sat down at the small eating table and meticulously checked her weapon, then put extra ammunition in her bag. That call had definitely spooked her, something that didn't often happen.

"I'm five minutes away," Swain announced an hour and fifteen minutes later.

"I'll be waiting," Lily replied. She put on her coat and hat, then slipped on her sunglasses, grabbed her bag, and hurried downstairs. She could hear the sound of a powerful car engine prowling up the narrow, winding street at a reckless speed, then the silver car rocketed into view and screeched to a halt directly in front of her. It was moving again almost before she got the door closed.

"What's up?" Swain asked, without any of the usual teasing in his voice. He wore sunglasses, too, and the way he handled the car was fast but businesslike, with no goofing around.

"I had a call on my cell phone," she said as she buckled up. "I haven't given the number to anyone but you, so I answered without checking the number. It wouldn't have done me any good, anyway, because it was blocked. The voice was electronically disguised, but it was a man, and he offered me a million dollars–American–to destroy the Nervi lab and kill the doctor in charge."

"Go on," he said, downshifting through a sharp curve.

She spelled out the rest of it for him, including every detail she could remember. When she got to the part about the avian influenza virus, he very softly said, "Son of a bitch," then listened to the rest without comment.

When she was finished, he said, "How long did you talk?"

"Five minutes or so. Maybe a little longer."

"Long enough to triangulate your position, then. Not an exact location, but the general area. If it was Nervi, he could blanket the area with people showing your photograph, and eventually he'd get a hit."

"I haven't made any acquaintances here. The apartment is sublet from someone who's out of the country."

"That helps, but your eyes are very distinctive. You must be part husky. Anyone who sees you will remember those eyes."

"Thanks," she said drily.

"I think you need to get what you need from the apartment, and stay with me instead. Definitely until he calls back. If it is Nervi and he does get another triangulation on your phone, it will be in a totally different district and that will throw him off."

"So he'll think I'm moving around, not staying in any one place."

"With luck. It's possible interference from the hotel itself would prevent anyone from locking on to the signal. Big build-ings really screw up the electronics."

Stay with him. It was a sound plan; they would be together, she wouldn't have to check in, and who would look for her in a luxury hotel?

There were several pluses to the plan, and only one minus that she could see. Silly of her to get hung up on it, but she was still reluctant to be intimate with him and she wasn't naive enough to think it wouldn't happen if they were sleeping in the same room. There were bigger things here to worry about than whether they would have sex, yet still she hesitated.

He gave her a hard, clear look that said he was reading her mind, but he didn't jump in to reassure her he'd keep his hands to himself and not try to take advantage of the situation. Of course he'd take advantage. That was a given.

"All right," she said.

He didn't gloat, didn't even smile. He just said, "Good. Now run through all that about the influenza virus again. I actually know someone in Atlanta who can tell me whether or not this is all feasible, before we rush in to save the world from some half-baked scheme that wouldn't work anyway."

She repeated everything she remembered while he worked his way through the narrow streets back to her apartment. Pulling up to the curb, he said, "You want to drive around for a few minutes while I go up and check that no one's in your apartment?"

Lily tapped the side of her boot. "Thank you, but I can do it."

"I'll be circling as best I can, given nothing seems to be laid out in a block. And while I'm circling, I'll be making that call."

"Sounds good to me." She climbed the stairs she had descended not half an hour before. When she'd left, she had pulled out a hair, wet it, and stuck it across the door and doorframe just an inch above the floor. The blond hair was as invisible as fishing line against the wood. She bent down close to look, and breathed a sigh of relief. The hair was still there. The apartment was safe. Unlocking the door, she went in and hurried around gathering her clothes and toiletries, everything she thought she would need. God only knew when or even if she'd ever be able to return for the rest of her things.

23

THERE WERE SOME OLD FRIENDS WHOSE TELEPHONE NUMBERS remained with you forever. Micah Sumner wasn't one of them, however, so while Lily was in her apartment gathering her clothes, Swain was trying to negotiate the narrow streets, shift gears, and punch in what felt like an endless series of numbers as he waded through the electronic mire required to reach information in the States, all at the same time. Then he didn't have anything to write the number down on, much less the fourth hand he needed to do it with, so when the computerized voice asked if he would like to be connected, he muttered, "Shit, yes," then pressed the number that corresponded to "Shit, yes."

By the fifth ring, Swain was beginning to doubt anyone was going to answer. But on the sixth one, there was some fumbling and a sleep-fogged voice said, "Yeah, hello."

"Micah, this is Lucas Swain."

"Well, son of a bitch." There was the sound of a huge yawn. "Haven't heard from you in a coon's age. Wish I wasn't hearing from you right now, either. Do you know what fucking time it is?"

Swain looked at his watch. "Let's see; it's nine AM here, so that would make it . . . three AM, right?"

"Bastard." That was said around another yawn. "Okay, why'd you wake me up? This had better be good."

"I don't know if it is or not." Swain cradled the phone between his jaw and shoulder as he changed gears. "What do you know about avian influenza?"

"Bird flu? You're shittin' me, right?"

"Nope, I'm serious as a heart attack. Is bird flu dangerous?"

"Not to wild fowl, but it is to domesticated birds. Remember seeing on the news several years back . . . 1997, I think . . . where there was an outbreak of bird flu in Hong Kong and they killed almost two million chickens to get rid of it?"

"Television was kind of hard to come by where I was. So it kills birds?"

"Yeah. Not a hundred percent of them, but enough. The problem is, sometimes the virus mutates and is transmitted from birds to humans."

"Is that more dangerous than regular flu?"

"Way more. If it's a virus the human body hasn't seen before, then there's no immune system resistance to it and you get sick as hell. Then you either die or you don't."

"That's comforting."

"We've been lucky so far. We've had a few mutations that allow bird-to-human infection, but none of the avian influenza viruses have made the magic leap that allows for human-to-human transmission. Like I said, so far. We're way overdue for a recombinant virus to hit us hard, but the avian flu that's been hitting Hong Kong doesn't look like a recombinant; it looks like a true avian virus. But it's infecting people, too. If it mutates that little bit needed for human-to-human infection, then we're in big trouble, because we'd have even less resistance to it than we would have to a recombinant virus that we'd seen at least a part of before."

"What about vaccines for it?" Swain drove around a curve and there was Lily's apartment building, but she wasn't standing on the street with all her worldly goods around her, so he drove past it to make another convoluted loop.

"We wouldn't have one. New viruses hit hard and fast; vaccines take months to test, to get them out to the general populace. By the time we could get an effective vaccine against an avian virus, a lot of people will have died. It's even harder to get one for avian influenza than it is for regular influenza viruses, because vaccines are cultured in eggs and—guess what—avian influenza will kill the eggs."

"Is this something the CDC is really worried about?"

"You're kidding, right? Flu kills a hell of a lot more people than the exotics that get all the sexy press, like the hemorrhagic fevers."

"So if some lab or something developed the vaccine ahead of time, then let the virus loose, they could make some serious money?"

"Hey, wait a minute." All sleepiness had fled Micah's tone. "Swain, are you telling me what I think you're telling me? That's a possible scenario?"

"I've just heard about it; I haven't checked it out yet. I don't know if there's anything to it. I wanted to see if it's feasible first."

"Feasible? It's brilliant, but it's a fucking nightmare. We've dodged the bullet the past few years, only regular influenza viruses have made the rounds, but we're holding our breaths and trying to get a reliable method of producing the vaccine before one of these damn bugs turns on us. Worldwide, even with antiviral drugs and medications to treat the complications, millions would die."

"Would it hit kids hardest?"

"Sure. Kids don't have the fully-developed immune system adults have. They haven't been exposed to as many bugs."

"Thanks, Micah, that's what I needed to know." It wasn't what he'd wanted to hear, but at least now he knew what he was dealing with.

"Don't hang up! Swain, is something like that going on? You have to tell me, man, you can't let us get caught flat-footed by something like this."

"I won't." He hoped; he'd have to take some fail-safe precautions. "It's just a rumor, nothing concrete. Flu season has already started, hasn't it?"

"Yeah, it's looking like a normal season so far. But if you find out there's some bastard looking to make a fortune with a virus like this, we need to know."

"You'll be the first," Swain lied. "I'll call you next week and let you know what's going on, good or bad." He *would* call, but Micah probably wouldn't be the first.

"Even at three fucking AM," Micah groused.

"You got it. Thanks, pal."

Swain disconnected, then dropped the phone in his pocket. Damn. Okay, so this scheme Lily's caller had told her about was not only feasible, but a real problem. Swain tried to think of alternate means of handling it. He couldn't call Langley because Frank was out of commission, there was a fucking mole in place who was feeding information to Rodrigo Nervi, and he had no idea whom he could trust. If Frank was there . . . well, one phone call and the whole damn laboratory complex would be toast tomorrow morning, but Frank wasn't there, so Swain had to turn it into toast himself. Somehow.

He could have given Micah the particulars, but what could the CDC do? Nothing more than alert the World Health Organization. Even if the WHO had the place raided without someone in the local police structure tipping off Nervi first, yeah, they'd find the virus, but the Nervi lab was working on a vaccine *for* the virus, so of course the virus would have to be there for testing, et cetera. It was a neat scheme, logically explaining away the smoking gun. He had to admire it.

He made it back to the apartment building, and this time Lily was there, carrying two carpet bags and with a familiar-looking tote hanging on her shoulder. He grinned as he looked fondly at the tote bag. Without it, he might never have found her.

He got out to stow the bags for her. They were on the heavy side, and he noticed she was a little breathless, which reminded him she'd said the poison had done some damage to a heart valve. He tended not to remember that, because she was such a capable person, but the fact was that only about two weeks had passed since she'd killed Salvatore Nervi and almost died herself. Even if the damage to her heart was minimal, there was no way she could have fully recovered her strength in such a short length of time.

He studied her as he opened the car door for her. Her lips

weren't blue, and her unpainted fingernails were pink. She was getting enough oxygen. She'd been rushing around, up and down three flights of stairs, so of course she was breathless. He would be, too. Relieved, he stopped her as she was about to get into the car. She looked up with a questioning expression, and he kissed her.

Her mouth was soft, and she leaned into him with such easy acceptance that his heartbeat kicked into a gallop. The street was no place for how he wanted to kiss her, however, so he contented himself with that brief taste. She smiled, one of those completely feminine smiles that left a man feeling drunk and confused and happy all at the same time, then slid into the seat and pulled the car door shut.

"Shit," he said as he got in the driver's seat. "I'm probably gonna have to dump this car."

"Because I could have been seen getting into it?"

"Yeah. Though we probably look like a couple going away on vacation, it's better not to take the chance. *Now* what will I get?"

"Maybe something a little less noticeable, like a red Lamborghini?" That wasn't fair, since the Mégane Renault wasn't in any way in the same class with a Lamborghini, but it was still a noticeable car.

He chuckled at the dig. "So I like good cars. Sue me."

"Did you get in touch with your friend in the States?"

"Yeah, but he was bitchy about the time difference. The bad news is, not only is this virus thing feasible, it's the CDC's worst nightmare."

"What's the good news?"

"There isn't any. Except Nervi isn't going to release the

virus until the vaccine is available, because of course he wants to be the first one innoculated, right? And it takes months to develop a vaccine. Since your friends did some damage to the program in August and presumably the mad doctor had to start over, I think we're safe in thinking they aren't going to release the virus during this flu season. They'll wait until next year."

She blew out a relieved breath. "That makes sense to me." She hesitated. "I've been thinking. I didn't know about the virus before, but now . . . This isn't something we have to do alone. Even though I'm not in good standing with the CIA right now, I could still use a pay phone and call my former contact there, let him know what's going on. They could handle something on this magnitude much better than just the two of us can."

Swain almost jumped out of his skin. "For God's sake, don't do that!" Her reasoning was sound, but she didn't know about the mole and he couldn't tell her without blowing the whistle on himself.

"Why not?" Her tone was more curious than anything else, but he could feel that pale blue gaze boring into him like lasers. She could cut steel with that look.

He didn't have a good reason on the tip of his tongue, and for a split second he thought the whole thing was going to blow up in his face, but then he had a flash of genius. He could pretty much tell her everything essential, without giving anything away. It was all in how he phrased it. "You know Nervi has contacts and influence there."

"He's an asset, an informer, but—"

"But he's also a very wealthy man. What are the odds someone there is on his payroll?" It was a simple explanation, and a true one. He was just leaving out a few details.

She turned back in her seat and scowled. "It's good odds. Salvatore was thorough, and Rodrigo is even more so. So we don't dare go to anyone, do we?"

"No one I've been able to think of, that he wouldn't have someone there on his payroll. Not the French police, not Interpol . . ." He let his voice trail off and shrugged. "I guess we have to save the world ourselves."

"I don't want to save the world," she said grumpily. "I like things on a smaller scale. I want it to be *personal.*"

He had to laugh, because he knew what she meant. As much as she'd wanted to bring down the Nervi organization before, now they *had* to do it.

The job was much tougher than he'd imagined at the beginning. With a virus like that having to be contained, the security would be on a par with that at the CDC in Atlanta. Getting in would require more than just having information about the security system; they would need inside help. Just how they got that help was going to be a bitch.

"We may have to take the chance that the guy who called you is on the up and up," he said. "Otherwise, we're screwed."

"I was thinking the same thing," she said, surprising him. Sometimes it was scary the way their brains seemed to work the same way and at the same pace. "The security in place because of the virus will be layered, and the virus itself kept in strict quarantine. We need someone inside."

"You'll have to meet with him. That's the only way we can know it isn't Rodrigo Nervi. If it is Rodrigo, he'll jump at the chance to have you come to him. He doesn't know about me— well, he might have an idea after the shoot-out the other day, but he doesn't know what I look like or anything—so I can watch your back."

She gave a grim smile. "If it *is* Rodrigo, he'll have so many men watching that you won't be able to do a thing about it. But I agree, that's the only way. I'll have to do it. But if it's Rodrigo and they grab me, do me a favor and kill me. Don't let them take me alive, because I expect Rodrigo will want to have some fun and games with me before he kills me. I'd just as soon skip that part."

Swain's stomach knotted at the thought of Nervi getting his hands on her. There were hard decisions he had to make, but that wasn't one of them. "I won't let that happen," he said quietly.

"Thanks." Her smile turned a little brighter, as if he'd given her a gift, and his stomach knotted even tighter.

Neither of them had eaten yet that morning, so with Lily's sunglasses and hat in place they stopped at a sidewalk café and had brioches and coffee. He watched her eat, his heart thudding as he wondered if this was the last day he'd have with her. He'd thought he could put if off longer, but circumstances were piling up on them. If her mystery caller was Rodrigo Nervi, there was no way they could know until the meeting, and then it would be too late.

He wished there was some other way they could do it, but there wasn't. The meeting had to take place. She had to accept the guy's proposal when he called tomorrow, set up a meeting, and be there. Then . . . the caller would either turn out to be Nervi, or someone else. God, he prayed it was someone else. He wanted more than one more day with her. He wanted more than one night.

He himself had gone into every job knowing it might be his last, that when you worked with violent people sometimes the violence turned on you. Lily was the same; she had put herself in the front lines and accepted the odds. That didn't make it any easier, knowing she was there by choice.

But if Nervi and his goons were the ones who showed up and he lost Lily, he swore to God the bastard would pay. Big time.

24

Swain turned in his Mégane and, at Lily's insistence, got a little blue four-cylinder Fiat from a different rental company. "No!" he moaned in horror when she told him what she wanted him to get. "Let's get a Mercedes instead. There are a lot of Mercedes around." He brightened. "I know. Let's get a Porsche. We might need the horses. Or a BMW. Both of those sound good."

"Fiat," she said.

"Gesundheit."

Her lips twitched, but she managed not to laugh. "You don't want anything noticeable."

"Yes, I do," he said stubbornly. "It doesn't matter who notices me because no one knows who I am. If I were looking for someone, I'd look at people who were driving Fiats, because that's what you get if you don't want to be noticed."

Using that same theory, she had put on a bright red wig as a disguise, so he actually made sense. But by now the amusement value was so great she wanted to see him drive one of the smaller Fiats for at least a day, just to hear how creative he could get with his complaining.

"You started out driving a Jaguar, then today you picked me up in a Mégane–if anyone saw us–so anyone looking for you would already know you like fast cars. A Fiat would be the last thing anyone would look for."

"No joke," he grumbled.

"A Fiat's a good car. We can get a Stilo three-door; it's fairly sporty–"

"Meaning, I can pedal it at ten miles an hour instead of five?"

She had to bite the inside of her cheek to keep from laughing, so ridiculous was the mental picture she had of him on a tricycle, his long legs folded up around his ears while he pedaled like mad.

He was sulking so much he wouldn't even approach the rental counter until she turned around and hissed, "Do you want me to put it on *my* credit card? Rodrigo would know about it before the hour's up."

"*My* credit card might expire from embarrassment at having something like this charged to it," he snapped, but then he squared his shoulders and stepped up like a man. He didn't flinch even when the car was brought around and the features pointed out. The Fiat Stilo was a quick little car, with nice acceleration, but she could tell he judged it woefully short on horsepower.

He put her bags in the back while Lily got in the passenger seat and buckled the seat belt. Swain slid the driver's seat back before he got in, making room for his legs.

He turned the key and started the engine. "It has a navigation system," Lily pointed out.

"I don't need a navigation system. I can read a map." He
put the car in gear, then made a high-pitched whining noise
through his nose as he accelerated. Unfortunately, the noise
exactly matched the pitch of the engine noise, and Lily lost her
battle not to laugh. She tried to hide it, pinching her nose and
turning her head to look out the window, but he saw her heaving shoulders and said sourly, "I'm glad *someone* thinks this is
funny. I'm staying at the Bristol; don't you think someone there
might think it's odd that I'm driving a Fiat instead of something
flashier?"

"You're such a car snob. A lot of people rent cars that have
good gas mileage. It's a smart thing to do."

"Unless they might have to make a quick getaway and they're
being chased by cars with bigger engines." His expression was
grim. "I think I've been emasculated. I probably won't be able
to get a hard-on while I'm driving this."

"Don't worry," she soothed. "If you can't, I'll let you get
whatever kind of car you want tomorrow."

Like magic his expression lightened and he started to grin,
only to have the grin morph into a grimace of acute pain as he
realized the choice she'd just given him. "Ah, shit," he groaned.
"That's diabolical. You're going to hell for thinking of something that evil."

She gave him an innocent look and lifted one shoulder in a
gesture that said, "So?" He was the one who had taken the issue
down the sexual path; if he didn't like where he'd ended up, it
was his own fault.

She was amazed that she could be so entertained, considering what they were up against, but it was as if by tacit agree-

ment they had decided to have today just for themselves, because today might be all they had. She had known some contract agents who, because of the nature of their work, lived
totally in the moment. She never had, but today she saw the appeal of not worrying about tomorrow. There was a poignancy
that hit home as she watched his expressions, an acknowledg-
ment of what could be between them if she had the chance to
let it grow. He made her feel soft inside, and warm with an affection that held so much promise it was almost frightening.
She could love him, she thought. She might already, just a little
bit, for his sense of humor and sheer *joie de vivre* that lifted her
own spirits from the depths. She had needed to laugh, and he'd
given her that.

"Let's renegotiate," he said. "If I can get it up, as a reward I
get to pick out a different car tomorrow."

"And if you can't, you have to drive this one for the dura-
tion?"

He snorted and said smugly, "Yeah, like that's gonna happen."

"Then where's the negotiation?" She stroked the seat. "I like
this car. I'm becoming very fond of it. Unlike you, my sexuality
isn't linked to a machine."

"Guys can't help it. We're born with a stick shift, and it's our
favorite toy from the time our arms are long enough to reach it."

"This car has a stick shift," she pointed out.

"Don't get technical. There's no testosterone here." He made
the high-pitched whining sound again. "See? It's a soprano. A
four-cylinder soprano."

"It's a great car for city driving. It's highly maneuverable,
economical, reliable."

He gave up. "All right. You win. I'll drive it, but I'll need therapy afterwards for the emotional damage you're inflicting on me."

She stared straight ahead through the windshield. "Massage therapy?"

"H'mmm." He considered it. "Yeah, that'll do it. But I'll need a lot of it."

"I think I can handle that."

He grinned and winked at her, and abruptly she wondered if she hadn't outsmarted herself and let him talk her into something she hadn't one hundred percent decided to do. Ninety-eight percent, yes, but not a hundred percent. That old sense of caution still nagged at her.

In that uncanny way he had of picking up on her wavelength, he turned totally serious. "Don't let me pressure you into anything you don't want to do," he said quietly. "If you don't want to sleep with me, all you have to do is say no."

She looked out the window. "Have you ever wanted anything and been afraid of it at the same time?"

"You mean like getting on a roller coaster, when you really want the ride but your stomach's already in your throat thinking about that first big drop?"

Even his anxieties were fun-related, she thought, and smiled a little. "The last time I was involved with someone, he tried to kill me." She said it casually, but the sorrow and tension that still gripped her to this day were anything but casual.

He whistled between his teeth. "That would ruin your day, all right. Was he crazy jealous or something?"

"No, he'd been hired to do it."

"Ah, honey," he said, with real sadness in his tone, as if he grieved for her. "I'm sorry. I can see where that would make you cautious."

"That's an understatement," she muttered.

"Gun-shy?"

"In a big way."

He hesitated, as if he wasn't certain he wanted to know. "How big?"

. She shrugged and said, "That was six years ago."

The steering wheel jerked in his hands and the car swerved, prompting the driver beside them to blow his horn in warning. "Six–*years*?" He sounded incredulous. "You haven't been involved with anyone for *six years*? Holy shit. That's–that's taking caution to the extreme."

He might think so, but then he hadn't almost been killed by someone he loved. She hadn't thought anything could hurt worse than Dmitri's betrayal, until Zia's death.

He thought about it another minute, then said, "I'm honored."

"Don't be. I wouldn't be this involved with you if circumstance hadn't thrown us together," she pointed out. "If we'd met socially, I'd have blown you off like yesterday's news."

He scratched the side of his nose. "You wouldn't have been tempted by my charm?"

She made a rude sound. "You wouldn't have got close enough for me to know you were charming."

"This may sound callous, but if that's the case, I'm glad you were getting shot at the other day. If you believe in fate, then it was meant to be that I'd be sitting there, at loose ends, just when you were on the losing side of a gun battle."

"Or it was sheer chance. It remains to be seen whether that

was good luck or bad luck—for you, I mean." And perhaps for
her, as well, though she thought she should count her blessings, that even if events went drastically sour, at least she'd had
laughter in her life again for a short while.

"I can tell you that," he said lazily. "It was the best luck I've
had in a long time."

She watched his face and wondered what it was like to live
inside his skin, to be so optimistic and at peace with one's self.
She couldn't remember feeling that way since she was a teenager, though she'd been happy while she had Zia.

After Zia's death, peace and happiness had been totally
alien. She had been so focused; all she'd thought about was
vengeance for her friends, for Zia. Now Swain was in her life,
and her goal had been transformed from something personal
to something so hugely important that she had to struggle to
grasp the scope of it. Her personal feelings had been made in-
significant, and reality had swept her to a different perspective.
She knew that although a person never stopped grieving for
lost loved ones, the quality of grief changed from gut-gnawing
agony to dull pain, to acceptance, to remembering the good
times—and sometimes all of those things were felt within a very
short time, in no particular order. Her focus had been shifted
from herself, her loss, to something outside herself, and with
that shift the pain had changed, become less immediate and
all-consuming.

She didn't know how long the surcease would endure, but
she was grateful for every moment of it. Swain was responsible,
she knew, for a lot of her shift in mood just by being his brash,
very American self. Of course, he could lift a woman's mood
just by walking down the street with that lazy, loose-hipped

gait of his. She knew because she had seen women watching him, and she knew the effect he had on *her*.

He reached for her hand and squeezed it. "Stop worrying so much. Everything will be okay."

She gave a rueful laugh. "You mean: my mystery caller will turn out *not* to be Rodrigo; he can tell us everything we need to know about the lab's security; we get in without any trouble, totally destroy the virus, kill Dr. Giordano so he can't do this again, and get away without anyone the wiser?"

He thought about it. "Maybe not everything; that's a big laundry list. But you have to have faith things will work out for the better one way or the other. We can't fail, therefore we won't."

"The power of positive thinking?"

"Don't knock it. It's worked for me so far. For instance, I was positive I'd get in your pants from the minute I saw you, and look at us now."

They were once more at a standstill, with a thousand things that needed doing and nothing they could do that day. Swain's security system expert didn't get in touch, but now that they knew what they were up against, they both thought the security measures in place would be far more complex than any the run-of-the-mill expert would ever see.

Just to see what they could find, they went to an Internet café to research influenza, before they went to the hotel. There was so much to read that in the interest of saving time, they each paid for computer time and divided the hits between them.

At one point during the afternoon, Swain checked his wrist-

watch, then took out his cell phone and punched in a long series of numbers. From where she was Lily couldn't hear what
he was saying, but his expression was serious. His conversation was brief, and when it was over, he rubbed his forehead as
if he had a headache.

While the computer was loading a large file, she went over
to him. "Is something wrong?"

"A friend was in a car accident in the States. I called to
check his condition."

"How is he?"

"Unchanged. The doctors say that's actually good. He lived
through the first twenty-four hours, so they're a little more optimistic than they were before." He rocked his hand. "He could
still go either way."

"Do you need to go there?" she asked. She didn't know what
she would do without him, but if this was a really close friend–

"I can't," he said briefly.

She took that to mean he literally couldn't, that he was persona non grata in the States and wouldn't be allowed in. She
touched his shoulder in sympathy, because she knew how he
felt. She probably wouldn't ever be able to go home again, either.

He was scrolling through the CDC Web site. The first time
he'd pulled it up, he hadn't found anything really interesting, but he'd kept clicking on related sites that had links to the
CDC, and he gave a satisfied grunt as a long list popped on the
screen. "Finally." He clicked on *Print*.

"What do you have?" Lily asked, bending down to read over
his shoulder.

He lowered his voice so no one could overhear what they

were saying. "A list of infectious agents and the safety precautions taken with each one." He nodded at the computer she was using. "What do you have over there?"

"A projection of illnesses and deaths during the next pandemic. Nothing useful, I don't think."

"This should tell us what we need. If it doesn't, my friend in Atlanta can fill in the blanks. I should have asked him a bunch of these questions this morning, but I hadn't had time to think about it and he called me a bastard anyway, since it was three AM there when I called him."

"Understandable."

"I thought so, too." Her hand was still on his shoulder, and he covered it with one of his. "Let's take this stuff back to the hotel to read. We can order room service, and you can get unpacked and settled in."

"We'll have to tell the hotel there are now two people staying in your room, instead of just one."

"I'll just say my wife has joined me. Not a problem. Keep your sunglasses on and don't let any of the staff see your eyes, and we should be in the clear."

"I'll look pretty silly sitting around a hotel room wearing sunglasses. Colored contacts will be easier."

"It isn't just your eyes that are so identifiable. It's the entire package, the color of your hair, your facial structure. Just duck into the bathroom when room service is delivered. Other than maid service, that's the only time we'll be interrupted." He logged off, then gathered all the pages that had been printed out. He paid for the service while Lily logged off her computer and did the same.

They stepped out into the street, and the wind whipped at

them. Though the day was sunny, it was cool enough, and the windchill cold enough, that a lot of people were wearing hats and scarves. Lily pulled her own hat down so it covered all her hair as they walked to where Swain had parked the car. He seemed to have remarkable luck in finding parking space in a city that was notorious for difficult parking, but she was beginning to think Swain was just one of those people born under a lucky horseshoe. If he'd leased a Hummer, somehow he'd have found a place to park it.

He forwent making any more disparaging comments about the Fiat, though she heard him making that high-pitched whining noise under his breath a few times. The days had gotten really short, with winter only a few weeks away, so the sun had already set by the time they got to the hotel and twilight was fading fast, making Lily's sunglasses unnecessary. She pulled them off but remembered that she still had a pair of pink-lensed sunglasses that she'd used as part of her disguise in London, and fished them out of her bag. The tint was light enough that she could see with the glasses on and wouldn't look like a total idiot for wearing sunglasses at night but was sufficient to hide the color of her eyes.

She slipped them in place and turned to Swain. "How do I look?"

"Sexy and stylish." He gave her a thumbs-up. "Just keep your eyelids at half-mast, as if you're jet-lagged, and we're home free."

He was right; no one paid any attention to them at all as he carried her bags through the lobby with her trailing behind. When they were in his room, he called the front desk and told them his wife had arrived, so there were now two occupants in his room; then he called housekeeping and requested extra towels. Lily busied herself unpacking, putting her clothing away in drawers or hanging it in the closet beside Swain's clothes, and her toiletries in the bathroom.

She got a jolt as she set a pair of her shoes beside his in the bottom of the closet. There was something intimate about the sight, her shoes so much smaller and daintier than his, that brought home to her the fact that she was now, for all intents and purposes, living with him.

She looked up to find him watching her, reading her discomfort.

"It'll be all right," he said gently, and opened his arms to her.

25

LILY WENT TO HIM, BURROWED HERSELF CLOSE TO THE COMFORT-
ing warmth of his body, nestled her head in the hollow of his
shoulder, and felt some of her tension ease as he wrapped his
arms around her. He kissed the top of her head. "I repeat, we
don't have to have sex tonight. If you're that uncomfortable with
the idea, we can wait."

"Can we?" she asked softly. "Normally I'd wait a lot longer
than this, because two kisses and one grope do not a relationship make–"

He gave a bark of laughter. "I guess not, but even though
logically I know we've known each other only a few days, part
of me feels as if it's been a lot longer than that. A week, maybe,"
he teased. "Have I really groped you just once?"

"Once is all that I remember."

"Then it's definitely just once, because you'd remember my

gropes." He rubbed his hand up and down her back, coaxing her tense muscles to relax.

"Tonight may be the only night we have," she said, trying for a matter-of-fact tone but unable to keep out a hint of wistfulness. The truth of that had been in the back of her mind all day. She couldn't afford to take her time, get to know him, ease into a relationship. Seen in that light, her decision was simple: she might well die tomorrow, and she didn't want her last night on earth to be spent alone. She didn't want to die without having made love with him, without sleeping so close in his arms that she could hear his heartbeat. She wanted him to be her love, even if she wouldn't have a chance to discover if he was *the* love. At least she would have the hope that he was.

"Hey," he chided. "Remember the power of positive thinking. Tonight is the first night, not the only night."

"Have you always been a Pollyanna?"

"Pollyanna saw something good in everything. I see nothing good at all about that Fiat."

Taken by surprise at his abrupt change of subject, she snickered. "I do. I got a good laugh out of your reaction to it."

He stiffened. "You mean you deliberately picked out that car just to jerk my chain?"

She didn't bother denying it, just gave a satisfied sigh as she rubbed her cheek against his chest. "I wanted to see you drive it for just one day. It's a perfectly good car; I once owned a Fiat, so I know how reliable and economical they are, but you act as if you're in agony."

"You'll have to pay for this," he said, shaking his head. "And not with all that massaging you promised, either. This is big. I'll have to think about this one for a while."

"Just don't take too long."

"You'll know tonight," he promised, tilting her head up for a warm kiss that lingered, multiplied, deepened. Unlike the night before, he took his time stroking her breasts, cupping them, thumbing her nipples through the layers of clothing. Lily half expected to be tumbled onto the bed, but he didn't even slip his hand under her top. She was glad; she wasn't anywhere near aroused. His caresses felt good, though, and when he released her, she was warmer and more fluid than she'd been before.

A brisk knock on the door signaled the arrival of housekeeping with an armful of towels. Swain went to the door and took the towels in the same motion with which he handed over a tip, not letting the maid in, though she would have gladly arranged the towels in the bathroom for them.

"Let's read over all these papers and see what we've got," he said after he put the towels away, indicating everything they'd printed out at the Internet café. "There's a lot of extra stuff in the articles that we won't need."

She liked that he wanted to take care of business before fun and games, so she joined him in the sitting area, where he had all the papers scattered out on the coffee table.

"Ebola ... Marburg ... We don't need all this," he muttered, dropping page after page on the floor. Lily picked up a stack of paper and began sorting through it, looking for any information on influenza.

"Here," she said a moment later. " 'How influenza viruses are treated in the laboratory.' Let's see ... 'laboratory-associated infections aren't documented,' but watch out for ferrets."

"What?" he asked, startled.

"That's what it says. Evidently infected ferrets pass the virus along to humans fairly easily, and vice versa. They make us sick, we make them sick. That's fair," she said judiciously. "What else . . . 'a genetically altered virus . . . unknown potential. Biosafety Level 2 is recommended.' What's Biosafety Level 2?"

"I have that here . . . somewhere." Rapidly he flipped through a section of papers. "Here. Okay. The threat is considered moderate. 'Laboratory personnel must be trained in handling the viruses, access to the lab is limited when work is being done,' but I guess we can safely say access to the Nervi lab is limited at all times. 'People have to wash their hands . . . no eating or drinking in the area . . . wastes are decontaminated before disposal'—that's good to know. I guess we could have safely gone in the sewer, after all."

"I'm just as glad we didn't."

"We may have to yet."

She wrinkled her nose at the thought. Even though the sewer had been her idea and she would go that route if there was no other way, she'd rather not.

" 'A biohazard sign must be posted,' " he continued. " 'Extra care taken when handling sharp instruments'—duh—these are all precautions the laboratory personnel take while handling the bugs. 'The lab must have lockable doors; no specific ventilation system is required.' Huh." He put down the papers and scratched his jaw. "This sounds like a basic lab, no airlock entrances, retina scans, thumbprint locks, or anything else. Looks as if we were borrowing trouble, because if Dr. Giordano follows these instructions, all we have to deal with is a locked door."

"And a lot of people with weapons."

He waved his hand. "That's straightforward." He tossed the papers on the coffee table and leaned back, lacing his fingers behind his head. "I'm surprised. I thought when you were dealing with infectious bugs, you had all sorts of hoops to jump through; but it's mostly personal security, not external."

They looked at each other and shrugged. "We're back where we started," Lily said. "We need information about the external security system. Once we get in, we look around for the door with the biohazard sign on it."

"X marks the spot," he agreed. They both knew it wouldn't be that simple; for one thing, the laboratory could be anywhere within the large complex. It could even be underground, which would limit their available exit routes.

Having found out what they needed to know, which was a lot less than they'd expected, there was no need to keep all the copies they'd printed. Swain picked up the ones he'd dropped on the floor while Lily gathered up all the other sheets; then they dumped everything in the trash.

She was at a loss for something to do now. The hour was still fairly early; they hadn't even had dinner. She didn't want to take a shower yet, and thankfully he didn't seem inclined to rush her into bed. Finally she picked up the book she'd brought and kicked off her boots, then curled up on the sofa to read.

Swain picked up his room key. "I'm going down to the lobby to pick up some newspapers. Do you want anything?"

"Nothing, thanks."

He let himself out. Lily waited to a count of thirty, then got up and swiftly went through his things. His underwear was neatly stacked in a drawer, with nothing hidden between the folded boxer-style briefs. She patted the pockets of everything he had hanging in the closet, finding nothing. There wasn't a briefcase, but she pulled out his leather duffel bag and searched it. There didn't seem to be any hidden pockets or a false bottom to it; his Heckler and Koch nine-millimeter weapon was there, neatly holstered. The bedside table yielded a thriller that was dog-eared at about the halfway point. She fanned the pages, but nothing had been slipped between them.

She ran her hand under the mattress, all the way around, and looked under the bed. His leather blazer was lying on the bed where he'd thrown it. She searched his pockets, and found his passport in a zippered inside pocket, but she'd already seen it, so she didn't take it out.

There was nothing to indicate he was anything other than what he'd told her. Relieved, she returned to the sofa and resumed reading.

He let himself back in five minutes later, carrying two thick newspapers and a small plastic bag. "I had a vasectomy after my second kid was born," he said, "but I bought some condoms, anyway, in case they'll make you feel more secure."

His concern touched her. "Have you done anything risky? Sexually, I mean."

"I did it standing up in a hammock once, but that was when I was seventeen."

"You did not. *Hammock* maybe, *standing up* a definite no."

He grinned. "Actually, the hammock dumped me out on my ass, and I haven't tried that again. It did a real number on the mood. I didn't get laid that day, after all."

"I can imagine. She must have laughed herself silly."

"No, she screamed. I was the one laughing. Even a

seventeen-year-old can't keep it up when he's doing belly laughs. Not to mention I looked like an idiot, and girls that age are real sensitive about image and things like that. She decided I was very uncool and went off in a huff."

She should have known he'd be the one laughing. Smiling, she propped her chin in her palm. "Anything else risky?"

He settled in the chair closest to her and stretched out his legs, propping his feet on the coffee table. "Let's see. Right after that is when Amy and I started going together, and I was faithful to her from day one until we got divorced. I've had a few close friends since then, relationships lasting from a couple of months to two years, but nothing casual. I've mostly been in places where there was no wild nightlife, unless you count the four-legged kind. Whenever I was in a civilized area, I didn't want to spend my time nightclubbing."

"For someone who's been in the wilds most of his adult life, you're very sophisticated," she murmured, suddenly uneasy as that discordant detail registered with her. She should have noticed before, but she wasn't greatly alarmed because she knew his weapon was in his duffel in the closet—and hers wasn't.

"Because I speak French and stay in luxury hotels? I stay in places like this when I can, because there've been times when all I had between me and the sky was air. I like driving fancy cars because sometimes I've had to get around on horseback— and that's assuming there were even horses."

"I wouldn't think French was very common in South America, though."

"You'd be surprised. I learned most of it from a French expatriate in Colombia. Now, my Spanish is much better than my French, and I also speak Portuguese, plus a smattering of German." He gave her a crooked smile. "Mercenaries are a polyglot group by necessity."

He'd never actually come right out before and said he was a mercenary, though of course she'd understood he was either that or something close to it. *People hired him to make things happen* was what he'd said, and she hadn't for one minute thought he was talking about corporate takeovers. Her uneasiness faded; of course he would speak several languages.

"Being married to you must have been hell," she said, thinking of his ex-wife at home with two little kids, not knowing where he was or what he was doing, if he'd ever return or die in some remote region and his body never be found.

"Thanks a lot," he said, starting to grin. His blue eyes twinkled at her. "I'm a lot of fun when I'm around, though."

There was no doubt about that. On impulse she got up and deposited herself on his lap, slipping her hand inside the collar of his shirt and cupping the back of his neck as she leaned into him. His skin was warm, his neck hard with muscle. He supported her with his left arm behind her back, while his right hand immediately began stroking her thigh and hip. She kissed the underside of his jaw, feeling the stubble of his beard rough against her lips and inhaling his scent, man mixed with the faint remnants of the aftershave he'd used that morning.

"What's this for?" he asked, though he didn't wait for the answer before giving her one of those slow, deep kisses that made her feel as if her bones were melting.

"For being a lot of fun," she murmured when he lifted his mouth; then she went back for seconds. His lips were more forceful this time, his tongue more demanding. His hand shaped her waist, slid under her shirt and up to her breasts. She caught her breath as he pushed her bra up and molded her bare breast with his palm. His hand was hot on her cool skin, his thumb gentle on her nipple.

She pulled her mouth free and took a deep breath, burying her face against his throat as warm pleasure began tightening her loins. She hadn't felt desire in such a long time that she had forgotten how it slowly unfurled, spreading throughout her body, making her skin ultrasensitive, so that she wanted to rub against him like a cat.

She wanted him to hurry, to get the awkward first time over with so she could relax, but for all his love of speed, hurrying didn't seem to be on his agenda tonight. He stroked her breasts until they were so sensitive the sensation bordered on pain; then he tugged her bra back into place and hugged her tightly to him. She knew he was aroused; either that, or he had a backup pistol shoved in his pocket, a big ten-round forty-five caliber from the feel of it. But he eased her back, kissed the tip of her nose, and said, "There's no hurry, we'll eat dinner, relax for a while. It won't kill me to wait."

"No, but me it might," she snapped, sitting up and glaring at him.

His mouth quirked into a smile. "Just be patient. You know the saying, 'All good things come to those to wait'? I have my own version of that."

"Yeah? What?"

"Those who wait, come good."

He needed slapping, he really did. "I'll hold you to that," she said, rising from his lap. She picked up the room service menu and tossed it at him. "Order."

He did, lobster and scallops, a bottle of Beaujolais, chilled, and apple tart. Determined to play it as casually as he did, she resumed reading while they waited for room service to deliver their order. He leafed through both newspapers, used his cell phone to call the States and check on the condition of his friend who had been in the car accident–unchanged, which caused his expression to set in lines of worry.

He wasn't carefree, she thought, watching his face. No matter how much he laughed and teased, his emotions weren't all on the surface. There were moments when he was lost in thought and there was no humor at all on his face or in his eyes; she had seen flashes of cold, grim determination in him. There had to be more to him than just good times, or he wouldn't have succeeded in his chosen field, though she wondered if someone actually chose to be a mercenary or gradually fell into it. He'd evidently made some money at it, so that meant he was good. That likeable, charming manner was just part of who he was; the other part would be fast and lethal.

Lily had shied away from relationships with normal men over the years, men who held ordinary jobs and had normal concerns. Not only would someone like that never understand how she did what she did, she had always been concerned that she would overpower a man like that in an intimate relationship. She *had* to be forceful and decisive, and that wasn't something she could turn on and off like a water tap. When it came to romance, she didn't want to dominate, she wanted to be a partner, but that meant by necessity she needed someone as strong in personality as she was. In Swain she sensed an easiness, a self-confidence that wasn't at all threatened by her. She didn't have to pander to his ego, or dampen her own personality so he wouldn't be intimidated. If Swain had ever been intimidated in his life, she would be surprised. He'd probably been gutsy and a hell-raiser even when he was a little boy.

The more she observed of him, the more she respected him. She was falling fast and hard, and there was no net beneath her.

26

After they ate, he watched Sky News for a while, and Lily read some more. They could have been a couple for years for all the impatience he was showing, but she remembered the erection that had thrust against her hip and knew otherwise. A man didn't get painfully hard when he wasn't interested. He was giving her time to relax, not pressuring her; he knew, of course, that eventually they would be going to bed together and the inevitable would happen then. She knew it, too, and knowledge was its own seduction. She couldn't look at him without thinking that soon he would be naked and so would she, soon she would feel him inside her, soon this coiling tension inside her would find a release.

At ten she said, "I'm going to take a shower," and left him to Sky News. The complimentary toiletries in the marble bathroom were designer brands, and smelled heavenly. She took

her time, washing her hair, shaving her underarms and legs–
an American habit she'd never lost–then smoothing scented lo-
tion all over herself before blow-drying her hair and brushing
her teeth. Feeling as ready as she ever would, and having killed
most of an hour, she put on one of the thick hotel robes and
tightly tied the belt around her before walking barefoot back
into the room.

"You're a bathroom hog," he accused, turning off the television and rising to his feet. His gaze went over her from her
shiny hair down to the tips of her toes. "I expected you to come
out wearing your pajamas. I've been thinking about getting
them off of you."

"I don't wear pajamas," she said, and yawned.

His brows snapped together. "You said you wore pajamas."

"I lied. I sleep nude."

"You mean you ruined a perfectly good fantasy just for the
hell of it?"

"It was none of your business what I wore to bed." She gave
him a smug smile and went to the sofa, where she picked up
her book and sat down, curling her legs under her. She was
pretty sure she'd flashed him all the way to Christmas–she
tried, anyway–because he abruptly turned around and went
into the bathroom without another word, and about thirty seconds later she heard the shower running. He was in a hurry
now.

Watching the clock on the bedside table, she timed him. His
shower lasted just shy of two minutes. Then she heard the
water running in the basin for forty-seven seconds. Twenty-two
seconds after that he walked out of the bathroom wearing a
damp towel knotted around his waist, and nothing else.

Lily stared at his freshly shaven jaw. "I can't believe you shaved that fast. It's a wonder you didn't slit your throat."

"What's a severed jugular compared to getting you in bed?" he asked, walking to the sofa and taking her hand, then pulling her to her feet. He switched off the lamp and towed her to the bed, turning off lights as he went until the room was dark except for one bedside lamp. He threw back the bedcovers, then turned to her.

Standing beside the bed, he cupped her face and kissed her. She tasted toothpaste; somehow in that race through the bathroom he'd managed to brush his teeth, too. She was in awe of his dexterity, because moving at that speed, if he hadn't cut his throat shaving, he should have at least jabbed himself in the eye with his toothbrush.

Despite that evidence of his urgency, he took his time kissing her. She put her arms around him and pressed her palms to his back, feeling the smooth damp skin, the flexing of muscles. During the kiss he lost the towel, and the belt of her robe came undone. Lily let her arms drop to her sides, and the robe slid off her shoulders, down her arms to pool around her feet. Then there was nothing between them except sighs and anticipation, and he switched out the last light, then lowered her to the cool sheets.

She reached for him as he got into bed beside her, letting her hands learn him until her eyes adjusted to the dark. She felt the crisp hair on his chest, his hard abdomen and sleek sides, slid her palms up his muscled arms and over the thick curves of his shoulders. He was busy with his own exploration, stroking her bottom, her thighs, then rolling her to her back and stringing kisses from her lips down her jaw and throat, then sliding his open mouth across her breast until one aching nipple slipped into it. He sucked leisurely, gently, and Lily made a soft sound of pleasure.

"I like that," she whispered, putting her hand on the back of his head to keep him there.

"So I see." He gave her other nipple equal time, leaving them both wet and hard, standing up like berries.

"What do you like?" She moved her hand lightly across his belly, just brushing across the tip of his straining erection, then reversed direction and searched out his flat nipples, teasing them until tiny points stood out.

"Yeah," he said roughly. "All of that." He shivered as ripples of sensation washed over him. Not at all reticent, he took her hand and moved it down to where he wanted it. She closed her fingers around his penis and he jerked, it jerked, pulsing in her grip. Experimentally she gave him a few lingering strokes; her fingers barely reached around him and her inner muscles clenched in response to that thickness.

He blew out a whistling breath and forcibly removed her hand. Lily growled a protest and reached for him with her other hand, managing another couple of strokes before he grabbed that hand, too. "You'd better let me cool down, or this will be over with before it gets started."

"After all the bragging you've done, you're good for only one round?" she murmured. "I'm shocked."

"Sassy, aren't you?" He pinned a hand on each side of her head, then levered himself over her. "I'll show you one round." At last, at last, his weight settled on her and her legs automatically parted to cradle him between them, her legs bending so her thighs gripped his hips. She could feel herself opening to him; he released her left hand to reach between them and position his penis. There was heavy pressure at the entrance to her body and she lifted herself into it, wanting to feel that first long, penetrating slide of flesh into flesh, but the pressure began to burn and nothing happened. He drew back a little and pushed again. This time she couldn't help a small gasp of pain as once again her flesh refused to accept him.

Chagrined, she felt her face begin to burn. "I'm sorry." She was embarrassed by her dryness. "It's always been difficult for me to just go with the moment. I can't seem to stop thinking."

He gave a rough little laugh, the sound puffing against her hair. He nuzzled her temple. "If *not thinking*'s a requirement, then I'm not doing it right, because I don't think I've ever stopped thinking. I take that back. For about ten seconds, I definitely don't think." His lips moved to her earlobe, and he nipped her with his teeth. "I'm the one who should apologize, darlin', for rushing you like this." His accent was stronger, a west Texas drawl slowing his speech. "A woman who hasn't made love in six years needs tender loving care, and I just skipped right over some mighty important steps."

"Steps?" He made it sound like programming a VCR. She thought about being indignant, but the little biting kisses he was giving her broke her concentration.

"Um-hmm." He was nipping at her neck now, then her collarbone. "Or rather, spots. Like this one right here." He lightly bit down on the ligament where her neck and shoulder joined, and Lily caught her breath as surprising pleasure roared through her.

She clutched his sides. "Do that again."

He was nothing but obedient, kissing and biting her neck until she was arching beneath him, her breath coming in quick pants. Those little bites were so arousing she thought she could almost climax just from them. He pinched her nipple, a hard, steady pressure that would have hurt just a few moments ago but now made her moan and push her breast against his hand.

He moved down her body, putting the tip of his little finger in her navel, biting the side of her waist, her hip, slipping his hands beneath her and squeezing her buttocks in a rhythmic motion. She tried to reach him to reciprocate some of the pleasure he was giving her, but he pushed her hands away. "Uh uh," he said in a rough, breathless tone. "I only have one step, and it's already been taken care of."

"What is it?" she managed to ask, though it was an effort to be coherent.

"Breathing."

She couldn't help herself, she had to laugh, and he punished her with a bite on the inside of her thigh that had the effect of stealing her breath and making her legs part even more. She knew what he was going to do, she'd been dying of anticipation as he worked his way down, but still, the first lick of his tongue shot sensation though her like electricity. She cried out, digging her heels into the mattress and arching her back off the bed. He captured her and dragged her closer for a deeper taste, a deeper probing with both tongue and fingers. The sense of penetration was acute, shivering through all her nerve endings like tiny shock waves that intensified with every slow in-and-out motion.

Oh, he was good. Even when she was ready for him, when she could feel the wetness between her legs, he seemed content to linger with kisses and caresses until she was writhing on the bed and all but begging him to stop, or not stop, it all seemed the same. Finally she grabbed his ears and rasped, "I'm ready," just in case he was in any doubt.

He turned his head and kissed her palm. "Are you certain?"

Infuriated, she sat up in bed. "Either do it now, or don't do it at all! You're driving me insane!"

He laughed and tumbled her back on the bed. Before she could recover her equilibrium, he was on her, pushing into her with a slow, inexorable pressure that made her breath hiss out of her lungs as he filled her. She held herself very still, her eyes closed as she tried to absorb all the sensations, the pressure and heat and heaviness.

He began a subtle back-and-forth motion, rocking inside her. Instinctively she tensed, tightening her inner muscles in an effort to contain him and control the act. He groaned, froze, then rasped out, "Do that again." This time it was he who held himself still while she loved him with that internal clasping. The act of tightening on him then consciously relaxing, then tightening again, brought her almost to the edge of climax–but not close enough.

He hooked his arms under her legs and held them high, taking total control. She couldn't limit the depth of his penetration in this position, couldn't lift herself to meet his thrusts, couldn't do anything except feel the long, slow strokes as he settled into a steady rhythm. He held himself positioned just high enough, in the perfect position for her to feel the maximum friction, yet the minutes passed and orgasm remained maddeningly just out of reach. Lily felt as if she were being pulled apart, the tension gripping her was so intense. His arms began trembling, his entire body was trembling, and she almost burst into tears as she realized he wouldn't be able to last much longer and she still hadn't been able to climax.

"I want to do it from behind you," he murmured, and pulled out. Before she could change positions, he lay down beside her and pulled her on top of him, on her back, with her head tilted back over his left shoulder. His hot breath teased her ear, and his hands stroked over her breasts, down her belly. He spread her legs, arranging them on either side of his, and reaching down, he held his penis in position while he pushed upward. She groaned as the thick length squeezed into her, shimmying in a paroxysm that carried her close to completion but stopped short yet again. She felt terribly exposed without him covering her. Cool air washed all down her heated body, her legs were spread wide, and with her head tilted backward, she was strangely disoriented, off balance.

"Shhh, I have you," he said in a reassuring rumble, and she realized she must have made a panicked sound. His hips flexed and rolled beneath her, working himself back and forth inside her. There was more of a tug in this position, a sharper sense of movement. He slid his right hand down her belly and curved his fingers down, between her legs, catching her clitoris in the fork of his first two fingers. He gently closed his fingers together, just enough, and held her as his strokes moved her up and down, back and forth, and the hot coil of sensation tightened inside her to an unbearable degree.

She made a strangled sound and dug her heels into the mattress, shuddering, tilting her hips down to take every inch of him she could, then surging upward against those maddening fingers. She was shaking from head to toe, her thighs quivering, her breath nothing more than sobs that caught in her throat. Closer, closer . . .

A low cry tore from her throat as she was abruptly hurled past the point of no return. Great pulsing waves radiated from her loins, ripping away her last vestiges of control. Finally,

finally–she was there and it was happening, more powerful than she remembered, blinding her to everything except the pleasure that held her racked and pierced.

Vaguely she realized she was crying, though she didn't know why. She was still shaking, so wrung out and limp she couldn't even lift an arm. She didn't have to. Swain slid out of and from under her, rolling on top of her and roughly pushing inside. His thrusts were hard and fast, taking him to the hilt each time. Sweat dampened his skin and he was shaking now, the way she had shaken, every muscle trembling as he drove deep and reached for his own pleasure. His rhythm frayed, disintegrated, and a long, deep groan rumbled in his chest, his throat, and with a harsh cry he arched back, pulsing inside her as he gripped her hips so hard his fingers left their marks on her skin. Then slowly he folded forward, still shuddering, jerking, his eyes closed as his trembling arms let his weight down on her.

His lungs were pumping like bellows, huge breaths going in and out. Lily still struggled for her own breath, trying to regain some use of her limbs, while her heart pounded so hard and fast she thought she might faint. She could feel her pulse even in her fingertips.

She had the dim thought that if this was to be her last orgasm, at least it had been a world-class one.

Finally she was able to lift her hand and weakly wipe the tears from her cheeks. Why on earth was she crying? Getting there had been a Herculean effort, but the end result had been worth it.

Face down beside her left ear, Swain groaned. "God. I felt that all the way down to my toes." He didn't lever himself off her, just lay there getting heavier and heavier. Lily didn't care. She wrapped her arms around him and held him as tight as she could.

"I'll get up in a minute," he promised in an exhausted voice.

"No," Lily said, but he was already laboriously moving off her to lie on his side facing her. He put one hand on her waist and pulled her to him, cradling her close, her head lying on his shoulder and arm.

"The first round is now officially over," he mumbled.

"I take it back. I don't think I can handle a second round," she managed to gasp, but his deep, even breathing told her he was already asleep. She took two deep breaths and felt herself sinking, joining him. For the first time in forever, she felt safe, wrapped tight in his arms.

27

LILY WOKE IN SWAIN'S ARMS, AND FELT AS IF SHE BELONGED there. She wished she could freeze time at that exact moment, so she never lost the sense of contentment and security. She didn't let herself think about the possible disaster the day might bring; she would do what she had to do, so there was no point in worrying about it. If she was lucky, tonight would be spent the same way last night had been.

To her surprise, she'd been up for two more rounds, though she was so sore now she almost regretted it. Almost. He'd awakened her at two o'clock by turning on the lamp, because this time he wanted to see her. She'd been embarrassed by the state she was in, sticky from going to sleep without having cleaned up, but he'd proved beyond a doubt that other than where cars were concerned, he didn't have a finicky bone in his body. "Sex is messy," he'd said with a slow smile as he'd hauled her back when she'd tried to leave the bed to go clean up. "And I'm the cause of it, so why should I mind?"

Having the lamp on didn't bother her, though somehow he'd known the first time would be easier for her in the darkness. She was thirty-seven, not a spring chicken, but she stayed in shape and her body type was naturally lean and small-breasted, so even when some parts started sagging, as they inevitably would, they couldn't sag very far. Certainly Swain seemed to appreciate every inch of her.

Climaxing the second time was easier, as if her body had remembered how. She wasn't as tense or desperate, plus Swain made it fun with his unabashed pleasure and very vocal appreciation. Afterward they had showered together, and she spread towels over the wet spots on the sheets before they got back into bed and slept for another couple of hours.

The third time, just after five o'clock, had been long and slow, all sense of urgency gone. She barely remembered stumbling back to bed afterward, and she had slept so soundly that if she dreamed, she didn't recall. Sunlight now spilled around the edges of the heavy curtains, making her wonder what time it was, but she didn't care enough to roll over and look at the clock.

He made an indistinct noise that was half sleepy man and half grumbly bear, then lifted her hair and kissed the back of her neck. "Morning," he rumbled, then nestled her closer.

"Good morning." She loved feeling all that muscular warmth at her back, loved the feel of his leg thrust between hers and the weight of his arm as he settled it back around her waist.

"Do I still have to drive that Fiat?" He sounded as if he were only half-conscious, but the subject had to be important to him for it to be the first thing he thought about upon awakening.

She patted his arm, glad her back was to him so he couldn't see her smile. "No, you get to drive any type of car you want."

"I was that good, huh?" he asked smugly, more awake now.

He deserved something better than a pat on the arm for that, so she reached back and patted his butt. "You were spectacular," she said with a faintly monotonous, mechanical drone in her voice. "Your technique was fabulous, and your penis is the largest I've ever seen. I am the luckiest woman in the world. This is a recording–"

He rolled over on his back and shouted with laughter. Lily slid out of bed and escaped to the bathroom while he was laughing, before he could retaliate. She looked at herself in the mirror and halted, struck by the softness of her features. One night of sex and she looked rejuvenated?

It wasn't the sex, she realized, though the deep relaxation of her body was a wonderful plus. It was Swain himself, the tenderness and consideration with which he'd treated her, and the feeling that she mattered to someone. It was the closeness, the link, the not being alone. For months now she had felt totally alone, removed from the world she could see around her as if nothing and no one could touch her, surrounded by a moat of pain and grief. Swain's enthusiasm, his personality, had pulled her out of that solitude, once again connected her with life.

Oh, damn, she was definitely falling in love with him. What a silly thing for her to do right now, with everything that was happening, but how could she stop it? She couldn't walk away, she needed his help, but even more she didn't *want* to walk away. She wanted everything he could give her, every minute. She couldn't even worry about whether he would be there forever, because what was forever? Today might be the extent of it for her, or tomorrow. All she had was now, and that was good enough.

Because there was only the one bathroom, she hurried so he could get in there. She didn't have any clothes in the bathroom and the bathrobe was on the floor beside the bed, so she had to walk out as naked as she'd walked in, which didn't matter because Swain hadn't yet bothered with clothes, either. He got up from the bed when she came out of the bathroom, his sleepy eyes lingering on her points of interest before he pulled her close for a long hug. His morning erection prodded her stomach, making her wish she wasn't so sore.

"Wanna take a shower together?" he said against the top of her head.

"I think I'd better take a long soak in the tub instead," she said ruefully.

He massaged her bottom, lifting her on her toes. "Sore, huh?"

"Oh, yeah."

"I'm sorry, I wasn't thinking. Twice was enough, I should've kept my hands to myself that last time."

"It was that third time that earned you your freedom from the Fiat." She stroked his ribs, moved her hands around to his back, and dug her fingers into the deep groove of his spine.

She felt his lips move against her hair. "In that case, consider your sacrifice worth it."

"Somehow I thought you'd say something like that." But she was smiling, too, as she rubbed her nose against his shoulder. "It's nice to know where I stand in your priorities."

He paused, then asked cautiously, "Was I supposed to say something really sweet right there?"

"You were, and you've failed in the romance department."

Another pause; then he nudged her with his erection. "Doesn't this count?"

"Considering you'd have that even if you were alone, no."

"It would already have gone down by now. You're what's keeping it up. See, I *am* romantic."

He was getting her back for her crack about the recording, but the slight shaking of his shoulders gave him away. She looked up into blue eyes that were sparkling with barely contained laughter, but since she was about to disgrace herself by giggling, she forgave him for it. She gave him a slap on the butt, then moved away to pick up the robe. "Get cracking, big boy. Are you hungry now, should I order room service?"

"I could definitely use some coffee, so you might as well order food at the same time." He checked the clock. "It's almost ten, anyway."

That late! She marveled at how well she had slept, but it also reminded her that her mystery caller could call at any time. While Swain was in the bathroom, she checked her cell phone, which she'd put in the charger the night before. The phone was on, and the service line showed a nice strong signal, so she hadn't inadvertently missed a call. She took the phone off the charger and slipped it into the pocket of the robe.

She called room service and put in an order for croissants and jam, with coffee and fresh orange juice. Swain hadn't professed a preference for anything other than traditional French fare for breakfast, so she went with that. In food, too, he'd proven to be remarkably sophisticated and adaptable. There was a lot he hadn't told her about his past, but then, she hadn't told him everything about herself, either, and probably never would. He was healthy, he was heart-whole, and for the moment he was hers. That was enough.

He poked his head out of the bathroom. "Do you want that soak now while I wait for room service, or do you want to wait until afterward?"

"Afterward. I don't want my soak interrupted by food."

"I'll shower now, then." He disappeared back into the bathroom, and a moment later she heard the shower running.

He came out just ahead of the arrival of their food, looking spiffy in black trousers and a simple white collarless shirt with the cuffs rolled up over his muscular forearms. He signed the check, while Lily stood with her back to the room looking out the window, then he showed the waiter out. He had just turned back from the door when Lily's cell phone rang.

She sucked in a deep breath and took the phone out of her pocket. A quick look at the window showed that the caller's number had been blocked. "I think this is it," she said, and flipped the phone open. "Yes, hello," she said, switching to French.

"Have you reached your decision?"

On hearing the mechanically distorted voice, she signaled to Swain with a quick nod and he came over to put his head right next to hers. She lifted the phone the tiniest bit away from her ear, so he could hear, too.

"I have. I'll do it, but on one condition. We must meet face-to-face."

There was a pause. *"That is not possible."*

"It will have to be possible. You're asking me to risk my life, but you aren't risking anything."

"You do not know me. I fail to see what a meeting would accomplish in the way of reassurance."

He was right about that, but she was already reassured. If Rodrigo had been the one making the call, he'd have jumped at her proposal for a meeting. Sending someone else to meet her, drawing her into the trap by using someone she didn't recognize, would have been a simple matter. This man was not Rodrigo, and wasn't working with Rodrigo.

She started to say that he was right, a meeting wasn't necessary, but Swain made an urgent signal and mouthed, "Meeting," then nodded his head. He wanted her to insist on the meeting.

She couldn't think of any reason why, but she shrugged and went along with him. "I want to see your face. You know mine, don't you?"

The caller hesitated, and she knew she'd guessed right. *"What does it matter if you know my face? I could tell you any name and you would not know the truth."*

That, too, was true, and she couldn't think of any logical reason for continuing to insist, so she went with illogic. "That's my condition," she said abruptly. "Accept or decline."

She heard him draw a deep, frustrated breath. *"I accept. I will be in front of the Jardin du Palais Royal tomorrow at two o'clock. Wear a red scarf and I will find you. Come alone."*

Swain shook his head, a determined expression on his face that told Lily he wouldn't budge on this.

"No," she said. "A friend will be with me. He insists. You are in no danger from me, monsieur, and he wants to be certain I am in no danger from *you.*"

The man laughed, which was transformed by electronics into a harsh, barking sound. *"You are difficult. Very well, mademoiselle. Are there any other conditions?"*

"Yes," she said, just to be contrary. "You wear a red scarf, too."

He laughed again and cut the connection. Lily closed the phone and blew out a breath. "It isn't Rodrigo," she said unnecessarily.

"Seems not. That's good. We may actually be getting a break."

"Why do you want to be there?"

"Because a man that reluctant to meet has something to hide, and I don't trust him." He picked up her coffee and handed it to her, then winked. "Guess what this means."

Lily blinked, still so focused on the call and its implications that she was at sea. "What?" she asked, bewildered.

"It means we have today." He clicked his coffee cup against hers in a salute. "And tonight."

With nothing to do but enjoy each other, he meant. A slow smile curved her lips. Moving to the window, she opened the curtains and looked out at the brightly sunny day. "If you get bored, we can make that trip to Disneyland," she said. She thought she could do it now, and enjoy the memories of Zia rather than suffering from them.

"Can you go naked there?" he asked, sipping his coffee.

Knowing exactly where this conversation was going, she pursed her lips and said, "Not likely."

"Then I'm not leaving this room."

28

THE NEXT DAY, SATURDAY, WAS ANOTHER COOL, SUNNY DAY THAT brought the tourists out in droves. Swain had thought tourists would have been thin on the ground this time of year, but evidently not. A lot of them had evidently felt the need to see the Royal Palace gardens, or maybe there was some sort of festival going on. There had to be something to account for the crowds.

Unfortunately, "in front of" the gardens turned out to be a rather vague instruction. The ornate garden park was large and bordered on three sides by shops, restaurants, and art galleries. One entered the park through a large courtyard dotted with striped stone columns, which he supposed was some artist's idea of . . . something, but they looked jarringly modern and out of place among the architecture of the 1600s. There was a long line of taller, more stately columns, too, which further reduced lines of sight. Between the columns and the throngs of people, many of whom seemed to be wearing a red scarf, spotting any one person was more difficult than he'd expected.

All in all, he considered this a piss-poor way to make contact, but it was somewhat reassuring. A professional would have picked a better way, which meant the guy they were dealing with was a rank amateur, possibly someone who worked at the Nervi laboratory and was alarmed by what was happening there. They would have a definite advantage over him.

Lily stood beside Swain, looking around. She was wearing sunglasses to disguise her eyes, as well as brown contacts in case she needed to remove the glasses, and the same cloche she usually wore to cover her hair. Swain looked down at her and caught her hand, pulling her closer to his side.

He thought of himself as an uncomplicated man in his wants and needs, his likes and dislikes, but there was nothing uncomplicated about this situation with Lily or the way she made him feel. He was caught in a hell of a dilemma, and he knew it. The best he could do was take care of one thing at a time, in order of importance, and hope to hell everything worked out. It couldn't work out with Lily, of course, and he felt a fist squeeze his heart every time he thought of what he had to do.

If only he could talk to Frank. Frank was alive, conscious, but heavily sedated, and still in ICU. In Swain's opinion "conscious" didn't exactly describe his condition, because according to Frank's assistant he could respond to such requests as "squeeze my hand" and occasionally mouth the word "water." To Swain, conscious meant you were holding conversations and having a rational thought process. Frank was a long way from there. He was in no shape for a phone call even if his cubicle had a telephone, which it didn't.

There had to be some other solution for Lily. He wanted to talk to her: sit her down, hold her hands, and tell her exactly what was going on. Things didn't have to go down the way Frank had decreed.

He didn't because he knew beyond a doubt how she would react. At best, she would walk away from him and disappear. At worst, she would try to kill him. Given her past and how wary and untrusting she was in general, he'd bet on the worst-case option. If she hadn't already been betrayed by a lover who had tried to kill her . . . maybe he'd have had a chance. He'd almost groaned aloud when she told him about that episode, because he knew it had set a terrible precedent in her mind. After barely escaping with her life that time, she wouldn't be inclined to give him the benefit of the doubt and talk before shooting.

Her emotions were on a hair trigger, and he knew it. She had been battered by loss and betrayal to the point that she had almost totally withdrawn, because she couldn't bear another blow. He knew very well that only circumstance had forced her to him, though he'd been quick to take advantage of the situation. She'd been starved for human contact even while she shunned it, her life totally devoid of laughter, fun, enjoyment. At least he could give her that, for a little while, and as he'd told her, he was one lucky son of a bitch because that was exactly what she could least resist.

The way she'd bloomed in the last few days broke his heart. He didn't flatter himself that the cause was his superior lovemaking technique or even his winning personality; it was the simple human touch that had done it, drawn her out of her shell, let her laugh and tease and accept affection as well as give it. But there was no way a few days could offset months, years of conditioning; she was still so delicately balanced that the least hint of betrayal would undo the trust he'd been building between them.

He was in a hell of a mess, because he was as caught as she was. If he'd touched her, she had also touched him. These past two nights, making love to her, had been . . . hell, they'd been the best time of his life. Losing her was going to rip his guts out, and he'd let things progress to the point that he'd lose her no matter what he did, because if he told her what he was and that he'd tracked her down, all she'd see would be betrayal. Son of a *bitch*. He'd thought he could handle it, have a good time and show her a good time for a little while, but he hadn't allowed for how important she would become to him. Nor had he known how emotionally battered she'd been, which would pretty much dictate her response if he spilled his guts to her now. He'd been stupid and arrogant, thinking with his little brain instead of his big one, and now he and Lily were both going to pay.

Okay, *he* deserved to pay, but Lily didn't. If anything, she was the good guy in this situation. So she'd killed a CIA asset; the son of a bitch had deserved to die, especially in light of what he'd been planning with the flu bug. Not that she'd known about that at the time, her motive had been pure revenge, but to Swain that was splitting hairs. What it came down to was, Lily hadn't quit. She just kept on throwing herself into the breach, willing to sacrifice herself to do what she thought was right. Not many people had that sort of moral fortitude, or plain stubbornness, whatever you wanted to call it.

The bottom of his stomach dropped out, and his heart started pounding as he realized exactly what had happened, how he'd been blindsided. "Jesus God," he said aloud. Despite the cool day, he broke out in a sweat.

Lily looked up at him, puzzled. "What?"

"I'm in love with you." He said it starkly, in shock at the realization of what he was feeling and the disaster looming in front of him. He ground his teeth together, his jaw locked as he fought to keep from blurting out everything. What he'd just said was enough to make him feel as if he'd leaped off a cliff.

Because of the sunglasses, he couldn't see her eyes very well, but he could tell she was blinking rapidly, and her mouth fell open a little. "What?" she repeated, but this time the word was very faint.

Her cell phone rang.

A fierce scowl twisted her face. "I'm *so* tired of these damn phone calls!" she muttered as she fished the phone out of her pocket.

Frustrated by the interruption, he grabbed the phone. "I know what you mean," he growled as he glanced at the little view window. He paused, staring at the number. He knew that number; it was one he'd called just a few days ago. What in hell–? "We have a number this time," he said to cover his pause; then he flipped the phone open and snapped, "Yeah, what is it?"

"Ah . . . perhaps I have the wrong number."

"I don't think so," Swain said, thinking furiously as the quiet voice confirmed his suspicion. "You were calling about a meeting?"

Perhaps the caller caught his voice, too, because there was

a long moment of silence, so long that Swain began to wonder if he'd cut the connection. Finally the caller said, *"Oui."*

"I'm the friend you were told about," Swain said, hoping this guy wasn't going to blow the whistle on him. He knew Swain was CIA; if he asked Lily about that, the jig was up.

"I do not understand."

No, he wouldn't, because his assumption–a correct assumption–was that Swain had been sent to France to take care of a problem, namely Lily. Yet here Swain was apparently working with her.

"You don't have to understand," Swain replied, "just tell us if the meeting is still on."

"Oui. I did not realize this park would be so–I am at the basin in the center. That is an easier meeting place. I will be sitting on the rim of the basin."

"We'll be there within five minutes," Swain said, and closed the phone.

Lily snatched the phone out of his hand. "Why did you do that?" she snapped.

"So he'd know for certain you weren't alone," Swain said. That was as good a reason as any, plus it was the only one that came to mind. "He's waiting for us at the center of the park, at the basin." He took her arm to lead her into the park.

She pulled her arm free. "Hold it."

He stopped in his tracks and looked back at her. "What?" He was afraid she was going to insist on talking about his out-of-the-blue statement, because in his experience women loved to talk things to death; but her mind was going in a completely different direction.

"I think we should stick to the original plan. You stay back, where you can watch me. Rodrigo may be slick enough to have known we'd be suspicious if he jumped at the chance for a meeting."

Let her meet alone with a guy who knew he was CIA? That wasn't going to happen.

"It wasn't Rodrigo," he said.

"How do you know?"

"Because the guy wasn't familiar with this park; he didn't know the entrance on a busy Saturday wasn't a great place to meet. Do you think Rodrigo wouldn't have checked that out? And look around you; would Rodrigo be likely to try kidnapping a woman with all these people around? This is someone who's probably on the level."

"Probably, but not certainly," she pointed out.

"Okay, look at it this way. If it *is* Rodrigo, would the presence of one person stop him from what he wanted to do?"

"No, but it would be impossible for him to do what he wanted without attracting notice."

"Exactly. Trust me, I'm not risking your life, or even my own. Rodrigo would have chosen somewhere secluded for a meet, because it would be stupid not to."

She mulled that over and finally nodded her head. "You're right. Rodrigo isn't a stupid man at all."

He laced his fingers with hers and started her moving. The feel of her slim hand in his made the bottom drop out of his stomach again, and her trust weighed on him like an anvil. God, what was he going to do?

"Just so you know, I heard what you said." She peered at him over the upper rim of her sunglasses. It gave him a jolt to see brown eyes looking back at him instead of pale blue ones, as if he'd been sucked into an alternate universe.

He briefly tightened his fingers on hers. "And?"

"And . . . I'm glad." It was simply said, and arrowed through him. Most women found it easy to say "I love you," much easier than men, but Lily wasn't most women. For her, loving and admitting to it must have taken every ounce of courage she possessed—and that was a lot of courage. She humbled him in a way he'd never expected, and had no idea how to handle.

They walked hand in hand into the huge formal park, which had once belonged to Cardinal Richelieu. The large basin with its center fountain sat in the middle. People strolled around, some just enjoying the gardens even though in November they weren't as lush as they would have been a few months ago, some sitting on the rim of the basin having their photographs taken to go in an album of vacation memories when they returned home. Swain and Lily strolled around the basin, looking for a lone man wearing a red scarf.

He rose to his feet as they approached. Swiftly Swain appraised him. He was a neat, trim man, about five-ten, with dark hair and eyes and the bony facial structure that shouted "French!" From the way his tailored jacket fit him, he either was unarmed or, like Lily, wore an ankle holster. He carried a briefcase, a detail that made him stand out from the rest of the park-goers; this was Saturday, not a time for office workers. He had no spy craft, Swain thought, or he'd know that he should blend in rather than stand out.

Their contact's dark eyes searched his face first, then went to Lily's. Surprisingly, his features softened. "Mademoiselle," he said, and he gave a little half-bow that was completely natural and respectful. Yeah, that was definitely the quiet voice Swain remembered. He didn't like the way the guy was looking at Lily, though, and he pulled her a little closer to his side in one of those gestures guys use to signal other men that they are edging into personal territory.

The Interpol man already knew his name, but to prevent a slipup in front of Lily that couldn't be explained, Swain said, "Call me Swain. Now, you know her name and you know mine. What's yours?"

The shrewd dark eyes studied him. The Interpol man didn't hesitate because he was unsure what to do, but because he was considering every angle. Evidently he must have decided there was no reason to be secretive, since Swain had his cell phone number and the resources to put a name with it if he chose. "Georges Blanc," the man said. He indicated the briefcase. "Everything you need to know about the system is in there, but after careful consideration I realize that a clandestine entrance is probably not feasible now."

Swain looked sharply around, making sure no one was within hearing. It was a good thing the man's voice was naturally quiet. "We should go somewhere more private," he said.

Blanc also looked around, and nodded his understanding. "I apologize," he said. "I'm not well-versed in procedure."

They walked toward a line of carefully manicured trees. Swain didn't care for formal gardens himself, preferring his nature in a more unruly state, but there were stone benches scattered about the park and he supposed on a quiet day there would be something serene about the setting. It seemed to appeal to a lot of other people, though this wasn't his cup of tea. They found one of those stone benches, and Blanc invited Lily to sit. He placed the briefcase beside her.

Suddenly alarmed, Swain stepped forward and seized the

briefcase, moving it away from Lily. He thrust it back at Blanc. "Open it," he ordered, his tone crisp and hard. A briefcase could easily contain a bomb.

Lily was on her feet and Swain moved so that she was behind him, at the same time reaching his hand inside his jacket. If the briefcase *did* contain a bomb, maybe he could shield her, though he doubted Blanc would explode a bomb while he himself was still standing so close. But what if Blanc didn't have the detonator, and someone watching them did?

Alarm flashed across Blanc's face, both at how fast Swain had moved and at the hardness of his expression. "There are only papers," he said, taking the briefcase and thumbing the catch releases. They sprang open and he lifted the lid, showing the sheaf of papers inside. There was an inner pocket and he held it open for Swain's appraisal, then riffled the papers. "You can trust me." He held Swain's gaze as he spoke, and Swain got the message.

Tension eased from his shoulders and he removed his hand from the butt of his weapon. "Sorry," he said. "I don't put anything past Rodrigo Nervi."

Lily punched him in the back. "What do you think you're doing?"

Trust her to get pissed because he'd tried to protect her. If she'd known what might be going on, she would have shoved in front of him to protect *him*, but she wasn't trained in this type of shit any more than Blanc was and for a couple of seconds she hadn't realized what Swain was doing. He'd be damned before he'd apologize for doing something she'd have done. He angled a narrow-eyed look at her over his shoulder. "Live with it."

She glared at him, then deliberately stepped around him

and once more sat down on the bench. "Please sit down, Monsieur Blanc," she said in her perfect French.

With an amused glance at Swain, Blanc did so.

"You said a clandestine approach might not be feasible now," Lily said, prompting him.

"Yes, the additional external security measures have made that difficult—especially at night, when there are additional guards at every entrance, in every hallway. There is actually less security during the day, when there are more workers."

That was logical, Swain thought. It wasn't good for their purpose, but it was logical.

"I propose to get you inside during the day."

"How are you going to do that?" Swain asked.

"I have arranged for you to be hired by the younger Nervi, Damone, who has arrived from Switzerland to aid his brother. Have you ever met him, mademoiselle?" he asked Lily.

She shook her head. "No, he was always in Switzerland. I gather he's something of a financial wizard. But why would he need to hire anyone for anything? Wouldn't Rodrigo do that, anyway?"

"As I said, he is here to shoulder some of the administrative burden. He wishes to have an outside firm look at the security measures and make certain they are as impregnable as it is possible to make them. Because this is for the protection of the laboratory, Rodrigo agrees."

"Rodrigo knows what I look like," Lily pointed out. "All of his employees do."

"But he does not know Monsieur Swain, does he?" Blanc said. "That is fortuitous. And I believe you are somewhat skilled at disguise?"

"To some degree," Lily said, surprised that he knew anything about that.

"So this Damone is going to hire us, sight unseen?" Swain asked doubtfully.

Blanc gave a slight smile. "I have been given the task of locating someone for him. He trusts me, and will not question my judgment. Damone Nervi himself will take you through security, into the laboratory." He spread his hands. "What could be better?"

29

"THIS ISN'T A SIMPLE JOB," SWAIN SAID. FOR THE SAKE OF PRIVACY, the three had repaired to a small café, where they sat at the most isolated table with their coffee and went over the brief-case's contents. They were using both French and English, having discovered this worked well for them. Blanc could express himself better in French, but Swain could understand it, and vice versa. Without appearing to think about it, Lily used both depending on whom she was speaking to. "It'll take at least a week to complete my shopping list," he continued.

To Swain's annoyance, Blanc immediately looked at Lily as if for confirmation. She shrugged and said, "I know nothing about explosives and demolition. Swain is the expert."

He hadn't told her he was an expert, but he appreciated the vote of confidence. As it happened, he did know his way around a detonator.

"The cover story you set up for Damone is good," he explained, "but now we have to back it up. From what you've said this Damone isn't stupid—"

"No," Blanc murmured. "Far from it."

"—and you can bet Rodrigo will at least be curious enough to check our credentials."

"At the least," Lily said wryly. "If he has time, he'll do a full-scale investigation."

"We'll have to make sure he doesn't have that time. We'll have to plant the explosives the first time we're in, because there might not be a second chance. Does Damone trust you enough that he'll take us into the laboratory *before* Rodrigo has a chance to investigate us?"

"He does," Blanc replied without hesitation. "I will tell him I did a thorough investigation myself."

Swain started to ask if Damone didn't know Interpol did no investigations, but swallowed the words because there was no way in hell he could explain to Lily how he knew Blanc was Interpol. Blanc wasn't the only one who had to tread lightly in these conversational waters.

"We'll need a panel truck or van, business cards, stationery, coveralls—all the outer requirements of a business. The van can carry everything we need; at least these blueprints of the complex give me an idea of the area we might have to cover. I don't suppose you know exactly where the lab in question is in the complex?"

Blanc shook his head. "Nor do I know if everything pertinent is in one area. Records may be scattered throughout the complex, though that would be shoddy record-keeping, wouldn't it?"

"Or smart, if there are now built-in redundancies, so if one set of records is destroyed there are backups. That's something we'll have to find out while we're there. Can Damone have Dr. Giordano himself give us a tour? Since it involves security for his own work, he would likely show us any redundancies so we could make certain they're properly protected," Lily said.

They were working with a lot of uncertainties here, but Swain remembered that Lily had a reputation for being able to read people. That was why, except for one thing, he'd been totally himself with her. He hadn't wanted her to detect any phoniness about him. Lily had met Dr. Giordano, gotten a sense of the man. He was proud of his work, she said; professionally it was sheer genius. So, yeah, he might well show them all of the safety measures in place for his research material. It had already been destroyed once; he wouldn't want that to happen again.

A worried expression grew in Blanc's eyes. "Will you set off the explosives with so many people around, or wait until night when there are fewer present?"

"We can't take the chance that someone will spot the packages if we leave them until night. They'll have to be detonated as soon as possible after placement."

"We could have a mock bomb-threat drill," Lily suggested. "Announce it immediately that at some undisclosed time during the day, the alarm will sound and they will be required to make a fast, orderly exit. If anyone sees something suspicious, they'll probably think it's part of the drill. In fact, we can make that part of the exercise: tell them that mock explosives are being planted throughout the building, and the test will be if all of them are spotted while the workers are going about their normal routine. They're not to conduct searches, just be alert, that sort of thing. A bonus to anyone who spots an explosive device. They're not to touch them, just report the location."

"Make the workers part of the plot?" Swain half-closed his eyes as he considered it. That would take a lot of uncertainty out of the plan, because then he and Lily would be *expected* to skulk around planting ominous-looking packages. Dr. Giordano might even show them some good hiding places for the explosives. The plan was so sneaky and brash that no one would be on guard against it. The biggest challenge would probably be disguising Lily well enough that Dr. Giordano didn't recognize her. "That's diabolical. I like it. We'd even have an excuse for taking in the explosives, if it's detected; we could show the workers exactly what Semtex or C-4 looks like, so they can recognize it in the future."

"You will use plastique?" Blanc asked.

"It's safest"—safest for the handler, that is—"and the most stable." Swain didn't know which he'd be able to get, Semtex or C-4, but as far as handling went, there wasn't a lot of difference between them. Both were stable, both were powerful, and both required detonators to go boom. Semtex might be more readily available here, since it was manufactured in the Czech Republic, but the new version also lost its plasticity after three years, so if Semtex was what he got, he'd have to make certain it wasn't too old to work.

"Set us up to meet with Damone a week from today," Swain told Blanc. "I'll be in touch with you if there's a delay in getting everything we need."

"You wish to meet with him on a Saturday?"

"If there are fewer workers in the complex on Saturday, that would be all the better."

"Yes, I see. I will try to arrange the meeting for that day."

"There is one other thing," Lily said.

"Yes, mademoiselle?"

"The million-dollar fee. I want it deposited in my account before we act. For one thing, we'll need the funds to buy everything we need."

Blanc looked startled.

"American," Lily specified. "That was the deal."

"Yes, of course. I will . . . see that it is done."

"This is my numbered account, and my bank." She scribbled down a name and number and gave it to him. "On Monday afternoon I will check my balance."

Blanc took the scrap of paper. Swain thought he still had a rather stunned look in his eyes, as if he couldn't believe Lily would actually take the money instead of acting out of the goodness of her heart. Swain figured she'd do the job even if she had to pay for the privilege, but since Blanc had offered to pay her, she wasn't fool enough to turn down that much money.

Swain paid for the coffee while Lily neatly placed everything back in the briefcase. She held out her hand to shake hands with Blanc, but the Frenchman instead carried her hand to his lips and kissed it. Exasperated, Swain reached out and freed her hand from Blanc's grip. "Cut it out. She's taken."

"So am I, monsieur," Blanc murmured. "I am not, however, unappreciative."

"I'm glad. Now go appreciate someone else."

"I understand," said Blanc, and again there was a deeper meaning behind his words.

Lily was chuckling as they walked away. "Frenchmen kiss hands. They don't mean anything by it."

"Bullshit. He's a man, isn't he? He means something by it."

"You'd know that from experience?"

"Oh, yeah." He took her hand himself. "Damn Frenchmen kiss everything they can. There's no telling where his lips have been."

"Does that mean I should boil my hand to get rid of the germs?"

"No, but if he kisses you again, I'll boil his lips."

She laughed softly, leaning against his arm. There was a slight blush on her cheeks, telling him that some part of her was enjoying his petulance. He put his arm around her shoulders and hugged her to him as they walked.

A week! Even though they would be busy the entire week, Swain felt as if he'd been given a reprieve. He'd have Lily for seven more nights, at least. In a week, Frank might be well enough to talk on the phone–if he didn't have any setbacks.

"I wasn't trying to cut you out of the money," Lily said abruptly, bringing his attention snapping back to her. "I'll transfer half to you."

"I didn't even think about the money," he said with total truthfulness. He was operating on Uncle Sam's time, here, even though his actions weren't sanctioned; he was already being paid. "Keep it. I have money, and from what you said you need to rebuild your savings." That also was the truth. Whether she would be alive to enjoy those savings was up in the air.

She'd have to be. He couldn't bear it any other way. Frank would just have to see reason.

That night when they were in the hotel room, she came up to him while he was sitting at the desk going over the blue-prints and schematics that had been in the briefcase. Blanc had very helpfully marked the function of each room on the blueprint of the laboratory complex, so Swain was able to narrow down the area they would need to cover. They wouldn't need to level the entire place, just select parts of it. For instance, there was no need for them to take out the bathrooms or meeting rooms; that would be a waste of plastique. When Swain had the total area condensed into square feet, then he'd be able to estimate how much plastique they needed.

Lily leaned against his back and draped her arms loosely around him, then planted a kiss below his ear. "I love you, too," she said in a somber tone. "I think. I'm pretty sure, though. It's scary, isn't it?"

"Damn terrifying." He dropped the pen he'd been using to figure the square footage of the rooms and turned in his chair so he could haul her down onto his lap. "I thought we'd just have some fun together; then the next thing I knew I was worrying if you ate enough for breakfast. You're like a Stealth bomber. My radar never showed a blip." He frowned down at her.

"Don't look at me," she protested. "None of this was my fault. I was minding my own business, having a little shoot-out in which I was outnumbered, when you charged into the middle of it. By the way, that was good driving, the way you slid the Jaguar around."

"I miss that car," he said reflectively. "And thank you, ma'am. That's called a state-trooper turnaround, for when you need to reverse directions and don't want to fool with details like stopping and backing."

"I thought you were happy with the Mercedes."

The afternoon before, they had returned the Fiat and he'd gone for yet another luxury car with a powerful motor, a Mercedes S-Class. Lily had actually been more comfortable in the Fiat, but evidently Swain's ego was directly connected to how many cylinders were under the hood of whatever car he was driving, so she'd gone along with it. The Fiat had been fun while it lasted, and since he was paying for it, she supposed he might as well drive what he wanted. She was just glad a Rolls hadn't been available.

"I am," he said. "Nobody makes a motor like the Germans. But the Jag was cool, too. And the Mégane handled good."

Lily wondered how they had segued from a discussion about being in love into one about cars. She looped her arms around his neck and nestled against him. Where did they go from here? And was there any point in worrying about the future until they were sure they had one?

"Stay in the–" Swain began.

"Don't even start," Lily interrupted. "There's no way I'm staying in the car."

"You'll be safer," he pointed out with impeccable logic.

"But you won't," she returned just as logically. He scowled at her. He hated that her logic was as impeccable as his. She scowled back, twisting her face into an exaggerated expression to mock him.

"I don't need anyone to cover me."

"Fine. Then I'll do it, since there's no danger."

"Shit." He scrubbed his hand over his face, then drummed his fingers on the steering wheel. At least the steering wheel belonged to a real car, a black Mercedes S-Class; that was the only comfort he could find at the moment.

This buy had him as nervous as a long-tailed cat in a room

full of rocking chairs. He had a prickling feeling on the back of his neck, from all his instincts screaming at him that this could get nasty. If he had been the only one involved, he could have handled it better, looked at it more as a challenge to his talents, but Lily was involved and that changed everything.

It had taken him three days to find a supplier for as much plastique as they needed, and the guy had insisted they meet in a bad section of Paris, where the explosives and money were supposed to change hands. As far as bad sections went, Swain supposed this was the pits. Slums were slums, and he'd been in a lot of them, but there was a bad smell here that put his back up.

The supplier's name was, supposedly, Bernard. It was a common enough name, so maybe it was his. Swain doubted it, but he didn't care if that was the guy's real name or not. All he cared about was making sure the plastique was usable, handing over the money, then getting out of there alive. Some unsavory characters made a very good living selling the same illegal merchandise over and over again; just kill the purchaser, then keep the merchandise and take the money.

Very probably some purchasers showed up with the reverse idea in mind: kill the seller, keep the money, and take the merchandise. Profit went both ways. That meant this Bernard would likely be as edgy as Swain. That was not good.

"I can't guard your back from here in the car," Lily said, checking what she could see of her reflection in the visor mirror. She was practicing her disguises. Tonight she was wearing black from head to foot under a black leather coat that had a boxy fit and disguised her lean but definitely female figure. Instead of her usual stylish boots she was wearing motorcycle boots with two-inch heels, which increased her height and were also clunky enough to obscure the size of her feet. She had bought skin-colored latex from a specialty store and was learning how to build up the lines of her jaw and brow to look more masculine. She was also wearing the brown contact lenses, and her blond hair was covered by a black knit cap that was pulled down almost to her eyebrows, which had been blackened to match the medium-size fake mustache she had glued under her nose.

He'd burst out laughing when he first saw her, but now that the only light was from the car's dash lights, the getup looked much more genuine. She looked masculine and scary. She had started to trim her eyelashes shorter so they wouldn't look so feminine after she put mascara on them to darken them, but Swain had stopped her. If anyone looked at her closely enough to notice her eyelashes, they were in trouble anyway.

She was holding her pistol in her hand. If she needed to use it, the seconds it took to pull it from her boot or from a pocket could be too long.

Swain was in a sweat about her stepping foot outside the car. If he'd had his way, he'd have had her encased in body armor, and maybe worn a vest himself. Unfortunately, he'd lost the argument about whether she should come with him or stay in the hotel, and now he'd lost the one about her staying in the car. It seemed as if he was losing every argument with her lately, and he didn't know what to do about it. He'd thought about tying her to the bed at the hotel, but he'd have to untie her eventually—and this was Lily Mansfield, not some soccer mom on vacation. He didn't know what she'd do, but he was sure he'd be in pain because of it.

A cold front had rolled in during the day, and what had been cool but pleasant had turned cloudy and downright cold as the sun set. Nevertheless, Swain had the windows partially down so they could hear anyone approaching the car, and he had angled the outside mirrors down, to catch anyone coming in low. As for the rest of the area, he and Lily just had to keep watch. The only direction from which he didn't expect attack was straight up, but that was only because he'd parked far enough away from the derelict buildings that no one could jump the distance.

He turned off the dash lights so there was complete darkness in the car, and reached for Lily's hand. She was wearing gloves, because her hands were another giveaway that she was a woman—and that was a problem they'd have to solve if she entered the laboratory as a man. He squeezed her fingers. She was steady as a rock, not showing a hint of nerves. When it came down to it, he'd rather have her at his back than anyone else who came to mind.

A car turned a corner, moving slowly toward them. The headlights were on bright, and he heard a familiar high-pitched whining noise. Bernard, the son of a bitch, was driving a Fiat.

Swain immediately started the engine and turned his headlights on bright, too. If Bernard didn't want them to see how many others were in the car with him, Swain returned the sentiment.

Since he had turned off the car's interior lights, too, there was no telltale light when Lily opened her door just enough for her to slide out; she sort of slithered, rather than getting out and standing up the way she normally would. With his brights blinding the occupants of the Fiat to that slight movement, they didn't see her leave the car and, still crouching down, move around to the rear.

Swain slipped low behind the steering wheel, positioning it so it blocked the top part of the headlights shining in his eyes. With that small difference in the glare, he could see the shapes of three heads in the Fiat.

The Fiat crept closer. When twenty feet separated the two cars, it stopped. To see if he could get Bernard to follow suit, he killed the brights on the Mercedes. The bright headlights had played a part, but now that part was finished. A few seconds later, the lights on the Fiat dimmed.

Well, thank God. At least now they weren't all blinded. He checked his rearview mirrors, but couldn't spot Lily anywhere.

The passenger door of the Fiat opened and a tall, heavyset man with a short dark beard got out. "Who are you?"

Swain stepped out of the Mercedes, George Blanc's briefcase in his left hand. He didn't like not having the engine block for cover, but took some comfort in the fact that the other guy had only a car door between him and a bullet, too—which wasn't saying much. A bullet went through a car door like a hot knife through butter. The only part of a car that provided much protection was the motor. "Swain. Who are you?"

"Bernard."

Swain said, "I have the money."

Bernard said, "I have the merchandise."

Jesus. It was all Swain could do not to roll his eyes. They sounded like a bad spy movie.

He wore his weapon in a shoulder holster under his leather coat, which was why he'd kept his right hand free. He was acutely aware, though, of the two other men sitting in the Fiat.

Bernard didn't have a weapon in his hands, but Swain was damn certain the two men in the car did.

Bernard didn't have *anything* in his hands. "Where's the merchandise?" Swain asked.

"In the car."

"Let's see it."

Bernard turned back to the car and opened one of the passenger doors. He pulled out a small duffel bag that was bulging with something. Until Swain saw for himself, he wasn't assuming the bag was full of plastique.

"Open the bag," he instructed.

Bernard grunted and set the bag on the ground, then unzipped it. The headlights from the two cars plainly showed the bricklike contents, wrapped in cellophane. "Take one out," Swain said. "From the bottom, please. Then unwrap it."

Bernard made an impatient sound, but he reached into the duffel, scrabbled around, and pulled out one of the bricks. He tore off the cellophane covering.

"Now pinch off a corner and roll it between your fingers," Swain instructed.

"It's new," Bernard said resentfully.

"I don't know that, do I?"

Another impatient noise. Bernard tore a corner from the brick of plastique and rolled it into a ball. "There, you see? It is still malleable."

"Good. I appreciate your honesty," Swain said with heavy irony. He opened the briefcase to show the money inside. American dollars, as specified, eighty thousand of them. Why did no one want payment in euros? He closed the briefcase and latched it.

Bernard stuck the ball of plastique back on its mother brick, and dropped it into the duffel. A slow smile moved across his face. "Thank you, monsieur. I will take the money now, and if you're very careful, all will go well–"

"Monsieur." The voice was Lily's, so quiet that only he and Bernard could hear it. "Look down."

He froze at the intrusion of that unexpected voice. He glanced down, but couldn't see anything; the headlights prevented it.

"You can't see me, can you?" Lily's voice was so low that if he hadn't known she was a woman, Swain wouldn't have been able to tell. "But I can see you. At this angle, I am afraid that my best shot is at your testicles. The bullet would angle upward, of course, tear out your bladder and colon, part of your intestines. You might live, but the question is, would you want to?"

"What do you want?" Bernard croaked, though of course he knew.

"Just the merchandise," Swain said. He felt as if he might croak the words himself. Lily's threat had made his blood run cold. "The money is yours. We aren't cheats, and we don't like to be cheated. Very calmly, we will make the exchange. Then you will tell your driver to back the car away, and you will walk beside it. Do not get in the car until it is at the end of the block. Is that understood?"

As long as Bernard wasn't in the car, he was a clear target. Walking alongside it was a guarantee that his driver wouldn't ram the Mercedes while Lily was still under it. The Mercedes was heavier, but a solid blow by the Fiat would still slide it some distance.

Warily Bernard approached. "Do not do anything!" he said, raising his voice for the benefit of his cohorts in the Fiat.

Swain extended the briefcase with his left hand, and Bernard extended the duffel bag with his left. Swain let go of the briefcase and for a split second Bernard was holding both brief-case and bag, but then Swain's left hand closed over the duffel's strap and he took custody of the bag. His right hand was inside his coat.

Bernard backed away, clutching the briefcase. "We have honored our agreement," he babbled. "There is no need to panic."

"I'm not panicking," Swain said calmly. "But your car isn't backing up, either, so a panic attack could be coming on."

"Idiot!" Bernard said fiercely, whether to his driver or Swain was a toss-up. "Back up to the corner, slowly. Do not shoot!" He was probably imagining a hot bullet plowing into his crotch.

"Lily," Swain hissed. "Get out from under the car, now!"

"I already am," she said from the other side of the car as she opened the door and slid inside.

Shit, she hadn't waited to see if Bernard did what he was told, but then how many men would ignore that particular threat? Swain tossed the duffel bag into her lap, then swiftly got in and slammed the transmission in reverse, spinning the car around with a sharp turn of the wheel, then accelerating with a squeal of rubber. Behind them, a car door slammed; there was a high-pitched whine as the Fiat's engine was revved up and it took off in pursuit. Swain thought it sounded like a sewing machine. Then a sharp crack sounded behind them.

"The fucker's shooting at us," Swain said grimly. If he had to change cars again, he was going to be seriously pissed.

"That's okay," Lily said, lowering the window and rising to her knees. "I'm shooting back." Shooting from a moving plat-form at a moving target was more along the line of asking for a miracle than using any real skill, but she levered herself half out of the window, steadied herself as best she was able, and squeezed off a carefully aimed shot. Behind them, the Fiat swerved wildly before once more straightening out, telling them that she'd scored at least a windshield.

Swain put the gas pedal to the floorboard and let all the horses run. The Fiat rapidly fell behind, and Swain snickered as he imagined them all pedaling frantically, knees working up and down.

"What's so funny?" Lily asked.

"If I'd still been driving the sewing machine, we'd never have made it."

30

"YOU SCARE THE HELL OUT OF ME," SWAIN SAID CROSSLY, STRIP-ping off his leather coat and tossing it across the bed, then shrugging out of his shoulder holster.

"Why is that?" Lily asked mildly, succumbing to an impulse she had every time she saw his coat. She picked it up and stroked the butter-soft leather, then slipped it on. The garment was too large, of course, hanging off her shoulders, and the sleeves reached way past her hands, but it was warm from his body and the feel of the leather was so scrumptious she almost purred.

"What are you doing?" he asked, diverted.

"Trying on your coat," she replied, giving him a look that said *Duh*. What did it look like she was doing?

"Like there was any way it was going to fit?"

"No, I just wanted to feel it." She pulled the edges together and stepped in front of the mirror, then had to laugh at her reflection. She was still wearing the mustache and black street clothes, and the knit cap pulled down over her hair. She looked like a cross between a street punk and Charlie Chaplin.

Gingerly she peeled off the mustache and latex, then removed the knit cap and ran her hands through her hair to fluff it. She still looked like a clown, so she removed the coat and tossed it back on the bed, then sat down and began removing her boots.

"Why do I scare you?" she asked, returning to his previous statement.

"*You* don't scare me; I'm scared *for* you. Though my balls did draw up when you told Bernard where you were going to shoot him, but I guess any man would have that reaction. Scared the hell out of *him*, anyway. Jesus, Lily, what if the Fiat had rammed the car while you were under it? Do you know how–What are you doing?"

"Taking off my clothes," she said with that *Duh* look again. She was down to her underwear and she unhooked her bra and dropped it on the bed, then skimmed out of her panties. Totally naked, she picked up his coat again and slipped it on, then walked back to the mirror.

There, that was more like it. The coat still swallowed her, but now it looked sexy, with her tousled hair and bare legs. She put her hands into the pockets and hunched her shoulders, then rolled her neck. She turned around to get a back view. "I love this coat," she crooned, lifting the hem just enough to show the beginning curve of her ass. She felt breathless and a little too hot, as if someone had raised the thermostat setting in the room. She lifted the hem higher.

"You can have it," he said hoarsely. His eyes were glazed. He came up behind her and gripped her buttocks in both hands. "You just can't ever wear it when you have other clothes on."

"That's awfully limiting." She had all she could do not to pant. Her nipples were so hard they ached, and he hadn't even touched them. Where had this intense sexual need come from? She didn't know, but she felt as if she would die if he didn't enter her.

"Take it or leave it." His palms were hot as he kneaded the rounded cheeks.

"Well, okay, I'll take it." She took her hands out of the pockets and stroked the sleeves. "You drive a hard bargain."

"That's not all I drive that's hard," he muttered, reaching between them to unzip his fly. "Bend over."

Because she was all but melting, her inner muscles clenched tight against the surging lust that gripped her, she bent over and braced her hands against the wall, going up on her tiptoes while he bent his knees. She caught her breath as he worked the broad head of his penis into her, then with a long, steady push sank to the hilt. He gripped her hips, anchoring her as he pulled back and thrust again.

Her feet almost came off the floor, and her head bumped the wall. He swore and slid one arm around her hips, holding her to him as he swung her around and took her to the bed. He didn't pull out, didn't change their basic positions, just bent her over the bed and began pumping.

Normally she needed direct stimulation in order to climax, but she was so ready for him just the friction of those long strokes was doing it for her. There was something about the combination of adrenaline, the sensuous leather on her bare skin, the knowledge that she was naked except for his coat, while he was still fully clothed, the primitive position, that was sending her responses soaring. She clenched her legs together, tightening herself around him, and the feel of that next stroke squeezing him deep into her was all that was needed. Choking back a scream, she buried her face against the bedspread and gripped fistfuls of fabric as the spasms of release shook every muscle in her body.

Swain leaned over her, bracing his hands on each side of her shoulders, driving so strongly that the impact of each thrust shuddered through her. He made a guttural sound, his penis growing impossibly hard; then he began short-stroking and his back arched and he began to climax, gripping her hips hard and grinding against her.

Five minutes later, they both managed to stir. "Don't move," he said thickly, drawing back and sliding the leather coat up so he could look at her bottom. He groaned and shuddered. "Oh, yeah, I think I've just discovered a fetish."

"Mine or yours?" she managed to say. Little lightning bolts were still zinging through her and she suspected the same thing was happening to him, because he hadn't softened very much.

"God, who cares?" He blew out a breath and gripped her buttocks hard, spreading the cheeks and dragging his thumbs down the crease until they met where her sensitive flesh was stretched tightly around his erection.

Her entire body flexed at the sensation as he massaged her; then gradually she relaxed under the soothing ministration. "This is depraved," she murmured sleepily. "We were shot at tonight; we should be upset, not turned on."

"Adrenaline does funny things to the system, and you have to burn it off somehow. But if this is how you react, I'll start shooting at you myself."

She shook with laughter, making him slip out of her. Groaning, he straightened and began to pull off his clothes. "C'mon, let's take a quick shower. I worked up a sweat."

She shrugged out of the leather coat and went with him into the bathroom. She'd have liked a long soak in the tub, but was afraid she'd fall asleep, so she settled for a shower. Refreshed, she put on clean underwear and one of his shirts, and a pair of socks so her feet wouldn't get cold. The room was untidy, with clothes scattered everywhere, but she wasn't in the mood to pick them up, and other than hanging up his leather coat–he had to take care of that coat–evidently neither was he. Instead, after pulling on a pair of pants and nothing else, he opened the duffel bag and began testing the bars of Semtex.

The good bars went on one side of him, the bad ones on the other. After all the bars were out of the duffel, there were only five bars that were too old to be used. "We're okay," he said. "There's enough of the good stuff. I allowed for some of it to be bad, just in case." He began packing the good bars back into the duffel.

Lily nudged an old bar with her toe. "What are we going to do with these?"

"I guess putting them in the trash might not be too smart. The only way I know of to dispose of plastique is burn it or blow it up, so I guess we'll have to take them with us to the laboratory, try to detonate them with the others. Even if they don't blow, they'll burn in the fire." He had acquired a combination tool–knife, pliers, miniature saw, and she didn't know what else, all in one handy-dandy implement that was banned on all airlines–and he used the blade to notch the old blocks so he wouldn't get them confused with the others. Then he replaced them in the duffel, and stowed the duffel on the top shelf of the closet.

"I hope the hotel's too classy to have nosy maids," he said, then yawned. "I could use some sleep. How about you?"

Lily had gotten progressively sleepier since getting out of the shower, and his yawn triggered hers. "Fading fast. What's our next step?"

"Detonators, radio controlled. We'll have to be a safe distance away when I set off the charges, and running hundreds of yards of det cord all through the lab might make someone suspicious. Once we have the hardware, then we'll work on the peripherals: the business cards and coveralls, the van. They won't be that hard to get, and a magnetic sign on the side of the van will take care of the customization."

"There's nothing else we can do tonight, then." She yawned again. "I definitely vote for bed." Now that the adrenaline rush was gone and the bout of earthy sex had relaxed her, she felt as if her bones were turning rubbery. She turned toward the bed and left him to take care of the lights. She was so tired all she did was pull off her socks; then she fell into bed.

She was vaguely aware of him peeling her out of his shirt, then skimming her panties down and off. She could have slept comfortably in both, but liked being naked in his arms. She sighed as he got into bed and cuddled her close to him. Her hand drifted across his chest. "Love you," she mumbled.

His arms tightened around her. "I love you, too." She felt his lips brush her temple; then it was lights-out for her.

Swain lay awake for a long time that night, holding her close and staring into the dark.

On Saturday, D-day, Lily took her time in front of the makeup mirror. The disguise had to be as good as she could make it, or this wouldn't work. If Dr. Giordano spotted her, all bets were off.

Her options had been either to cut her hair short and dye it or to buy another wig. She didn't mind coloring her hair, but she didn't want to cut it as short as a man's unless there was nothing else to be done. Luckily, very good wigs were available in Paris. The one she bought was longish for a man, but not inordinately so. Nor had she wanted to duplicate the brown color she had used as Denise Morel, or her own blond color. That left black or red. She had opted for black, as it was a much more common color than red. In fact, most of the world's population had black hair. Over the wig she wore a cap printed with the initials of the fictitious security company Swain had invented, Swain Security Contractors, SSC. He had gone with an American name, since there was no way he could convince anyone he was anything but American.

She had practiced with the latex of the sort used in movie makeup. She was nowhere near as good as a makeup artist, but she didn't have the luxury of years of practice to perfect her technique. She could widen her jaw a tad, build up the bridge of her nose so she had a classic Roman profile instead of a near-beak—which was the only way she could think of to disguise her profile, which was every bit as distinctive as her eye color—darken her brows and lashes, and add the mustache to hide her full upper lip. She had decided against building up her brow ridge, because she never could get it right and always looked Neanderthal. Dark brown contacts–darker than the hazel brown she had worn as Denise Morel–and wire-framed glasses completed the facial disguise. She had to be skillful with the base that colored the latex the same shade as her skin, because she didn't want anyone to notice that she was wearing makeup.

She had even covered the tiny holes in her pierced earlobes with the latex. A man might have one ear pierced, might even wear an earring to work, but most men definitely did *not* have both ears pierced. She supposed some did, but she didn't want anything about her to attract attention.

The cold spell that had ushered in December was still with them, which was a blessing. To hide her figure she had wound a wide elastic bandage around her breasts, and the dark blue coveralls she wore were loose enough to disguise the shape of her hips. The weather was cold enough that she added a light-weight fiber-fill vest over the coveralls, and that last touch completely hid her figure. Thick-soled work boots with lifts added three inches to her height.

Her hands were a problem. Her nails weren't polished and she had clipped them very short, but her fingers were slender and undeniably feminine. Because of the weather she could wear gloves while she was outside, but what about inside? She couldn't help Swain plant the charges and keep her hands in her pockets at the same time. The best she could do was use blue eyeshadow to outline the veins on the backs of her hands and make them look more prominent and, as a crowning touch, add adhesive bandages to two of her fingers to give the impression that she sported the nicks and cuts of someone who did work with her–his–hands.

At least she wouldn't have to talk much. Swain was the

mouthpiece; she was the labor. She could pitch her voice into a lower register, but that was hard to maintain. To coarsen her voice for when she *did* have to talk, she had forced herself to cough enough to irritate her throat.

Swain, of course, thought her hoarse voice was sexy. She was beginning to think she could sneeze and he would find it sexy. As often as he'd made love to her over the past week and a half, she suspected he'd lied about his age and was really just twenty-two, with premature gray in his hair. Not that his attention wasn't flattering; in fact, she soaked it up like a plant starved for rain.

However, it wasn't as if they hadn't been doing anything other than going at it like bunny rabbits. Either Swain had a talent for locating the sleazoids in the city, or he had some really questionable acquaintances. While Lily—always disguised—had handled the peripheral things they needed, such as locating a van that fit their requirements and having two magnetic signs made, getting the business cards printed up as well as forms with very official-looking technical checklists on them and "SSC" at the top, clipboards, a variety of tools, their coveralls and boots, Swain had been associating with some very rough characters in order to buy the detonators they needed.

He had wanted to build the remote control himself, something he said was easily done with the remote-control system from any radio-controlled toy—such as a car or an airplane, available in any good toy or electronics store—but decided that using a custom control would look more professional, so he had forked over the money required, and bitched about the cost for days.

Then, going by the information contained in the blueprints,

he had set about determining where the charges should be placed, and how strong they should be. Lily had never really thought about demolitions from a mathematical standpoint, though she'd known Averill had taken pride in calculating the strength of his charges to exactly what was required to do the job, and nothing more. Swain had explained it all, reeling off numbers as if they were general knowledge: this much Semtex would do this much damage. He used the terms *plastique* and *Semtex* interchangeably, but when she asked, he acknowledged that they weren't exactly the same. C-4, plastique, and Semtex were all in the same family of explosives, but *plastique* was the more widely known term and was used all-inclusively, but incorrectly. Lily hated when details were wrong; too often her life had depended on getting the details right, so she insisted he say Semtex when he meant Semtex. He'd rolled his eyes, but humored her.

He'd spent hours showing her how and where to place a charge and set the detonator. The detonator was the easy part, but he was very particular about where the charges went. He had numbered the locations, then prepared the charges for each and labeled each charge with the number corresponding to where he wanted it to go. They had studied until they could reel off each location and its number without hesitation, memorized the blueprints, then driven out into the country, where he had marked off the distances to give them a better feel of the size of the complex and how long the job would take.

The good news was, they had a cover for being in the complex. The bad news was, depending on what they found when they got in there, placing all the charges could take a couple of hours or more. The longer they were in there, the better the chance of discovery. Swain was safe; Lily was not, especially if for some reason Rodrigo showed up. He would know from Damone that "security experts" were touring the facility, and he might be curious. If he did appear, Swain would handle the meet-and-greet while Lily busied herself elsewhere and hoped Rodrigo wouldn't insist on meeting the other "expert."

Dr. Giordano was the other danger, as far as recognizing Lily was concerned. Likewise, she would try not to attract his attention, though that would be more difficult. After all, the facility was his and his work was his pride and joy. He would be very interested in Swain's opinion of the security measures in place. Since Swain was supposedly the owner of SSC, he would be more the focus of attention than Lily, but she couldn't hope to escape completely.

Neither of them had forgotten that this was to be Dr. Giordano's last day on earth. Lily remembered how kind he'd been to her when she'd been so ill, but at the same time she knew he was at the heart of an evil scheme. So long as Giordano was alive, the knowledge of how to mutate a virus so it would pass from human to human could be used to produce a pandemic. If not avian influenza, then it would be something else. Viruses were deadly enough without his help. The pandemic might occur anyway, at any time, but she'd be damned if she would let it be deliberately timed so someone would make a lot of money.

The plan was, after the charges were set, they would hold a mock bomb-threat drill, timing how fast the buildings could be emptied. When everyone was outside, Swain would detonate the charges and almost simultaneously Lily would execute Dr. Giordano. The percussion and fire from the explosions would certainly cause panic, perhaps some injuries. They themselves would slip in earplugs before detonation, and make certain they were standing behind something for shelter. In the confusion they would get into the van and drive away–they hoped. Nothing was taken for granted.

A luxury hotel wasn't the best place they could have chosen to prepare explosive charges. Everything had to be tidied away every day before the arrival of the housekeeping service, and they didn't want to put the charges in the van as they were completed, in case the van was broken into. The last thing in the world they wanted was some punk in possession of that much Semtex.

"Are you ready, Charles?" Swain asked. *Charles Fournier* was the name they had chosen for Lily. Swain got such a kick out of it he'd been calling her Charles even when they were alone.

"I think this is the best it's going to get," she said, getting up from the vanity and pirouetting for him as best she could in the heavy work boots. "Do I look okay?"

"Depends on your definition of 'okay,' " he said. "I wouldn't ask you out on a date, if that's what you mean."

"That'll do," she said, satisfied.

He grinned. "I don't even want to kiss you. That mustache gives me the willies." He had just finished packing the charges, some in the duffel bag and some in a box. The detonators were in a separate box, and as a precaution he'd taken the batteries out of the remote control.

He was dressed in coveralls that matched hers, with *SSC* embroidered on the left breast pocket, but underneath he wore a white dress shirt and a tie, to denote he was the boss and draw attention his way. The coveralls were unzipped enough to reveal the tie, and they were loose enough to hide the line of the shoulder holster he wore. She had opted for her familiar ankle holster, though with these boots, getting to her pistol was more difficult than usual. They weren't entering a fast-draw competition, though; when the time came, if everything was working right, she'd have plenty of time to pull her weapon.

He carried the duffel bag and the box containing the charges, while she carried the box with the detonators. They had the elevator to themselves, but they didn't indulge in any small talk, or go over the plan one more time. They each knew what they had to do.

"You drive," Swain said when they reached the van, taking the keys from his pocket and tossing them to her.

Her eyebrows went up. "You're trusting me to drive?"

"A: I'm the boss and I'm the driven, not the driver. B: a van's no fun to drive."

"That's what I thought," she said drily. The van must handle as agilely as a beached whale for Lucas Swain to have willingly turned over the keys.

They were supposed to meet Damone Nervi at the complex at three PM. Swain had chosen that time because in the afternoon people are tired and less alert than they are in the morning. When they reached the complex, Lily couldn't help looking at the small park where the gun battle had erupted just two weeks before. The incident had been mentioned in the news; then when no additional excitement was added by someone dying, it had been completely dropped the next day. She was pleased to see that even though it was a weekend, the cold weather had kept most people from enjoying the park. It was mostly deserted, except for the very occasional hardy soul walking a dog. The fewer people who were about, the better.

As they approached the gate where two guards waited, she coughed several times again, to roughen her voice. One guard held up his hand and she obligingly eased to a stop, then lowered her window. A blast of frigid air made her glad she was wearing the vest. "Monsieur Lucas Swain to see Monsieur Nervi." Before she could ask, Swain handed over his international driver's license for the guard to check. She fished out her new fake license and handed it over, as well.

"Fournier," the guard said, reading the name off the license. They checked the names against a list, which, she noticed, had only the two names on it, so completing their task didn't take very long.

"Go to the main entrance on the left," the guard instructed, returning the licenses to them. "Park in the slot marked for visitors. I will call Monsieur Nervi and notify him of your arrival. Beside the door is a buzzer; press it and someone inside will release the lock for you to enter."

Lily nodded as she slipped the license back into her pocket, and raised the van window to shut out the cold air. She coughed several more times, because she didn't think she had sounded hoarse enough when talking to the guard. The more she coughed, the worse the cough sounded, as if her throat was getting into the spirit of things. It was already a little sore, so she needed to be careful not to overdo.

Two men stepped out of the entrance. One was Dr. Giordano. "That's the doctor on the left," she said to Swain. "The other man must be Damone Nervi."

There was, in fact, a strong family resemblance, but where Rodrigo was a very good looking man, Damone Nervi was probably the most handsome man she had ever seen, though in no way was he effeminate. His looks were classic, from his thick black hair to his smooth olive-toned skin. He was tall and trim, elegantly dressed in a double-breasted charcoal gray suit that draped on him the way only the Italians could get a suit to fit. Dr. Giordano was smiling in welcome, but Damone's face was set in an aloof, rather stern expression.

"Something's off," Lily murmured.

"How?" Swain asked.

"Supposedly we're here at Damone's insistence, so he shouldn't look as if we're as welcome as the plague."

"An apt simile," he observed. "Yeah, I see what you mean. The doctor's smiling, Damone isn't. Maybe he isn't a smiley type of guy."

Sometimes the most simple explanation was the best one, but Lily couldn't shake her vague uneasiness. She parked the van in the appropriate slot and tried not to be obvious as she studied the two men.

Swain didn't wait. He left the van and strode confidently to the entrance, where he gave both men a brisk handshake. His bearing had changed, Lily realized, the habitual lazy saunter had been replaced by a walk that said, "get out of my way." Everything about his body language had subtly changed, and he looked like an aggressive, no-nonsense businessman.

According to their plan, she got out and went to the back of the van, opening the doors and getting out two clipboards that each held a thick sheaf of printed forms, plus two circuit testers that were totally useless for anything they were supposed to be doing but which Swain had decided looked impressive. They might even test a circuit or two, just to look as if they were doing something.

Laden with this paraphernalia, taking care she held every-thing as a man would hold it rather than clutching the clipboards to her chest as women did, she approached the three men. "My associate, Charles Fournier," Swain said, indicating her. "Damone Nervi, Dr. Giordano. The doctor has agreed to give us a tour, show us all the security measures in place in order to save time."

Her hands were occupied to prevent her from shaking hands, so everyone contented themselves with nods and greetings. Dr. Giordano was still relaxed and welcoming; if anything, Damone's expression had gotten more stern. Lily's uneasiness grew in proportion. Why was Damone acting as if this "inspection" hadn't been his idea from the beginning?

Damn. Could all of this have been orchestrated simply to draw her into a trap, into a private building where anything could happen to her and no one would ever be the wiser? Was Rodrigo even more cunning than she'd imagined? She had to admit that if so, he'd merely borrowed a page from her own book and drawn her into the trap by not jumping at the first few chances to capture her. Taking her off the street would have been noticed, and while Rodrigo had the political capital to make an incident go away, why spend it when he could simply be patient and lure her into a place where no one would notice anything? For all she knew, the lab was empty of personnel and the vehicles in the parking lot were just window dressing.

If she had miscalculated, she had caused not only her own death but Swain's also. She thought of all that laughter and zest for life being snuffed out, and went cold inside. The world would be a darker place without Lucas Swain in it. If anything happened to him because of her–

But now Damone had turned away, and Dr. Giordano was chiding him for being so morose because his fiancée had cancelled a scheduled visit. "Perhaps you should visit her," the doctor teased, slapping Damone on the back. "Women like it when we men come to them."

"Perhaps tomorrow," Damone said, shrugging and looking faintly sheepish.

Lily relaxed. Her imagination had been running away with her; Damone was simply in a bad mood because his girlfriend hadn't visited.

Dr. Giordano pressed a series of numbers on a keypad at the door, and it buzzed open. "We used to each have a card which we slid through a scanner, but people were forever losing their cards and the security company decided a keypad would be more secure," he said as he stepped inside and they followed.

"That's true," Swain said, "so long as no one gives the entry number to unauthorized people. However, I've been here two minutes, and I can already tell you that the number sequence for entry is six-nine-eight-three-one-five. You didn't block the keypad with your body when you keyed in the number. Even worse, the keypad is tonal. I could hear it." He pulled a tiny digital recorder from his pocket. "I activated this when you started to unlock the door, just in case." He pressed the *play* button and a series of six different-toned little beeps sounded. "With this, I could open the door even if I didn't know what the numbers were."

Dr. Giordano looked acutely embarrassed. "I assure you, I'm not usually so careless. I did not think I should be on guard against you."

"You should be on guard against everyone," Swain replied, really getting into his role. "And the keypad should be changed so you don't hear the tones. That's the real weakness."

"Yes, I see." Dr. Giordano pulled a notebook from the pocket of his lab coat and made a notation in it. "I will have this taken care of immediately."

"Good. After the tour, there are two exercises I'd like to conduct, if I may. My associate and I will plant fake explosives in various parts of the complex, and we will see how long it takes any of the workers here to spot something they consider suspicious. If no one notices anything, I'd like to make an announcement about what we have done, and invite them to look around, and notify you whenever they spot anything out of the ordinary. That raises their awareness, first knowing that these packages were put in place without being noticed, and again by in effect teaching them where to look and what to look for. Lastly, I'd like to conduct a bomb-threat evacuation, to time how long it takes everyone to clear the buildings, see what routes they use, and possible alternate routes. This would really be best done when your workforce is at its maximum number, but today was the only day available, so we'll work with what we have."

Lily was impressed. Swain was doing a hell of an acting job. Not only that, she hadn't known he had that tiny recorder. He must have acquired it while he was picking up the other electronics he thought they'd need.

"Of course, that's brilliant," Dr. Giordano said. "Now, if you'll please follow me?"

To Lily's consternation, Damone fell in step beside her while Swain walked beside Dr. Giordano. The last thing she wanted was one-on-one conversation with anyone. Because her hands were full, she couldn't cover her mouth, but she turned her head into her shoulder and gave two hard coughs.

Swain looked back at her. "Charles, that cough is sounding worse. You should take something for it."

"Later," she croaked, and for good measure coughed again.

"You are ill?" Damone inquired politely.

"A cough only, monsieur."

"Perhaps you should wear a mask. Dr. Giordano is working with influenza viruses, and anyone who is already sick would be especially vulnerable."

Dr. Giordano turned his head and said with concern, "No, no, we won't enter that lab."

"Do your workers often fall sick from the viruses and bacteria they're working with?" Swain inquired.

"It happens, of course—so often that no one keeps records. But I am trying to develop a vaccine for a particularly virulent strain, and anyone who enters that lab must show no signs of illness, plus I instituted strict measures requiring the wearing of masks and gloves."

It was good to know the doctor was taking care his bug didn't spread to the general populace before the vaccine was available to make them millions of dollars, Lily thought. She stared at his back, at his well-shaped head. He seemed such a nice man, but he was the cause of it all. Because of him, Zia was dead.

Lately—since Swain—she had been able to sometimes think of Zia without the crippling pain of grief, with more a fond and sad remembrance. But looking at Dr. Giordano and knowing he was the reason she no longer had Zia, everything rushed back at her in full force. She clenched her jaw to keep from moaning aloud, and fought the burn of tears. It wouldn't do for "Charles" to start weeping.

They had all—she and Averill and Tina—fretted because Zia seemed to catch every bug that went around. By the age of ten she had already had pneumonia twice. Whether her immune system had been weakened by the deprivation of her first few weeks of life, or she was just unlucky, didn't matter. Every winter Zia had been ill several times, and she had always caught at least one summer cold that would inevitably turn into bronchitis. She would have been almost certain to catch such an influenza as Dr. Giordano was planning to unleash on the world, and what were the odds she would have been one of the unlucky ones who died?

In trying to stop that from happening, Averill and Tina had set in motion a train of events that had led to that very outcome anyway. The irony of it was bitter.

Hard on the heels of pain came a hot rush of hatred, so strong that she shook with it. She sucked in a harsh breath, trying to wrestle her emotions back under control before she did something stupid and blew everything.

Walking beside her, Damone gave her a curious look. Lily covered for herself by turning her head and giving another cough. She just hoped the latex on her jaw held up under all this stress. Even more, she hoped that Damone didn't notice that she had a mustache, but not even a hint of a five o'clock shadow on her face.

They walked down a long hall and turned right. "This is my office," Dr. Giordano said, indicating a door with his name lettered on it in gold, and another keypad entry. "Next to it is the main laboratory, which I would like to show you. It is where I do my most important work. Monsieur Fournier, you should perhaps remain outside."

Lily nodded. Swain took one of the notebooks and circuit testers from her and said, "We won't be long." She leaned against the wall the way she'd seen men do, the picture of patience as the three men went into the laboratory. She was just glad Damone hadn't chosen to remain with her.

They were out within ten minutes, Swain making notes. She hoped he'd used his trusty little recorder to get the tonal codes of the keypad when Dr. Giordano had entered it, because that time the doctor had been very careful to shield the keypad with his body when he was punching in the sequence. They would need to get into both the lab and the office to set charges.

"Charles," Swain said absently, "I want you to check the GF modulator on the 365 BS detector in the doctor's office."

"Yes, sir," Lily croaked, diligently writing down the gibberish. She had no idea what a GF modulator was, or if such a thing even existed, and the only BS she knew of was what was coming out of Swain's mouth almost every time he opened it. It sounded impressive, though, and gave her an excuse for being in Dr. Giordano's office.

It was that way throughout the tour; whenever they "inspected" an area that Swain deemed on their hit list, he would reel off a set of instructions designed to get either himself or Lily back in that area. Not once did he repeat himself, probably because he couldn't remember all the numbers and initials he'd used before. Dr. Giordano was obviously impressed by Swain's comprehensive knowledge, though Damone's expression was more enigmatic. Lily suspected Damone would be a hard sell on anything, which further underscored how much he must have trusted Georges Blanc, in order for him to have accepted Blanc's recommendation.

At last they were finished, and Swain gave a brief smile. "That will do, I think. Now, if you gentlemen will excuse us, we'll check those items I mentioned to Charles, and then we'll sneak around hiding our little surprise packages. This will probably take . . . an hour, perhaps a little longer. Then we'll have some fun with your employees that I hope will impress on them how vigilant they should be, and then we'll have that evacuation drill."

"Of course," Damone said, and gave a very Continental little bow. "Thank you both for coming. If you don't mind, I won't remain here. Dr. Giordano knows far more about the facility than I, and he is the heart of all the research here. It has been very good to meet you." He shook hands with Swain, then extended his hand to Lily and she had no choice but to accept his handshake. She tried to grip his hand firmly, and gave it one brisk shake before letting go and slipping her hands into her pockets.

Damone gave her a long, unreadable look, but said nothing and took his leave. Something in her relaxed a little in his absence. He'd been nothing but polite, but she had often felt his gaze boring into her as if he sensed something odd about her but couldn't quite decide what it was.

After Damone had left, Lily and Swain returned to the van and began dividing the charges between them. Her notes told them where the charges needed to go. Swain had shown her how to use the detonators; there was nothing to it. Destruction was always a lot easier than construction.

"Almost finished," Swain said. "You okay? You almost lost it there at the beginning."

So he'd noticed that her emotions were getting the best of

her. "Yes," she said, her eyes dry and her hands steady. "I'm ready."

"Here we go, then. I'd kiss you for good luck, but your upper lip is hairy."

"Just for that, I'm going to wear the mustache to bed tonight." Joking felt strange, given what they were about to do, but in a way the humor anchored her. She just hoped that, come night, they both would be still alive and together.

"That's a scary thought." He shrugged his shoulders, as if working out the tension. His blue eyes were deadly serious as he surveyed her. "Be careful. Don't let anything happen to you."

"Same here."

He looked at his watch. "Okay, let's hustle. I want all of these planted within half an hour."

They reentered the building and, after one long look, went in opposite directions. Neither of them looked back.

31

Because Swain had numbered the rooms on the blueprint and marked the charges accordingly, Lily knew which charges went where. He'd shown her where to place them for maximum effect, but hidden well enough that they were likely to stay hidden until they could get the buildings evacuated.

It's almost over. The thought kept running through her mind as she walked the hallways of the complex, not making any attempt to avoid detection. Almost no one paid her any attention, and no one questioned her. It was as if, just by being inside the complex, she'd proved her right to be there. The Nervis and Dr. Giordano had become acutely aware of security after the first incident, but for everyone else it seemed to be business as usual. The workforce was light, anyway, since it was the weekend. Those who were there were probably dedicated to the point of being blind to everything else, or tired and resentful that they were working when most others weren't. The end of the workday was growing near, and a lot of people were just killing time.

It's almost over. For four long months she'd had one aim: vengeance. But this had grown into something larger than her personal vendetta against the Nervis, something more important. What Averill and Tina had started, she was about to finish, in honor of a young girl who had died while she was still trembling on the cusp between childhood and adolescence.

Lily's own life had taken a bizarre turn when she was eighteen, but she'd hoped to see Zia live a normal, happy life: marry, have children, be in step with most of the world's population. Those who went with the flow, who fit in with the crowd, often had no idea how very lucky they were. They belonged. She had wanted Zia to belong, to have the things she herself either had never had or had been forced to give up.

What a special child Zia had been! As if she had somehow known her life would be short, she had spent it in a fizz of effervescence. Everything had been a source of wonder and joy to her. And she'd been a chatterbox, trying to get everything said that could be said, talking at a mad pace until they'd had to laugh and tell her to slow down.

It was almost over, Lily's quest. She placed a charge against the wall behind the filing cabinets that held Dr. Giordano's documentation of his experiments and results, and stuck a detonator in the mound of Semtex. Soon all of this would be nothing but ashes.

Almost over, she thought as she placed the explosives in the office where all the records were put on computer disk and stored. A small charge under each computer, and another bigger charge where the disks were stored. Everything had to go. There could be nothing left of Dr. Giordano's research.

Swain was taking care of the doctor's office, and the two laboratories in which the live virus was kept. Unfortunately, that was also the area where the vaccine was being developed.

Lily wished there were some way the vaccine process could be saved, because in a year or so there could very well be a desperate need for it. There was nothing they could do, no way they could protect that part of Dr. Giordano's research. She just hoped that when the time came, some other lab had been working on the same thing and would be able to step up to the plate.

She went down a long, steep flight of stairs to the basement and set the largest charges under critical walls, to make certain the destruction was complete. By the time she climbed back to the top, she was out of breath and her heart was pounding.

She could no longer tell herself she was still recovering her strength. There was no doubt about it: any exertion made her short of breath. She couldn't tell if the breathlessness was getting any worse, but she faced the truth: when she was able she would have to find a good cardiac specialist somewhere and see about getting that pesky valve fixed.

A lot of what she would do next depended on Rodrigo Nervi. She would have to leave France; there was no question of that. Leave Europe, in fact. Swain hadn't said anything about afterward, and neither had she. First they would see if there *was* an afterward. She tried to imagine a future by herself, and couldn't. Whenever she saw herself now, she was with Swain.

Where would it be safe for him to go? Not back to South America, and neither of them would be safe going back to the

United States. Mexico, perhaps, or Canada. That would get them close to home. Jamaica was a possibility. Swain didn't like cold weather, so she didn't think he would choose Canada, though that would have been her first choice. Perhaps they could summer in Canada and spend the winter farther south.

A harried-looking man wearing a lab coat and carrying a thick notebook went past her with only a nod. Glancing out through a window, she saw that the sun was setting; the short December day was almost over. Their timing was good; at this time of day, everyone was thinking of home.

The charges had all been placed, with no problems or interference from anyone. It had been so easy it was almost frightening.

She made her way back to Dr. Giordano's office. Swain was already there, sitting on the comfortable sofa in the office and drinking a cup of coffee. Dr. Giordano indicated the carafe. "Please, help yourself," he said. "The coffee will be good for your throat."

"Merci," she said. She had coughed so much she had definitely irritated her throat. The first sip of hot coffee soothed the membranes and she almost sighed with pleasure.

"You have a definite problem," Swain was telling the doctor. "We planted the charges without anyone asking us what we were doing, or becoming alarmed. Awareness is your first defense, and your people are so absorbed in their work they are thinking of nothing else."

"But scientists are like that," Dr. Giordano protested, lifting his hands in a very Italian gesture. "What can I do? Tell them not to think about their work?"

Swain shook his head. "The obvious solution is to have people inside who *aren't* scientists–trained security personnel–rather than relying so completely on electronics. You should have both. I'm surprised your security company didn't suggest that."

"But they did. Our work here is so sensitive I elected not to have people in the complex who didn't understand the safety measures we must take with these viruses."

"Then that's a trade-off you have decided to make. It does leave a big hole in your security, but if you are aware of it–" Swain shrugged, as if to say there was nothing he could do. "I'll have my recommendations put in a report to you. Implement the ones you want. Now, are you ready to have your people see if they can spot the charges?"

Dr. Giordano looked at his watch. "Their time is short. I am afraid this must be a brief lesson."

"Of course."

They went to the intercom system, and Dr. Giordano pressed the switch that opened the loudspeakers. He cleared his throat, then began an explanation of what had been going on that afternoon. Lily imagined that all over the complex workers were looking at each other, then uneasily examining their surroundings.

Dr. Giordano checked the time again. "You have five minutes in which to see if you can spot any of these mock explosives. Don't touch them, just call me and report."

He clicked off the loudspeaker and asked Swain, "How many of these charges are there?"

"Fifteen."

They waited, watching the time. Four calls came in during the allotted five minutes. Dr. Giordano sighed, looking sad, and announced the results over the loudspeaker. He turned back to Swain with a "what can I do?" expression on his face.

Lily sat down and rubbed her right leg as if it were aching. She felt an unaccountable sadness, now that the time was here. Considering her earlier rage and hatred, why should she feel sad now? But she did.

She was so tired of killing. She wondered if there would ever be an end to it. Rodrigo Nervi would search for her until the end of his days; she would have to look at every stranger as a possible threat, never relaxing in public.

Swain got up. "You didn't tell them about the bomb threat drill. That's good, I think. Your people have been remarkably unaware, so let's see if I can perhaps stir them to a little more action. May I?" He indicated the intercom system, and Dr. Giordano waved a hand in permission, smiling. Swain turned on the loudspeaker again and in his rough French said urgently, "The explosives are real! There has been a mistake! Get out, get out, *get out!*"

He turned and began swiftly ushering Dr. Giordano out the door. Behind them, Lily started to retrieve her pistol from her boot, but Swain looked over his shoulder and gave a sharp shake of his head. *"Move the van,"* he mouthed.

She couldn't believe they hadn't thought of that before. The van was parked too close to the building. If she didn't move it to a safer distance, they wouldn't have transportation. Swain couldn't do it because she had the keys, and he was already busy taking the batteries for the remote control from his pocket, trying to insert them while he was moving at a fast clip.

People were hurrying out of various rooms and laboratories, confusion on their faces. "What is it?" one woman asked. "This is a joke?"

"No," Lily said briefly. "Hurry!"

As they went out the door, for Dr. Giordano's benefit she said, "I have to get something from the van," and ran for the vehicle.

Evidently taking her action as something they themselves were supposed to do, those lab workers who drove instead of taking the train began running for their own vehicles. The guards at the gate, seeing this unusual activity, stepped out of their little building with their hands on the butts of their weapons, leaving them still holstered but ready to draw on a second's notice.

Lily started the van and rapidly backed it out of the parking space. Dr. Giordano gave her a startled look, but Swain said something and distracted him by pointing at what the workers were doing, at the same time walking at a fast clip to a safer distance and urging Dr. Giordano along with him.

She pulled the van between Swain and the guards, blocking their view but also positioned in such a way that it gave them some protection from the coming blast. As she got out, she heard Swain say, "Is that everyone, do you think?"

"I don't know," Dr. Giordano replied. "Not many were working today, but as to how many–?" He shrugged.

"You should always know, otherwise how can you get a head count?" Swain asked reasonably, and, to Lily's surprise, turned and handed the remote control to her.

"You do the honors," he said.

She had watched him test the device, and he'd explained to her how it worked, but why was he deviating from the plan? She didn't have time to ask, because Dr. Giordano was already looking puzzled. Before he could ask questions or become alarmed, she activated the device. A little green light glowed, showing it was on, and she pressed the button that sent the radio signal to the detonators.

There was a sort of deep, muffled *whoomph;* then all hell broke loose.

Parts of the complex blew up and out, the percussion of the blast hitting them like a blow. Black smoke and fire billowed, and a dark cloud of debris arced overhead. People screamed, ducking and protecting themselves as best they could. Flying glass pierced several people like arrows. One man went down under a chunk of the debris that rained down on them like rocks thrown by a giant.

Dr. Giordano turned to Swain with an expression of horror on his face. Lily reached down for her weapon, but Swain already had his hand inside his coveralls. He pulled out the big H & K, shoved it directly against Dr. Giordano's chest, and pulled the trigger twice. Dr. Giordano slumped to the ground, already dead.

Moving swiftly, Swain pushed Lily toward the van. She climbed into the driver's seat, but he kept pushing, so she clambered over into the passenger's seat, and he took the place behind the wheel. The engine was still running. He slammed the door, put the vehicle in gear, and started it rolling forward as one of the guards ran past them. The other was on the phone in their little building, shouting frantically into the receiver. He was still on the phone when they went out the gate.

Damone was in Rodrigo's office when the phone rang. Rodrigo answered it, and his olive complexion turned a strange ashen color.

Damone got to his feet. "What is it?" he asked when Rodrigo hung up.

Rodrigo's head was bowed, his shoulders slumped. "The laboratory has been destroyed," he said hoarsely. "Explosives. Vincenzo is dead." Slowly he raised his head, horror dawning in his eyes. "He was killed by the security consultants *you* took into the complex."

Damone took several deep breaths. Then, very quietly, he said, "I couldn't let you release that virus."

" 'Couldn't'–?" Rodrigo blinked rapidly, trying to make the words mean something else. But they remained the same, and Damone stood there with a very calm expression. "You–you *knew* what they were going to do?"

"I paid them to do it."

Rodrigo felt as if the world had shifted on its axis, that nothing he had thought was real had any substance. In a blinding moment of clarity, he knew. "You were behind the first explosion. *You* hired the Joubrans!"

"Unfortunately, Vincenzo was able to duplicate his work, so I had to take more drastic measures."

"Because of you, *Papa is dead!*" Rodrigo roared, surging to his feet and reaching for the weapon that was always in the desk drawer.

Damone was faster, his own weapon much closer to hand. He didn't hesitate. He pulled the trigger three times, putting two holes in Rodrigo's chest and an insurance shot to the head. His brother sprawled over the desk, then crashed to the floor, over- turning the wastebasket.

Damone let his hand drop to his side, and a tear rolled down his face.

It had come to this, from events he had set in motion back in August. He sucked in a deep breath and wiped his eyes. The road to hell was truly paved with good intentions. All he had wanted was for that virus to be destroyed. He couldn't let his father go through with his plans to release it.

Giselle, his wonderful, brave, fragile Giselle, would never have survived if she had contracted the influenza. She had had a kidney transplant just the year before, and had to take drugs that suppressed her immune system, and even the vaccine could not have saved her. She had been reluctant to accept his proposal because she couldn't give him children, and she knew how important family was to Italians in general, but he had eventually convinced her. He loved her more than he could express, more than he could explain even to himself. For her, he had taken steps to destroy the virus.

He had never thought his father would discover who had set the first explosion, and he'd been heartsick when he learned the Joubrans and their daughter had been executed, as a lesson to those who would cross Salvatore Nervi.

But the Joubrans had had a friend, this Lily Mansfield, and their deaths had sent her on a quest for vengeance that put his papa in the grave.

She had been the perfect choice to complete the Joubrans' mission. With George Blanc's help—Damone had almost panicked when she demanded a meeting, but an urgent call to Blanc had persuaded him to appear in Damone's place—he had devised a plan to get her and her friend inside the complex.

He hadn't been prepared for how he would feel when he actually saw her, the woman who had killed his father. For a moment he had wanted to kill *her*, punish her for his anguish at what he himself had caused. He was certain that "Charles Fournier" was this woman in disguise, though it was such a good disguise he'd been taken aback and unsure that there wasn't a third person involved. But he had deliberately forced her to shake hands with him, and the feel of that slender, feminine hand in his had convinced him.

So. She had accomplished the mission—and forced him to pay her a million American dollars to do it. He hadn't intended to follow through on the payment, but she had outsmarted him by insisting on payment in advance.

He wished she had died in the explosion. Perhaps she had; he didn't know yet if there were any fatalities other than Vincenzo. But if she had escaped alive, he would call a truce. Lily Mansfield was safe from the Nervi organization. She had reacted to an event he had caused, and in the same way that a snowball rolling downhill becomes an avalanche, so things had proceeded to this point.

He had murdered his brother. His immortal soul was perhaps damned for this, but he thought the lives he had saved by destroying the virus would be weighed in the balance. And he had saved Giselle.

Damone stepped to the door. The sound of the shots had of course been heard, but no one had entered. He opened the door and saw several nervous men standing just outside, wearing uncertain expressions. He looked over the faces and picked out that of Tadeo, Rodrigo's man. "Rodrigo is dead," he said gently. "I have assumed control of all operations. Tadeo, would you please make certain my brother's body is treated with all due respect? I will take him home, bury him next to Papa."

His face pale, Tadeo nodded. He knew the way things worked. He could become Damone's man, or he could die.

He chose to live. He murmured some quiet words to the other men, and they went inside the office to take care of Rodrigo's body.

Damone went into another room and placed a call. "Monsieur Blanc. It is over. Your service to me has ended."

32

"WHY GREECE?" LILY ASKED AS SHE SWIFTLY GATHERED HER things in Swain's hotel room.

"Because it's warm, and because it's the first flight out that I could get us on. Do you have your passport?"

"Several."

He stopped what he was doing and gave her an oddly tender smile. "The one in your real name. That's what I booked your ticket under."

She winced. "That might cause problems." She hadn't forgotten that she had to be on guard against the CIA, too, though so far she seemed to have gone in under the radar on that one. After what had happened today, whether that would remain true was anyone's guess. "Turn on the television. Let's see if anything is being reported on the news."

Either the explosion was being kept quiet or they had

missed the story in the news item rotation, and they didn't have time to wait through another segment. Rather than call a bellman, Swain carried their luggage down himself, then checked them out of the hotel.

"We have to go to my apartment," Lily said when they were in the car. They had ditched the van several blocks away from the hotel, and walked the rest of the way.

Swain gave her a disbelieving look. "Do you know how long that will take us?"

"I have to get my pictures of Zia. I don't know when or if I'll be able to come back, so I'm not leaving them behind. If I see we're going to miss our flight, I'll call and cancel the reservations and book us on the next one."

"Maybe we can make it," he said, a devilish grin on his face, and Lily braced herself for the ride of a lifetime.

They did make it to her apartment building in one piece, but Lily kept her eyes closed most of the way and didn't open them no matter how close the screeching brakes and blasting horns were. "I won't be a minute," she said when he pulled to a stop.

"I'm coming up with you."

She gave him an incredulous look as he climbed out of the car and locked it. "But you're blocking the street. What if someone wants to get by?"

"Then they can damn well wait."

He climbed the stairs with her, his left hand on the small of her back and his right hand on his pistol butt. Lily unlocked the door, and Swain went in first as she reached in and flipped on the light switch, sweeping right to left with his pistol until he was certain no one was waiting for them.

Lily stepped inside and closed the door. "We can leave our weapons here." She dragged a lockbox out of a cabinet. "This is sublet for a year, and I have eight months left."

They both put their weapons in the box, and she locked it, then put it back into the cabinet. They could have put the weapons in their checked luggage, disassembled and in a lockbox, declared them to the airline, and perhaps had no trouble collecting them on the other end, but she doubted things would go that smoothly. It was always easier to acquire weapons once she got to where she was going than to try to take one with her. Besides, they didn't want the airline personnel paying any particular attention to them.

She got Zia's photographs and added them to her tote bag, and they were out the door. As they were going down the stairs, Swain said, grinning, "Was that the bed you bought from a nun?"

Lily snickered. "No, it came with the apartment."

"I didn't buy the nun story for a minute."

Though he drove like a demented bat out of hell, it became obvious they weren't going to make it to the airport in time to catch the flight. Lily called and canceled their reservations and made new ones for another flight, and after that he actually took his foot off the gas pedal occasionally, so she dared to keep her eyes open.

"Why did you shoot Dr. Giordano?" she asked, watching the traffic instead of him, because the fact that he'd deviated from the plan bothered her. Had he noticed that moment when she'd become emotional, and been afraid she might botch the shot?

"I wondered when that subject would come up," he muttered, and sighed. "I did it because it was personal to you, and because you didn't need the guilt I knew you'd feel afterward."

"Salvatore Nervi was a personal hit, too," she pointed out. "I don't feel one shred of guilt about him."

"That was different. You actually liked Dr. Giordano, before you found out what he was doing. Killing him would have hurt you."

He was probably right, she thought, leaning her head back against the headrest. In setting up the hit on Salvatore, she had been carried along on a tide of pain so great it had over-whelmed everything else. But between then and today, she had found sunshine again; somehow, killing Dr. Giordano would have blotted out some of the sun. She didn't understand it. Giordano was a righteous hit, perhaps the most righteous of all—but she was glad she hadn't done it. It was that gladness that both puzzled and upset her. Was she losing her edge . . . and had Swain noticed? Was that why he'd done it?

He reached over and took her hand. "Stop fretting about it. It's done."

It was done. Over. Finished. She felt as if a door had closed behind her, sealing off her past. Other than go to Greece with Swain, she had no idea what she would do next. For the first time in her life, she was adrift.

They reached the airport and turned in the Mercedes to the rental company, then made their way to the ticket counter and checked in. They had a couple of hours to kill before their flight and they were both hungry, so they went into one of the airport restaurants. They chose one of the rear booths from which they could watch the entrance, though checking in had been totally uneventful. No one had tried to detain them; no one blinked an eye at Lily's name. It was unnerving.

The restaurant was one with multiple televisions on the wall so the patrons could keep up with news, sports, and weather while they ate. They both looked up when they heard the name "Nervi" mentioned.

"In shocking news tonight, Damone Nervi has announced that the explosion that devastated one of the Nervi properties late this afternoon has resulted in the death of his older brother, Rodrigo Nervi. The brothers lost their father, Salvatore Nervi, less than a month ago. Damone Nervi has assumed leadership of all the Nervi holdings. The explosion that killed Rodrigo Nervi is believed to have been caused by a faulty gas line. Authorities are investigating."

Lily and Swain looked at each other. "Rodrigo wasn't there," she hissed.

"I know." He looked thoughtful. "Son of a bitch. I believe there's been a coup."

Lily had to agree. Damone had evidently seized the opportunity to kill Rodrigo and make the murder look like an accident. It must have been an impulse, a spur-of-the-moment decision precipitated by the destruction of the laboratory. But Damone was widely reckoned as the brilliant one, the one with the Midas touch; would he have acted so impulsively, when the outcome could just as easily have resulted in his own death?

The only other possibility was that Rodrigo's death wasn't an impulse at all. And that could be only if–"My God," she blurted. "He planned the whole thing."

Three weeks later, Lily woke from a late afternoon nap to hear Swain out on the terrace, talking on the satellite telephone he'd wrangled from somewhere, saying angrily, "Damn it, Frank–No. No. Fuck it, *no*. All right. I said *all right*, but I don't like it. You owe me, big-time. Yeah, I said *you* owe *me,* so you'd better be damn sure you're right." He slammed down the phone and walked to the low wall of the terrace, where he planted his hands on his hips and glared out at the blue Aegean.

She slipped from the bed and went out through the double doors onto the terrace, walking up behind him and sliding her arms around his waist. She laid her head against his bare back and kissed his warm shoulder blade. "You finally got to talk to Frank?" Frank was his friend who had been in the car accident. Two weeks earlier Frank had been moved out of ICU into a regular hospital bed, but he'd evidently been guarded by some-one who had been adamant that he not be disturbed. The day before he'd been moved into a rehab facility, but judging from the way Swain had sounded, their first conversation hadn't been to his liking.

"The hardheaded son of a bitch," he growled, but he caught one of her hands and pressed it to his chest.

"What's wrong?"

"He wants me to do something I don't want to do."

"Such as?"

"Take a job I don't like."

That wasn't welcome news. In the three weeks they'd been in Greece, on the island of Evvoia, they had slipped into a lazy routine that felt like heaven. The days were often cloudy but definitely warmer than in Paris, with highs often reaching into the seventies. The nights got cold, but that was all the better for cuddling in bed. Today had been almost perfect, sunny all day long, and so warm Swain had been shirtless most of the day. Now that the sun was setting, the temperature would drop like a rock, but for just a few minutes more they were comfortable.

They made love; they slept late; they ate whenever they wanted; they strolled through town. They were staying in a house on the mountain slope above the port town of Karystos, with a spectacular view of the sea. Lily had fallen in love with the house, a simple white house with bright blue shutters and an air of peace. She could have stayed there with him forever, though she knew the idyll would eventually end.

Evidently it was going to end sooner than she'd expected. If Swain took this job he didn't want to take–and Frank was obviously twisting his arm to take it–he would have to leave the island. She could stay here without him, of course, but the big question was: Did she want to? An even bigger question was whether she'd have the option of going with him. They still hadn't discussed the future; the present had been so very pleasant she had luxuriated in it, letting the days drift past.

"If you take the job, where will you have to go?"

"I don't know yet."

"Then how do you know you don't want it?"

"Because I won't be here." He turned in the circle of her arms and kissed her forehead. "I don't want to leave."

"Then don't."

"Frank's pulling one of those 'do it for me' deals."

"It's obvious he can't do it himself. How long will he be in rehab?"

"At least a month, he said, and God only knows how long it'll be before he's back to normal."

"If you take the job, how long will you be gone?"

He was silent, and her heart sank. A long time, then. "I could go with you," she offered, though she hadn't meant to. If he wanted her with him, he would say so. Surely he did, didn't he? He said "I love you" every day, several times a day. He showed it in the obvious enjoyment he took from being in her company, in the attention he paid to her, the way he touched her.

"You can't," he finally said. "If I take it, that won't be an option."

That was that, then. "When do you have to decide?"

"In a few days. Not right now, at any rate." He cupped her chin and turned her face up, studying her features in the growing twilight as if he were trying to memorize them. His blue eyes were darkly intent. "I don't know that I can do it," he whispered. "I don't want to leave here."

"Then don't," she said simply, and he laughed.

"I wish it was that easy. Frank . . . well, he's a hard man to turn down."

"Does he have something on you?"

He laughed, though the sound was more wry than humorous. "It isn't that. He's just one of those persuasive people. And I hate to admit it, but I trust him more than any other man I know." He shivered suddenly, as the dropping temperature finally got the best of him. "Let's go inside. I can think of several things I'd rather be doing than worrying about a job I might not take."

He didn't mention it again, and because he didn't, Lily left the subject alone. They went inside to a simple supper of new potatoes cooked with dill and capers, feta cheese in olive oil, bread, and Boutari wine. They had hired a woman from town named Chrisoula to come up and do the cooking for them every day; at first she had wanted to prepare large evening meals, in the Greek tradition, but they had impressed on her that they preferred to eat more lightly at night. She didn't like it, but she complied. For one thing, this meant she got home at an earlier hour, where she could enjoy the long evening meal with her own family.

The house had no television, and neither of them missed it. In the three weeks they'd been there, Swain had bought a news-paper twice. That lack of outside interference had been just what she needed, a chance to just *be*, no pressures, no looking over her shoulder. On the warmer days she sat on the terrace for hours, soaking up the sunshine, letting her psyche heal. She had put one of Zia's pictures out in the bedroom where she could see it, and a day later Swain had taken the pictures of his kids out of his wallet and propped them up beside Zia's. Chrisoula thought all three kids were theirs, and they didn't disabuse her of the notion, which wouldn't have been that easy in any case, because neither of them had a good grasp of the Greek language and Chrisoula's English wasn't much better. They managed to eventually communicate on most things, but it was an effort.

That night, knowing that Swain might leave soon, Zia was very much on Lily's mind. Some days were like that, with memories ambushing her at every turn, though now she would go days without crying. And because she was thinking so much about Zia, she wondered if Swain had days when all he could think about was his kids.

"Don't you miss them?" she asked. "Chrissy and Sam?"

"So much it hurts," he readily replied. "I figure it's what I deserve."

She had known he felt guilty about his kids; she just hadn't realized he embraced the guilt. "Instead of wearing that hair shirt, why don't you move closer to them? You missed most of their childhood, but that doesn't mean you have to miss

their adulthood, too. One of these days you'll be a grandfather. Are you going to keep yourself away from your grandchildren?"

He turned his glass of wine around and around, staring
thoughtfully at it. "I'd love to see more of them. I just don't
know if they'd like to see more of *me*. When I do see them,
they're friendly, they're fond of me, but maybe that's because
I'm on the periphery of their lives. If I try to horn in . . . who
knows?"

"So ask them."

He gave a quick grin. "A simple answer for a simple problem, huh? To a little kid, nothing matters as much as just being
there, and I let them down. That's the hard truth."

"Yes, it is. Are you going to let it go on being the hard truth
for the rest of your life?"

He stared at her for a long minute, then drank the rest of his
wine and set the glass down on the table. "Maybe not. Maybe
one day I'll work up the nerve to ask them."

"If Zia was still alive, there's no way I wouldn't be there."
That was another hard truth, and implicit in the statement was
She isn't alive, but your children are. She didn't know why she
was hammering at him about this, except that she'd been
thinking of Zia and Swain might not be here much longer for
her to say this to him. They had covered this ground once before, but it didn't seem have to sunk in with him—either that or
he was so acutely aware of the mistakes he'd made that he was
punishing himself by staying away from his kids. The more she
knew about him, the more she suspected the latter.

"All right," he said with a wry smile. "I'll think about it."

"You've been thinking about it for years. When are you
going to *do* something?"

The smile turned to a bark of laughter. "God, you're as bad as a snapping turtle."

"Turtles nag?"

"The old saying is that if a snapping turtle bites you, it won't turn loose until it hears thunder."

She tilted her head. "I don't think I've heard thunder since we've been here."

"I know we haven't. Okay, I promise I'll call my kids."

"And–?"

"And tell them I know I was a lousy father, but ask would they hate it if I saw them more often?" He made it a question, as if he wasn't certain that was the correct answer, but his blue eyes were dancing.

She clapped her hands, like someone applauding a performing child.

"Smart-ass." He was laughing aloud now, getting to his feet and taking her hand to pull her up and into his arms. "I was going to show you something special tonight, but now I think you'll just get the same old, same old."

If he thought that was punishment, he was way off target. Lily hid a smile as she pressed her face into his shoulder. She loved him so much she would enjoy her time with him down to the last minute, and not worry about whether or not he took this job his friend Frank wanted him to take. Wasn't that part of what she'd just been talking to him about, making the most of your time with the people you love, because you don't know how long that time will be?

She wouldn't think how unlucky she was to love him and lose him. Instead she would consider herself lucky for having met him at a time in her life when she had needed him so much.

The next day was another unusually sunny day, with the temperature warming as rapidly as it cooled down at night. By April, the daytime temperature would be in the nineties; by July, soaring over a hundred wouldn't be unusual. But the weather in early January was pleasant, if sometimes a bit rainy, especially when compared to Paris at this time of year.

Chrisoula prepared them a lunch of meat patties, flavored with herbs and fried in olive oil, served on saffron rice. They ate on the terrace, enjoying the weather. Because the stones of the terrace reflected the sun's heat, Lily wore a loose, gauzy white dress that she'd bought in town, though she had a shawl nearby in case she needed it. She liked being able to wear whatever she wanted without having to worry about whether it concealed her ankle holster, and she had embraced the island's tourist fashions with enthusiasm. The locals probably thought she was crazy for wearing summer fashions in January, but she didn't care. She wanted to wear sandals, and she had bought a silver anklet that made her feel feminine and carefree. She might stay on Evvoia even if Swain left, she thought. She loved it here.

"Who was your handler?" he asked abruptly, telling her that his thoughts had been far different from her lazy enjoyment of the day. "The guy who got you into the business. What was his name?"

"Mr. Rogers," she said, smiling ironically.

He almost choked on his wine.

"He never gave me his first name, but you can bet it wasn't Fred. It doesn't matter; I doubt that was his real name anyway. Why are you asking?"

"I was watching you and thinking how young you look, and

wondering what kind of bastard could approach a kid with a job like that."

"The kind who gets the job done, regardless."

After lunch she napped on one of the chaises on the terrace, and woke to incredible pleasure brought by Swain's tongue. He had lifted her skirt to her waist and removed her underwear and knelt with his head between her spread thighs. Lily gasped, her body arching in delight even as she choked, "Chrisoula will see—"

"She left a few minutes ago," Swain murmured, and gently slipped two of his fingers into her. She climaxed rapidly under that double stimulation, and was still quivering with the last spasms when he loosened his pants and covered her with his body. His penetration was smooth and slow, the fit perfect now after making love so many times during the past month. He was tender and attentive, holding off until she had climaxed a second time, then going deep and holding himself there while he shuddered with his own release.

Making love alfresco was wonderful, she thought after they had tidied themselves and she was once more completely dressed. The air had felt like silk on her skin, heightening her response. She stretched, utterly relaxed, and smiled at Swain when he brought over their glasses of wine. She took hers and he sat down on the chaise beside her legs, his warm hand sliding under her skirt to lazily caress her thigh.

"Why did Chrisoula leave so early?" she asked as she sipped the fragrant wine, thinking she hadn't slept that long. Chrisoula hadn't had time to prepare their dinner.

"She wanted to go to the market for something. I think." Swain smiled. "Either that or a pig was on top of her house."

"I'm betting it was the market." Sometimes their attempts at communication had laughable results, but Swain threw himself into it with enthusiasm.

"Probably." His stroking hand had worked its way down to her ankle. He played with the silver anklet, then lifted her foot and pressed a kiss to her ankle. "We could be having the pig for dinner, though, so we'll see how far off I was in my translation."

"What do you want to do for the rest of the afternoon?" she asked, finishing her wine and setting the glass aside. She didn't know that she would be able to move a muscle. Two orgasms had left her bones feeling like butter. She hated to waste such a gorgeous day, though, so if he wanted to go into Karystos, she would make the effort.

He shook his head. "Nothing. Maybe read for a while. Sit right here and watch the bay. Count the clouds." He patted her ankle, then stood up and walked to the terrace wall, where he stood, sipping occasionally from his own glass. She watched him, everything female in her appreciating the width of his shoulders and the narrowness of his ass, but especially enjoying that lazy, sexy saunter of his that said this was a man who took his time at what he did. Even Chrisoula responded to him, flirting and laughing, and she was a good twenty years older. Not to mention that when she flirted, he usually had no idea what she was saying, though that in no way kept him from replying to what he thought she'd said. Lily had no idea of the exact meaning, either, but she could tell from Chrisoula's blushes and body language that she was definitely flirting.

A feeling of great lassitude swept over her and she let her eyes close. She was so sleepy, so relaxed . . . she shouldn't have had that last glass of wine . . . it was putting her to sleep–

She forced her eyes open, and found Swain watching her with an expression on his face that she didn't recognize, alert and watchful, no hint of humor at all.

Fool, an inner voice said. She had been caught in exactly the same way she had caught Salvatore Nervi.

She could feel the numbness now, spreading through her body. She tried to stand up, but she barely managed to sit before collapsing back against the chaise. What could she do, anyway? She couldn't outrun what was already inside her.

Swain came back to squat beside the chaise. "Don't fight it," he said gently.

"Who are you?" she managed to ask, though she could still think clearly enough to figure it out. He wasn't a Nervi employee, so there was only one other possibility. He was CIA; whether one of their black-ops personnel or a contract agent himself; the end result was the same. Whatever his reason was for helping her with the Nervis, after that was finished, he had completed his own mission. She had completely fallen for his act, but then she'd noticed before what a superb actor he was, and that should have been a warning. By then, however, she had already been in love with him.

"I think you know."

"Yes." Her eyelids were so heavy, and the numbness had spread to her lips. She fought for coherency. "What happens now?"

He stroked a strand of hair back from her face, his touch gentle. "You just go to sleep," he whispered. She had never heard him sound so tender before.

No pain, then. That was good. She wasn't going to die in agony. "Was it real? Any of it?" Or had every touch, every kiss, been a lie?

His eyes darkened, or she thought they did. It could be that her eyesight was fading. "It was real."

"Then . . ." She lost her train of thought, fought to get it back. What was she–? Yes, she remembered now. "Will you . . ." She could barely speak, and she couldn't see him at all. She swallowed, made an effort: ". . . kiss me while I sleep?"

She wasn't certain, but she thought she heard him say, "Always." She tried to reach out her hand to him, and in her mind she did. Her last thought was that she wanted to touch him.

Swain stroked her cheek, and watched a light breeze flirt with her hair. The pale strands stirred and lifted, fell back, lifted again as if they were alive. He bent down and kissed her warm lips, then sat holding her hand for a long time.

Tears burned his eyes. God damn Frank. He wouldn't listen, wouldn't budge from his original plan, and if Swain couldn't do the job, he'd by God send someone who could.

Yeah, well. If it hadn't been for the small matter of a mole that still had to be located, Swain would have told him what he could do with his fucking job. But he had the recording Blanc had gotten to him during that week of preparation for taking down the Nervi lab, and when he got back to Washington, he had that to take care of. He'd heard Lily stirring in the bedroom yesterday afternoon and hadn't been able to tell Frank everything that was going on, just the gist of what Dr. Giordano had been doing and a brief argument about what Frank wanted him to do with Lily.

He had sent Chrisoula away this afternoon because he had wanted one more time with Lily, wanted to hold her close and look into those remarkable eyes as she came, wanted to feel her arms around him.

It was over now.

He kissed her one last time, then made the call.

Soon the unmistakable *whump whump whump* of a heli-copter sounded over the mountain slope. It sat down on a flat spot just off the terrace, and three men and a woman got out. They worked silently, competently, wrapping Lily and prepar-ing her for transport. Then one of the men said to the woman, "Get the feet," and Swain whirled on him.

"*Her* feet," he said savagely. "She's a woman, not a thing. And she's a fucking patriot. If you treat her with anything but respect, I'll rip your guts out."

The man eyed him with consternation. "Sure, man. I didn't mean anything by it."

Swain clenched his fist. "I know. Just . . . go on."

A few minutes later, the helicopter lifted off. Swain stood and watched it until it was a tiny black speck; then, his expres-sion set and blank, he turned and went into the house.

Epilogue

Six months later

LILY WALKED DOWN THE HALLWAY TOWARD DR. SHAY'S OFFICE for what she hoped was the last time. Six months of intensive deprogramming, therapy, and counseling was enough. After her initial rage at waking and finding herself in custody, she had been grateful for this second chance and had been as co-operative as possible, but she was ready to leave.

The entire six months hadn't been taken up with therapy, though. Two months in, she'd had surgery to repair that leaky, damaged valve in her heart, and recovery from that hadn't happened overnight. She felt completely well now, but the first few weeks after the surgery had been rough, even though the cardiac surgeon had used the minimally invasive technique. Any surgery on the heart required that the heart not be beating, so she'd been placed on a heart-lung machine while the work was being done. She still felt uneasy about that, even though it was in the past.

Dr. Shay wasn't Lily's idea of a typical shrink, assuming there was such an animal. She was a short, chubby, jolly elf of a person, with the kindest eyes Lily could imagine. Lily would have killed for Dr. Shay, and that was part of the reason she was still at the private clinic.

She had herself worried about whether she would ever be able to fit into a normal life, but the therapies Dr. Shay had designed had shown Lily how far she'd been from that normality. Until she had gone through those exercises that tested her impulses, she hadn't realized how ready she was to kill, how that was always–*always*–her initial reaction to confrontation. Over the years she had become very good at avoiding confrontation because of that, without ever realizing that was what she was doing. She had minimized the risk by not associating with many people.

She had gone through the exercises again and again until she retrained herself, and through many sessions with Dr. Shay until her anger and pain were more manageable. Grief was a terrible thing, but so was isolation, and she had made things worse on herself by being so isolated. She needed her family, and with Dr. Shay's encouragement she had worked up the nerve to call her mother a few weeks before. They had both cried, but Lily had felt a sense of incredible relief at once more connecting with that part of her life.

Swain was the only part of her life that she hadn't discussed with Dr. Shay.

She hadn't been allowed visitors or any contact with the outside world until she'd called her mother, so it wasn't surprising that she hadn't seen him or heard from him since that day on Evvoia when she'd thought he'd killed her. She wondered if he even realized that had been what she'd thought.

She didn't know if he would get in trouble for the way he'd conducted his mission, how much the Agency even knew about it, so she simply hadn't mentioned him and neither had Dr. Shay.

She knocked on Dr. Shay's door, and a voice she didn't recognize said, "Come in."

She opened the door and stared at the man who sat behind the desk. "Come in," he repeated, smiling.

Lily entered the office and closed the door behind her. Silently she sat down in the seat she usually took.

"I'm Frank Vinay," the man said. He looked to be in his early seventies, maybe, and he had a kind face but the sharpest gaze she'd ever encountered. She recognized the name with a sense of shock. This was the Agency's director of operations himself.

A few dots connected, and she said, "Swain's Frank?"

He nodded. "I'll admit to that."

"You were really in a car accident?"

"I really was. I don't remember anything about it, of course, but I've read all the reports. It put Swain in a bind, because he found out there was a mole who was reporting to Rodrigo Nervi, but he didn't know who it was and I was the only person he could say for sure *wasn't* the mole, so he had no one to call. He was totally on his own with that operation—except for you, of course. Please accept your country's thanks for what you did."

Whatever she had expected to hear, that wasn't it. She said, "I thought you would have me killed."

The kind face turned somber. "After all your years of service to the country? I don't operate that way. I read the reports, you know; I saw the signs that you were stretched thin, but I didn't

pull you in the way I should have. After you killed Salvatore
Nervi, I was afraid you were going to disrupt the complete network, but I still never contemplated having you terminated unless you gave me no choice. This was my first option," he said,
indicating Dr. Shay's office. "But I knew there was no way you
would believe it if the plan was presented to you. You would either run, or kill, or both. You had to be taken, so I sent my best
hunter after you. It was a fortuitous selection, because another
field officer might not have worked the situation as capably as
he did when circumstances changed."

"When he found out about the mole, and I found out what
was really going on at that laboratory."

"Exactly. It was a complicated situation. When Damone
Nervi discovered what his father and brother were planning,
he took steps to prevent the virus from being released by hiring
Averill Joubran and his wife to destroy the work, and that set
the whole ball of wax into motion."

A man as handsome as a movie star, was how Mme. Bonnet
had described her friends' visitor. That was Damone Nervi, all
right.

"So he knew all along who I was, that day at the laboratory," she murmured. "And he knew I killed his father."

"Yes. He's an amazing man. He wouldn't have minded if
you'd been killed in the explosion, mind you, or if one of the
guards had shot you as you and Swain were leaving, but he did
nothing to compromise your mission."

He was a bigger person than she was, Lily silently admitted.
She had almost lost control and attacked Dr. Giordano—but she
hadn't, she realized. That was how Damone Nervi must have
felt. Hah. He *wasn't* a bigger person, after all.

"The thing is, we may not have done any good at all," she said. "The avian flu virus may mutate on its own, at any time."

"That's true, and there's nothing we can do to stop it. But the CDC and the WHO are working hard to develop a reliable method of producing the vaccine, and if the virus mutates before that happens–" He spread his hands. "At least no one is releasing it deliberately, and making a fortune from the deaths of millions. Which brings me to another health issue," he said, smoothly switching subjects. "How are *you* doing?"

"I feel well, finally. The surgery wasn't a picnic, but it worked."

"I'm glad. Swain was there, you know."

She felt as if he'd thrown a body block at her. "What?" The word came out as a weak gasp.

"For your surgery. He wanted to be there. When you were placed on the heart-lung machine, he almost fainted."

"How . . . how do you know that?" She almost couldn't speak, so profound was her shock.

"I was there, too, of course. I was . . . concerned. It wasn't a minor surgery. He saw you in recovery, but had to leave before you were awake."

Or he'd *wanted* to leave before she was awake. She didn't know how to take all this in, or what to think.

"You can leave here anytime you want," Mr. Vinay continued. "Do you know what you want to do?"

"See my mother and sister, first of all. After that . . . I don't know. I need a new line of work," she said wryly.

"If there's any field in which you'd like to be trained. . . . We can always use someone who's dedicated and resourceful, and loyal."

"Thank you for the offer, but I'll have to think about it. I honestly have no idea what I want to do."

"Maybe I can help out a little," he said, getting to his feet with some difficulty. He used a cane now, she saw, leaning his weight heavily on it. "He's waiting. Do you want to see him?"

There was no need to ask who was waiting. Her heart leaped, and her pulse began racing. "Yes," she said without hesitation.

He smiled. "I'm glad. I didn't know if you understood how difficult things were for him."

"I didn't at first," she said honestly. "I was so shocked to realize . . . but then I began to think."

He laboriously made his way around the desk, and patted her shoulder. "Have a good life, Liliane."

"I will, thank you . . . Mr. Rogers."

Frank Vinay smiled, and left the office. Ten seconds later, the door opened again and Lucas Swain stood there, as good-looking as always, but now he wasn't laughing. The expression in his blue eyes was almost . . . scared.

"Lily," he began. "I–"

"I know," she interrupted, and with a laugh launched herself at him. His reflexes were excellent; he opened his arms and caught her.